Books by B. V. Larson.

## STAR FORCE SERIES
*Swarm*
*Extinction*
*Rebellion*
*Conquest*
*Battle Station*
*Empire*
*Annihilation*
*Storm Assault*
*The Dead Sun*
*Outcast*
*Exile*
*Gauntlet*

## REBEL FLEET SERIES
*Rebel Fleet*
*Orion Fleet*
*Alpha Fleet*

Visit BVLarson.com for more information.

# Blood World

(Undying Mercenaries Series #8)
by
B. V. Larson

**Undying Mercenaries Series:**
*Steel World*
*Dust World*
*Tech World*
*Machine World*
*Death World*
*Home World*
*Rogue World*
*Blood World*

Copyright © 2017 by Iron Tower Press.

This book is a work of fiction. Names, characters, places and incidents are either products of the author's imagination or used fictitiously. Any resemblance to actual events, locales or persons, living or dead, is entirely coincidental. All rights reserved. No part of this publication can be reproduced or transmitted in any form or by any means, without permission in writing from the author.

ISBN-13: 978-1973357124
BISAC:   Fiction / Science Fiction / Military

*"Soldiers are marching flasks of blood, flesh and bronze. None of it matters save for the flame inside."*
– Marcus Aurelius, 171 AD

## -1-

My daughter Etta took on a new fascination in her eleventh year. Her fledgling interest grew into a full-blown obsession right around her twelfth birthday in late spring.

The whole thing reached critical mass when she got her new, very expensive birthday gift. I wouldn't have sprung for it, except my parents were doing better with money now and had gone in halfway with me. On top of that, Etta had specified she'd only wanted one thing for a present. How do you tell a kid "no" when there's only one thing on her list, and she really wants it?

After spending all that money, I was pleased to see her use it every night. Like every parent who buys a child an expensive toy—or in this case, an expensive alien-made scientific instrument—you can't quite be sure it won't sit on a shelf after a week or two.

But Etta wasn't that kind of girl. Her new obsession had a firm grip on her young mind. She became an expert with the auto-scope right away, and she spent most of her free time fooling with it.

The auto-scope amounted to an intelligent, star-gazing device that could spot, track, identify, and perfectly visualize any star or planet in the heavens.

Tonight, she had her star-gazing rig set up on the back porch. It was a warm evening in May down in Georgia Sector, and I was rocking on the porch swing while Etta worked the device, her face glued to its eye piece.

"Dad?" she asked. "Have you been to Tau Ceti?"

"You know I have, girl. Tech World, we called it back in the day."

"What do they call it now?"

I winced. The truth was grim: my legionnaire friends called the world of the Tau "Trash World" these days. The planet's ecosystem had yet to completely recover from the devastating thermonuclear strikes launched by *Minotaur's* broadside cannons.

But even that wasn't the worst of the damage that had been inflicted. The Tau people's main spaceport, Gelt Station, had suffered as well, sending their economy into a tail-spin.

Etta eyed me carefully.

"They call it Trash World, don't they?" she asked. "Did you have something to do with that new name, Father?"

That was the trouble with little girls. They tended to grow up and start figuring things out.

"Uh..." I said, making a vague gesture. I faked a smile and took in a deep breath. "My legion was out there, it's true. A lot of bad things happened at about the same time. But that doesn't make everything our fault."

She continued eyeing me instead of staring into the lighted interior of her faintly humming auto-scope. The scope's eyepiece put an oval of white light on her cheek.

"It's true then," she declared after measuring my expression. Then she turned her attention back to her machine.

"What's true?"

"What they say at school."

I shifted uncomfortably on the porch swing and took a swig of beer. I knew I should keep quiet, but I couldn't.

"What do they say?" I demanded.

Etta kept her face aimed into that circle of light as she spoke. "That Legion Varus destroys everything it touches."

"No!" I said loudly. "That's *not* the truth. At least… not always. Sure, we get the roughest missions. Sometimes, bad things happen when we're deployed to a hot spot. But that doesn't make it all our fault! That's like blaming the fireman for the fire he's trying put out!"

"Hmm…" she said. "I almost believe you."

My beer was still in my hand, but I set it aside, finding I no longer enjoyed the taste.

"Why are you asking about Tech World, anyway?" I demanded, becoming irritated. I was thinking of all those installments I paid every month to send Etta to a private school. That was a whole bunch of money to waste on being insulted. My family could do that for free.

"Come here," she said a moment later. "Look into my scope."

There was an odd tone in her voice. It was almost like she knew she was going to blow my mind.

For my own part, I welcomed the shift in the conversation. I moved to the scope and towered over her. So far Etta's strength was mostly in her personality and mind. Someday she'd become a big girl, and she was already lightning-quick with a blade, but for now she was still just tall and willowy.

Stooping, I looked into her scope. What I saw there was amazing.

"The resolution… the image… so perfect! I can see Gelt Station spinning slowly over the clouds. It's as plain as day! But that's twelve lightyears away… How can this thing possibly…?"

"It's not real," she said quickly. "Well, I mean, it really *is* Tau Ceti, and the scope is aimed that way and zoomed in so tightly it appears you can see the planet in question. However, the image the auto-scope is displaying is being relayed over the grid. The scope cheats, you see, interpolating what you want to see, and bypassing its own optics with—"

Laughing, I straightened up. "I get it, professor. You know who you sound like?"

"My grandfather? The Investigator?"

3

"Yeah, him. Do you remember him? It's been years."

"Of course I do. When I lived on Dust World, he was my only living relative who admitted to the relationship."

Frowning again, I wondered about that. Etta had always been a troublemaker, both on Dust World and Earth. There was a little too much of me and her mother in her, I supposed.

She was a wild thing, essentially, and raising her was like raising a half-wolf hybrid. Worse, I was pretty sure she was smarter than I was.

Sitting back down on the porch swing, I took up my beer bottle again. It was a little on the warm side, but I swilled it down. As I did so, I watched Etta. She was changing shape, too—just starting to grow hips and boobs. She was going to turn into a cute, dangerous little woman soon, and I was going to be in a fresh new world of hurt.

*Damn.*

Etta turned to look at me. "What are you thinking about now?"

"Nothing."

"Liar."

"That's disrespectful, girl!"

"Sorry," she said in a tone that indicated she didn't mean it.

She was my daughter all right. I sighed, and she turned back to her auto-scope.

"Hey," I said, deciding to switch up the mood, "aim that thing at L-347, will you?"

"I don't know that star… but okay, I've found it in the index."

The auto-scope whirred and spun to the south. It aimed into the trees, and I figured the target must be low on the horizon.

Etta looked into the scope anyway, and she clucked her tongue. "I've got it, but there's not much to see."

"Look for L-347 Prime, the only planet close to the star."

She twiddled her knobs and muttered to herself. She was so serious. She looked like a tech already.

"Got it…" she said. "Huh… megaflora?"

I stood and approached. My heart was suddenly pounding. Could this little alien-made machine really look across the gulf of lightyears to check up on other star systems? The mere idea...

"L-347 is better known as Death World," I said, horning in on the eye piece and staring. "Will you look at that! I'll be damned, that really *is* Death World! I can see the clouds, the massive forests. Those plants—they can think, you know. Some of them."

Etta was looking at me, and she was smiling.

"What?" I asked turning my eyes back to the scope. I was hooked.

"You like my new toy. Do you still regret the cost?"

"Nope. Not anymore. You got me. What am I really looking at? A conglomeration of images from the past? Some kind of wiki spiced-up to look like a live stream?"

"Better than that. Earth has a new data feed from the Galactics. The Mogwa commissioned a permanent deep-link. We're now hooked up to *their* grid. The Galaxy-wide Imperial grid. These data streams therefore come from the Core Worlds themselves."

Stunned, I looked at her. "Seriously? I'm looking at a live-stream of Death World in this scope on my back porch?"

"Not necessarily. It depends on the source material. See the icons at the bottom of the display? They indicate this image is less than a hundred hours old. That could be anything from live to four days or so in the past. Pretty good, in either case. But one thing you can be certain of: that visual of Death World is the latest that exists anywhere in the galaxy. At least, the latest that *our* side has."

I turned back to the auto-scope, and I laid my hands on the machine. It had no keyboard, but it did have a touch-interface. The system used Empire-standard icons and gestures, but I didn't understand the navigation right away.

"Show me how it works," I said, "and how much did this really cost, by the way? Your grandma was evasive. She just kept saying that she paid half."

"More than the family tram," Etta said.

"That's not too bad. The tram's a piece of crap."

Etta giggled, and she showed me how to work the auto-scope. Soon, I had Gamma Pavonis in view, then Cancri-9.

"Steel World..." I said, feeling a surge of nostalgia. "That's where it all started for me. My service with the legions began right there on that harsh planet."

"I know," she said, "but it's hard for me to believe. Do you realize Earth legions haven't been out there for more than two decades?"

"Has it been that long?"

She looked at me kind of funny.

"Father?" she asked. "How old are you—exactly?"

"Uh... what year is it?"

She shook her head. "You have to be forty-something. Maybe fifty? It's alarming. You look like you're twenty-five. I'm catching up to both you and mother."

"Yeah..." I admitted. "You're really going to feel weird if you start to look older than we do."

"I'm never going to do that. I'm going to join the legions as soon as I'm of age."

I looked at her seriously. "I don't know about that, girl... No, I take that back. I *do* know: that's a bad idea."

"I'm not afraid."

"No? Well... that's because you haven't died yet. After you go through the guts of a revival machine a few times, you might feel differently."

She fell quiet. I could tell she was in one of her stubborn moods.

Right then, I realized Etta probably would end up joining the legions, just like she said. That was the kind of girl she was. Once an idea implanted itself in that overactive brain of hers, a crowbar and six gorillas didn't have a prayer of prying it back out again.

The thought of Etta in the legions broke the spell the auto-scope had cast over me. I straightened, feeling a pang in my back. How long had I been out here on the porch, looking at every world I'd ever visited? The night had gone from warm to cold, so I figured it had been hours.

Looking at my tapper, which was embedded in my forearm and needed a shave, I clucked my tongue. "It's late, and it's a school night. Time for bed."

"I'm not finished with my planned observation of the Triangulum Galaxy."

"Yeah, well… it's late."

She crossed her arms. "That's because you spent all night hogging my scope."

"True…"

"Father, do you know what they'll attempt to teach me tomorrow in that so-called school?"

"What?"

"We're to learn and sing the Galactic Anthem-all sixteen versions, one for each of the known Superior Races. It's humiliating."

"Humiliating? Why?"

"To sing songs praising the Galactics? They're our conquerors, our—"

I did something sudden and dangerous then. I grabbed Etta and clamped my hand over her mouth.

She had a knife out, quick as a cat, but I'd expected that. Using my off-hand, I shook her wrist until she dropped it.

Breathing hard and pissed beyond measure, she glared up at me. Slowly, I removed my hand from her face.

"Tell me," she hissed, "why I shouldn't damage you in your sleep tonight?"

"First off, because I'm your father. Second, because I'm trying to save your disobedient tail, whether you know it or not, girl."

Moving slowly, I let go of her. She was combat-trained and naturally vicious. The girl had a bad temper in her to boot—a mean-streak. Nothing we'd tried had ever fixed that.

I kept my eyes on her hands and knees, suspecting she just might strike a soft spot.

"Explain yourself," she growled, still breathing hard and giving me the stink-eye.

"You can't talk like that about the Galactics," I said in a calm, measured voice. "Not at school, not at home—not ever."

"Why not?"

"I know we're on our own home porch, but our tappers spy on us. So, possibly, does your nifty new auto-scope, here."

She glanced at her forearm, then the auto-scope, frowning in alarm.

"Are you serious?"

"Absolutely."

Then I told her how they'd measured my emotional state for years. How such automated spying had affected my promotions within the legion, and how it had come as a shock to me as well when I'd learned of it.

"Hegemony can listen to us? Any time they want?" she asked, horrified.

"Yes, I think they can. But the trick is: they don't. Not most of the time. There are only so many Hog agents out there looking for subversion. So, they use AI listening-programs to trigger on keywords, phrases—"

She brightened. "A simple solution presents itself. Sensitive topics should be discussed in code."

"Uh..."

"Yes..." she said, pacing the porch. The old floorboards creaked under her tread. "At first, I was thinking I'd have to damage my tapper. But now—"

"Hold on," I said, regaining her attention. "Look, it's not a big deal for you—not yet. Even the AI probably doesn't care what a kid thinks or says about anything. It's me who's the danger, here. I'm a legion officer. I have a colorful history. If they're listening to anyone, it's me."

"And by inference, whoever you're talking to..." she said, her eyes unfocused, thinking hard.

"Right. You've got it now."

She picked up her knife, waved it in my face momentarily then put it away with a flourish.

"You took dangerous action," she said. "I don't like being disarmed."

"No killer does."

"But I think now, in retrospect, that you were correct to do so."

"No hard feelings, Etta?"

"None. I'm tired now, and sad."

"Why's that?"

"Because I no longer completely trust my auto-scope. It's disappointing. I'm going to bed."

"I'm sorry," I said.

"Why?" she asked, and I could tell she meant it.

I struggled with a way to explain what I was feeling. "For parents, it feels terrible to have to shatter your kid's innocence."

"There's no need to apologize… but, Father?"

"What?"

"Are there many more such shocking things to learn in my future?"

I heaved a sigh. "Well… you probably don't have as many surprises coming as most young girls do, because you're pretty worldly already. But yeah, you've still got a lot to learn."

"Another alarming thought… Goodnight."

She stood on her tiptoes, and I automatically bent my knees. She managed to brush my cheek with her lips, and then she vanished into the house.

Heading to my own shack out in back of the main house, I settled down on my stained couch and tried to fall asleep.

I couldn't help but think of all the things Etta had to learn about the world—and all the things the world had to learn about her.

*Boyfriends, for instance.*

That was the first topic that came to mind. Etta had a lot to learn about that phase of life. What would she do when some sorry bastard tried to cop a feel for the first time? Damn… that was going to be one hellacious night to remember for everyone.

Listening to the forested swamp outside my shack, I drifted off to sleep at last.

## -2-

First thing in the morning, a fist began thumping on my door.

For me, this was an occurrence that was both familiar and alarming. I'd been dragged out of bed to be arrested on any number of occasions, both falsely and with good reason. In either case, I didn't care for the experience.

Springing off my couch, I reached for a weapon. Like most legionnaires, I had one within arm's reach pretty much every moment of the day and night. After any man has died his first dozen times or so, he finds it hard to sleep without a deadly implement near at hand.

My fingers closed in a jerk around the butt of a laser pistol. It was a sleek, wicked thing. The gun had no dangling cord that connected to a power cell. It was a low-yield internally powered unit, which meant it was only good for three or four burns before it went dry.

But that should be enough.

The hammering subsided, but it began again a few seconds later. Whoever it was, they weren't patient by nature.

I didn't call out. I didn't suggest my rude visitor should settle the hell down. To do so would only serve to put them on their guard.

Instead, I popped the door open and pushed the slim barrel of my pistol into the craggy face that waited outside.

"Primus Graves?" I asked a second later, dumbfounded.

Even after twenty years in the service of Legion Varus, this man had never come down to Georgia to see me. He'd never shown the slightest inclination.

"You really live here in this shack, McGill?" he asked, looking past the muzzle of my gun into the dark interior of my humble home.

"Yes sir. I like it."

He glanced at the laser pistol, as if noticing it for the first time.

"Well? Are you going to assassinate me or ask me to come inside?"

"Uh… come on in, sir."

I lowered my pistol, but I didn't put it away. I stepped back, and he pushed past me.

He sniffed a few times speculatively, but he didn't say anything. I left the door open to let things air out.

"What brings you down here to my neck of the woods?" I asked him, indicating the couch, because that was the only seating I had.

"I'll remain standing, if you don't mind."

"Suit yourself, Primus. You want a beer, or something? I've got—"

"McGill, I'm here to apologize."

My mouth fell open. That was a stunner. "I don't think I've ever heard those words come out of you before, sir. What's up?"

"You've been volunteered."

For several long seconds, he stared at me, and I stared back. I blinked a few times as his words sank in.

In Legion Varus, being "volunteered" was never a good thing. After any soldier had died a time or two, he soon got over the idea of volunteering at all, so when decorum required an officer to come up with a victim for a hazardous assignment, he generally chose that person himself. Calling this process "volunteering" was a joke so old amongst legionnaires it had become part of our lexicon.

As I tended to be an outspoken man, I'd been "volunteered" for special duties more than most. That part didn't surprise me. What did give me pause, however, was the fact that I'd apparently been volunteered for something so heinous in nature that Graves seemed to think it was worth traveling all the way down here to Georgia Sector to tell me about it.

"Uh…" I said, "I've been volunteered for *what*, exactly, sir?"

"I can't tell you that. But you'll find out soon enough. I just wanted to come here, man-to-man, and let you know it wasn't me. Not only that, I don't think it's right. There, I've said my piece, and I'll be going now."

"Huh…" I said. I was feeling a bit concerned now. It took a lot to worry a man like me, but Graves was pulling it off. "If this is some kind of joke, sir, I—"

"Have you ever heard me tell a joke, Centurion? Much less travel a thousand miles down from Central to deliver it?"

"No, sir."

"Right. I'll see you Monday at dawn. We'll start at Central for the briefing. Don't be late."

He was already heading for the door. I followed in a confused fog of thoughts and questions.

"I take it I've been reactivated, sir?"

"If it makes you feel any better, the whole legion is involved. The general mobilization message will be going out tonight."

"That makes me feel tons better, Primus."

"Good. See you Monday, McGill. Don't be late."

Just like that, the door closed, and he was gone. A rented floater was waiting out on the main road. He climbed in and let it whisk him away. Presumably, he was going back to the sky-train station and flying back to Central.

What could be so grim, so unpleasant, that Graves would feel the urge to do such a thing? To come all the way down here to apologize in person?

He could have sent a text—but of course, there was no such thing as a private message sent tapper-to-tapper. Graves had to know that, because even I did.

Instead, he'd come to talk to me in person. That just didn't sound good at all. It didn't sound *right*.

Any further notions of sleep were out of the question after Graves left. I went inside the main house, ate breakfast with my family, and pretended all the while I felt good inside. I did such a good job of faking it that, for a while, I actually *did* feel better.

But then that night, the message went out. Legion Varus was being activated again at last. My momma heard about it almost before I did. News on the grid traveled from one tapper to the next very quickly these days.

"James?" she asked. "Is this true?"

I looked at her, and our eyes met. I didn't bother to lie. She could see the truth in my eyes.

"Oh…" she said. "It's been so long. I'd almost forgotten how it feels each time they order you to fly away to the stars again."

"I'm sorry, Momma."

"Don't be. I understand. Your sacrifices have held this family together. The last thing I want is for you to feel bad about leaving us to do your job. Don't worry about us at all. We'll take care of Etta, and we'll be fine."

I smiled a real smile. "That's good to know."

"Have you told Etta yet?"

"Told her what?" asked a third voice from behind her.

Etta stood in the doorway, outlined by the bright light of day through the auto-screen door.

"I'm going away again, Pumpkin," I said.

"Don't call me that. You never call me that."

Stepping forward, I reached for her, and she rushed to me and clasped me around the waist. That was a special feeling. She really cared now. She really understood the loss of a relative to the stars.

Before, when we'd first started raising her, she'd been distant and cold at emotional moments. But today, she seemed like a very normal young girl.

## -3-

Monday morning came in a blur. The packing, the good-byes, the sky-train ride—they didn't seem real.

To me, it was like one day I'd been enjoying my free time in Georgia and the next I was gliding down over Central.

I didn't have a window seat, as they never fit my frame. I was crammed into an aisle seat, with the bulkhead in my face dead ahead. The sky-train shivered as it reentered the thicker atmosphere, plunged through the clouds, and sailed toward the spaceport.

Craning my long neck, I could see the Earth below. Central was down there, a squat ziggurat of black stone. The windows were all black glass, and they reflected gleams of pink morning sunlight up to dazzle my eyes.

Leaning back into my seat again, I relaxed—but I couldn't sleep. That was unusual for me. I'd long been known as a man who'd someday sleep through his own funeral after my righteously delivered, long overdue perma-death.

But... not this time. I was cursing Graves. His act of honor had thrown me off my game. I'd already spent more time worrying about this mission than I had any other in my long and storied history of assignments.

Giving myself a shake and sucking in a deep breath, I told myself to forget about it.

That almost worked. I felt better by sheer force of will, and the tingling in my gut went away for a while.

Landing at the spaceport, I headed for public transport. It was early on Monday morning, so rush-hour was in full force. I began to worry I'd be late.

"Worry" was perhaps the wrong word. The truth was I was vaguely concerned. But part of me figured that if they really had volunteered me for the worst duty I'd ever served, well, the brass could damned-sure wait for me to show up. It might even make some of them feel better about their decision to have me play the victim.

"McGill!" a familiar voice shouted. I winced at the recognition.

Instead of answering, I hit the automated baggage claim touch-plate and picked up the lone bag it spit out.

Turning with my ruck slung, I spotted Winslade. He was a thin man with the eyes of a rodent.

"What is it, Primus?" I asked.

"What do you think? I'm here to pick you up," he said, spitting out each word.

He reached out to examine my arm. I flinched away at first, but then I reluctantly let him see my tapper.

"Messages silenced, as usual," he complained. "Why am I not surprised? If you'd read your messages, you'd know I was going to be waiting here for you."

"Oh yeah… I did silence all that. I was just trying to get a little shut-eye on the sky-train, sir."

"Sleep is for the dead, McGill. You should know all about that. If you wanted to sleep in this morning, you should have flown here last night."

"Excuse me, Primus," I said, "but why have you been sent to pick me up? I mean, doesn't Turov have adjuncts for errands like this?"

I knew Winslade was Turov's lapdog. He liked the job, but he didn't like having his servant's status pointed out. Doing so brought him pain and me a commensurate surge of pleasure.

With a grin, I offered to let him carry my bag. He shoved it away angrily.

"Follow me, Centurion," he growled and stalked off.

I was expecting him to lead me to a private air car, but instead we boarded a skimmer. The vehicle was capable of flight, but it was more like an armored flying bus than a cushy ride.

"A skimmer? Seriously?" I complained.

Winslade gave me a sour glance. "Disgusting, isn't it? I've been sent out to collect a half-dozen Varus lowlifes just like you. Not only is the task demeaning, the skimmer smells like a primate exhibit."

My jaw sagged open. I'd been joking about the skimmer. To me, any flying contrivance was just fine. Taking the public transport tunnels would have worked out, too.

But what had really surprised me was the fact the skimmer was already loaded. Carlos was aboard, Kivi, Sargon…

"It's old home week!" I said, grinning and waving as I climbed aboard.

My friends greeted me with enthusiasm.

Carlos was sporting a scraggly beard and a beer gut, but otherwise he was the same as he'd always been. "McGill?! Good God, now we *know* we're all dead!"

"That's right," I told him. "There's no point in fighting it."

"We'll fight it, sir," Sargon said confidently. "We always do."

"Good to see you again, Centurion," said another familiar voice from behind me.

I whirled around in shock. "Adjunct Harris? They got you roped into this too, did they?"

"Volunteered," he said grimly. "No choice. No options. No escape."

There was something in his voice and his stare that caught my attention. For a moment, I didn't hear the rest of them. They were all catcalling and laughing like we were going to a high school reunion luau.

After Harris and I locked eyes for a moment, I got it. He'd been visited by Graves, too. He'd been given that special, private apology. The very thing neither of us had ever gotten from Graves. Not once in twenty long years.

Kivi was tugging at my shirt, and I turned to her and forced a smile.

"Kivi! You're looking hot this morning."

"Always," she said. "I'm only twenty-four again."

"Uh... What?"

"I had an accident about a month ago. You know how it is..."

It took me a second, but I got it. She *did* look younger, not a day older than the afternoon we'd last met.

"Oh now," I said, "you offed yourself? That wasn't necessary."

"Wasn't it? You noticed the difference right away. I wasn't sure we'd ever be called up again, so I decided to get one last... um... freshening."

My mind worked on that for a half-second. If a girl was so vain about her looks that she'd arrange her own death just to look a few years younger, well, it would be best to tell her it had worked.

"By damn," I said, "every second I look at you, I can see another missing wrinkle. You always look good to me, but I guess it was worth it."

"It was stupid," Carlos butted in. "She didn't need to do it. I mean, hell, we'll probably all die over the next month, anyway. Zap! New body for free. And you know what else? If Central ever finds out, they'll charge you for the procedure. With interest."

"Hmm," I said, wanting to tell Carlos to cool it.

Kivi and he had been an ongoing thing when we'd last met. A glance at Kivi's reaction to Carlos' comments told me there was trouble in paradise. Her lip curled up to reveal her teeth, and her eyes narrowed like those of a hungry fox.

"Uh..." I said, as silence suddenly reigned. "Well, I think youth looks good on you Kivi. I'm sure Carlos just meant—"

"He meant nothing," Kivi snapped. "He's just bitter after our break-up. It's been a year, Carlos. Grow up."

The skimmer lurched into the air, and I found a seat in a hurry. Kivi flounced her butt down right next to me.

"Uh..." I said. "You sure you want to sit right there? I'm a man who takes up a whole row."

"I'll sit in your lap if we'll fit better."

It was a mean thing to say to a man like me. I felt a hot surge at the thought of her bouncing on my lap, but I had to shake my head.

"What about Carlos? He's right there."

"I'm not into beards."

"Yeah, but... he's a friend."

"He cheated on me."

"Really? Carlos?"

"Well... not in action, but he flirted all the time."

I laughed. "I always do the same and so do you."

"I know," she said. "But it's different with you. Any girl who gets near James McGill knows what's she's in for. It's expected, not a surprise. You take that or you leave it up front. I miss that simple honesty."

"Hmm..." I said, disturbed on several levels by her comments.

But that was Kivi. She was a troublemaker of the first order.

Most Legion Varus people were like that. We were all unstable, energetic and sometimes downright irritating. That's why we'd been accepted into the worst legion in human history after being rejected by all of Earth's respectable outfits.

Kivi kept talking and flirting with me while Carlos kept hunching his shoulders and pouting a few rows away. I stopped listening to her, as it was easier that way, just saying "uh-huh" now and then to keep her happy.

While Winslade did a poor job of flying us all to Central, bumping us around in the air like we were on a carnival ride, Kivi entertained herself by rubbing her body up against my side. That was nice, but it was also upsetting at the same time.

Glancing at Kivi then the brooding faces of Carlos and Harris, it occurred to me that the psych tests we'd all taken back in the day at the Mustering Hall really *had* worked. We were still a legion of misfit toys.

Despite all the pouting, I felt at home being in their midst again. We were like a big, dysfunctional family full of assholes and loudmouths. We belonged together somehow.

After a short flight, Central loomed ahead. The unmistakable manmade mountain grew steadily until it blotted out the sky, and then we flew into the vast pool of shade cast by its massive shadow. The warm, late spring sun that had been shining in the windows died, and the skimmer's cabin cooled by at least ten degrees.

The pyramid-shaped building continued to swell until it seemed impossibly big. Constructed entirely with flat black polymers and shiny metals, it was the largest single structure Earth had yet to produce.

The mere sight of it brought back a flood of memories, both good and bad.

But it was the moment when we landed that changed everything. The group quieted, grabbed their stuff, and filed out.

We all felt it. Vacation had officially ended the moment the skimmer's skids touched the landing pad.

Legion Varus was back in the game, a lean pack of killers that no one else had ever wanted.

That meant anything might happen next.

## -4-

"I see on my tapper that Group Nine has landed," the familiar, gravelly voice of Primus Graves said in our headsets. "Legionnaires, please proceed to the express elevators and select the option that takes you down to the vaults. They've been conducting experiments down there, and they're in need of fresh volunteers."

A collective groan went up from the group. All six of us felt a rock of disappointment grow in our guts. At least Harris and I had been forewarned, but for the others this shocker was something new.

"This is *bullshit*," Carlos began. "I can identify every flavor of shit ever made, and this is a bad one. Mark my words, people."

For once, Harris didn't tell him to shut up. Carlos noted the adjunct's lack of a response, and he eyed Harris' glum expression suspiciously.

"You knew about this, didn't you, Adjunct?" he demanded. "You *know* what's coming!"

"No I don't, Specialist," Harris said. "I just know it's going to be something bad. Isn't it always?"

Carlos was our bio specialist, which made him the team's medic. For the first time, the thought impinged upon me that our small group *did* make up a full combat team. We had Kivi as our tech, Carlos as our bio, Harris and me to lead and

Sargon as our veteran, the heavy-weapons man. All we needed to form a full squad was enough regular troops to fill out the ranks.

Could that be an accident? I didn't think so. Primus Graves wouldn't have flown all the way out to Georgia Sector to apologize in advance for something that was happening at random.

What had he called us? *Group Nine?* That title seemed chilling now, in retrospect. Group Nine didn't sound military, it sounded like something a nerd would call a hapless batch of lab rats.

We walked across the landing pad and approached the elevators. We were challenged by guards, checked thoroughly, and shunted onward into Central itself.

The elevator dinged and we all watched as the doors slid open. The metal box that was to take us all the way down to the vaults was a special one. It was bigger, dirtier, and even more dimly lit than the regular elevators.

I'd been down to the vaults before. Instead of carrying people up to the lofty offices of the highly ranked, this elevator took you down instead—more than five hundred floors down— to where the Earth itself began to get hotter.

As we filed into the elevator, Winslade stepped to one side and crossed his arms. I reached out and put an arm around his shoulders. He frowned at this.

"Unhand me, Centurion."

"Winslade," I said quietly, "if I find out you led us here and set us on a one-way trip into an incinerator, you know what I'm going to do?"

"Apologize?" he asked.

"What?" I asked in confusion.

"I'm coming with you, fool! Stand aside!"

He stalked into the elevator, pressed the last button on the list, and crossed his arms again. Harris and I glanced at one another in surprise. Oddly, although neither of us *liked* Winslade, the fact he was coming along for the ride did help put us at ease.

"Sorry, Primus," I said.

"Not as sorry as you're going to be when I jot down some special notes on your next performance report."

I kept my mouth shut after that. Despite our long history, I felt like I'd overstepped the bounds of good taste. After all, he was my superior officer—only by one rank, but that was enough.

We had an odd relationship, just as so many people did in Legion Varus. Among legionnaires, rank was respected—but it wasn't *everything*. I suspected that had to do with our lengthy service and our many difficult deployments.

The elevator lurched into motion at last. It hummed and made grinding noises. Our ears cracked repeatedly as we descended, and no one said much.

"Uh, sir?" Harris asked Winslade at last.

"What is it now?"

"If we're going down into some kind of an experimental operation, well, I'm beginning to expect the action will involve a teleport suit."

Harris' idea gave me pause. A teleport mission...? I hated those. I'd been on quite a few, and they were rarely as fun as they sounded.

"But now that I think about it," Harris mused, "I'm not sure that a teleport mission adds up..."

"Why not?" Winslade demanded. "Get to the point, please."

To me, he sounded nervous.

"Well..." Harris began slowly, "no offense, Primus, but why would *you* be coming along? I mean, a commando raid doesn't need brass."

"Who said we were going on some kind of teleport raid in the first place?"

I finally spoke up. It was in my nature to do so.

"Harris is right. This whole thing is strange, even for Legion Varus. If you've been briefed, sir, now's the time to start talking. We weren't born yesterday. We're hundreds of meters underground and going deeper. It's not like we're going to tell anyone."

Winslade shifted his eyes from one questioning face to the next. He opened his mouth then closed it again.

"The truth is," he said, "I don't know what all this is about. Admittedly, I'm higher ranked than anyone on this so-called 'team', but I'm still in the dark—the same as the rest of you."

"You don't even know why you're here, in particular?" I pressed. "I can understand everyone else in the group. We each have a functional purpose. But *you*, sir? You're brass—no offense."

"None taken," Winslade said, each word spoken with slow bitterness. "But no, I'm unaware of the reasons for my involvement. There was some mention of weight, I believe... An issue of balancing—something like that."

We all exchanged baffled glances. Kivi, our tech, spoke up next.

"Weight..." she mused. "Could they have been talking about displacement? That sounds like teleportation again."

"Maybe, but—" Harris began, but he was cut off.

The elevator door had dinged.

We all looked at it expectantly, but it didn't open right off.

We waited for a few more tense seconds, but it still didn't open.

"Something's wrong," Kivi said.

My eyes drifted to the panel, then the indicator lights. "It's says we're at the vault level. End of the line. Why won't it open?"

"Maybe this is part of the test," Sargon suggested. "You want me to force this thing open, Centurion?"

"No," Primus Winslade commanded quickly. "Let's avoid damaging government property like a pack of apes, shall we? Tech, check the panel, please."

Kivi advanced. She touched the panel with her arm, checked her tapper then gave a gasp of surprise.

"What now?" Winslade demanded.

"Check your tappers," she said urgently. "All of you."

We did. They were all blinking the same yellow lightning-bolt icon at us. We'd been disconnected from the grid.

"Is that just because we're down here so far underground?" Carlos asked.

"I don't know," Kivi said. "There should be routers down here to relay our signals. James? What do you remember about being down here in the past?"

I looked blank. "Uh... it's been a long time. But I don't recall a problem with my tapper."

"They're screwing us already," Carlos said with certainty. "No messages. No one to call for help. I bet a revive request would just bounce."

"Open that panel and fix it, tech," Winslade ordered.

While Kivi broke out her portable computer and interfaced with the elevator's control unit, Sargon gave me a meaningful glance. I shrugged in return.

I knew what he was thinking: was I in operational command or was Winslade? He had the rank, but I had the experience. If something *was* wrong down here in the secret vaults under Central, I had the superior skills to deal with it.

But I shrugged briefly in response to Sargon's unspoken question. I had no grounds to usurp Winslade. For the time being, for good or for ill, he was in charge.

Kivi turned back to us, frowning. Her mouth opened to speak—but she never made her report concerning the status of the panel.

At that moment, something big—something *heavy*—rammed into the elevator doors on the far side.

We didn't know what it was, but we could hear it, and we could see what it was doing.

The metal doors made a *crumping* sound and dented inward, forming a diagonal line of bulging steel nearly a meter long in the dead center of the closed doors.

Outside, we could hear heavy thumping, like massive feet in rapid motion. A grunting, woofing sound followed.

"Something's out there!" Kivi said, scrambling away from the door.

"Ya think?" Carlos asked. "Get back to that panel. Take us up a level or two!"

"Hold on," I said. "Maybe this is the experiment Graves mentioned."

"Yeah, right..." Carlos said, "I'm sure it is—and I'm equally sure it's gone totally wrong."

"Too bad we're unarmed," Winslade said, breathing hard.

I glanced around the group. Hard eyes met mine.

Another *crump* sounded, and the door dented in further. This time, the line that pressed into the elevator car didn't intrude as deeply, but it did form a faint "X" by crossing the first line at an angle.

I nodded to my team.

"Okay," I said, "pull out whatever you've got. No one is going on report."

All of the Varus people, except for Winslade, produced weapons. It was in our blood, our psyche, to travel armed these days.

A hidden razor popped out of my boot. Kivi slid a wand out that crackled with a shimmering nimbus of power.

"EMP?" I asked her, "or is it a shock-rod?"

"Both," she said with a wicked smile. "I designed it myself to fit into a make-up kit."

"Excellent," Winslade said, looking around with approving glances. We all had some kind of blade, stunner, or other deadly item. He looked at Carlos last and frowned.

"What's that?" he asked, pointing to the long, shining wire in the bio's hands.

"It's dental floss," Carlos said. "You want me to give you a cleaning?"

"That won't be—"

The crumping sound came again. This time, the door gave way.

A massive head rammed its way into the elevator car with us. Kivi screamed and fell, as she'd been closest to the control panel.

"It's a jugger!" Harris roared in shock. "How could a jugger be down here?"

The head lunged from side to side, trying to bite people. We instinctively threw ourselves backward and away from it. Kivi, using her feet to kick at it, got a boot caught up in those jaws. The jugger ripped away the boot and chewed on it in excitement.

Then the head pulled back and out of view.

Breathing hard, we lined the rear walls of the elevator.

"What in the holy fuck is going on?" Harris demanded.

"I think I know," Carlos said. "They put a jugger down here to ambush us. Maybe it got loose, or maybe we took too long to come out of that door and feed it dinner. Whichever, we're good and screwed in here. No way this elevator is going back up with the door all folded in like that."

"We'll have to exit this car," I said. "If we can get to the next one down the line, maybe we can ride it back up."

"Screw that noise," Harris said. "We have sticks and knives, here. If we crawl outside of this car, it will eat us one at a time."

"What do you suggest, then, Adjunct?"

Harris' eyes drifted upward to the roof of the elevator. "There's a small access door up there. Probably for maintenance. The lightest of us could crawl up top and—"

"An excellent suggestion," Winslade said. "Kivi, as our resident lightweight—"

"Are you kidding?" she said. "You weigh about the same as I do, Primus. You've probably got more arm-strength, too."

"Don't bet on it," Carlos chuckled.

Winslade cast him a withering glance. "Very well. I'll go up first and see what can be done. If we can reach the next elevator down the line, just possibly—"

The jugger appeared to get bored with waiting for us to come out. He rammed his head into the hole again, snapping and making everyone jump. His small forearms worked on the thin metal that held him back, peeling it away from his neck.

"Don't let him get in here!" I shouted. "Attack him! Stab for the eyes!"

My razor came at him from one side, Kivi's shock-stick lashed at the other. The jugger whipped his head from side to side, which served to work his shoulders in a fraction deeper. He threatened us, slashing the air with his four-inch fangs.

I opened up a bleeding line in his upper lip. Kivi teased one nostril, and there was a bright flash and a cracking sound.

The jugger's eyes flew wide, and they focused on Kivi. He let out a deafening roar and pulled his head back again.

"You've been marked for death, girl," I said.

"I think so..." she agreed.

We all breathed hard and stared from a crouched position for the next minute or so. Outside, silence reigned.

"Someone check that hole," Winslade said. "See if the monster is still stalking around out there in the corridor."

"Someone?" Carlos asked.

Winslade looked at him. "Oh… right. This group never volunteers for anything. You do it," he said, pointing at Carlos.

"Why me?"

"Because you're useless," Harris barked at him, "and you brought dental floss to a dinosaur fight."

"I'm going, I'm going…" Carlos said, and he crept to the ripped-apart door.

He rammed an arm through and yanked it back quickly. He checked his fingers, and smiled. "All still there."

"Scout and report, Specialist!" Winslade urged him.

Sucking in a deep breath, Carlos shoved his head into the opening. He looked quickly from side to side then pulled back again.

Kivi let out her breath next to me. Maybe she still cared about Carlos—a little.

"I didn't see anything," Carlos whispered. "Coast looks clear."

"Winslade?" I asked quietly. "It's now or never, sir."

"Right… Leg me up, Sargon."

Winslade moved with grace when he was lifted bodily into the air. The cargo elevator was taller than most, but with Harris and Sargon each holding up a leg, Winslade managed to shimmy up and out of the car.

"He's probably going to escape and leave us here," Carlos said in a low tone. "You guys know that, don't you?"

No one replied. The thought had occurred to everyone already.

Listening underneath the open hatch, we heard Winslade grunting and scrabbling up there like a roof-rat.

"What do you see, Primus?" Harris called up through the hatchway.

"A lot of cables, dirt, and grease," he said. "Hold on… yes, there is another car nearby. The top hatch appears to be open…

I think I can make it, but if one of these cars starts to move on its own, I'm dead for sure."

"That would be a crying shame, sir," I shouted up the hatch. "But we're kind of running out of time down here and…"

"I know, I know…"

We heard him leap then. He landed with a thump and a grunt of effort.

"He's on the second elevator," Carlos said. "He has to be."

"Oh no…" I heard Winslade say faintly from above.

"What's wrong, Primus?" I called up to him.

"I'm at the second elevator, but I'm afraid it's no good to us," he shouted.

"Why not?" demanded Harris loudly.

"Because it's full of dead legionnaires. What's more, they're wearing dragon's head patches. Legion Victrix troops. Sorry bastards."

We all looked at one another in shock.

"Did I call it, huh?" Carlos demanded. "Did I call it, or what? This is all *bullshit*. We're guinea pigs down here. *Dead guinea pigs!*"

"You're probably right," I said, "but I'm not giving up, because I don't want to die in the jaws of this dino. Anyone want to go throw themselves into that monster's mouth and maybe choke it on the way down? That strategy appears to have worked out for Victrix."

No one volunteered.

"Okay then. Juggers are dumb, let's be smarter. How are we going to survive?"

They looked at one another. Kivi spoke up first.

"We need better weapons. If that group in the next elevator was wiped out, that means the thing managed to get inside and kill them eventually."

"Primus?" I called, shouting up through the access hatch. "Is there anything interesting inside that elevator with the bodies?"

"Yes," he called back. "I'm way ahead of you, McGill. There's a gun on one of them. I'm going to try for it."

"Good. Be careful, sir!"

The rest of us exchanged glances. Kivi frowned at me.

"You shouldn't have encouraged him. He'll get killed."

"So what?" Carlos asked. "He's been as useful as tits on a boar so far."

"Shut up," I told them all. "Sargon, stand near the breach, on the right side."

"Why?"

"In case Winslade can't get back using the hatches. He might have to—"

Right about then, we heard thumping feet and panting breath. It was coming from the other side of the elevator door.

"Sargon! Get ready to pull him in!"

Sargon stood at the hole, and I moved forward to the other side.

Winslade's hands appeared first, and we grabbed them and lifted him through the hole. He dropped the laser pistol he'd brought along, and it clattered on the floor of the elevator.

Winslade made it about halfway when he appeared to get stuck. Sargon's muscles bulged, and I could tell he was about to rip the man through the hole.

"Hold on," I said, "you'll cut him up bad on that metal."

"That's right, you oaf," Winslade said. "My boot is stuck, that's all. Let me work it free, and—"

Winslade broke off, and his words changed into a cry of alarm. His head turned, looking back through the hole he'd been wriggling through.

A gurgling sound, low and deep, came from a throat that wasn't human.

The jugger was back.

"Pull me!" Winslade cried. "PULL!"

We pulled. We pulled *hard*. But the jugger already had a firm grip on Winslade's kicking legs.

Winslade slid forward, and sharp metal rasped on his belly and ribs. His clothes were sliced away in lines. Blood began to well.

Then he slid backward again, yanked into the dark corridor with incredible force. Sargon and I were nearly pulled off our feet.

Winslade's eyes bulged in shock and pain. He seemed beyond words now. He was in a state of agony, shock, and terror. I could only think, in those desperate moments, that a billion creatures had died in a similar fashion throughout history. That being eaten alive by something huge with massive jaws and incredible strength couldn't have been an uncommon way to go out even for humans in centuries past.

Grunting, straining and roaring with effort, we pulled on those skinny arms of his. The one I gripped slipped part-way out of the socket, popping and crackling. It had to have broken, but I still hung on. I didn't want the jugger to get his dinner. Not this time.

At last, the jugger seemed to give up. Winslade came firing out of the hole like a cork out of a bottle.

Thrown off balance, Sargon and I fell on our backs.

For some reason, Kivi chose that moment to start screeching about something. I didn't get it. I was all smiles.

Winslade, too, seemed happy. He smiled at me, his teeth bloody.

"Thanks, McGill," he said in a faint voice.

Then the light went out of his narrow eyes, and that's when I noticed that we only had half of Winslade.

The other half of him was outside in the corridor, being greedily gulped down by the jugger.

## -5-

Carlos made the next move, after he gave up trying to resuscitate Winslade. He got up, grabbed the laser pistol Winslade had dropped, and took pot-shots at the monster outside.

The gun barely glimmered.

"The charge is gone," he said in disgust, tossing it aside. "Winslade died for nothing."

Everyone looked depressed and desperate after that. We'd been desperate before, don't get me wrong, but now we were really feeling it.

"What are we going to do?" Carlos asked. "We can't get out of here. We're rats in a trap."

"Has anyone got something to poison him with?" Kivi asked suddenly.

We all stared at her for a second.

"I'm fresh out of cyanide," Harris said, "if that's what you mean."

"Cyanide…" she said, then she got down on her knees and dug in her bag. She produced a cosmetics kit. "There's cyanide in some cosmetics."

"That's a long shot," I said. "I don't think you're going to kill this thing with mascara."

"Yeah…" she said. "He's way too big. How about flammables? Anyone got a lighter?"

No one did. We huddled against the back of the elevator car and sweated. The jugger, for his part, was out there striding back and forth. Now and then, he beat his tail against the door or tried to rip a fresh hunk away from the hole he had made.

"If he got into the other car," I asked. "Why doesn't he just rip his way in here?"

"Maybe he's not hungry enough yet," Carlos suggested.

His thought didn't seem to liven the mood any.

"I've got an idea," I said, "how about batteries? If we can get him to swallow some, he might not like that."

"The batteries in our tappers are small," Kivi said. "Like the size of a thumbnail."

"Yeah… But there's your computer—"

"Wait!" Carlos shouted. "I know! That laser pistol!"

We all looked at it. Kivi knelt and went to work. She had the battery out and bouncing in her hand a moment later.

"This might work," she said. "There are dangerous chemicals in here, charged or not."

"All right then, we've got a plan!" I said.

"We do?" asked Carlos. "Who's going to swallow that battery then jump into our scaly friend's mouth?"

Looking around the elevator, my eyes landed on Winslade. The others followed me, and Kivi put her hand to her mouth in revulsion.

For a long moment, no one said anything.

"I'll do it," Carlos said seriously, breaking the silence. "I'm the bio, after all."

"I don't want to watch," Kivi said, facing the wall.

Carlos knelt, borrowed my razor, and cut a good-sized chunk out of Winslade. It was grisly, but we'd all seen worse.

Rolling up the battery in the fresh meat, he handed it to Sargon.

Looking disgusted, the veteran nodded. "I'll deliver it."

He stalked to the elevator door. Tapping lightly on the door with his knuckles, he tried to get the jugger to show himself.

"Here, kitty…" he called.

Nothing happened for a minute or two.

"Come on, jugger. I got something good for you here. A snack!"

"Just throw it outside, Sargon," Kivi suggested.

"Yeah…" he said. "I guess I'll have to."

But then, in the moment of his distraction, the jugger rammed his head inside again.

I'm not sure what went wrong in that moment. Maybe the jugger had been playing with us. Maybe he had been capable of pushing himself farther into the elevator car than he had been letting on all along.

Either that, or the smell of fresh blood, so near and enticing, had driven him to great efforts.

In any case, he lunged, ramming his entire head and one grasping forearm into the car with us. That claw latched onto Sargon's leg and dragged him closer to the snapping jaws.

The forearm was scaled and thick. It was as big as a fat man's leg, and much stronger. Sargon was a big man, the strongest in the group, but he couldn't resist the tug.

The main problem was one of leverage. He didn't have anything to hold onto. The floor of the elevator was like the floor of all elevators, smooth and completely devoid of handholds.

Still, Sargon thrashed and flailed. We rushed in too, trying to help. Kivi whacked the frigger on the nose with her stunner again. That made him hiss and shake, but he didn't let go of Sargon.

For his own part, maybe sensing he was doomed anyway, Sargon timed and tossed his package into the snapping jaws. The jugger gulped, and the battery went down.

That moment of distraction almost fixed everything. Harris and I each hooked our hands under one of Sargon's armpits, and we lifted and pulled.

Sargon rose up into the air, pulled in two different directions at once like a wishbone.

Sensing he might lose the tug-of-war this time, the jugger made a final, desperate play. With Sargon's body lifted in the air, he twisted his great head, turned, and took a big bite out of the veteran's guts.

That was it. Game over. Sargon died and the jugger retreated, enjoying his ill-gotten gains.

None of us spoke after that. Kivi had tears in her eyes, but she didn't make a sound.

"How long?" Harris rasped at last.

"How long until what?" Carlos asked. "How long until we're all dead?"

"No, fool. How long until that battery eats a hole in his stomach?"

"Oh..." Carlos looked thoughtful. "I remember talk of this in medical school... A poisoning involving a twenty millimeter lithium battery takes about two hours to burn through, if it lodges in the esophagus. After that, it can burn into the heart or lungs... This battery is way bigger, but it will still take a while. I'd guess four to ten hours."

Harris stared at him, and sweat ran off his face. He nodded. "Better than nothing. But I don't think we're going to be alive that long."

I thought it over. I thought hard. This whole thing was pissing me off. I wasn't sure if this was a test, or an accident, or what. No matter what it was, I wasn't enjoying any of it.

But most of all, I wanted to win.

"Listen up," I said. "This dino is dead in time, so the safe play would be to get everyone up that shaft and on top of the elevator. From there, we might be able to wait all day until he dies."

They glanced at the access hatch, and most of them nodded thoughtfully.

"But," I said, "let's think about the other group—those poor Victrix bastards next door. They had a pistol, a better weapon than we had. Does anyone remember what Winslade said? Had they tried to get out of their hatch like we did?"

"Yeah," Kivi said. "I remember. He said the hatch was up on their elevator car before he got there."

"Exactly. And despite all that, they died."

"What's your point, McGill?" Carlos asked. "Because if it's just that we're all as good as dino-shit, I'm with you there. But that's not exactly constructive."

"My point is this: waiting things out isn't going to work. Avoiding conflict isn't going to work. You remember those tests in the Mustering Hall, back in the day? When did passivity ever win an award? Those tests are always rigged. For all we know, that jugger can blast through our door and eat us anytime he wants to. Hiding in here isn't the way to win."

"What then?" Harris asked.

I pointed at the torn apart hole in the elevator door, and the jugger beyond that stalked the dark corridors.

"That's our goal. We're going to kill that thing. We aren't going to run from him, or hide from him. We're going to kill him."

All of us slid our eyes toward the dark circle in the center of shredded metal. No one spoke, but we all felt the same urge to violence.

He was a predator, but humans were born killers, too.

More importantly, we were pissed-off Varus Legionnaires.

## -6-

We took careful stock of our weapons. The collection was pitiful.

"One burnt out laser pistol, no battery," I said. "One razor—but the jugger didn't seem to care much when I gave him his first shave with it."

"We've got my chain," Harris said, uncoiling the links which wound around his knuckles.

"And my wire," Carlos said, stretching it out and letting it snap back. It was housed in a small, circular pack that reminded me of a tape measure.

"I still have my wand," Kivi offered, "but the charge is gone."

I nodded, looking at each item in turn. My eyes landed on Carlos' odd weapon.

"I assume that thing is meant to whip around someone's throat? To garrote them?"

"Not just that," he said. "It's an alien-made monofilament. It can saw through steel."

"Really?" I asked. "How long is it? If you pull it all the way out?"

"I don't know… at least three meters."

We pulled and pulled. It turned out it was about four meters long.

"Careful," Carlos complained, "you'll stretch out the spring inside the housing, and it won't snap back again."

I took it from him, earning myself a frown. I deliberately yanked on it until it came loose from its carrying case. Then I dropped it, and it fell in a tangled mass on the floor. It coiled itself like a snake at our feet.

"You frigging broke it, McGill!"

"I'll buy you a new one."

They watched as I tested it and pulled on it experimentally.

"This is it," I said. "We can make a noose and set it up like a rabbit-snare."

They stared at me without comprehension. I snorted.

"A bunch of city rats," I said. "Watch."

Making a quick slip-knot, I soon had a shining loop of wire with one long end hanging from my upraised hand.

"All right," Harris said, "but how are we going to get it around that monster's neck?"

"More importantly," Kivi added, "how do we tie it to something? We're in a frigging elevator, here."

Looking around at the smooth walls of the elevator, my eyes lit on the hatchway above us.

"Up there. It's got to be tied off up there."

"Hold on!" Carlos said, shaking his head. "How is this going to work? If that jugger gets far enough into this elevator car to get his head into a loop of wire, he's going to have to be almost completely inside with us."

I eyed the scene, and I nodded. "That's right. You got a better idea?"

"Sadly, no."

We set it up. Kivi went up onto the roof, fumbling around, and then—I'm not exactly sure what caused it, but the jugger went berserk.

Was this response due to the creature getting bored? Or had he been tipped off somehow that one of his prey was trying to escape again?

I recalled that when Winslade had gotten out onto the roof, the jugger had come inside for dinner then, too.

Kivi screamed, and I think the rest of us howled with her.

The jugger wasn't fooling around any longer. Digging with his massive foreclaws, whipping his head from side to side, he managed to ram his way through the widened hole in the door.

"Tie it off, Kivi!" I shouted. "Tie it off!"

We'd given her a loop of metal to work with, but who knew if the line would be long enough, or if there would be a flange just the right distance from the hatchway to do the job? None of us had ever been up there, except for Winslade and now Kivi.

Spreading out, we prepared to die as the jugger forced himself into the elevator car with us. I jumped forward, slashed open his claws, and jumped back. Harris whipped at him with his chain—but neither attack seemed to have any effect.

Carlos took charge of the noose. He stuck his head through it, and he waggled his tongue at the jugger. He spat at him, called him names, and gave him a good look at his middle finger.

Juggers aren't geniuses, but they aren't animals, either. This one knew that he was being mocked. He came through the door in painful surges, like a demon being born from a metal womb.

Free at last, he stalked forward, darting his head down in one lunging, snapping bite.

Carlos, bless his salty heart, offered up his grinning face, right on the other side of that big, shining loop of metal.

The jugger snapped off his head, and Carlos was dead, just like that. Blood gushed, and the jugger looked satisfied as he gulped the head down.

"Give it a yank, Kivi!" I shouted.

She did so, and I saw the noose tighten.

Alarmed, the jugger did what all creatures do when caught around the neck: he tried to back out. This only pulled the noose tighter, of course.

The damned thing took a long time to die. That's the main thing I remember about the long, long minutes that followed.

Panicking and trying to pull away one moment, then lunging forward to kill us in a rage the next, we got a front row seat. The jugger thrashed and roared. Whenever he got smart and tried to use his stumpy arms to pull away the noose, Harris and I danced in, messing with him, distracting him, making him lunge and snap at us.

Each time he did so, of course, the noose tightened. Soon, it was cutting into that tough, scaly neck. Blood welled up all around.

The monster thrashed and fought hard, but eventually, he died.

Feeling relieved but a bit sick to our stomachs, we retrieved Kivi by helping her climb down out of the ceiling hatch.

"What do we do now?" Harris asked me.

"We march out of here. Proud as punch."

"What if there are more tests?" Kivi asked. "Or more juggers out there, waiting for us in the dark corridors?"

"Then we kill them all," I said confidently.

Not waiting for a consensus, I walked out of the ruined elevator door, crawling over the jugger's lengthy tail in order to do so. Standing in the corridor outside, I put my hands on my hips.

"Group Nine reporting!" I called out. "We had a little trouble on the way down, but we're ready for that first experiment now!"

We waited. Thankfully, they didn't make us wait long. A figure appeared ahead of us and walked up to greet us.

"McGill?" Graves asked me. "Where's the rest of your team?"

"They're taking a nap back in the elevator shaft, sir. They got bored with your little game."

He chuckled. "I like your attitude. I always have. I wish I could tell you this is over, Centurion. That you've won the prize—but I don't like to lie."

"Uh..." I said thoughtfully. "So that jugger, he wasn't the reason you came to my place to apologize in advance?"

"No."

"Can I ask then, Primus, what the point of all this is?"

"You can, but I won't answer. Not unless you win. And for your sake, I hope you don't. The prize sucks."

Confused and glancing at one another, we followed him into the darkened tunnels.

We passed a dozen elevators, and we saw at least twenty dead legionnaires. There were plenty more in the corridor to step over, too. All of them had been ambushed as we had. In many cases, it appeared that the poor saps had forced open the door early on and gotten themselves slaughtered right off the bat.

But among all those dead troops, I only counted a single dead jugger: ours.

That made me proud, no matter how this bullshit was destined to end.

## -7-

We followed Graves for what felt like a half-mile. The tunnels were dank, dark, and kind of stinky. People don't always smell too good when they were dying in a state of mortal terror—and giant lizards never do.

Reaching a station of sorts, we were patted down, sprayed off with cold water from a pressure hose, and then ushered inside. There were grim-faced guards at the entrance.

"Hogs?" Harris asked. "We're being hosed down by hogs after all that? That's an insult."

Hogs were what real legionnaires called Hegemony troops. They outnumbered guys like us fifty to one, but as they usually stayed on Earth, we didn't have much respect for them.

Harris gave the next hog he saw the bird, but I slapped his hand down.

"What?" he said, glaring. "Since when do you love the hogs?"

"I don't," I said, "but they're armed, and we aren't right now. This might be another test."

Grumbling that I'd changed, Harris shut up and followed me. Every step he glowered at the stained puff-crete floor like a dog on his way to the vet's.

"Finally," Graves said when we'd made it through the checkpoint. "This is the center of our diplomatic operation. Please familiarize yourselves—"

"Say *what?*" Harris demanded. "Did I hear you right, Primus? How is this a diplomatic operation?"

"That's what it's called. Really, it's more of a training ground for future diplomats."

Even I had to laugh at that. "I can't wait to see the embassy."

"Um, sir?" Kivi asked. "Can I ask what planet is going to be receiving this very special team of diplomats you're training here?"

Graves looked at her coldly. "No. You can shut up."

He proceeded to show us around the place. It wasn't a huge deal. There were maybe two hundred people down here in this dungeon, most of them techs and bios.

"Where's the teleport room?" Harris asked.

Graves eyed him. "There is none."

"How are we going to get out there, then, Primus?"

"Out where?"

"To whatever world the diplomats are schmoozing."

Graves blinked. "Ah… you misunderstand. The trials will continue in the morning. These are your quarters. Rest up, and when your teammates come back from the revival center tell them to do the same. The second heat will begin tomorrow, and the VIPs will be watching this time."

Baffled, we were left behind in the passages outside our quarters. The room we'd been assigned to wasn't well-appointed. It was about ten meters square with uncomfortable beds stacked up along two walls.

"Home sweet home," Harris said, claiming a bottom bunk with a flourish.

"McGill?" Kivi asked me.

I turned, and I saw an emotional look on her face.

Uh-oh, I thought. This was it.

Several times in the past, when we'd come under heavy fire on some strange planet, Kivi had sought solace by sharing my bed. Sure, there wasn't any privacy here, with Harris being no more than a dozen feet off, but that hadn't fazed her in the past. She was a very physical girl.

"Uh…" I said. "What's up, Kivi?"

"Tell me about Carlos. I couldn't see well from up there on top of the elevator car. What did he do to get that jugger into the noose?"

"Oh… you want to know about that? He shoved his head right in there, teasing that overgrown lizard until he got his head snapped off."

She frowned, shaking her head. "A joker to the last, huh?"

"No girl," Harris said, his voice rumbling up from his chosen bunk. He was lying on his back with one arm thrown over his eyes to block out the bluish light in the room. "He sacrificed himself to save us all. He got the lizard to charge and shove its big ugly head into that noose. That doomed him."

"That's right," I said. "Carlos was the hero in the end."

"The hero…?" she asked, befuddled.

Harris cleared his throat. "Now, if you two are going to screw, please do it fast and quiet-like. I could really use some sleep. I got a feeling we're not through with our volunteer assignment down here at the south end of Hell."

"You got it, Harris," I said, and I gave Kivi a quick up-down of my eyebrows.

"What?" she asked, scandalized. "As-if!" She stalked away making pffing sounds.

Harris released a rumbling laugh from his bunk. "You're losing your gift, McGill. Either that, or the girls are getting smarter."

I frowned, not liking either possibility. But I didn't dwell on it. I headed for the public showers, and I took a long soak in a steamy room.

After about seven minutes in, another figure showed up. I turned with a smile, expecting it to be Kivi. Maybe she'd changed her mind—but it wasn't her.

"Natasha?" I asked in surprise. "You're down here too?"

"Yeah. We came in after you guys. We're Group Twenty-Two."

"Did you do it? Did you kill your lizard?"

She looked startled. "No—is that even possible? We ran to the end of the corridor while it chewed on Lofton. Two of us made it to the exit."

"The exit?" I asked, a frown on my face. "There was an exit?"

"Yeah, of course. Did you miss the whole point of the exercise?"

While she asked this, she unceremoniously stripped down and climbed into the stall next to me. The warm water washed off a layer of grime and blood, just as it had for me. I handed her the soap absently.

"The exit..." I said thoughtfully.

We'd never even considered the option of simply running down the hallway. No wonder we hadn't won outright. Sure, we'd killed our lizard, but that hadn't been the goal of the game. I shook my head, musing. Maybe it was for the best that we'd done it wrong.

"Say, Natasha—?"

"Forget it, James. I'm too tired. Even if you could get me out of here on a lifter tonight, the answer would still be no."

"Huh? Oh... no, no, nothing like that. I wanted to know what you've learned about this contest. What's this all about?"

"The answer is still no," she said guardedly. She didn't even look at me.

That made me feel a tiny pang. We'd had a good thing once. Of all the girls I'd shared a bed with, she was one of the sweetest. She'd fallen hard for me long ago, I knew that, and I regretted the fact I hadn't done better by her.

"Look," I said, "we're both Varus. I'm asking you what the hell is going on. Did you know that Graves actually flew all the way down to Georgia Sector to apologize for volunteering my ass into this thing?"

That made her turn and frown at me. She shut off her water, and I tried hard not to look down and watch the last runnels of water roll off her breasts. She hadn't aged a day—but then, neither had I. That was probably the only nice side-effect of dying all the time.

"Are you serious? Graves? Apologizing?"

"Yeah. He made a big effort to do it, too."

"That sounds bad..."

"Very bad. He's never given a shit about any of us before. What could be so bad that a man with a heart of stone like him would do that?"

"It can't be that lizard-chase. That wasn't any worse than the abuse he gave us as recruits."

"Right," I said. "That's what I figured."

"Could you hand me that towel, James?"

"What?"

She sighed. "Stop staring and give me a frigging towel."

"Right, sure… sorry."

I tossed her a towel and she covered up. I frowned as she did so. First Kivi, now Natasha. I was striking out, two-for-two.

I reassured myself with the facts: I hadn't even been trying.

## -8-

I took a solid nap, but it didn't last long.

A horn blared, blasting us out of our hard bunks. We were all but tossed out onto the cold, unforgiving floor.

"Damn…" Carlos said, climbing back to his feet in slow motion.

Reaching down, I gave him a hand up.

"Just got back from the revival chamber?" I asked.

"Yeah… I'm still feeling it."

"Well, that was the first bell. You've got time to shower."

"Okay."

He staggered toward the exit. We all watched him, but only Kivi moved.

"I need one too," she said, trotting after Carlos.

Winslade chuckled. I turned in surprise. His laughter was always kind of nasty-sounding, and today was no exception.

"You're back with us, sir?"

"Imagine my joy," he said. "Looks like that bio friend of yours has his squeeze-toy back again."

"Sure does," I admitted.

"How does that make you feel, McGill? To get outdone by a pug like him?"

"Pretty good, actually." I proceeded to tell him how the rest of the fight with the jugger had gone down.

Despite himself, Winslade seemed impressed. So did Sargon, who listened in as well.

"So… he teased the lizard's head into the noose…" Sargon said. "That's pretty clean. The kill was his."

"Right," Harris agreed. "McGill came up with the idea of a snare, but Carlos brought that wire to the party, and he teased the saurian into that fatal charge. He deserves the credit."

"A mutual admiration society?" Winslade asked. "I didn't think Varus grunts kept score in matters like this."

No one said anything, but we were all thinking the same thing. Winslade had been brass too long—maybe forever. Even before he'd gotten high rank, he'd been a suck-up attaché for high-level officers. For all I knew, he'd never spent a day in the trenches as a plain recruit.

Sensing the distance between us all, Winslade threw his legs off the bunk and sucked in a sharp breath through his nostrils. He seemed to regret it immediately.

"What's that stink?" he demanded. "Ah yes, of course, the goop from the revival machines. All right, as your commander, I'm ordering you *all* into the showers."

I glanced at him meaningfully and cleared my throat.

"What…? Oh… all right then, we can give our hero five more minutes alone with Kivi first."

The group waited for the five, then headed for the showers as a group. As I'd already cleaned myself, I lingered behind.

"What about you, sir?" I asked Winslade.

"I took a shower immediately after my revival. I recommend it highly, it's become my habit."

Nodding, I thought hard about how to approach the next subject. It wasn't going to be an easy one.

"Hmm…" Winslade said. His eyes narrowed and he regarded me with suspicion. "I can almost see the large wheels in your head doing a slow revolution every minute or so. What did you want to discuss, Centurion?"

"It's about leadership, sir," I said. "You see, I have it on good authority that we're going to be treated to a series of tests like the one we just went through. In order to do the best we can—"

"The answer is no, McGill."

I glanced at him in surprise. Everyone seemed to be saying that to me lately.

"You haven't heard—"

"No, I'm not going to relinquish command. Certainly, you've shown yourself a cunning leader. You're a natural alpha-dog—but you're still the dog in this pack, if you catch my meaning."

"Sir, I wasn't going to suggest you follow my orders. That would be inappropriate, given our ranks."

"Good, if that's settled then—" he said, sliding his butt off his bunk and taking a step or two toward the door.

My big arm shot up, barring his path.

He looked at it like it was the tail of the jugger we'd just fought.

I dropped my arm immediately. "Sorry sir," I said. "What I was trying to say is perhaps we could adjust our leadership roles for the good of the team."

He crossed his arms and looked up at me with surprise and suspicion.

"I'm almost amused," he said. "Diplomacy? Out of James McGill? It's like watching an ape put on lipstick. Please, by all means, proceed."

As usual, Winslade wasn't making this easy on me. He rarely did. I felt my temper rising—but I controlled myself, just barely.

"What I'm suggesting is that you perform as our liaison. If you could use your silver tongue on the brass, maybe you could gather clues that would help us out. On top of that, you'd be in charge of our overall strategy. For instance, do you realize that in that last room, we could have done better?"

I quickly told him about the true goal of the exercise: to run away.

"Hmm…" he said. "That was my first instinct, wasn't it?"

"Exactly so, sir. I tend to get bullheaded in these situations. But in real combat scenarios, I would suggest you use my skills as team-leader to execute your orders in the best way possible."

Winslade looked thoughtful. His tongue darted out, snaked over his lips, then darted back again.

I wanted to laugh at that, but I didn't.

"Interesting…" he said. "I get what you're suggesting. You play the grunt, like a noncom breaking down doors and suchlike. I, on the other hand, would be in the rear of the formation, making the big decisions."

My best Georgia smile lit my face. "That's *exactly* it, sir. What do you think?"

"Very well. Centurion McGill, you are in operational command of these petty exercises. I, however, will decide our goal in each instance. To make things clear to the troops, I'll announce my decision, and I'll verbally pass temporary leadership to you for purposes of executing my general orders."

"Excellent, Primus. But please make sure the orders are open-ended enough—give me a little breathing room, sir."

"Will do."

And thus was forged a working relationship. I knew everyone else on the team would be happy about it. All of them hated Winslade anyway, and more importantly, they didn't trust him. That sort of disconnect could be deadly in any combat scenario.

* * *

The next morning at dawn we reported for duty. By that time, our team felt like a team—not just the faceless Group Nine riding in an elevator and griping. Winslade and I had made our leadership arrangements official, and the group had taken to the idea right away.

I reflected that we'd pulled together as a team fast, and that was partly done out of necessity. Even Winslade felt the urgent need to cooperate. The jugger had given us a taste of what might be coming, and we all knew enough about violent exercises to realize we had to function like a well-oiled machine in order to survive.

The morning briefing started out in a deadly silence. Normally, if you put a few hundred legionnaires from a dozen different outfits into one big room, you got a lot of noise.

But not today.

"Troops," Imperator Turov said, strutting back and forth at the front of the room. "Welcome to the vaults. Down here, we do things we don't discuss anywhere else."

She'd had a little stage built so we could see her clearly, I guess. I found the setup unusual. It was about a meter high, and she was the only thing on it. Essentially, it was impossible for me not to stare at her.

"Today," she continued, "we're embarked on an unusual bit of diplomacy."

There was that word again: *diplomacy*. It didn't fit at all in my book. What the hell did giant sauropods, legionnaire grunts or even that pack of nerds with tablet computers who seemed to be watching our every move from the side of the room have to do with *diplomacy*?

Putting my mind into gear to figure things out, I considered the situation. First off, Turov was a woman to be reckoned with. I could scarcely believe she'd been placed in charge of another major project, as she generally screwed up whatever she touched. The fact she was still in a leadership role was testimony to her connections among the suits on the Ruling Council.

Despite her history, here she was, wearing a skin-tight uniform and…boots. Those boots weren't the norm. Once my eyes landed on them, I felt a jolt of suspicion. The boots were black and glossy, and they *looked* like legionnaire standard-issue, but I could tell right off they weren't regulation. I'd swear to it.

They were too high in the heel—that was it. In fact, after I took the whole outfit in, I came to realize she'd snuck lifts in there somehow, and the boots therefore gave her an extra two inches of height, if I had to guess.

Knowing her, I understood immediately that she wasn't just trying to look taller. Sure, she was a bit on the short side with matching petite, shapely features all the way around. But what those lifts really did, especially from the perspective of a grunt down low in the crowd, was to raise her butt up and shape it nicely.

A distraction? An idle vanity? Who knew and who cared? All of us guys were enjoying the view.

Even as I watched her with the rest of them, I felt mildly troubled. Deep down, I just didn't trust Galina Turov. She always had a third angle running that was obscured by the first two things you noticed. She was that kind of tricky.

"…so…" she continued, and I made an effort to tune back in, "Chief Inspector Xlur will be here shortly. I want to make this very clear: I want *absolute* decorum. I *demand* it! Any soldier who embarrasses Earth will pay for it dearly. Xlur hasn't graced our planet with his glorious presence in many years, and this time, his visit will go *perfectly*!"

Her mention of Xlur shocked me. My eyes jumped right up off her ass as if she'd poked them with twin needles.

My gaze met hers, and for an electric moment, I realized she *was* actually singling me out from the crowd and making eye-contact with me. It was quite possible she'd been trying to do that for some time now, while I daydreamed, examining her shoes and her tail-section.

After a moment's thought, I figured out why she was trying to get my attention. Galina and I had been involved in a disagreement with Xlur some years ago, right before Legion Varus shipped out to Machine World. That had been a dark and desperate day, even by my standards. The long and the short of it was Xlur had ended up dead, and we'd ended up swearing each other to secrecy concerning the details.

I sensed that Turov was expecting me to do something, to make some kind of response. Possibly, while I'd been distracted, she'd said something important.

Without any idea what I was agreeing to, I gave her a small nod.

That broke whatever spell she'd been under. She stopped strutting around, and she looked away from me quickly. Her entire demeanor shifted.

Turov halted and stood still, assuming a wide military stance. Her hands were clasped behind her back. Her vision swept over the ranks as everyone else reacted to her news, murmuring among themselves about the prospect of having a Galactic in the same room with us.

"Xlur is a Mogwa," she said after we'd quieted again, "as you all should know. Remember, our province is only one of thousands in our beloved Empire, and no Frontier citizen is more interesting than a worm to a Mogwa. Xlur wields total power within the boundaries of Frontier 921. He is, for all intents and purposes, a living god on this green Earth."

Our initial shock passed, and the crowd quieted down. Most of us, especially the troops from the respectable outfits like Germanica and the Iron Eagles, now stood at sharp attention. The Germanic pukes in particular were as stiff as boards, and their eyes were wide in alarm. Almost no one wanted to screw up in front of a real live Mogwa.

Naturally, there were exceptions to this general response. Pretty much all the dissenters were among my own teammates. We'd met more than our share of Galactics over the years, and we weren't overawed by them.

Kivi crossed her arms and looked down. Carlos shook his head and kicked at the floor with the toe of his boot.

Sargon, taking the part of veteran seriously, used his own boot to wake Carlos up. With a hiss and curse, Carlos straightened. Kivi did the same, before she caught a boot in the butt as well.

"Well done, Veteran," Harris murmured.

Sargon said nothing, but I could tell the praise made him proud. Harris had been our veteran for many years, and he'd only been moved up into the officer ranks recently.

"Good..." Turov said, eyeing the crowd and apparently liking what she saw. "I can see you understand the importance of this day. Chief Inspector Xlur will operate as one of the judges of this contest. He will not vote—but he will be watching with keen interest."

I glanced at Winslade, hoping he had some insight into what kind of contest we could expect. More lizards?

Noticing my scrutiny, Winslade merely widened his eyes and fractionally shrugged his shoulders in response. Apparently, he didn't know what we had in store for us either. On the other hand, he could be faking it. You just couldn't tell with Winslade. He was as slippery as a snake oil salad.

"Let's get down to it. The results of the first day's contest were inconclusive. The best teams—Group Four and Group Twenty-One, suffered only a single loss each."

At the mention of their numbers, one pack from Germanica and another from The Iron Eagles cheered.

That made me frown a bit. Sure, Group Nine had lost half our people, but we'd killed our lizard. That ought to count for an extra death or two.

"Due to this lack of a clear winner, we've decided to eliminate half the contestants due to their incompetence. Every group that had no or only one survivor is hereby dismissed. I thank you for your service."

Up and down the lines, there was a shuffling. About ten groups walked away, shaking their heads. Some cursed, some cheered weakly.

The other groups grinned at them and flashed eyebrows. This was met with angry words, and in a single case, a fist was thrown.

It came as no surprise to anyone that the belligerent soldier was from Solstice. They had a rep that was almost as bad as Legion Varus. In fact, it occurred to me as the unruly Solstice veteran was thrown out of the room, that if one of our Varus groups had been kicked out and sneered at, there would have been more punches thrown—maybe a lot of them.

Turov watched this display sourly.

"There! You see that? That demonstrates the lack of discipline that probably caused them to die like rats in the first place! Don't allow them to trouble your thoughts again! You're better than them! All of you!"

A ragged cheer went up, although the remaining half was beginning to wonder what they'd won through their success.

Carlos wasn't under any illusions. "I screwed us," he said in a low tone. "I'm sorry guys. I think I should have let that lizard eat us all, like so much ground-up cat food."

No one said anything, but I couldn't help but wonder if he would prove to be right in the end.

Turov smiled and slammed her small hands together, making a popping sound. "Congratulations, winners! You will go on! You will be outfitted, and prepped, and you will prove yourselves again! Remember, Xlur will be watching!"

Again, the ragged cheer broke out. It was far from full-throated, however.

Turov cleared off the stage, and the wall behind her yawned open. After a moment, it became clear it was a smart-wall, one that could be reconfigured to the dimensions and shape required.

"Up!" Graves shouted from behind us. "Up on that stage! Advance, take a weapon, and move into the pits!"

*The pits?*

We turned away from him, back toward the stage. We could see now that the area behind it was quite large. A series of depressions were visible when we climbed onto the raised area and advanced.

Between us and these "pits" were racks of weapons. They were all basic in nature. Knives, spears, swords and a few throwing axes.

"Whoa," Carlos said, "this is going to suck more than I thought."

Sargon ignored him and vaulted onto the raised area. I understood the whole stage-thing better now. It had never been a stage. In order to create pits, they'd been forced to raise the floor, as the bottom of the vault was pure puff-crete, one of the hardest substances known to man.

Sargon wasn't fooling around. He rushed the racks and grabbed for a spear.

I happened to know, from past experiences, that he was a gifted man with a spear. He could throw one like he was born to it.

But unfortunately, he wasn't alone. Another big fellow with hair braided tightly against his head had rushed for the weapon racks as well. Both of them, apparently, were interested in the spear, valuing its reach.

The second man was from Germanica. He tried to snatch the spear away from Sargon.

"Hold on!" I shouted, running up to them. "Hold on, now!"

"We haven't got any instructions yet," Harris called out. He was right behind me.

Sargon and the other man eyed one another in cold anger. Then, suddenly, Sargon shrugged and gave him a smile. His grip loosened, and the Germanica asshole yanked the spear away.

"This will end up in your guts, Varus!" he shouted, laughing.

Happy, the Germanica man turned away and walked with an exaggerated swagger toward his team, who hooted at us. He shook the spear overhead like a trophy.

In his last moments, he opened his big mouth again, no doubt intending to hurl a fresh insult toward my people—but he never got the chance.

Sargon had grabbed up an axe. Without hesitation, with an even stride, he walked up behind the Germanica man and split his skull right down the middle.

The sound was like that of a melon striking a sidewalk. Blood exploded, but Sargon snatched up the fallen spear from dead fingers with a wide grin. He even waved it at the dead man's friends.

"Oh, gee-zus—" Harris began. "Damn it, Sargon!"

The Germanica people lost it. They snatched up weapons from the racks, shouting with rage.

I sensed things were getting out of hand early, so I took up the axe Sargon had discarded. After all, it had been pretty effective.

## -9-

"DIE, VARUS!" the Germanica people roared as one.

"HALT!" boomed a deafening voice, amplified by a throat mic from the end of the stage.

It was a narrow thing, but we did all pause, snarling at one another.

Tribune Deech approached at a leisurely pace. She looked at the dead man and put her hands on her wide hips.

"This is a violation of the rules," she said. "No one is supposed to strike until you're in your assigned pits and given the go-ahead."

"No one told us that," I said. "My man was challenged, and he took action."

"McGill...?" Deech said, recognizing me and looking me over. "Your team is off the rails already, huh? Why am I not surprised?"

"Can you tell us the rules, sir? We obviously don't know them."

"All right. It's pretty simple. We're placing two teams in every pit for two minutes. Whichever group defeats the enemy and crawls out with the most members standing wins. You broke those rules, so you lose by default."

The Germanica group hooted and laughed.

"But no one told us anything," I said again stubbornly.

"That's true..." Deech said thoughtfully. "Imperator Turov was supposed to do it, but she seems distracted today. Two more damned sentences added to her speech would have done it."

"Tribune Deech!" another voice called out, and a tall figure approached. "Perhaps I can be of some assistance with your animals."

We all looked up. It was none other than Tribune Maurice Armel. He had a French accent, a wispy mustache riding above a set of sneering lips, and most importantly, he was the leader of Legion Germanica.

"Maurice," Deech said. "I'd welcome your input."

"The rules are the rules," he said. "I know such cold logic hurts, especially when it's applied to a group of feral, emotion-driven creatures such as yours, but—there it is."

Deech looked annoyed, but I was worried. She was, at the bottom of her heart, a woman who believed in law and order. Quite possibly, she was the straightest arrow in Legion Varus. Maybe that's why they'd made her our overall commander.

A faint smile played over Armel's face now. He knew Deech well. He knew our tribune was a sucker for an argument like that, one that appealed to the strict letter of the law.

"We can fix it," I said loudly. "I'll give up Sargon. He'll step aside. He's our best man in a pit-fight. That way, it will be five-on-five from the start."

Armel made a big show of considering my proposal carefully. He squinted, and he rubbed at his swarthy chin. But at last, he ended this act with a regretful shake of his head.

"I'm afraid not," he said. "You've clearly planned this whole thing out. Legion Varus is infamous for such trickery, such foul deceit. I wouldn't even be surprised to learn—"

"How in the hell could we plan something?" I demanded, losing my temper at last. "We didn't even know what the rules were until—"

"McGill," Tribune Deech said in a commanding voice. "Stand down."

I shut up. I had some respect for Deech, even though we didn't always see eye-to-eye.

"We'll forfeit this round," Deech said. "It's unfortunate, but I don't see any other way to solve this, and we need to move ahead."

"Very, very gracious of you, Tribune," Armel said. "In fact, if you'd enjoy having a drink together while we observe the rest of this glorious contest, I'd like to invite you—"

"Don't worry about it, McGill," Winslade said loudly, turning his back on the two tribunes and the grinning Germanica assholes. He patted me on the shoulder. "They got lucky, and they know it. We would have torn them apart."

"What?" Armel said, narrowing his eyes and turning his head to follow us. "What was it one of your apes said, Deech?"

Winslade gave me a subtle wink.

Instantly, I got the message. *Damn*, I thought, I should have come up with it myself.

"There's no shame in it," I said loudly, turning back to face them. "Everyone has to know when to fight, and when to run. There's no shame in that at all, Tribune."

Armel was stock-still, his gaze burning in my direction. I could tell he was at war internally. It was entertaining to try and guess which side of him was going to win out: his brain, or his sense of pride.

"You would dare call a Germanica team... *cowards*?" he asked.

"Well now," I said, crossing my arms. "You're the one who came up with that word, not us. You must have thought it up all by yourself. But now that you've put it out there... this whole thing does seem fishy. Could it be that Germanica was the one doing the scheming here? Seriously Tribune? All this just to get out of a fair fight?"

Behind my back, my team had gathered. We were solid now, I realized. We weren't catcalling and making obscene gestures—but we were grinning smugly.

"No one will say such a thing," Armel announced. "No Varus trash will ever *dare* to claim a Germanica man piddled himself in fear. I hereby accept your offer. You have only to ban this shaved ape named Sargon from the pit, and my team will defeat yours honorably."

"Done!" Tribune Deech said. "Pair off against your opposing groups, everyone! This contest will last for two minutes. The team with the best combination score, based on kills and men left standing, will win."

A murmur swept the crowd, punctuated by a few energetic whoops and threats.

"To kick off the event," Deech continued, "I'm going to count down slowly from ten. When I get to one, everyone will have a single second to get your ass into that pit and start fighting. Good luck, and do your best!"

A roar went up from the assembled teams. We'd been readying ourselves mentally and physically all this time, stretching, gripping our weapons, and rubbing talc into our sweating palms.

"...Ten!" shouted Deech.

Pounding feet sounded all over the raised stage. Groups assembled on opposite sides of each pit. Our mouths opened of their own accords. Our lungs sucked in air, and we let it hiss back out through our teeth.

"...Nine!"

I felt my heart pound, and I waved my axe overhead in challenge to Germanica, they snarled in return. We were ready.

"...Eight!"

Off at the far end of the chamber, a sound distracted us. A section of the smart-wall began to peel away. Behind this was what amounted to rows of seats and cordoned off areas.

A throng of onlookers sat there, perched on what looked like cushy chairs.

"What the fuck...?" Harris asked next to me, and I seconded the emotion. We had spectators?

"...Seven!"

"Hey!" Kivi said, pointing into the stands. "Look up there... isn't that Xlur himself?"

It was indeed the Chief Inspector. Physically, the Mogwa was a spidery alien with a central thorax of waxy black. Xlur's six limbs operated as either arms or legs. Each of his terminating hands—or feet—could be used to manipulate objects.

"...Six!" Deech boomed.

"McGill," Carlos said at my side. "I want you to know how uncool this whole thing is."

"...Five!"

"What?" I asked, turning to him in confusion.

"You could have let it go, man. You could have let us forfeit out, and we'd be done with this shit. But noooo, you just had to—"

"...Four!"

"Carlos," I interrupted, "you look across that pit."

Reluctantly, he did so.

"...THREE!"

"You really wanted me to let Armel humiliate us? Really? Then you can stay out of this."

"What?"

"...TWO!"

"You heard me! Stay out of the pit! You stand up here and save your skin. Why don't you piss yourself too, while you're at it?"

"*ONE!*" Deech roared at last, and a huge cry rolled up from the fighters. Even the audience of high-ranking officers joined in.

I threw myself into the pit, and my eager gang followed. Even Winslade jumped in without hesitation.

Winslade's example might have shamed Carlos. He hopped in after us, screaming out a single word: "VARUS!"

## -10-

I was angry. I don't mind admitting it. Sure, that's not the best state of mind to be in at the start of a serious fight, but it's not the worst, either.

As an opener, I took a chance. Sometimes, that's what a leader has to do: get things started.

Cocking back my arm, I gripped Sargon's axe and heaved it into the thick of the enemy.

The pit itself was about ten meters across, if I had to guess. That might sound like plenty of room—but it isn't. There were ten of us inside that limited space, and it felt like we were ten mice trapped in a shoebox.

With only a split-second to dodge, the lead man in the approaching group managed it—but the guy hiding behind him didn't. I nailed him full in the chest.

The axe chopped right through his breastbone and kept going. Damn, that thing was sharp! It must have a monofilament blade on the head.

Whatever the stage surrounding our pit was made of, it must have been something porous, because the axe thunked into it and pinned the squirming, dying legionnaire there.

Now, with only four souls left to face five, Germanica's team didn't look so smug. Of course I'd managed to disarm myself, so I fell back, letting my team wrap around me and move forward.

Harris had chosen a long knife from the racks. There was no surprise in that, as he was an expert with that particular weapon. He took the point position of our group without being ordered to, and he did so with relish.

Unfortunately, he was faced by a man with a sword—a rapier. Harris tried to get in close, but the enemy was a wiry fellow, quick on his feet. He seemed to know what he was doing with a long blade, and he stop-thrust Harris and hurt him bad.

I dared to turn my head, looking from side to side at the rest of this mess of a fight. Winslade and Carlos were both sparring with their opponents, tapping weapons and making fake jabs—without going for the kill.

At the center of the ring, Kivi was standing behind Harris. I could tell she was looking for an opening. The swordsman struck again, and he ran Harris clean through.

Kivi saw her chance. She darted in while Harris had the swordsman's weapon bound up with his ribs, and she clocked the man on the left knee with a weighted club. He went down, howling.

That might have meant a victory for us, but Harris began convulsing. He died on the wood chips littering the floor of the pit.

I tried to dash in and snatch up Harris' fallen knife, but these Germanic friggers were on top of their game. I got my hand pinned down by some kind of forked stick.

*Damn,* that hurt, but the tines of the big fork didn't penetrate the puff-crete under the wood chips. I was able to rip my hand loose and send the owner sprawling on top of Harris. It was a woman, and she hadn't been prepared for the strength of my yanking motion.

I could move again, but my right hand was a wreck. I held it up against my body, kind of curled, dangling and bleeding at the same time. I figured the tendons were gone.

Seeing a shot at glory, the girl grinned and pulled back for another savage thrust with her trident-thing. Backpedalling wasn't going to cut it, because the rim of the pit was only a few feet behind me. I dodged, but I could see right off that wasn't going to work, either. She meant to plant that thing in me, and all I could do was try to take it in a less vital spot.

But then, the game shifted again. Winslade bounced into view behind her. He slid in a weapon that looked for all the world like an icepick. He stabbed several times. He was good—if he caught you from behind.

The girl who'd been trying to fork me collapsed, stunned and choking.

I got my balance after that and snatched up Harris' knife with my good hand. I had it in my left, but that didn't bother me. You didn't get far in Legion Varus if you couldn't defend yourself while wounded.

Looking around, I was confused. Where was the enemy? They all seemed to be down, bleeding.

"TIME!" Deech boomed from above us.

We backed off, tossing our weapons down. The fight was over.

The last Germanica fighters tried to rise, but they couldn't stand. All of a sudden, I got it: Kivi had been running around, smacking kneecaps. She'd put down three that way.

The enemy fighters weren't all dead, or even mortally wounded, but they couldn't stand up unaided. In comparison, we'd lost Harris and no one else.

"Varus WINS!" Carlos shouted at the top of his lungs.

I shook my head at him. Now that the action was over, he was all full of grins and war-whoops.

The scoring committee took their sweet time getting to our pit. Armel, Turov and Deech made up the three judges.

Both Armel and Turov looked like they smelled something bad when they walked up to our pit—something real bad. In their defense, they probably did.

"Let's see," Deech said with a faint smile on her lips. "What's the count here? One, two, three… four Varus still standing?" She managed to sound surprised.

My good arm rose up, and I shook my fist overhead.

"And… oh my, where are your Germanica troops, Armel?"

"They're nose-down in the sawdust, that's where!" I shouted at them.

63

The tribunes both gave me a brief glare, so I forced myself to shut up. It was hard to do. Nothing seemed to get my blood pumping more than an arrogant officer like Armel.

"All right then," Deech said. "That's a score of four-up, plus six-down. The total score for Group Nine is ten points."

"What?" Armel demanded, whirling around on one sharp boot heel. "I know you have a sense of humor, but this isn't the time or place for comedy, Deech."

"I don't understand."

That was a lie. As a near-professional liar, I could see that plain as day. Deech wasn't good at lying, most people weren't. Oh, she could spot liars a mile off—but that wasn't the same thing as coming up with your own convincing twists to the truth.

"Let me spell out the situation for you," Armel told her. "Five men entered this pit on each side. That means the Varus score is *nine*, four standing, plus five down."

"Ah," Deech said. "You're right, I *did* make an error. I forgot to count Sargon over there. With him added to the group, Varus would have eleven."

Armel's face reddened. He took in a long, deep breath and blew it out again, making his whispery mustache flutter.

"Are you saying these things only to irritate me? If so, it's most immature."

"Tribunes," Imperator Turov said, stepping between them. "This is unnecessary. Why argue about the score—unless it decides the winner?"

Both officers looked down at her. Even wearing heels, Turov was a head shorter than either of them.

"Unfortunately," Deech said, "it will make a material difference to the outcome. Clearly, as the third judge and our commander, the choice will come down to you, Imperator. How should we score this contest?"

Turov walked to the pit and looked over the fallen. Orderlies from the bio unit that was on duty to handle the event were helping the wounded and carrying off the dead.

"I choose Varus," Turov said at last. "They put on a better show. That's what these aliens want in the end, isn't it? A good show?"

After rendering her verdict, Turov headed back toward the comfy seats. Her hips rolled as she walked—even more than usual. That had to be an effect caused by her new boots.

Armel fumed, and Deech managed not to smile.

"The score is final," she said, "and with this second contest, it's conclusive. Varus tied with several groups in the first heat, but the second was a clear victory. We don't need to continue."

"Only because they applied low blows," Armel complained bitterly. "Let us pray their alien counterparts will have weak knees to strike at!"

"I sincerely hope that they do," Deech said.

Armel turned on me, and he looked wrathful for a moment, but then his face softened as new idea overcame him.

"James McGill..." he said. "Never has a man so richly earned the fate that awaits you and your unit. In the end... well, I truly hope you don't come to regret this triumph. That would be a shame."

"Uh... thanks, sir... I think..."

Laughing, Armel whirled and marched away. When he'd gone, I turned to Deech.

"Sir?" I said, "I'm not sure I understand this whole thing. We're to face aliens next? Is that it?"

"Yes," Deech said, and she looked down at her scoring chart. "I... I'm sorry you weren't properly informed. Every legion was called upon to choose a cohort as their champions. Of course, it wouldn't do to have full units brawling at once, so we reduced the cohorts to small teams."

Winslade stepped forward and spoke up. "Tribune?" he said, "I'd like to point out that I'm not actually in the direct chain of command between you and McGill, here."

"That's right," Deech said. "Graves is in charge of this cohort. But the Imperator made a special request. Your name was placed on the roster as a representative high-level officer. She said something about it being good for your character."

Winslade looked pale, as if he'd been slapped. He pressed his lips together so hard they looked bloodless and puckered.

"I see," he said.

I got it, too. Turov had put Winslade in the doghouse. Who knew what he'd done to deserve it in her eyes? It could have been anything from failing on a private mission to forgetting to rub her feet at night.

"Burn..." Carlos said quietly behind us.

Sargon smacked him, which was a good thing, because that way I didn't have to do it.

"What's next then, Tribune?" I asked Deech.

She glanced over at the visiting dignitaries in their comfy seats then turned back to me. Was it my imagination, or was she checking out Armel the same way I'd been checking out Turov? It was a chilling thought.

"Take a break," she said to my team, "and heal yourselves. There's to be a banquet in your honor tonight."

"A banquet?" Sargon asked, perking up. "I love good food."

"Excellent," Deech said. "You'll learn more tonight, but this whole thing is somewhat shrouded in mystery. It was arranged by the Mogwa, after all. We're players in this game—but we aren't pulling the strings."

Deech looked back toward Xlur, and I stared with her. A crowd of kiss-asses surrounded the alien, talking and sipping drinks. I hoped they'd enjoyed our spectacle of violence, which had apparently served the Mogwa as entertainment. From my position, they appeared happy.

"Look at them," Carlos said, "all sucking up to Xlur. He's got something like sixty toes, you know. I bet they'd lick them all if he asked."

Glancing after Deech, I saw she'd moved on. If Carlos was going to start saying rude things, that was probably for the best.

"Should I smack down this specialist for you again, Centurion?" Sargon asked me.

"No..." I said. "No... because he's right. I also want to apologize to everyone on my team in advance."

"What for?" Sargon asked.

"In case it goes really badly," Winslade filled him in.

"It's tits-up already, if you ask me. It's all Kivi's fault, too. Damn girl, did you have to be born so tricky?"

"I'll kneecap you tonight," she said, "then you can ask me that question again."

Carlos laughed and grabbed for her. They began making out, and I smiled remotely. At least they were happy.

For now.

## -11-

To my way of thinking, an invitation to a banquet is something a man just doesn't turn down. Heck, when the mess hall laid out the daily spread of chow, I was always the first in line. Always.

So, it came as no surprise to anyone that knew me that I was up front at the officer's mess that same night. My arm was in a sling, but that was just to immobilize it. The bio people had done their wet-work and shot me up with happy-drugs to boot. As a result, I was in a pretty damned good mood.

"Hiya, Imperator!" I called as Galina joined me in line.

She ran her eyes up and down my lengthy person and narrowed them.

"Are you drunk, McGill?"

"No sir! I'm a winner!"

She sighed. "Yes… I'm glad you're happy about that."

"What kind of a hellhole meat-grinder have we won, anyway?"

Her eyes flashed back to meet mine. "Who has been talking to you?" she snapped.

I blinked, not quite getting it. "Uh… lots of people. Mostly, they're congratulating me on the beat-down we gave Germanica. Did you realize that Legion Germanica is one of the most hated outfits on Earth? The public looks up to them, sure, but the other legions—"

"Shut up."

"Yes sir."

A few minutes passed, and more people kept filing in. At last, to the rear of the procession, I saw flapping movement.

Xlur's six limbs churned, and all four hand-like appendages hit the ground in a unique pattern. Only a Mogwa walked like that. To me, he looked like a cross between an ant and a chimp walking on all fours.

"Sure is strange to think about," I said, eyeing him.

"What do you mean?"

"That some kind of bug-monkey critter like that can boss us around on our own home planet."

"Don't talk like that," she growled at me. "Ever."

"Right, Galina. Sorry."

"I'm your superior officer. You will address me with respect, McGill."

"Oh damn! I'm sorry, your first name just slipped out."

Turov eyed me critically for a moment. "I think I made a mistake inviting you to this event. Just about anything might fall out of your mouth tonight. I think you're going back to your unit."

"Aw now, come on, Imperator! Don't do that, I'm really looking forward to some good chow."

Before she could answer, an unwelcome voice called out loudly from the rear of the line. It was none other than Tribune Armel.

"There he is! We are in great luck! Come, Chief Inspector, you simply *must* meet an amazing person. He's a rising star from Legion Varus. He's only a centurion now, but mark my words, someday James McGill will run Varus. Some say he does so already!"

"Oh, hell…" I said in a low tone.

"That red-assed bastard," Turov hissed at my side.

Jumping ahead in line, Armel marched past a dozen frowning officers like they weren't there. At his side was the wobble-gaited Xlur.

Coming up to the head of the line with Turov and me, Armel gave us both a wide grin. We nodded stiffly in return.

"Tribune Armel," Turov said. "It's such a surprise to see you escorting the Inspector. I thought Equestrian Drusus was going to perform this honor."

"I was under that impression too, Galina," he said. "But apparently, Drusus had other pressing matters to attend to."

Galina gave him a brief, hate-filled stare. She didn't like people using her first name, especially if she outranked them.

Tribune Armel had a single sunburst as a rank insignia, which was more or less equivalent to a one-star general of the past. Turov, for her part, had two sunbursts. Drusus, the commander at Central, wore three.

"Well, in any case," she said, forcing her face to soften, "we are greatly honored to see you at our table, Inspector Xlur."

For his part, Inspector Xlur had been taking it all in. He was an arrogant prick of an alien, but he wasn't dumb. Not by a long shot.

"Turov…" he said, working his tapper briefly. "Yes, I've found the reference. We've met before. But what is this oversized beast? What did you call him?"

He indicated me with a single pointing finger among many.

Turov and Armel both opened their mouths to answer, but I beat them to it.

"I'm Centurion James McGill, sir," I said. "It's an honor."

Xlur's eye-groups went to his tapper again. "Yes… the McGill-creature. I recall an encounter from the day of my… accident."

"Ah-ha!" Armel hooted. "So, you've met McGill before, have you? I'm sure you must have a very favorable opinion, in that case. I like to call him a shining gem, hidden at the very core of Legion Varus."

"You are an odd being," Xlur said to Armel, then he turned back to eye me again. "Unfortunately, I lost some of my memory files that day, probably due to the inferior networking systems on this dark, backwater planet. In any case, I can't remember any details about the McGill."

"Dinner is served!" Turov announced, opening the velvet rope that held us all in check.

A flutter-fingered waiter rushed us, waving us back, but when he saw the ranks on those epaulets, he retreated and shut his mouth tight.

Turov showed Xlur to a table and waved a hand at me and Armel, indicating a different table. "You two will sit over there."

"No!" Xlur's translator box boomed suddenly. "I wish to regain something of my prior thoughts. I will dine with the McGill—and this odd, loud being as well."

Turov showed her teeth in the tightest smile I'd ever witnessed. "Of course, Chief Inspector. The banquet is in your honor, after all."

We took our seats around a beautifully laid out table. The silverware wasn't only silver though. There were gold handles on every knife, fork and spoon. But that wasn't the most amazing element of the ensemble. What really got me was the glassware.

Grabbing up what looked like the stem of a chalice cut from a solid gemstone. There was no glass, just the stem. I waved it at a passing waiter, who immediately approached.

"What would you like, sir?" he asked me with an accent that reminded me of Armel's.

"Give me some of the red stuff," I said.

He snatched up a dark green bottle and tilted it to pour. I let him pour it seemingly into my hand which gripped the iridescent stem.

My chalice was a fancy alien-made device. The intelligent glass sensed the falling liquid, and a field flickered into life. It captured every drop of wine, and formed a swirling globe that caught the light of the candles in our centerpiece as well.

"Hot damn," I marveled, "would you look at that? I've heard about this kind of mug, but I've never held one in my hand before."

"Taste your beverage, McGill," Armel said. His chalice was half-empty already. "I want to hear how much you appreciate this particular variety of 'red stuff' as you call it. You should be aware that it cost Hegemony several thousand credits a bottle."

"In that case," I said, "maybe you shouldn't gulp it so fast, sir."

His eyes darkened, and his face turned red, but before he could shout at me, Xlur spoke up.

"Turov," Xlur said. "Do I understand your system of ranks? Are you in command here?"

"You are correct as always, Chief Inspector," she said.

"In that case, I'm appalled. You allow your subordinates to speak as they wish. Is that a failing in your leadership, or an affectation?"

"I'm sorry if they're bothering you, Chief Inspector. Should I have them silenced?"

The way she said this last word gave me a pang of concern. It didn't sound like she meant she was going to lightly scold us.

"Normally, I would demand it," the Mogwa said. "But tonight I want to experience the confusion and filth that is Earth. I'm curious about your dim-lit ball of dirt. For some reason I keep hearing about it, although I can't fathom what the fuss is about."

"We are the Empire's local enforcers in Frontier 921," Turov said, clearly deciding to take Xlur's words in the best possible light. "We're proud to have served the Empire so well."

"What an inconsequential statement," Xlur mused. "Perhaps it's my translation box. It fails to perform well when interpreting fringe languages."

"I'm so sorry to hear that," Turov purred. "Perhaps I could have some of our best techs see if they could fix it?"

"Absolutely not," Xlur said stiffly. "That would entail a breach of licensing laws."

"A pity."

About then, to everyone's relief, the food showed up. We were served wonderful dishes, including sea-brisket, squab and venison soup. I'd never tasted anything like it—and it was all good.

Xlur even seemed to be enjoying his food. He tried a few earthly flavors, particularly enjoying the squab.

"Is this a flying insect?" he asked.

"A bird, Inspector," Turov answered. "It does fly, however, yes."

"It's excellent. You will have a thousand of these transported to my personal ship by morning."

Turov's eyes flew wide, but she recovered quickly. She popped her hands together, and a waiter rushed to us.

"What is it, sirs?"

She relayed the request without so much as a smile or an apologetic shrug. The waiter looked sick, but he nodded.

"I'll see what the kitchens can do."

He raced off, and I could only imagine the hubbub Xlur had created with his off-handed request. A few minutes later, I saw waiters deployed all over the mess hall retrieving every squab they'd laid out on other people's plates. This caused some complaining, but after a few whispers and pointed fingers indicating our table, dissenters quickly fell quiet. Everyone knew our Mogwa guest had the right to eat our firstborn children, if he'd wanted to.

After the food was consumed, Xlur stopped listening to Armel and Turov. He instead eyed me with a cluster of optical organs.

"You're quiet," he said to me suddenly. "That's unusual."

"Uh…" I began. "Well sir, I'm the low-ranked man, and I don't want to step on the words of my superiors."

"A wise rule of conduct," the Mogwa agreed. "But it's a rule that you've rarely, if ever, practiced."

"Chief Inspector," Turov interrupted in her sweetest tone, "if McGill has decided to mend his ways, wouldn't it be best if we all encouraged him on this new path?"

Xlur looked back at her. "You speak to me as if I were a child. I'm not offspring—I'm an adult Mogwa. Are you aware of this?"

"Of course, Great One," she said.

She looked flustered, and all our easy talk died.

Xlur turned back to me. "I know who you are now. I've been reading reports with my off-brain while we consumed this meal. You spoke to Grand Admiral Sateekas personally, when the battle fleet came to erase your planet."

"Um… yes, I might have."

73

"You were in his reports. Some passages were glowing, others were highly derogatory. Anyone reading those after-action reports would think the McGill ruled this bush-kingdom."

"No sir," I said. "I'm just a soldier. Sometimes, I get into spots where I'm in over my head, that's true, but I'm not that important."

"So… Sateekas lied? Is that the nature of your accusation? What would be his motivation to do so?"

"Uh…"

"Chief Inspector, please—" Turov began.

"Do not speak!" Xlur boomed at her suddenly, loudly. "I'm now suspecting a great secret lurks here. I'm not sure what it is, but I have verified that this being was present when I last visited this dirtball and died. He was also instrumental in the turning back of the Empire's local battle fleet. Today, he is here again at my table. Did you somehow believe these events would go unnoticed?"

Turov froze, her eyes wide. Her mouth hung open, but she didn't make a sound. She'd been ordered to be silent in the same breath she was asked a question, and it looked like she was going to play it safe.

Xlur seemed satisfied with her freaked-out stare. He turned back to me.

Armel, for his part, watched the proceedings with a mixture of interest and concern. He'd set up all this, of course, but I didn't think he'd meant for things to get so serious. He wore the expression of a man who tossed hot ashes over a hated neighbor's fence, only to see flames licking at the roof an hour later.

Sensing the shift in mood at our table, the rest of the mess hall had fallen quiet. Two dozen high-ranking officers were all craning their necks, staring and worrying.

"I've yet to hear the McGill-creature's response," Xlur said. "Explain yourself."

"Um… what was the question again, exactly?"

The truth was, I'd had quite a bit of wine. Worse, I'd been sailing high on pain-meds when I came in the door. What I wanted most right now was a soft bunk and hard nap.

Turov's hand came up to cover her eyes. She looked between a web of fingers, and her eyes pleaded with me to fix things.

"Idiocy," Xlur said, and he turned back to Turov. "I'm reading an odd data stream on my tapper as I scan the McGill."

"He is indeed an odd one, Lord," Armel murmured.

"Before daring to return to this barbaric planet," Xlur said, "I took certain precautions. A new app measures beasts of all sorts for mental acuity, truthfulness, obedience ratings and general health. McGill is providing unique input. The app is baffled."

"Yes!" Turov said, seizing on the opportunity like a drowning man reaching for a life preserver. "We've had similar confusing measurements. We test our recruits, and McGill has always been an enigma. He seems at one moment ingenious, and the next dimwitted."

"This explains so much," Xlur said, leaning back and seeming to relax. All around the mess hall, dozens of others sighed in relief with him. "Why he is not promoted. Why he acts erratically. Why you have endured him without permanent execution."

"All that, and more," Armel said quietly.

Xlur looked at him. He ruffled his limbs. "You, creature, have never performed an action of import to the Empire. I tire of your misplaced comments. Speak again in my presence, and I'll demand that your organs are removed."

Armel froze. He didn't look happy, but he *did* shut the hell up. I was left wondering which organs Xlur was referring to.

Xlur turned back to Turov. "I thank you for this experience, servant," he said. "I've always had questions concerning this place. Dark events have unfolded with unnatural frequency on this lonely stretch of the frontier. Can you tell me why I shouldn't request the McGill-creature be put down? As a chaotic mutant, he might be dangerous to all of us."

Galina blinked, surprised by the question. She looked at me, then at Armel. Neither of us spoke, as the question had been directed to her.

"We have found him useful at times, Lord," she said simply.

"I can see that. Intriguing…"

"My comment was in no way meant as a refusal, Chief Inspector," she said. "Would you like him to be permed? You have only to make the request."

Armel came back to life at this shift in the conversation. His face brightened, and it seemed to me that his mustache curled a little higher at the corners of his mouth.

Xlur pondered for a moment.

"No," he said at last. "I will leave the choice up to you. Earth has done amazing things for such a small power on the edge of the endless night. As I haven't been personally affronted, I have no cause to order such a thing—not today, in any case."

"Excellent. Shall we retire for the night?"

"Yes," said the Mogwa, "but I will not be staying on your cold little planet another night. I'm going up to my ship immediately. Are you prepared to deploy your delegation?"

"Yes," Turov said. "We've chosen our champions. We will send them immediately."

"See that you do. We aren't prepared yet for hostilities. They must be appeased—for now."

"I understand, Chief Inspector. Good night."

The Mogwa left, and everyone watched him go.

After he'd exited the room, the dinner broke up, but I don't think most of the humans who attended were able to sleep well or digest their food easily that night.

That was a shame, really, considering how good the meal had been.

Fortunately, I was an exception to this rule. I was stress-free. The Mogwa I'd murdered years ago had met me, and I'd survived. By my accounting, that made the evening just about perfect.

## -12-

In the morning, I was unsurprised to see a blinking red message on my tapper. I'd been called into Turov's office.

That involved a very long elevator ride to start off with. When I'd gone about a thousand floors up and the doors dinged open, I found myself squinting in a gush of honest-to-God sunlight.

Walking down a long, quiet hall lined with offices full of hog brass and their underlings, I finally reached the end and started to tap on the door.

The door melted away, and I stepped inside.

"Neat trick door," I commented.

A sour Winslade sat like a secretary in the front office. He jerked his thumb at the next door behind him, where Turov must be holding court.

I paused on my way past his desk.

"Hey," I said. "They put you back to work already? Flying a desk?"

"Apparently," he said, without looking at me.

Winslade and I had a terrible past. We'd killed one another with a vengeance on many occasions. He was, in fact, a weasel of the first order.

But despite all of that, when we got into the real shit together, and the bullets and the blood were flying, we typically found we could rely on one another. Our last few days in elevators and pit-fights had proven that.

"Hey," I said. "For what it's worth, you did good down there. Just as good as any of my team. You're a Varus man, in my book."

Winslade looked up at me. His eyes were full of suspicion for a second. I could tell he was thinking I was making fun of him somehow.

But I wasn't, and he saw that pretty quickly.

Shrugging like he didn't care, he looked down again.

"Thanks," he said.

And that was it. There were no hugs, tears, or sloppy kisses. I didn't know if we were friends now or still enemies, but then I didn't much care, either. I always call them as I see them about stuff like that—stuff that matters.

Barging into Turov's office like I owned the place, I gave her a big smile.

"McGill," she said. "Do you know how hard it was to sleep last night?"

"Was something bothering you, Imperator?"

"Yes, something was bothering me! We almost got erased *again*! That damned Armel—he just had to go and pull a prank at dinner."

"Armel is a funny guy," I said. "He's got quite the sense of humor."

"That wasn't funny!" she said angrily. "He was out of his depth. Snide, drunk, and out of control. Even you know when you're in real trouble—and you're better at getting away with stunts."

The thought occurred to me that I could egg her on right now. Maybe, if I pushed like Winslade enjoyed doing, I could work her up into a frenzy and get Armel flogged or demoted or something. The idea was tempting, but I didn't like playing the weasel just for fun, so I shut up and stopped stoking her flames any higher.

"Imperator," I said, switching topics, "I'm getting some bad vibes about this mission. Where, exactly, are we going?"

She didn't meet my eyes. She looked down instead, fooling with her tapper.

"That's classified."

"Oh, come on. I'm a centurion, and I'm going on this mission, apparently. Where am I headed? Some people are talking about the Wur, about there being a problem out in the far corners of the Cephalopod Kingdom."

Turov huffed, shaking her head. "The Wur are a problem, that's true. They're like a deep cancer, a rot at the core of the Cephalopod sector of space. But we're not deploying against them this time."

"Who then? Don't I have a right to know?"

"Yes, but I'm not sure I can trust you to keep your mouth shut until the transport leaves Earth."

"You trusted me to kill a Mogwa for you," I pointed out. "You trusted me to give you your Galactic Key back. Both are big perming violations—"

"All right, shut up," she said, and she turned back to her tapper, working on it in earnest.

"What are you doing on your tapper, anyway?" I asked. "Got a new boyfriend?"

"Ha! I wish. Here, look at the wall."

My eyes followed her gesture to the largest, blankest wall in her over-sized office. A shade lowered covering the window, filling the office with gloom.

For just a moment, I figured maybe she was going to make a surprise pass at me, and I looked in her direction again.

Galina looked good, as always. Her outfit was a size too tight, and her body moved like that of a graceful dancer—but she wasn't reaching for me.

The wall she'd indicated lit up. I felt a pang of disappointment, but that quickly faded and I became interested in the image on the wall. It began to transform as I watched. The lights dimmed further as the wall brightened, and I found myself staring at a high-resolution star map.

"This is our slice of the galaxy," she began, "viewed from just outside its edge. Remember that our galaxy is really a very large disk, and most of it is flat."

"I wasn't born yesterday."

"Good. We'll see how much your knowledge has improved since you've joined the legions. Frontier 921, like all frontier provinces outside the Core, is about five hundred lightyears thick. Each province is a slice of this relatively thin, spinning disk of stars."

"Right," I said, "and here's old Sol, on the right edge of this map." As I said this, I pointed it out in order to show off. Our home sun blinked when I brushed it with a finger. "Now, off to my right would be the Galactic Core—but that's maybe thirty thousand lights away."

"You're doing well. I'm shocked."

I moved my hand over the wall. To my surprise, my finger brought up information on any star it brushed against. "Let me see if I can get my bearings. Frontier 921 extends in a roughly cubic region with about five hundred lightyears on each border."

"That's right," Turov said, "but we've changed the borders recently to include the Cephalopod Kingdom. There are several hundred thousand stars in the entire region now—but most of them are useless. Many are brown dwarfs or tiny red suns, so cool and dim they almost don't qualify as stars at all."

"Huh…" I said thoughtfully, running my eyes and fingers over the map. I quickly found Gamma Pavonis and poked at it. "Here's Machine World, right here."

"James, this level of interest and knowledge on your part is unexpected."

"Yeah…I've spent some time lately looking at stars with my daughter's auto-scope."

"I'm astounded," Turov said, and again I let her implied insult slide.

"I've been curious about the real extent of our chunk of real estate for a long time," I told her, even though the truth was I'd hardly cared until a few nights ago. "Just how many star systems in our territory are worth fighting over?"

"Not many," she said. "We ignore a hundred stars for every one of them that's interesting."

"So few… Even with the squid-owned stars? What's wrong with them all?"

"Many have no planets, or they're circled by only a few burnt husks. Some systems are too full of radiation, dust, or other hazards to be much use."

"What's that leave us with, then? A thousand?"

"Less. Even with the Cephalopod Kingdom added in, we're dealing with maybe five hundred stars that support any kind of complex life."

"How many are under our military control?"

Turov cleared her throat. "That depends on who you ask. As a Hegemony officer, I'd tell you all of them. But that's unrealistic. There are at least a hundred systems that are governing themselves, or which have no form of government at all."

She stepped near the left edge—away from the side that was closer to the Core. At her touch, a region lit up and showed a large, dull-red zone. There were a few reddish patches like this closer to Earth, but I could tell right off most of the rebel stars were out on the border of known space.

"The fringe of the fringe," I said. "Those are former Cephalopod worlds, right? Can't say I blame them if they're rebelling."

"You can't blame them? They're suffering—and making their people suffer. Chaos and anarchy are never pleasant things, James."

*Chaos and Anarchy?* Was that what she called freedom and self-governance? I glanced at her, but I didn't comment because she looked serious. Turov liked order—especially if she was in charge of it.

"Okay," I said, "I'm guessing I'm headed out here, into the lawless region. Right?"

"That's correct," she said. "We need to make some allies out there. We've found a critical world. One that has exactly what we're looking for."

"Uh... and what would that be?"

"We're losing ground out there, James," she said, evading the question. "Every month or so another world breaks off ties and declares independence—or just goes dark."

"What are we going to do about it?"

"We're going to build our own battle fleet."

I eyed her, and I decided she was serious. "Thousands of ships? Enough to terrorize all these star systems? How?"

"Shipyards are springing up everywhere in the loyal systems. We've received an emergency clearance to ignore the patents of the Skrull. They aren't happy about losing their monopoly, but now they have new jobs as trainers and foremen to teach the rest of us."

"Wouldn't it just be easier for the Empire to send Battle Fleet 921 to the biggest rebel worlds and smash them up a little?"

"Probably, it would. But Grand Admiral Sateekas has almost finished his tour. He has been recalled again to the Core."

"The civil war breaking out again? Aren't the Galactics getting along?"

"No, they aren't. The ceasefire has become tense. The whole thing might spark up into a fresh conflict at any time. That's why the battle fleet is withdrawing again—leaving us in charge. You recall the deal we made a year or so ago, don't you?"

"How could I forget? I negotiated the details myself."

"Don't remind me."

I laughed good naturedly at the memory, but she didn't join in. "Sateekas said we'd have to agree to go to war with some neighboring power if we wanted to keep the squid worlds. Is that what's happening out there?"

"Not yet. There is another growing power just beyond that red zone—but we're not ready to face them yet. Interstellar war fleets aren't built in a day, James. We need to get our own house in order first. To that end, we're building a coalition of forces under Earth's banner."

"Who's paying for all this?" I asked. "I bet the Empire hasn't given us a dime."

"You are correct in that assumption. But now we're allowed to tax the industry of faithful Empire worlds in this province. We're funding our own build-up locally."

"Huh…" I said, looking back at the map.

I was impressed. Earth was just one tiny planet on this vast scale. We sure had some out-sized gonads even to try to rule a half-million star systems, empty or not.

"You still haven't told me what I'm doing here today. Why I'm pit-fighting with Germanica."

She heaved a sigh. Did she... yes, if I wasn't mistaken, she looked a tiny bit guilty.

That worried me. In order to make someone like Turov feel sorry for him, a man had to be in a pretty bad spot. After Graves' similar reaction, I was doubly concerned.

"You're going on a diplomatic mission," she said at last. "You are going to try to forge an alliance."

"That doesn't make any sense at all," I said. "First off, I'm no diplomat. I don't like flag-waving marches or tea-ceremonies."

She chuckled. "There will be precious few of either on this journey. What you must do is prove to the inhabitants of a critical planet that Earth's legions are impressive."

"Uh..." I said, absorbing that. "Why?"

"The world in question is highly warlike. The inhabitants are only impressed by forceful displays."

"So? Why can't we just drop a bomb on them? Make them submit."

"We're not trying to start a fresh war. We're trying to get them to support us—as they did the Cephalopod's. The squids were their last masters."

Right then, I was beginning to get an inkling of what she was talking about. But I didn't quite believe it. Not yet.

"Um... I take it they're not impressed by marching around in formation? Our spiffy uniforms won't do the trick?"

"No—and money doesn't mean much to them, either. They're only impressed by honorable combat."

"Arena fighting? Combat scenarios? Like the fun you put us through yesterday?"

"That's right."

I turned back to the big map. "Show me this world. Where is it?"

She tapped on her wrist, and a single spark lit up on the left edge of the wall.

"Damn, that far out? That's half-way to Rigel!"

"It's about three hundred lightyears away," she confirmed.

I whistled. "Months in warp. That sucks right there—unless…"

I craned my neck to look at her. "You weren't thinking of shipping me out airmail, were you? Using a teleport suit?"

"No, we looked at that option, but it's not feasible. It would take too many suits, and you will need supplies—no."

Tapping on the target star, I got a name to come up.

"Epsilon Leporis," I read. "An orange giant, K4 class. Huh… Leporis? Isn't that the rabbit constellation?"

"Yes. The hare which is chased by Orion, the hunter."

"What's so special about this star?"

She shrugged. "We really don't know. We haven't been out there. We're working from Cephalopod maps and using them as guides."

"What kind of people am I going to meet out there?"

She squirmed as if uncomfortable. Normally, I enjoyed watching a pretty lady in a tight outfit squirming, but today I had a bad feeling about it.

"Come on, Galina," I said. "You're holding back something. Where's the punchline?"

"There's someone I'd like you to meet," she said. "She can answer more of your questions."

She exited the office, and I frowned in her wake. Her mincing steps left me wondering what I'd gotten myself into today.

It wasn't the first time I'd had that feeling, and I was sure it wouldn't be the last.

## -13-

Waiting around in Turov's office, I soon moved to her high-backed chair and lounged in it. As she took several long minutes more, I started going through her desk drawers.

Finding nothing of interest, I leaned back again and put my boots on her desk.

The next thing I knew I was lightly snoring, and my feet were rudely swept aside by a small, angry hand.

"Get off there!" Galina said. "Were you actually asleep?"

"What…? Oh no, sorry… Just thinking about all these—hey!"

I'd finally looked past Galina to the tall woman standing in her wake. She was lovely, but oddly proportioned. Her neck was a little too long, as were her limbs.

Right off, I knew what she was. Only Rogue-worlders looked like that, a people we called tech-smiths. They were human, but only barely. They'd been specially bred for their scientific skills. The Cephalopods had used them as slaves until recently.

But all that wasn't what left my jaw hanging low. What I found hardest to believe was that I *knew* this woman.

"Floramel?" I asked in a hushed tone. "Is that really you?"

"Yes, James," she said. "Did you miss me?"

"Every starry night," I said, and we smiled at one another.

Galina rolled her eyes and looked slightly annoyed.

"I should have known," she said, putting her fists on her hips. "Centurion McGill, this is Floramel, the scientific lead on this entire project. I don't know why I'm telling you this, as you two have obviously met."

Floramel and I approached each other. I wanted to give her a hug, but I didn't want to freak her out. Her people took any kind of physical contact as a direct prelude to sex—either that, or as an attack.

Accordingly, I waited for her to reach for me. She did, after a moment's hesitation. She reached up to my broad shoulders and gave them a purposeful squeeze with hands. I grinned, knowing what that meant.

"I think I'm going to be ill," Turov said.

Floramel turned toward her when she said that. "Do you need to go to the infirmary, Imperator?"

"If I did, I would hate to see the state of my office when I returned. No, you two shall exit. Take him to your labs, Floramel."

We turned away to exit, but Galina called after us. "Ah, Floramel?"

"Yes, Imperator?"

"You *do* know that James is a registered sexual predator, don't you?"

"Ah now, that's just plain rude, Galina."

"Don't call me that. Get out!"

We hastily left her office. I didn't know what had gotten into Galina. She hadn't made any kind of pass at me since I'd gotten to Central, but still, she was acting like I was her property. Sometimes I didn't get women.

"James?" Floramel asked. "Was the imperator joking?"

"Yes," I said. "She has an odd sense of humor."

"I think she was jealous of me," she said. "I've been studying human social behavior since my revival, and—"

"Floramel," I said, stopping her in the corridor and smiling. "Let me just take a look at you. I'm so happy. You haven't aged a day. Why didn't you contact me? I had no idea you'd been revived."

She cocked her head thoughtfully. She wasn't a dumb lady. In fact, she was probably the smartest one I'd ever hooked up with.

"You've had sex with the imperator?" she asked me suddenly. "Is that even allowed?"

I made a choking sound. All my dodging, bullshit and small-talk had gotten me exactly nowhere.

"That's a rude thing to ask about, Floramel," I said. "You must know you're not the only girl I've been with."

"Hmm... I have an odd feeling about this situation. Are you in love with her?"

"No," I said. "Most definitely not. In fact, I can assure you, I haven't touched her since before you and I met."

That was true, and I felt good telling her. There had been plenty of other women, of course, but I sensed now wasn't a good time to bring that up.

"Good," she said, and she started walking again. "I must apologize for my lack of professionalism. I felt I had to ask these questions after the imperator's odd behavior."

"I understand."

"To answer your prior queries, I was revived about eight months ago. For nearly two months, I was a prisoner. At first, somewhat abusive debriefings became a daily routine for me."

"I'm sorry about that. But you can understand why they wanted to make sure you weren't an enemy spy of some kind, right? After all, you did rebel against Earth and the Empire."

"Yes," she said. "Only after I gave them a considerable list of technical information did I win some degree of freedom. I'm now allowed to roam several levels of Central unescorted."

I frowned at that. "You mean you haven't been outside Central since you got here? You haven't really experienced Earth?"

"No."

"That's a damned shame. Hold up a second."

We were standing in the elevator lobby now, and I used my tapper to call Turov. She took her time answering, and finally Winslade came online.

"What is it, McGill?"

"I want to talk to the imperator directly."

"That's not possible right now. She bounced the call to me."

"Well, bounce it right back again. I need permission to take Floramel out on the town."

"What? Are you kidding me? You're calling to arrange a date for yourself? This sort of behavior—"

"Winslade," I said, "relay the request. I need to be at the top of my game on this mission. It's critical to Earth."

Grumbling, he put me on hold for a while.

When he came back on the line, he was laughing. "She said you can bang her blue if you want to."

Stabbing at the buttons, I ended the call.

"What was that?" Floramel asked me. Fortunately, she'd wandered off to stare down the sloping sides of Central to the busy streets below.

"I think we're good to go, girl," I told her. "Let me show you around town."

During the long elevator ride to street level, Floramel explained to me about the vital technical information her people had placed upon the data core. She'd given it to me before her world had been destroyed, and it had consisted of her people's physical blueprints and mental engrams.

"In other words," I said, "in order to learn your tech secrets, Earth had to revive you."

"That's right. I hope you aren't upset by my ruse, James. Our technical achievements *were* on those data files—just not in the manner you assumed."

I chuckled, and I shook my head. "Don't worry, Floramel. I'm not upset. Not in the least. You did exactly what you had to in order to save yourselves. An acquaintance of mine has often suggested that we all need exactly that kind of lever to prevent being permed."

"Really? Does he give this advice often?"

"Yes, actually, he does."

"Hmm… sounds like Claver."

I almost fell over when she said that name. We were going through a stern row of security hogs guarding the exit at the time, and a veteran looked at us with pitiless eyes.

"Did this off-worlder drug you, Centurion?" he asked in immediate suspicion.

"What? No. She shocked me—but not literally."

Still frowning, he waved us on our way. We exited in a hurry.

"Claver?" I asked her at the massive doors. "Did you say *Claver*? How did you meet that particular rodent of a man again?"

The last I'd seen Claver, he'd been stealing secrets from Floramel and her tech-smiths. They'd been quite upset with him at the time.

"Rodent of a man…" she repeated. "That's an insult cast upon his character, isn't it?"

"It sure is. Tell me how he's related to this project."

Floramel did, and I was grinding my teeth by the end of the tale. Somehow, Claver had edged his way back onto Earth and regained some level of status again at Central. I could hardly believe it.

"That weasel," I said, muttering to myself.

"Will you mention a snake, next?" Floramel asked curiously. "Or perhaps a worm, or a—"

"Yes. He's all of those and more. You should steer clear of him the best you can. I'll see if I can get him kicked off the premises."

"I doubt you'll be successful," she said. "He's going with us to the frontier. He's an important member of this expedition."

"Is he now? I wonder why Turov didn't mention that?"

"Perhaps she anticipated a negative reaction from you?"

I had to laugh. Floramel was getting smarter about human interaction, but she was still very literal, even after eight months of immersion therapy on Earth.

"One more big question," I said. "What about the target world? What do you know about it? About its people?"

Floramel hesitated. "I know…" she began slowly, "I know it's a secret. I know I'm not supposed to talk about it—not with anyone."

I sighed, and I gave her hand a squeeze.

"That's okay," I said. "I'll figure it out eventually."

Taking her around the city, we visited a museum of art and technology, which she enjoyed very much. Next, we hit a nice restaurant and finally a bar. For me, things were finally going in the right direction.

After the bar, we had no trouble locating a hotel room.

Now, one might think I was taking advantage of the girl, but nothing could be farther from the truth. Upon our first meeting earlier today, she'd squeezed my shoulders. For a Rogue Worlder, that signaled she was ready to go to bed.

Like I said, she was a very direct person.

*Long legs.* That's what I remembered best from that night. Those long legs had a way of wrapping a man up in them, and not letting go.

It'd been over a month since I'd been with a woman, so I had plenty of stamina. Eventually it gave out, however, and we slept together.

In was the middle of the night, I woke up and found myself breathing hard.

Floramel was gone. I stumbled across the room, and I found her staring at herself in the bathroom mirror.

"What's wrong?" I asked in a voice that was husky with sleep.

"I don't feel like myself."

"What do you mean?"

"I still *look* like a tech-smith, but I'm becoming too much like one of you—a pure human."

I yawned and eyed the toilet wistfully. I'd had more than my share of beer tonight, and I was feeling the urge.

"Well, um, could you—"

"I want to apologize, James," she said seriously.

"Uh… for what?"

"I can't maintain this fiction any longer. I must tell you what you're going to face out there at Epsilon Leporis."

She was so serious, I felt my mind growing worried and waking up. I hated that feeling in the middle of the night.

"How long have you been sitting up, anyway?" I asked.

She ignored the question.

"You brought me home with you, to Earth," she said. "You... I would still be dead if it wasn't for you. I was permed."

She was staring at the mirror again, buck-naked and looking great. But at that moment, all I could do was cast wistful glances at the toilet.

"Girl, I totally understand what you're going through," I told her.

"You do?"

"I've been through it more times than I can count. Death, revival, thinking about what was and what might have been. It's a grim modern reality we all have to deal with."

"Yes..." she said. Suddenly, she stepped past me and went back to bed.

With a sense of great relief, I used the toilet thoroughly.

Coming back out and snapping off the light, I slipped into bed with her, under a single cool sheet.

She was so still and so quiet, I wondered if she'd gone to sleep again. But she hadn't.

"They are known as the ninth tentacle," she said.

"Uh... what?"

"That's what the Cephalopods call them—their ninth appendage."

"Hmm... who are we talking about, exactly?"

"Some of them march in squares of nine. Others are very tall and thin, and they stink like animals. Still another type is so huge, such slobbering idiots, they can barely be trained not to consume the enemy soldiers they strike down."

I felt a chill go through me.

"Littermates?" I asked. "Trackers? Giants?"

She levered herself up suddenly, making the sheet whisper and rasp.

"I'm sorry, James. I wish I wasn't the one who had to tell you this."

"Let me put this together... You're saying this planet, a world circling Epsilon Leporis, is the home world of the genetically altered soldiers the squids used to fight against Earth?"

"Not just Earth. They've bred and cloned millions—billions. The world is a red hell with an orange sky. They know nothing of civility—at least not the baser types you've met with."

"How do you know so much about them?" I asked.

"I—*we* created them—for the Cephalopods. At least, we created the means to mass produce them from their prototypes."

"How in God's name did you do that?"

"It's complex biology. Vats… artificial wombs… Tech not unlike the revival machines you know so well. That's why I feel a terrible guilt tonight. I've never felt such a sensation before."

"Are you worried about me, heading out there to deal with them, or about all humanity for twisting up your own genetic cousins?"

The second I asked that, I felt a pang of my own. I'd driven a knife into her in the middle of her confession. But it was hard not to be bitter. I'd seen millions of people die, right here on Earth, when these clones of hers had invaded our green lands to the north.

"I'm worried about all of us," she said. "I feel bad for all our crimes, those that have already impacted humanity, and those yet to bear fruit…"

My mind fogged over, thinking about what gruesome technological terrors her people may have invented that I didn't even know about yet. I found myself unable to take in the full scope of it.

Quietly, Floramel stood up and began putting her clothes on in the dark.

I watched her for a few seconds, unsure how I should respond. We'd just had a great time in bed—but could that really erase all the sins this woman had just owned up to?

"Floramel, wait," I said at last, getting up and touching her arms with my hands.

"You… you don't reject me?"

"That depends," I said, "what would the squids have done to you and your people if you'd refused to comply with their orders?"

She shrugged. "Tortured and killed our leaders until the rest complied—or until we were all dead."

"Did anyone die that way?"

She nodded. "My parents, among others. Both of them."

"I'm sorry."

"Don't be. It was a long time ago. I barely remember as I was a child. That was their solution you see, to remove the oldest of us and work purely with younger, genetically altered generations."

I touched her again, and now my hands were gentle. I gave her a hug, and she returned it. I couldn't recall having gotten an honest hug from her before.

She let her clothes fall away from her again, leaving us in a bare embrace. We spent the next hour of the night nuzzling, screwing, and generally comforting one another.

But when she finally fell asleep again, I found that I couldn't join her. She'd transferred nightmares from her head into mine.

*Damn*, how I hated those squids.

## -14-

Tribune Deech was a hard-ass old battle axe—or at least that's how the legionnaires in Varus thought of her. It wasn't an entirely fair assessment. Sure, she had a stern face, and she was at least thirty-five physically, having stored her permanent record at that age. But the real problem was she'd come from the Iron Eagles.

For a Varus man, that meant trouble. Iron Eagles was one of the three most prestigious legions Earth maintained. They'd been the third to ever be commissioned, after Germanica and Victrix. Of the three, they had the reputation of being the best fighting unit humanity had yet to produce.

The trouble was one of culture. Varus was a tough outfit, too. We'd seen plenty of action, we weren't afraid of anything, and we tended to get the job done—no matter what. The Iron Eagles, however, were much more by-the-book. They were elite, there's no denying it, but they were more like eagle scouts when compared to the pirates who ran wild in Legion Varus.

As a result of this culture clash, Tribune Deech and I, well, we just didn't often see eye-to-eye.

"Let me get this straight, Centurion McGill," she said to me the next morning when I checked in about forty minutes late. "You left Central last night, taking our top scientist with you, and got lost in the city?"

"We didn't get lost, not exactly, sir. We knew exactly where we were."

"But you turned off your tappers. No one could locate you on the grid. Do you realize a full unit of techs and MPs spent the night combing the city for you two?"

Floramel, who was standing next to me, looked mortified. She stared at the puff-crete floor, humiliated and upset.

I was standing in a much jauntier pose. My beret was riding on my head, just where it ought to be, and my Legion's wolf's head patch was proudly displayed on my sleeve. After last night, when I'd finally gotten an inkling of what was in store for me on Epsilon Leporis, I was having a hard time taking Deech seriously.

Winslade was off to my right, wearing a smug expression. He liked watching me get a good dressing-down almost as much as Harris liked to see me get executed. Sometimes, I wasn't sure why I ever gave that weasel a break.

"Dr. Floramel," Deech said, turning toward her next. "Are you aware that you were breaking your oath? That your freedoms here at Central are dependent on always being traceable?"

Deech was calling her "doctor" because she was, after all, a foreign scientist. As the Rogue Worlders had never bothered with family names, "Dr. Floramel" was about the best thing she could come up with.

"Yes, Tribune. I apologize without reservation."

"Indeed? Well... I think the real problem here is McGill. He's led countless good people astray, if the stories are to be believed."

"Whoa now," I said, "don't let idle gossip sway your opinion, Tribune. A lot of people tend to think my methods are unorthodox, but they have a hard time arguing with the results."

Winslade jumped in, unable to restrain himself. "Tribune Deech? If I may be so bold, this man was under my command recently, and I feel I might be able to come up with an appropriate punishment for his insubordination."

I glared at him. Winslade wanted to be my jailer? That was the last thing I wanted. He was kind of pissing me off, too.

Where did he get off talking about administering punishments after what we'd pulled off together in the pits only yesterday?

Deech looked Winslade up and down.

"No," she said at last. "He's under Primus Graves' command. He'll handle it."

"But, sir...?"

Deech was already walking away. She'd spun around on her heel, and she never looked back at us.

Like I said, she was a hard-ass. I had some respect for her, but not as much as I did for Graves or Drusus. That kind of thing had to be earned in my book.

"McGill," Winslade hissed at me, "why didn't you say something?"

"Uh... like what? You're the one who jumped in and started talking."

"What if Deech begins to pry? Not everything about this mission is well-known."

I blinked at him, not getting the message entirely. "So what if Deech knows we're going to Epsilon Leporis? Is it really that big of a secret?"

"Who told you about that, McGill?" Graves demanded from my right.

I turned to face him, and I manufactured a welcoming smile. "There you are, sir! I'm supposed to report to you, I guess. What are your orders?"

"My orders are for you to tell me who leaked classified information. Was it Floramel, here? She's one step above a prisoner of war. Did you realize that, McGill?"

Floramel looked like she wanted to shrink into the floor. After living for decades under squid rule, she was terrified of authority figures.

"No, sir!" I said loudly. "It wasn't her. Imperator Turov told me."

Winslade made a gargling sound.

"You really should get that looked at, Primus," I told him, tossing him a concerned glance. "We're going into deep space soon, and I wouldn't want to see you put down over a bad illness."

Graves looked back and forth between us.

"Imperator Turov…" he said. "She's also the one who authorized your exit from Central in the first place, isn't that right, McGill? With our prized lead scientist in tow?"

"That's right, Primus. She surely did."

Winslade was glaring now, but I didn't entirely get why. Turov outranked all of us. If she wanted to go off-script, well hell, she could get away with it. She wore more brass sunbursts than anyone present.

"Well then," Graves said, "I'll have to report this to Equestrian Drusus."

That got everyone's attention. Drusus was the man at the top of this pyramid we called Central. He wore three sunbursts, and he outranked everyone in the sector. You'd have to go to the Chiefs of Staff in Geneva to find someone of higher stature.

Winslade began ticking off his fingers then. "One… two… three levels? You're really going to bounce this up that far, are you, Graves? Why can't you handle a discipline issue yourself?"

Graves turned on him. They were both the same rank, in the same legion, but there was no love lost between the two.

"McGill is my problem, Primus," Graves said. "I'd appreciate it if you'd exit gracefully from this situation."

"Request noted," Winslade said primly.

He then turned around on his heel and stalked away.

Graves and I looked after him.

"You know where that little man is headed, don't you sir?" I asked.

"To Turov. He'll rat on us, of course. Don't worry, I'm well aware of his loyalties. What I don't get is how you always get yourself into these things, McGill. Does Floramel here know what kind of rep you have on Earth?"

"Uh…"

"That's what I thought," he said, and he turned toward Floramel. "Ma'am? Do you know what a cad is? A scoundrel? A playboy? A philandering man-whore?"

"Oh, now," I said, "that's just not cool, Primus."

"I…" Floramel said, looking concerned, "I have some idea. Not all of those terms are familiar, but are you saying Centurion McGill will tell a woman anything to procure sex?"

"Exactly! You've been warned. He's trouble—and not just for you."

I shook my head, flabbergasted, but Graves was already walking away. Left with Floramel eyeing me carefully, I turned to her with my best smile.

"What's on your mind?" I asked.

"How many women have you slept with since we last met?" she asked simply.

"Uh…" I said, not knowing how to answer that question. If I told the truth, which was that I wasn't sure and had no exact count, she probably wouldn't be happy. But then again, I didn't want to lie.

"I see," she said, studying my face. "Graves spoke the truth. I've been deceived. Here on Earth, and back home on Rogue World."

She turned away to go. I reached out a hand and gently stopped her. Leaning close, I spoke into her ear.

"I didn't lie about other women," I said. "You never asked about them. For what it's worth, whatever we shared was real to me. We've experienced a lot, here and out among the stars."

She looked down at my hand. "Am I under arrest, Centurion?"

"No, of course not," I said, letting go of her instantly.

Floramel walked away, and just like that, I'd been dumped. I frowned after her and Graves. People could be so touchy sometimes.

"McGill?" Winslade asked, puffing as he came trotting back to me. "Tell Graves I have direct orders for him from Imperator Turov. She's been trying to get hold of him on his tapper, but he isn't answering. What did you do to make him pull a stunt like that? Unplugging is a move out of your playbook, not his."

I gazed after Floramel, only half-listening.

"Don't worry about it, Winslade," I said over my shoulder. "Graves has already administered his punishment. Drusus won't need to get involved—not now."

"Really? What should I tell Turov?"

"Tell her she can untie the knots in her panties. This crisis is over."

Grinning, Winslade worked his tapper.

"You didn't...?" I asked him.

He nodded, lifting his tapper so I could see. "I took the liberty of recording your words and relaying them directly. Don't worry, the imperator enjoys junior officers making public references concerning her undergarments. She really does."

Winslade walked away, laughing. Whatever respect I'd gained for the man yesterday in the pit I'd lost all over again today.

## -15-

Before I knew it, Legion Varus had shipped out. *Nostrum* was the name of our fast transport, and I was happy to see she was still in good shape after our last deployment.

*Nostrum* was a sleek, comfortable ship. Unlike the usual rented Imperial transport I'd experienced, she had an officially human-centered design. In comparison to older ships we'd lost in past campaigns like *Corvus* and *Minotaur*, *Nostrum* provided real comfort and an excellent simulated view of the stars.

Almost every chamber had a ceiling or a wall that appeared to show the cosmos as we passed by it all. That was a damned good thing on this journey, because we were headed pretty far out, and it felt good to be able to mark your progress.

"You see that one?" Natasha asked me about a month into the journey.

"That's Rigel, isn't it?"

"That's right. We're headed that way, and the blue-white giant seems to get bigger every day."

She was right. Rigel was getting big. It already looked like a headlight at the far end of a tunnel. The blue shade was distinct, and I had to wonder how bright it would look when we finally reached Epsilon Leporis.

"Forty thousand times as bright as our star," Natasha said in a dreamy tone.

There wasn't any kind of technology, science, gizmo or natural wonder that didn't turn this girl's brain on. I admired that about her. She wasn't just a thin girl with a pretty face, she was as smart as anyone I knew. Smarter even, maybe, than Etta.

But Etta had street-smarts part of me argued. Just thinking about my daughter made my expression falter.

"What's wrong?" Natasha asked, watching me.

"Just thinking about home. About my family."

She reached up a hand and ran it over my back absently.

Kivi walked by right then, and she curled her lip into a disgusted twist. She made a little spitting sound, too.

Then she passed by, and she disappeared.

Natasha dropped her hand from my back. I missed her touch immediately.

"What's wrong with her?" she demanded, staring down the passageway. "She's got Carlos wrapped around her little finger. Isn't that good enough for her?"

"Nope," I said. "All men belong to Kivi—according to Kivi."

"I deal with the other techs in our unit every day. She's the only one who's never been friendly."

"That's because you're too skinny and too cute. That's two strikes in her book."

"Irritating woman."

My gaze shifted back to the stars. "How long until we make planetfall?"

"Three weeks," she said. "Long enough to get in one more round of training."

I winced at that. I'd already died twice since we'd left Earth. Just thinking about the last time made my throat hurt. Absently, I rubbed at the base of my neck.

Staring at Rigel, I didn't even notice at first that Natasha was staring up at me.

"You're different," she said.

"How do you mean?"

"You haven't made a pass at me, and I've been standing here with you for nearly half an hour."

"Uh… am I missing a bet, here?"

She laughed. "I didn't say that."

Natasha looked down and fooled with her tapper, but I could tell she was just avoiding my eye. She had my radar up now, whether that had been her intention or not.

Some people might think I'm about as subtle with a woman as the proverbial bull in the china shop. But that's old news. I like to think I've become more refined in my methods these days.

"You still working with Floramel down in the shops?" I asked nonchalantly.

Her face snapped back up to gaze at me intently.

"It's true, then!" she declared. "You *are* still involved with her. I'd heard you'd gotten together back on Earth, but I—"

Leaning over, I snaked a kiss. She pulled back in alarm at first, but then she let me do it, pressing her lips to mine briefly.

"What was that?" she asked when I went back to looking at the stars.

"Just something I felt like doing," I said, "and no, Floramel and I didn't last long. Even before we got aboard *Nostrum,* she became cold and distant. She's married to her work, I think. Besides, I think it bothers her that I die all the time."

"That bothers me, too. I don't see how you frontline troops can keep your sanity. I haven't died for years."

I chuckled. "I have a feeling we're going to fix that problem of yours right up when we get to this particular hellhole."

"What did Floramel say about it? I know she's been out there."

"Yeah,… nothing good. I gather it's hot and arid, with a smoky sky like orange flame."

"I've studied the star. It's aging, becoming bloated. It's already swallowed the nearest planets. Think about how our sun would look it if had grown big enough to consume Mercury."

I thought about that, and I didn't find it encouraging.

That was the moment. I knew it was, from my vast experience. My arm lifted slowly, surely, up to slide over her shoulders.

It felt like the most natural thing in the world to do—for both of us.

But I never got to make another move on her. Right about then, everything went to Hell in a hand-basket, as my grandma used to say.

Klaxons went off all over the ship. The deck heaved, settled, then the wall became the floor, and we slammed into it.

The image of Rigel and all her sister stars winked out, replaced by a blank panel of iridescent white.

"What's happening?" I demanded, lifting Natasha and setting her on her feet.

"If I didn't know better, I'd say we were making an emergency exit out of our warp bubble."

That threw me for a loop. In my considerable time spent traveling in space, warp-bubbles had always been safe—at least, for the ship itself.

The Alcubierre Drive moved our ship faster than the speed of light, not by applying terrific thrust, but rather by warping space in a bubble around the ship. Such a bubble, or field, had to be carefully maintained in order to keep the ship moving, and so my first suspicion was that our ship had suffered some kind of catastrophic systems failure.

Natasha had the same thought. "I have to get to the Engine rooms. I'm sorry, James."

"Don't be!" I told her. "Just move your butt!"

She did, and I watched her race all the way down the passageway until she vanished. Walking the other way, toward my unit's module, I wondered why a woman's tail-section looked better walking than it did running. It made no sense to me, but neither did a lot of the cosmos.

"McGill?" a voice called out of my tapper.

"Primus Graves? What's happening, sir?"

"We've been knocked out of warp. Tune into command chat."

As a ground-pounder, I normally kept the officer-only command chat channel turned off. During *Nostrum*'s long flight, I'd have been treated to an endless stream of techno-babble from the flight crew if I hadn't.

Obeying Graves, I soon got an earful.

"We're completely out of warp. Radiation has stabilized."

"Have we got a breach?"

"Negative. No venting detected by the AI."

Those first voices had been crewmen, guys I didn't know. But then a voice broke in that I did recognize.

"This is Tribune Deech. Captain, can you give me an update? What is our situation?"

"Tribune—I don't understand it. All systems on the drive checked green, but all of a sudden, it was like we hit turbulence."

"Could it be a pocket of mass?" she asked. "A comet, or some other chunk of dark matter between the stars?"

"I don't know, sir. The ship's warp bubble should plow through or around that. Only a really big mass, like a planet, could do this—but in that case, we'd all be dead."

"Captain, it's clear that we hit something. Or that our engines failed us. What's your best theory?"

The Captain hesitated. "It's only a thought, but it seems like we hit another warp bubble."

"Really? How would that be possible?"

"Another ship passing through the same space at the same time. A one-in-a-quadrillion shot I know, but that's what it seems like."

"What would happen, exactly, if you are correct?"

"The two fields would disrupt one another and both ships would be tossed out of warp. Damage could result to one or both ships, or their drives."

"Very well, assess and report. Come back to me in five minutes. Deech out."

"Uh... all right, Tribune," the captain said.

I could hear in his voice that the *Nostrum*'s captain was put out. After all, Deech was ordering him around like he was a shuttle pilot. Aboard this ship, while in flight, he was supposed to be the judge, jury and executioner—even though technically Deech outranked him.

Switching back over to a private line with Graves, I was concerned.

"Sounds like we're in trouble, sir," I said. "Permission to mobilize my unit?"

"What for?"

"You heard the captain, sir. One in a quadrillion chance? I don't even play the lottery. If another ship hit us, it did so on purpose."

"But how could another ship even locate us in warp, much less time it right to disrupt our warp bubble?"

"I don't know any of that, sir, but I don't believe in coincidences of this kind. Remember, we're in hostile space. This whole region is old squid-territory, and it's far from friendly to Earthers."

"Hmm…" Graves said. "Our orders are to secure everything and hold on, but I think it's not a bad precaution to put a unit into combat gear. We can always revive you later, if things go wrong."

"That's mighty considerate of you, sir," I said, but he'd already closed the channel.

Figuring I had clear orders to mobilize, I kicked it into gear and contacted my adjuncts. Harris, Toro and Leeson all reported in, and they were surprised at my demands.

"Suit up," I said. "I want everyone in the central chamber of our module in ten minutes. Lock and load, people. This is no drill!"

Not one of them argued with me. They knew better by now. They just jumped into action. Tuning into my unit's chat line, I heard the general hubbub of officers and noncoms screaming at the regulars.

My unit was gearing for battle, and for once, it wasn't going to be some kind of knife-fight in an artificial pit.

## -16-

*Nostrum* spun for a short time, but she was a new ship with high-class stabilizers. She righted herself and returned to her previous course.

Her warp drive, however, had been knocked out of commission. I could hear the rumbling, almost like a deep, sick cough as it shivered through the spine of the great ship.

"Centurion?" Harris asked, meeting me at the entrance to our module. "Some of the troops are a little banged up, but we've got ninety-five percent effectives."

"Ninety-five percent? Tell those who are hugging their bunks I'll recycle them if they can't carry a rifle in three minutes."

"Yes sir!" Harris boomed, and he whirled on the unit regulars, seeking out slackers of every stripe.

Leeson walked up and chuckled. "Harris is still a veteran in his heart," he said. "You set the right man on them."

"Yep," I said, "he reminds me of a terrier hunting up rats in the barn."

Making a steady stream of threats and accusations, Harris raced around the various bunk rooms and managed to roust all but two of my troops into gear.

"What happened to the last two?" I asked him a moment later.

"Well... one of them is Adjunct Toro, sir..."

"I'll talk to her personally. What about the other one?"
"Uh... That was Lau."
"Was?"
Harris avoided my eye.
"I thought he was sleeping, sir," he said, "but it turns out he's dead."

I nodded, checking Lau's room. There was a blackened burn-hole in the man's forehead. It was obvious Harris had found him goofing off and had taken extreme action.

I could tell Harris was worried I'd chew him out or even put him on report.

"You're right," I said to Harris, who was peering over my shoulder uncomfortably. "It was an honest mistake—and Lau made it."

"Thank you, sir!"

Next stop was Toro's quarters. She had a tiny single bunk in a private cubicle. It wasn't roomy like my own commander's quarters, but it was better than you got as a grunt.

"Toro?"

"McGill? Thank God it's you, sir! Harris was just in here..."

She trailed off, spotting Harris in my wake.

"Sir," she said, "I'm injured. It's nothing serious, but I'm going to have to pass—"

"Adjunct Toro," I said, "this ship is under attack."

"Attack? How could that be? We're in warp. I thought it was another of your drills—"

"Turn on command chat, listen in, and get an education."

Toro did so while I watched the rest of the troops gear-up and form squads. Turning around, I found Toro limping up to me.

"I'm sorry sir," she said, looking worried. "I had no idea."

For a few seconds, I toyed with my pistol. I'd seen Graves make motivational speeches in just such a manner many times.

"As a new centurion," I told her, "people seem to think they can scoot by with me—but they're mistaken."

"Of course, Centurion! I wouldn't—"

"Personnel who are critically injured in early action," I continued loudly, "before there have been enough causalities to glut the revival teams, are often best recycled."

She swallowed hard, took out an injectable and jammed it into her knee. "I feel better already, Centurion."

"That's good. Don't fall behind—oh, and Toro? Your platoon is on point for the rest of this action."

"Got it!" she said, and she hustled out into our module's main chamber.

Amused, Harris came up to me after she went by. "You've got the touch, McGill. I wouldn't have expected it—but it's undeniable. Graves himself couldn't have gotten these people moving any faster."

I made no comment. Harris was right—or at least, I liked to think I was in Graves' league. In any case, I'd definitely developed a serious disdain for slackers.

That isn't to say I wouldn't let a good man slide in other ways. If a couple wanted to share a bunk at night, for instance, well... that was their business. I didn't care at all as long as they fought hard on the line come morning.

By the time we were fully mobilized and marching down the central passage of the ship's spine, we'd wasted seven precious minutes. I was a little annoyed, having felt we should have been able to do better.

"McGill?" Graves called a few minutes later.

"Primus? 3$^{rd}$ Unit is ready for action. We're—"

"I know where you are. Keep going and take the tubes up to Gold Deck. I'm deploying your unit outside the Cent-Op chambers. You'll cover the main guns down to the automated-magazine chamber. Don't take any crap from the crew. Tell them you're approved security troops, courtesy of Legion Varus—but try to stay out of their way."

The losers in fleet liked to think they could take care of their own defense, but as real combat troops, we knew better.

"Isn't that where they control the broadsides, sir?" I asked Graves. "Is there any trouble in local space?"

"Not yet, but if you were invading a ship like this, which vital subsystem would you take out first?"

"Uh... the enemy ship's guns, sir?"

"Bingo. Move out!"

Pin-wheeling my arm, I got the unit trotting. Toro's group was in the lead, as I'd directed. She was sweating inside her helmet, but she didn't complain or even make eye contact as she jogged by. I felt proud of her. It wasn't the first time a Varus soldier had fought on a bum knee, and it wouldn't be the last. I'd done it myself on several occasions.

After Toro's platoon, Leeson's moved out then Harris brought up the rear of the column. I ran with Leeson in order to keep an eye on both ends of the formation.

Legion Varus, like all of the independent outfits, was broken into ten cohorts of around twelve hundred men each, plus auxiliaries. My unit, the third, contained a mix of heavy and light troops. Harris had the light troops, Toro the heavies, and Leeson's platoon contained most of the specialists.

In an open battle on a planet's surface, the light troops would usually lead the formation. That's because they could run faster and they carried snap-rifles, weapons capable of light damage at long range.

But when carrying out operations in an enclosed space, there was no room to maneuver. Most commanders liked to lead with their heaviest troops in close-quarters, and I'd opted for that strategy.

Heavies like Toro's troops wore powered armor with exoskeletal strength to help with the load. Every member of her team was a regular, an experienced soldier, well trained with morph-rifles and force-blades. Partly due to their powerful kit, I felt good about putting her group in the lead.

When we reached the tubes that carried people up and down between decks, I called a halt then ordered the first squad forward. Toro handled all the details. I watched with interest.

"Anything happening outside the ship, Centurion?" Harris asked me.

"I'm listening to command chat, the same as you. Nothing yet."

Harris nodded and popped open his faceplate to scratch stubble. "Let's hope this is all some kind of screw-up by our techs."

"Yeah… as long as we can get back into warp, that would be the best outcome."

He looked at me in sudden alarm. "You haven't heard anything about engine damage, have you sir?"

"I know we're not able to go back into warp right now. They're working on it."

Harris looked worried, but he didn't say anything.

"We're pretty far out from Earth," I said, giving voice to his thoughts.

He nodded. "Over two hundred lights from home. That means a rescue is going to be long in coming, if it becomes necessary. In fact, the brass back home might call the whole thing a failure and leave us to rot."

"Nah," I said. "This ship is too valuable. They don't have very many fast transports like *Nostrum*—not yet."

I patted a strut as if to comfort the ship.

Harris flickered a smile at me. I wasn't sure if he'd bought my bullshit or not, but at least he seemed to appreciate the effort.

"I'm going forward to see what's taking Toro so long to get her heavies up that tube."

"Give her a kick in the ass for me, sir."

Moving along the line, I clacked my armor into that of others for fifty steps or so before catching up with Toro.

"What's the hold-up, Adjunct?" I demanded.

"Sir! Uh… the first squad hasn't released the tube yet. The doors are still shut."

I glanced at her. "When was your last report from your lead squad?"

"Um…"

I looked down, and I saw she'd been fooling with her knee again. She had the front plate over her leg joint open, and I saw blood in there.

Using my helmet's HUD, I logged into her local chat and contacted the squad leader—or at least, I tried to.

Then I brought up my status display. I immediately sucked in my breath. We were getting red readings. The squad had been wiped out.

"Flip down your faceplate, Adjunct!" I shouted at Toro.

She did so and a moment later, she looked shocked.

"I didn't know, sir."

"Relay that status to the rest of the unit. Take the manual route."

"The stairs, sir?"

"Right. I'm contacting Graves."

Gritting her teeth, she began shouting and urging her troops to advance up the stairway, but I thought the better of it and stopped her.

"I don't want to lose another squad of heavies. For all we know, radiation has leaked through up there. Harris?"

"What's up, Centurion?"

"Your lights are on. Scouting mission, up that stairway. I need info like yesterday."

"Oh shit… On it, sir!"

Harris' people went racing by a few seconds later. Harris gave Toro the finger as he ran by.

In the meantime, I'd been trying to contact Graves. He wasn't answering. No one was answering up there on Gold Deck.

Rolling back my neck, I stared up at the ceiling, wishing I could see through the decks to where Gold Deck was laid out. What the hell was going on up there?

Logging onto command chat, I cleared my throat.

"This is Centurion McGill. Be advised, I've lost a squadron of heavies while trying to advance to Gold Deck. Their life signs are all showing as red. I'm also out of contact with Primus Graves and Gold Deck in general. If anyone has information, please share."

A chorus of voices came back at me. I'd been off the command chat line for a few minutes while leading my squad. It was too confusing to have local voice, unit chat and command chat all going at the same time.

"McGill, this is Winslade. Is your unit ready to fight?"

"Yes sir," I said. "We're in a full kit at the bottom of the—"

"Then get up here, please. We're under assault. It was very sudden. Most of the crew up here on Gold Deck is already dead."

A chill ran through me. What could have killed so many so fast? What could have struck so quickly that the general alarm hadn't even gone out yet?

I didn't know, but as I moved into the stairwell, which was really more of a switchback passage with handholds, I figured I was going to find out soon enough.

## -17-

About a thousand steps. That's what it took to make it all the way up to Gold Deck.

It wasn't as bad as it sounded, however. People in powered armor almost had their legs moved for them. What's more, the artificial gravity was toned down in the stairways, and you hardly had to touch the steps. You could sort of hop and just glide over five or six at a time.

Once we all got into the rhythm of it, the motion was kind of like ice-skating. The experience might have been fun if we weren't thinking of the sudden death that seemed to lie ahead of us.

Harris was the first one to report back. His light troops had lost us long ago, pulling ahead of Toro's heavies even though I'd told them to stay together.

"Contact!" he boomed in my ear.

Up above, I could hear the chatter of snap-rifles on full-auto.

"What have you got, Harris? Report!"

We all kept moving upward, and for a few seconds, I wondered if Harris had been hit.

"Uh... I don't know yet, sir. We've spotted movement... we're engaged. They're firing back at us."

"With what?"

"Seems like explosive pellets, or bullets. Something ballistic."

"Can you press through?"

"We're bunched up on these damned stairs."

"Leave one squad engaged, fall back with the rest. I'm moving up the heavies."

I gave Toro a nod. She was a little pale, but she was game. Leading her 1st squad, she headed up while Harris' lights came back down, squeezing past.

It occurred to me we were too vulnerable to explosives on this damned stairway.

"Kivi!" I called out. "Get some of your buzzers up there. I want to see the action. Leeson, spread out into the level below Gold Deck."

"Blue Deck, sir? The bio people aren't going to like that."

"Screw 'em."

He chuckled, but he complied. He got his men off the stairway, and when the bulk of Harris' lights came down the stairs, I shunted them off to the side, too.

"Toro," I said, "you've got the ball. Break us out of this shit."

"On it, sir."

She sent in her best, a squad of heavies with morph-rifles slung and force-blades out. Each heavy trooper had weapons that were constructed of electro-magnetic fields. Through an alien trick of physics, these shaped force-fields had a sharpness beyond that of any metal blade. They also burned whatever they touched, and they could be extended outward from the length of a dagger to several yards.

Watching on my HUD and my tapper, I got Kivi's buzzer feed and gasped.

The heavies burst past Harris' troops. Most of them were on the ground. Their light weapons had proven relatively ineffective.

The heavies were hit with a storm of heavy explosive bullets as they rose up out of the stairway and rushed through the doorway. The big double doors themselves were smoking and broken, hanging by their hinges on either side.

What made me gasp wasn't the mess on the floor, or the incoming hail of fire.

It was the first sight I caught of the enemy. They were giants. Armored giants, of the type I hadn't laid eyes on since Earth had been invaded years ago.

"We've got littermates!" I boomed. "Heavy troops, two full squads of them! Toro, send up all your weaponeers with belchers. We're going to burn them down."

"Weaponeers advancing."

Harris came up to me then. He was panting and had his hands on his hips. "Is that the best idea, sir? They'll go crazy if you—"

"Shut up, Harris."

He did so immediately, and I didn't even look at him.

My mind was whirling. What were littermates doing out here, in the middle of nothing? Sure, I knew we were headed for Epsilon Leporis. That was their homeworld and all. But we weren't close yet. We still had nearly a hundred lights to go.

It didn't matter, I told myself. It didn't matter at all. I was going to kill them, I was going to kill them all, and it was that simple.

The heavies engaged in close, losing two in the charge to incoming fire. Fortunately, we were on a spaceship and didn't have to run across a half-mile of open ground. They were fighting hand to hand a moment later, and I took that opportunity to rush up with a group of weaponeers.

"All at once now," I told them. "Narrow aperture, take careful aim."

The weaponeers formed a firing squad around me. Toro's heavies were fighting an odd sword-fight with the enemy, trading hammer-blows with the bigger soldiers. The enemy, however, had relatively primitive swords made of metal. If they hit straight on, their swords were sheared off as often as not, flashing sparks as the fields struck steel.

Still, Toro's group was outmatched by the weight of the enemy. They couldn't take them down without help.

When I had five weaponeers prepped up, I ordered them to fire at once, for the heads.

Four hit their targets. Smoking and wreathed in flames, they went down in a heap.

Their brothers went berserk then, and they stopped playing around with Toro's heavies. They dropped their swords and grabbed the heavy troops with massive fists, trying to tear the men apart with their bare hands.

Blood sprayed and smoked. Most of it was from the enemy's side—but not all. Two heavies were taken apart—literally. Their limbs were ripped off, their armor ignored.

Toro's troops hacked them down. Leeson's weaponeers advanced and shot the flopping bodies, several of which were still struggling to rise.

"Well, well, well," said a familiar voice behind me.

I turned slowly. It was Winslade. He had his arms crossed, and a smug smile on his face.

"Don't tell me this was all some kind of exercise, Primus," I said dangerously.

"Seemed real enough to me. Didn't it to you?"

Before I could wring his neck, another voice spoke up off to my side. It was that battle axe Deech.

"Stand down, Centurion. You fought well. The scenario wasn't fair—but it wasn't meant to be."

I blinked at her then looked around as more Gold Deck people appeared in a steady stream.

"Is this really happening, sirs?"

"Yes," Deech said, "and for what it's worth, I didn't want to do this. It's part of our commitment, you see."

"That's right," Graves said.

"You too, huh?"

"Let's not sour your success with complaints, McGill. The element of confusion was required. We're trying to impress the natives of Epsilon Leporis, remember?"

"Well…" I said, kicking at a steaming body at my feet, "did we impress them?"

Graves nodded. "Enough to be allowed to continue. We've proven we're worthy of our invitation."

"Was everyone in on this? Everyone but me?"

"No one below the rank of Primus knew anything," Deech told me. "That's why we simulated an attack on Gold Deck.

Our sparring partners specified that they wanted a convincing test of our forces. In this case, the purpose of the test was to see how one of our small units performed without higher level officers to direct them."

"This is really weird," I said, feeling angry and somewhat cheated.

Deech looked at Graves. "You can handle the rest of this, Primus. I've got other things to attend to in my office."

She sauntered away, and Winslade followed immediately in her wake. It looked to me like he was trying to court a new master. I looked after them both sourly.

"That's Deech," Graves said as he came up beside me and clapped me on the shoulder.

His gauntlets rang against my epaulets and that irritated me. Everything about this irritated me.

"She always passes the buck," Graves went on. "Do you know that she made a huge point of sitting out this entire contest? Winslade and I were in complete command of the situation—at least, that's what she said until it became clear you were going to win. Then, she rushed out here to get her face into the after-action vids."

"Sir," I said, "this exercise was total horseshit."

"Oh, come off it, McGill," he said. "Just think of all the times you've pissed me off with some kind of trick."

I did for a second, and I shrugged. He had a point, but I didn't feel like admitting it.

"What happened to that first squad we sent up?" I asked.

He led me to the transport-tube landing zone. It was kind of like a big elevator lobby without any mirrors. A mass of bodies were strewn there.

"They were all murdered the second they stepped off the elevator?" I asked.

"Right. That was supposed to happen to more of your men to even out the contest. But then you rushed up the stairway and flanked the ambushers. Good call, by the way."

"We outnumbered them badly from the start," I said. "Did they really think they could win?"

"They did, because they had many advantages. The thinking was that you'd lose more of your men right here at the tubes than you did. If you hadn't outmaneuvered them, they probably would have skunked you."

"Why'd you pick me for this surprise drill, sir?" I asked.

He looked at me questioningly.

"I didn't. You picked yourself. Remember when you contacted me and suggested you should mobilize your unit just in case?"

"Yeah?"

"That's when you volunteered."

I heaved a sigh. It was the oldest lesson in Legion Varus lore: *never volunteer for anything*.

On that simple point, I'd failed.

"Wait a second, Primus," I said, "what about the warp-bubble accident? Were we kicked out of warp or not?"

"Yeah..." he said thoughtfully. "I thought that was over-dramatic. It seemed dangerous, too. I'm not really sure how that all played in. We could have just come out of warp, rendezvoused with these troops from Blood World—that's what the natives call it, by the way—Blood World."

"Sounds inviting."

"It's not meant to."

"About the warp-collision," I said, thinking it over. "Was that meant to make the entire scenario seem more real?"

"Not in any briefing I attended. It wasn't mentioned at all. We were simply told we would meet with a Blood World ship, take on boarders, and play out this battle. That's all."

Turning my head back toward the pile of gigantic bodies, I frowned. "Maybe we should consider reviving a few of these guys and asking them some questions."

Graves chuckled. "There are several key problems with that idea, McGill. First off, they don't have tappers recording their engrams. We could copy their bodies from DNA samples, but they would be mindless."

"Oh... right. Are they catching a revive back on Blood World then?"

He looked at me like I was stupid. It was an expression I was well-familiar with.

"Of course not," he said. "These monsters wouldn't even fit in a standard-issue revival machine. They came here, and they died, and that's it."

"You mean I permed all these guys?"

"That's right—if you can even call it that. I mean, for normal people who've never even heard of a revival machine, it's just called dying, isn't it?"

"I guess so…" I said, somewhat disturbed.

Graves walked away, shaking his head at my foolishness, but my eyes lingered on the stack of dead. Sure, they were somewhat alien and monstrous, but they were mostly human underneath. It seemed kind of unfair for the Legions to use them as target practice when we could just bounce back the next day.

Troubled, I left Gold Deck behind and headed down to the labs. I had a lot of unanswered questions buzzing in my head.

## -18-

On the way down to the labs, I took the opportunity to strip off my armor and weapons, tossing the whole kit into my unit's module. There was plenty of blood and scorch marks on my gear, and I didn't think anyone down below wanted to see that.

When I reached the labs, I was in for a surprise. Floramel was working in the depths of *Nostrum's* lower decks, right alongside Natasha.

Just spotting the two of them, working together, made me halt in my tracks. These two women both had a claim on me. Natasha's claim was far older, but Floramel's was fresh and new.

Standing there for a few long seconds, I wasn't quite sure what to do.

The labs themselves were spacious, super-clean, and full of strange equipment. This was the deck that belonged to the techs. Unlike Blue Deck, the level that every ship had which was inhabited purely by bio-specialists and their victims, this one never seemed to be named after a color. People just called it "the Labs" or "Engineering" and left it at that.

I suspected it was because the region wasn't quite as restricted as other areas were. Gold Deck was for commanders and flight personnel only. It usually encompassed the ship's bridge and the offices for all the brass aboard any given transport. Gold Deck's unique purpose formed a good reason to restrict access.

Likewise, Blue Deck was crewed by the paranoid bio-types. They operated like a priesthood, caring for their incredibly expensive—and incredibly useful—revival machines. Oh, sure, any bio could cure a cold or cancer if she felt like it, but the main service they provided was the revival of dead troops, and everyone knew it.

The tech people were different. They were important, sure, but they were more down-to-earth and approachable. They handled a wide variety of problems—everything from servicing shipboard equipment to coming up with analyses about astrophysics and alien psychology. The breadth of their responsibilities forced them to work with others every day, and that seemed to make them easier to deal with.

A finger tapped my back while I stood in the doorway. Startled, I turned and looked down. There was Kivi, giving me a disgusted sneer.

"Can't decide which one to hit on today, McGill?" she asked.

I marveled at my poor timing. Kivi was a tech specialist herself. How likely was it that she'd show up right now? Together with Natasha and Floramel, I was in the presence of every tech girl I'd ever been involved with. The odds would have seemed longer, except for the fact they were all techs, this was their deck, and I'd taken no precautions such as contacting anyone before I came down here.

"Uh…" I said, trying to think.

"Don't bother coming up with a lie," Kivi said, and she scooted by me. As she did so, there was plenty of contact.

Now, you have to understand that a man just hasn't been brushed up against properly until Kivi's done it to you. She was a master. She rubbed every important part of herself against my side as she went by, making it all seem natural, accidental, and thrilling at the same time. We both knew full well there was plenty of room for her to scoot by in that open doorway without touching me at all—but that wasn't how Kivi operated.

I knew her game. She wasn't really promising me anything, nor was she too clueless to squeeze by neatly. She was trying to torture old James McGill. She wanted revenge on me after having caught me checking out two other women right in front of her.

Unreasonable? Yes. Pure Kivi? Definitely.

Using my full knowledge of her nature to my advantage, I enjoyed the fleeting contact and let it go. I didn't chase her, make a comment, or even let my eyes drift after her well-rounded posterior.

Soon she was gone, and I was able to think clearly again. I came to a firm decision. I walked up behind the Floramel and Natasha team, bold as brass, and laid one hand on each of their backs. My head poked between them as I did so.

"What are you two working on?" I asked loudly.

Startled, the girls eyed me, but they didn't pull away. Neither one of them knew I was touching the other. Sometimes, it pays to be large and have a long reach.

"We're trying to figure out what happened to the warp field," Natasha said.

"Incorrect," Floramel said. "We *know* what happened. We're trying to figure out *why* it happened."

Natasha's shoulders bunched up a bit in irritation. I couldn't blame her for that. Floramel liked to be precise, and all too often, that urge came out sounding like she was calling other people morons.

"Okay..." I said, "but what's that thing on the table?"

"It's a section of the outer hull, James," Natasha said patiently.

"That thing? Looks like a head-sized lump of charcoal."

"Extreme heat has been applied," Floramel explained, "along with some warping, radioactive fields and torsion. In combination, this abuse caused this section of the hull to be reduced to this damaged state."

"You're telling me this lump of crap came off the outside of our ship?" I asked, and I gave a long, low whistle. "So, what's the verdict? Did we hit another vessel or not?"

"Yes," Natasha said.

"No," Floramel said at almost the same instant.

I looked from one to the other. "Uh…"

Natasha wore a tight expression. I got the feeling Floramel was starting to get on her nerves.

"She means," Natasha explained, "that we didn't *literally* strike the other ship. We hit its wake. If we'd hit the other ship itself… well… we'd all be dead by now."

About then, Floramel pulled back a little, and I blew it. I left my hands on both of the girls. She noticed this, and she looked confused.

"I don't know what it is that you're proposing, James," she told me.

"Huh?"

"You're touching both of us. This behavior doesn't quite correspond to your traditional gripping of the shoulder—but the nature of the signal is still unmistakable."

Frowning, Natasha stepped back. Even though I dropped my hands to my sides, she began to glare at me like she'd been molested or something.

"Oh, come on," I said to them both. "We're all friends here, working on a critical scientific mission. Grow up, ladies. Continue the briefing."

It was a bold-as-brass play, but it was all I had. Fortunately, it seemed to work. Both of them turned slowly back to face their lump of melted space-crap again.

I suppressed a sigh of relief.

Natasha began explaining about heat-thresholds, force fields and the unique properties of melting-point temperatures in vacuum. Occasionally, Floramel corrected her on a tiny technical detail. I found the lecture less than fascinating.

My hands—those bored, treacherous bastards—crept up again and almost touched each of the girls. To me, it sometimes seemed like my fingers have minds of their own.

I managed to fight my sinister urges and clasped my hands behind my back for good. With a pasted-on smile, I strictly maintained the pretense that I cared about their burnt space-rock. It was a sheer force of will.

"Uh-huh," I said about two minutes later, sensing it was an appropriate moment to jump in. "Look, ladies, this is fascinating, but I'm no tech. What I need to know is what happened? Did the Blood Worlders send out a ship and run it into our warp-bubble or not?"

"That's not entirely clear," Natasha said. "We think they tried to match our course and speed, but perhaps they got too close and caused the disruption... by the way, did you say 'Blood Worlders'?"

"I did indeed. That's what they call themselves. Colorful, isn't it? Conjures quite an image."

"Yes, lovely," Natasha said, turning to Floramel and giving her an up-down appraisal. "Have you heard that name before, Floramel?"

"Yes," she said. "The littermates didn't coin it themselves. Their brood-mothers did."

Natasha suppressed a shiver. "In any case, I think we've done all the analysis of this chunk of debris we can. I'm willing to rule the incident was an accident."

Both of us looked at Floramel. "I'm not willing to do so," she said. "I'm of the opinion our warp-field was disrupted purposefully."

"But why?" Natasha asked. "The most believable scenario is the simplest one. The ship came here to meet us, got too close, and both our fields were disrupted. When we dropped out of warp they crossed over to Gold Deck to spring their trap on McGill. Case closed."

I had to admit, she made a convincing argument. I turned my eyes to Floramel, who was still looking at the space-rock doubtfully.

"People think the Blood Worlders are stupid," she said, "but they aren't. Not all of them. Those who are in charge are very cunning."

"Okay," I said, "but to *be* cunning, you have to have a motive. What were they trying to do?"

She shook her head. "That I don't know. I just know they managed to knock us out of warp. We're still not flying again—did you know that?"

"I noticed that," I said. "All the field projectors are dead. The back half of the ship, which is usually thrumming all the time, seems quiet."

"Do you want to walk with me down there and check it out, James?" Natasha asked.

"Sure."

This was a mistake. Floramel immediately looked upset.

"Uh…" I said, "you want to come along too, Floramel? Any tech will do. I'm not welcome in the engine room. They won't want to answer my questions unless I'm escorted by a tech."

It was an ass-covering play on my part. Floramel was still suspicious of my motives concerning her and Natasha, and I didn't want her to feel I'd left her out.

"Oh… is that the intention? Then no, I'll stay here. I need to finish my measurements on this hull sample."

"Suit yourself," I said, giving her a friendly nod and a smile.

I left, and Natasha followed.

"You're still trying to rekindle with her, is that it?" she asked me.

"Is that a problem?"

"Not for me," she said a little too quickly.

The last time Natasha and I had connected, it hadn't seemed like a big deal. We'd been fighting and dying on a rock-pile planet called Rogue World. Tech-smiths like Floramel had lived there under a blue-glass dome—but that was over a year ago.

"I'm not chasing her," I said. "Not really. It's just that Floramel is different. She doesn't totally get our social rules here on Earth. I don't like the idea of hurting her in a careless way."

"Better to break hearts up-front and guilt-free, hmm?"

"Come on, Natasha. You and I haven't been intimate for a long time."

"It was on Rogue World. Where you met Floramel."

I got it then. She was jealous of Floramel. Not because there weren't any other women around—there always were. But because she'd decided Floramel was the one who'd stolen me away.

Maybe I'd misjudged how much Natasha cared about minor hook-ups. It wouldn't be the first time.

"Hey," I said, "we can do this trip to the engine room some other time."

"No," she said. "Let's do it. I want to know what happened, too."

"Okay. Glad you're coming along. I feel like we're missing something."

"I feel it too."

When we reached Engineering, I knew right off my instincts had been proven correct. Something was very wrong down here in the aft of the big ship.

The guards outside the main hatch were lying on the deck, and both of them were stone dead.

## -19-

The bodies were posed in a way that told me instantly it hadn't been an accident. Someone—or something—had killed the guards.

"My tapper is dead," I told Natasha. "I can't report in."

"Mine too—it's some kind of stealth-jamming. Hold on."

She worked on her tapper, which was connected to a larger, portable unit in the small ruck she always carried. Every tech had a real computer on their backs, not just a standard-issue tapper.

My gun came out, and my visor slammed down. I stepped toward the bodies in a crouch. I didn't see any clear cause of death. They were lying on their backs, hands held up rigidly in front of them. Their mouths and eyes were open, staring at nothing in surprise.

"Don't touch them!" Natasha said.

I glanced over my shoulder at her and withdrew my gauntlet.

"What's wrong?"

"I'm sensing high voltage—the bodies are flowing with current. They're cooking even now."

I stood up and retreated.

"We've got to report this," I said. "We've got to back up to where our tappers will work again."

"Hold on, I've penetrated the jamming field."

"Good, patch me through to Graves on Gold Deck."

Natasha worked for a second then gave me a nod.

"McGill?" I heard a fuzzy voice in my helmet. "What's this about?"

"Emergency, Primus. I'm down in Engineering and—"

"You're not supposed to be in Engineering, McGill."

I opened my mouth, but then I halted. Could this all be some kind of on-going game?

My mouth twisted up with disgust. I flipped up my visor again, shaking my head.

"It's not safe, Centurion," Natasha hissed at me.

"Yeah, right…" I said. "Primus Graves, I have to protest. You really should announce these oddball contests."

"What are you talking about?"

"I'm talking about the electrocuted crewmen at my feet. If you're going to have combat trainings live onboard ship, you really should—"

"Where are you again, McGill?"

"At the entrance to Engineering, sir. Like I said."

He was quiet for a second. "No trainings, drills or other special events are scheduled for that zone. In fact—I can't raise Engineering at all. Are you doing that?"

"Uh…" I said, flipping my visor back down again.

I stepped away from the bodies on the deck. All of a sudden, they were even more alarming than they had been the first moment I'd spotted them. If Gold Deck really didn't know what was going on down here, well, the whole ship was in danger.

"Sir, we've got a problem—a serious problem. Tap into my vid feed from my body-cams."

Graves did as I asked, and soon he cursed. "Alright, I don't know what's going on. I'm mobilizing a unit and sending them down there to back you up. In the meantime, advance and investigate. Graves out."

A few moments later, yellow flashers began to spin all along the passageway. At least Graves had sounded the alarm.

Looking at Natasha, I shrugged. "We've been ordered to investigate. Contact everyone in our unit. Tell all the adjuncts to bring my people down here."

"Didn't Graves just say that he was sending back-up?"

"Yes, he did, but he never said I couldn't call my own. Bring them down, Natasha, that's an order."

She worked her tapper after that without complaining. That was one thing I liked about her. She could get kind of prissy when it came to other women in a social situation, but when the bodies hit the floor, she was all business.

With my sidearm in my hand, I advanced to the main hatchway alone. I stepped over bodies, one at a time, with great care. When I turned back to look at Natasha, I saw the wires she'd been talking about. Cables were running to each of the dead crewmen, and they'd been carefully hidden on the far side of the corpses, so anyone approaching wouldn't notice until it was too late.

They were wired up like Christmas trees. Tracing the wires to some open panels in the bulkheads outside of Engineering, I reached in and grabbed up a handful of copper and optical fiber cables.

Yanking loose a meter or so of copper wire, I carefully dropped it so it made contact with the hatchway and the metal deck.

The results were both spectacular and immediate. A blue flash sparked, and the copper wire curled up, glowing white hot and burning away the insulation.

"There's voltage in the hatch," I said, "Natasha, can you fix this? I can't get in."

"James, why don't you wait for back-up? Whoever did this might be waiting on the far side with a weapon."

"True, but I've got my orders, same as you."

"All right."

She came forward, worked on an open circuit panel and soon pronounced the power had been cut off. I touched the door by flicking my finger across it, and I felt no jolt.

I put my tapper up to the touch-plate lock, but there was no reaction.

"It's not going to open automatically," she said. "I had to kill the mechanism. The hatches are on pure manual now."

"Right," I said, and I tried not to wince as I applied my shoulder to the hatch. Spinning the wheel, I heard gears roll and click. The hatch swung slowly open with a groan of metal.

There was something inside—a whole bunch of somethings.

I gaped at them in utter shock. They were small—less than a meter tall, but they looked somewhat human. They were thin and wiry, with stringy, overly-long arms and legs. Their muscles were starkly outlined on their bodies, as if they had very little body fat. They didn't wear much for clothes, either.

"What kind of freaky goblins are these?" I asked no one in particular.

They scattered as I forced my way through the hatch, which only opened about a foot. A few were working on a panel nearby. They had tools, and they seemed intelligent and organized.

I heard a click, and I felt a squeeze. The hatchway I'd just forced open had begun to close again.

"You little pricks," I said, and aimed my gun at the group at the panel.

They raced off in every direction, like a pack of monkeys rushing up trees. One ran down the hall away from me, another ran past me, under my feet, and out into the passage behind me. Still another raced right up the wall, using just about anything for a handhold. I remembered seeing a rat race up a ladder into my grandma's attic years ago, hopping from rung to rung like he was built for it. This sight was just as startling.

Pressing and straining, I tried at first to get through the hatchway. But it was no use. I wasn't strong enough, and after a second, I realized I was pinned.

Sighting my pistol on the nearest little gremlin, I nailed him.

He must have thought he was safe, watching me with those big wet eyes from the roof of the passage—but I'm a pretty good shot, even when my ribs are beginning to crackle.

He shrieked when I burned him and fell dead onto the deck.

That's when I noticed there were more bodies—full-sized human bodies—all over the deck. Our engineering crew had been slaughtered.

Struggling to pull back, I almost made it. The pneumatics powering the hatch popped and hissed, trying to force the hatch shut. I got one foot back, then the other. I felt a little tug on my hand, and I figured it had to be Natasha, trying to help.

But in the end, it was my helmet that screwed me. It was too big and bulbous to get through the hatch. I would have taken it off, but I couldn't do that either, as my arms were pinned.

Then, my ribcage gave out. The air was driven from my lungs, and I could feel my spine cracking. Breathing in little gasps, my vision went in and out in waves.

Something ran up to me, and I saw it was a gremlin. It had a cord in its hands with a long needle at the tip. It came close, wary, walking in a crouch as if ready to spring away.

I tried to lift my gun. Lord, how I tried. I would have done just about anything to even twitch my fingers up enough to aim and fire my pistol one more time—but I couldn't. My hands were numb, and my pistol fell to clatter on the deck, having slipped free from my squirming fingers.

The creature dropped the cable and sprang away for a second, but then it crept back again. It looked up at me, and it gave me a small, happy grin.

Then it jabbed that needle into me, and it applied the juice.

I heard Natasha, as my body danced and fried and began to steam a little. She must have been outside, pulling at my exposed limbs, trying to pull me back to her side of the hatch.

Trying to help.

But she'd become attached to me, her muscles as rigid as mine.

Helpless, we died together in a deadly embrace. My final thought was that we'd become a new trap for the next victims to encounter.

## -20-

Revivals aren't always what they're cracked up to be. I'd avoided dying for nearly two full years now—and I'd almost forgotten the sights, the sounds, and the nauseating sensations…

Of all my senses, my ears started working first. That wasn't unusual. Balance, vision, clear thought—these things came later.

"We've got a big one," a female bio said. I didn't recognize her voice.

"It's McGill," a familiar voice said. "Get him on the gurney. I need information."

That was Winslade. I'd have known his voice anywhere. To me, it wasn't even slightly surprising to hear him speak as I returned from whatever Hell I'd been languishing in.

"McGill?" Winslade said, near at hand. "Can you hear me? We're under some kind of attack. Snap out of it, man."

"He can't talk yet, Primus. Do you mind?"

A bright light shined into my eyes. It was painful, shocking. I tried to roll my head and squinch my freshly-grown eyes shut, but the bio kept blinding me.

One of my big hands came up almost on its own, and it grabbed her wrist. I gave her a light squeeze, and she hissed.

"You're breaking my wrist!"

"Sorry," I rasped, and I let her go.

She flicked off her light and retreated.

"He's always an ape with women," Winslade said. "Remember that, in case he asks you for a date later on."

"You should look out for yourself, Primus," the bio warned him.

Behind him, I'd risen from the gurney like a reanimated corpse—which was, I guess, a pretty accurate description of my current state.

My heavy hand landed on Winslade's shoulder before he could turn or scoot away. I pulled him close, and I gave him a one-armed bear-hug that pushed the air out of his lungs.

"What in God's name are you doing, McGill?" he demanded in a gasping voice.

"I'm giving you my report, sir," I said. "That's what it felt like—but a hundred times worse. That hatch… It just kept squeezing and squeezing until I was as dead as dead can be."

Releasing him, I let him take a breath, cough, and glare at me.

"You're a bad grow," he pronounced. "You've got to be. You've assaulted two people in your first two minutes out of the revival machine."

"Oh, come on," I said. "Man-up. I was just having a little fun."

I grinned at him, my bleary eyes still squinting and blinking.

He sneered, but he lifted his hand off the butt of his sidearm.

Figuring I wasn't going to be recycled right away, I got off the gurney and stood. I forced myself to balance through sheer will.

Winslade took another involuntary step backward.

"Things are bad, McGill," he said. "We've lost Engineering."

"You don't say? What was it, those little gremlins?"

"Gremlins?"

"That's what everyone calls them," I lied.

Winslade looked confused for a moment, but then he shrugged. "Fine, gremlins it is."

"So you're telling me you didn't invite them aboard? I've been telling everyone they're your best friends."

"You *what*? Oh—I see. Another misguided attempt at levity. Well, listen-up Centurion. Graves is dead. Half your unit died with him. Is that funny too?"

"What happened?" I said, frowning in real worry.

"I've been trying to tell you," he said between clenched teeth. "Graves took two units down there—one of them yours. After seeing several dead bodies—including yours—they formed up and assaulted the hatches."

"How'd that go?"

"They failed. Engineering, as you may or may not know, is built to withstand a serious assault."

"Two units failed to retake the ship?" I asked, whistling. "I don't see how they could. Those little gremlins are tricky, but they don't seem *that* dangerous."

"I've sifted through the after-action reports of the survivors, and I understand the enemy employed numerous deadly traps."

"Yeah," I said, putting on fresh clothes and digging my Centurion's bars out of the rank-insignia box. "The gremlins are tricky little buggers. Let's go talk to Floramel."

"Whatever for? Haven't you been listening? We have a tactical situation on our hands. I haven't dared send in a larger force with heavier weapons for fear of destroying our engines entirely."

"So, they haven't damaged the Alcubierre Drive?"

"No, not yet."

"Good," I said, walking out into the passages of Blue Deck. "God, how I hate the smell of this place."

Winslade followed me as he clearly didn't know what else to do.

"I think we need to talk to Floramel," I told him, "because these gremlins are hers. Her tech-smiths made them. They're some kind of relative of ours, like the littermates and the slavers."

"But they're so small. You really think they were genetically bred from human stock?"

"I'd bet on it. The way that last one grinned at me as he rammed an electrified needle into my shin—yes sir, only a human could be that gleefully evil. By the way, Primus, where's Tribune Deech?"

"She's seen fit to place me in charge of retaking Engineering."

I glanced at him and gave him an up-down appraisal. "I've heard she operates like that. She doesn't like to take on dangerous, failure-prone tasks on her own."

Winslade stiffened as if slapped. "That's absurd. She's delegated the task to me because of her absolute confidence in my leadership skills."

"Uh-huh."

We'd reached the labs by this time, and I could hear a large number of troops had gathered below on the aft decks. There must have been a full cohort down there.

I shook my head. "That's too many men. They'll just get in each other's way."

Winslade gave me a sour look. "They're placed here defensively. I wanted to make sure the gremlins can't penetrate the rest of the ship. They're small and thin enough to wriggle through the ship's conduits like rats."

"Interesting…"

The labs were full of techs, every one of which was working in a fever. After all, Engineering was part of their territory, so to speak. They'd taken this attack as an assault on all of them.

We found Floramel in her office. I knocked politely, but when she didn't answer, I waved to Primus Winslade. He used his tapper to override the lock, and I stepped inside.

The interior was dark. A tall, shapely figure was seated at Floramel's desk, but she didn't move. Right off, I feared the worst.

"Floramel?" I asked.

"Oh, please," Winslade said, and he snapped on the lights with a flick of his fingers.

Floramel was sitting there, with her face in her hands.

"What's wrong?" I asked her.

Winslade made an odd sound. He was sucking air through his teeth in disgust.

I waved him back. Rolling his eyes, he retreated and stood in the doorway, assuming a bored pose.

"Floramel?" I asked. "You aren't hurt, are you?"

In the back of my mind, I was thinking of the gremlins. They seemed to like tricks. It would be just like them to have propped Floramel up as another booby-trap.

Then she moved, and I breathed a little easier.

"It's all my fault," she said in a husky voice.

"How could it be?"

"The homunculi—they were my project."

"Uh... you mean you *made* these things? Personally?"

"Yes. I oversaw their development. They were one of the last experimental designs we created for the Cephalopods. I never thought I'd see them again. They were all shipped off-world, and I—"

"What were you thinking?" Winslade demanded suddenly.

Floramel jumped a little. I don't think she'd realized he was still standing in the doorway.

I gave him a deadly stare. "Do you mind, sir? The lady is in a bad way."

Huffing, he turned on his heel and left. "You have five minutes, McGill. After that, I'm going to apply my own methods."

Not liking the sound of that, I worked hard to keep my expression pleasant when I turned back to Floramel. In return, she studied me fearfully.

"What a horrible man. What's he talking about?"

"Yep, he's horrible. But he's in charge today, so we have to pull ourselves together."

Her lip trembled a little.

"You died down there," she said in a hushed voice. "I watched it. They transmitted it all over the ship. I hated myself when I watched you die. I even felt bad for that grasping woman—Natasha."

"Yeah... Listen girl, I know you're in an emotional state. You seem to have lost much of your aloof nature. I mean, you've changed a lot since you've moved to Earth."

Floramel nodded, and she looked lost.

"It's so different on Earth," she said. "Living among neural-typical humans is difficult. I think I've become more like them."

"That's bound to happen. Culture shock, they call it."

She studied me for a moment, and she nodded slowly.

"Now," I said gently, sitting my big butt on her desk. "We need to talk about these gremlins. How do we kill them and kick them off our ship?"

"They're your brothers," she said. "Or at least, your cousins."

"Right…" I said gently. "Later on, we'll do our very best to make friends. I promise. But for right now, they've got to go. You can see that, can't you?"

Her distress was obvious, and deep down in my guts, I began to suspect a new reason for her uncharacteristically emotional state.

She'd admitted she'd had a personal hand in the creation of these little bastards. Could it be she still held some fondness for them? Were they, to Floramel, something akin to small pets—or even wild, errant children?

"Listen," I said, "back on Earth, things like this happen now and then."

She looked at me in surprise. "They do?" she asked.

"Well, not *exactly* like this. But sometimes a person takes in a pet when it's small. They treat it like an infant, but when it grows up, its true nature always comes out. Beloved things sometimes turn vicious with age, like a tiger, or a chimp that goes berserk as an adult."

"The homunculi aren't animals, James."

"No, no, of course not. They're infinitely worse. They're smarter and meaner than any monkey I've ever heard of."

I told her then of being lanced with an electrified needle. Of how the gremlin grinned at me, enjoying my agony.

By the end of my story Floramel was crying again. Gently, I touched her cheek and swept away a tear. I'd never seen her cry before.

"Time's up, McGill!" Winslade called from the doorway.

Throwing up my hand, I gave him a stopping gesture. He sighed and began to pace outside again.

"Will you do it?" I asked her gently. "Will you help us get our ship back?"

"I will," she said, her voice sad and dull.

Somehow, I didn't feel triumphant about my successful persuasion. Floramel was an honestly sweet girl. She was so wise and so innocent, all at the same time.

But dammit, those tiny demons had to go!

## -21-

We stood outside Engineering—well outside.

Floramel marched forward slowly, stopping about fifty meters away from the end of the passageway. Bodies were strewn all over the deck in front of the hatchway, which had been blackened by Graves and his earlier attempt to breach it.

"Children?" Floramel called out. "This is Floramel calling to you. Come out and speak with me."

This startled me. I was standing behind her, ready to fight. She was unarmed and looking helpless in her vac suit. She had her hands clasped in front of her, and her head tilted upward at the end of that long, lovely neck of hers.

I found myself feeling protective. These little friggers had already killed Natasha and me, plus about two hundred others. If we hadn't been desperate, I would never have approved of this attempted pow-wow with the enemy.

"Tell me again, McGill," Carlos' voice buzzed in my ear, "when are we going to charge in there and slaughter these monkeys?"

"Hold on, Carlos," I radioed back. "Give Floramel her shot."

Carlos and a full unit of troops were well back, in defensive positions at the other end of the long passageway that led to Engineering.

I knew why Carlos was angry. We'd both been killed by these guys in devious ways. Graves and his troops had penetrated further, and the main hatch was already hanging half off its hinges.

"Children?" Floramel asked softly, but there was no response.

Then she did what I'd specifically told her not to do. She walked forward, coming to within twenty meters of that exposed hatch. The first of the dead bodies lay right at her feet.

"Dammit, girl," I said in her ear on a private channel. "Step back here. If they nail you, we have to nail them."

She paid me no attention at all. Maybe she'd figured out she was the last chance these gremlins had to live. In that case, she was right.

Frankly, I was amazed they'd survived so long. We'd tried all the easy stuff. We'd flushed the deck with radioactive gas. We'd electrified the deck and then tried to shut off the power entirely.

The trouble was that in each case, they'd been able to override our remote control actions. Engineering was at least as well wired-in to the ship's controls as Gold Deck was. They'd been able to shut down every move we made.

The only systems the gremlins didn't have control of were the helm, life support and navigation. They were working on that tirelessly, however. Our techs could sense their interference, hacking and workarounds. For every attack we sent their way, they sent one right back.

Sooner or later, this was going to change from a stand-off to an outright fight to the finish. If they managed to cut power to the rest of the ship, or gain control of our engines and begin flying the ship, Winslade had issued firm orders: we were to go in and take them all out, even if it meant losing the ship.

A core breach. That's what we feared most. We'd been pussy-footing around with these gremlins precisely because they were holed up in Engineering. The drive was there, with about a terawatt's worth of fusion reactors. If we ruptured the cooling jackets or otherwise did permanent damage to the engines, well, it was all over for Legion Varus. We'd have to signal Earth that we'd lost the ship to pirates, and blow ourselves up.

If the hogs back home were in a charitable mood, they'd revive us all on Earth. It was a humiliating defeat that none of us wanted to endure.

"Floramel!" I hissed down the hall after her.

She'd begun stepping over bodies. Any one of them could kill her. They'd all been wired up to zap the unwary.

Before she reached the hatch, a figure appeared ahead of her. Then six more tiny heads popped up.

"There you are!" she said. "It's been so long since I've seen you."

"You are the designer?" one of them asked in a tiny voice.

"Yes. I'm Floramel. I—"

They swarmed forward. Bounding over the wired-up bodies with astounding speed and agility, they were all around her in an instant.

I had my rifle up to my shoulder. I sighted the nearest of them, and I put my crosshairs on his tiny scalp.

"Why would the designer be here?" asked the gremlin. "Why aren't you home?"

"Our old home was destroyed, children," Floramel said gently. "It's all gone. Even the rock beneath our dome has been melted away into fragments."

A general hissing went up from the gremlins. They were circling now, all around Floramel's feet. It was a weird sight, like seeing a goddess stand as tall as a tree surrounded by villagers.

"Who?" a gremlin asked.

"Who destroyed our world? I…" Floramel faltered. She'd had a nice lilt in her voice up until now. She'd been glad to see her tiny creations again. But now, perhaps she'd sensed that she shouldn't tell them who was responsible for the destruction of their original home.

"The Empire," another one said, answering for her. "We know."

"I'm sorry," Floramel told them. "As sorry as you all are. But there has been enough death and destruction. We must—"

"No!" one shouted. "We mustn't!"

"Children, please."

"You're a slave to these apes. We've seen them from the inside. We've cooked them and tasted their flesh. They aren't us—but they are *like* us. Did you make them, too?"

"No, they're the original form. You, me—all of us are descended from these humans."

The gremlins cocked their heads and regarded me curiously for a moment.

"They seem so slow and stupid," one said. "How can they be our gods?"

"They aren't gods. They're our ancestors."

"Primitive proto-beings?"

"If you like."

I *didn't* like it. Not the way this conversation was going, or Floramel's unwarranted attachment to these tiny devils.

Standing, I lowered my gun and took ten steps forward. The gremlins shifted warily.

"This one is mean," one said.

"He's big, but he's dumb."

I forced a grin. After all, we were supposed to be on a diplomatic mission. If Floramel could charm these imps, maybe I could do the same.

"Listen kids," I said. "I'm in charge of the security down here. We're all on the same ship. How about we make a deal?"

"What kind of deal, big-man?"

"Here's a bargain: We'll give you a ride back to Blood World, with a module aboard our ship just for you. You'll be fed, clothed and given whatever you need. When we get to your planet, you can go free without any repercussions."

"Sixteen of us have died on this huge, cold ship," one of the gremlins complained. He stepped forward from the rest as if he was their leader. "How will you pay for that?"

"Well," I said, "I'm sorry about that, but a lot of us died, too."

A general laugh went up from the group. They grinned at me, but I wasn't sure what was so damned funny.

"Sorrow isn't payment," the gremlin informed me. "Only pain pays a blood-price."

"That's right," said another, walking forward confidently. He looked up at me and he grinned. He grinned hugely.

"Big-man," he said, "would you like to dance? I've seen you dance, and I enjoyed—"

That was about it for old James McGill. You have to understand, I'm a dishonest man. I'm a man who knows all the ways a truth can be bent, this way and that, until it breaks like a dry twig.

Now, I'm not an evil sort. At least, I like to think I'm not. My lies are almost always told to ease over the difficult parts in life. They grease the sharp edges and painful sorts of things we're all forced to swallow from time to time.

But my intimate knowledge of deceit gave me powers others didn't possess when it came to spotting subterfuge, treachery and downright orneriness. In short, I knew these devils were lying to me, and they had no intention of letting us bargain our way back into Engineering. It just wasn't going to happen.

Last of all, in that singular moment before I lost control, I recognized the gremlin at my feet—the one that was grinning up at me, asking funny questions about dancing… Grinning wide.

It was none other than the same little dick who'd jabbed me with an electrified needle not two hours earlier.

And now he was teasing me about it. Enjoying himself. When I realized that—I snapped.

It's been said before, and it'll be said again—a Legion Varus man isn't to be trifled with. We simply don't take well to being played. It's just not in our natures to laugh with an enemy. Instead, we tend to take matters into our own hands and kill whatever gets in our way.

Not being a philosopher or a psychologist, I don't have any fancy way of explaining what gripped me over the next few moments, but I can tell you plainly what happened.

A cold, deadly calm came over me. A murderous stare haunted my eyes. It was as if the light of the stars themselves glittered in my pupils, and let me assure you, there's no light more merciless or terrifying than that.

The gremlin who'd dared to tease me—he knew he'd made a mistake. He'd overstepped his bounds and then some.

Maybe he'd thought that with Floramel there, he was safe to do and say what he wanted to the big-man. But he'd thought wrong.

He bounded in a single leap backward, moving through the air like a trapeze artist.

But it wasn't enough to escape. My hand swept up and caught him. I didn't bother to do anything complicated. I just crushed him and threw his lifeless doll-like body at the rest, who scattered like raccoons firing off a tipped-over garbage can.

"James!" Floramel called out in horror.

She might have tried to do something like restrain me, but it was no use. I was wearing powered armor, and I didn't even feel her touch.

My heavy boots crushed down the dead men all around us as I charged after the gremlins who hooted and bounced away in a dozen directions. I felt a tingle coming up from my boots, but I wasn't fried. I'd taken the precaution of insulating my body to prevent such traps from stopping me again.

Another gremlin caught a bolt from my rifle, which I whipped up one-handed from my shoulder where I'd slung it. He went ass-over-teakettle down the passage, looking like a tiny man-shaped fireball.

The rest of them vanished through the open hatchway, and just like that, our peace-talks came to an abrupt end.

I turned around slowly to see Floramel's eyes were full of horror and tears.

"Dammit…" I said.

There were some things you just never wanted your lady to see—and this had been one of them.

She ran off, crying, and I didn't try to stop her. I heaved a sigh instead.

That's when I felt it—a tiny prick in the back of my left leg, right behind the kneecap.

The electricity flowed, and I did that dance the other gremlin had asked for. I danced until I fell, then I kept dancing, eyes blinking fast.

My flesh smoked and my lungs locked up.

It seemed like it went on for a long time. Maybe the gremlins had been studying us, working hard to determine just how much current they could apply to incapacitate a human body without quite killing the subject.

Either that or it was just dumb luck.

In any case, I was in agony. My heart was fibrillating, my muscles were locked so tight I couldn't barf. I couldn't even breathe or cry aloud. I just kind of gurgled and shook.

Then, thankfully, I died.

## -22-

"Twice in a row, McGill?" Winslade asked with a hint of amusement. "I've got half a mind to send you back down there. Maybe you'll beat your personal record for failure today."

Struggling, I found the strength to get up into a sitting position.

"Where's..." I rasped, "Where's Floramel?"

Winslade chuckled. "Chasing skirts again already? I'm afraid you've gotten your last taste of that one. After you lost your mind during that impromptu peace conference, she specified she doesn't want to work together with you—on anything. Ever."

I didn't hear the rest of his snotty speech. He probably told me what kind of a loser I was, and that I'd blown everything—but I didn't care.

Inside, I was feeling a broad range of conflicting emotions. Part of me was glad I'd laid into those monstrous runts. They'd paid the price for playing with a Varus man.

But I wasn't entirely at ease. I'd blown it with Floramel—probably permanently. It was obvious she felt some kind of unearned love for the gremlins. Going berserk and killing them in front of her? That had to be the equivalent of stomping cats in front of a cat-lady. Relationship-death at its finest.

Still another part of my mind was worried I'd blown everything on a bigger scale. That I'd possibly doomed all

Legion Varus to drift out here in interstellar space for years—maybe forever.

"…are you even listening to me?" Winslade demanded. "Specialist? Check this man—is he a bad grow?"

She came close and poked at me. I allowed it.

"He's fine. He looks depressed, but if I know James McGill, he's probably just bored and tuning you out."

I glanced at the bio in surprise then I recognized her. It was Centurion Thompson. That was unexpected because bio people of officer rank rarely worked in the revival rooms.

Frowning for a second, I checked her lapels. She wasn't a centurion anymore. She was a specialist—and I realized Winslade had called her that.

Two steps lost in rank? That seemed odd. What had she done to fall so far from grace?

Thompson almost seemed to follow my thinking.

"Sir?" she said to Winslade. "Maybe I should keep this man under observation for a few minutes. If he's a good grow, I'll send him up to Gold Deck."

"Thirty minutes," Winslade told both of us. "That's it. I expect to see you on Gold Deck by then. We're having a discussion you don't want to miss."

"Roger that, sir," I said.

He left, and I frowned at Specialist Thompson.

She looked back at me warily, without saying anything. We'd had a bad relationship from the start, Thompson and I.

She was thin and had a pinched face, but she'd never lacked for energy or a sense of duty.

"Well?" I asked. "I got rid of Winslade. What was it you wanted to say?"

We studied one another for a few more moments then she shook her head, releasing a bemused puff of air from her lips.

"I can't believe this," she said. "I used to be the centurion, and you were the specialist. I can't say I like the switch."

"Yeah…" I said, eyeing her warily as she checked me over.

Years back, Thompson had tried to kill me with a needle. I'd reversed the situation on her, but I'd never quite trusted her since.

I reached out and touched her rank insignia. She flinched away, but then she got it.

"How'd it happen?" I asked, ending our uncomfortable silence.

She took a probe out of my ear and looked at me. She put her hands on her hips.

"What I want to know is: why didn't *you* get demoted?"

"Uh... what?"

She shook her head and continued the examination. "I'm guessing it was dumb luck. I was associated with Turov—the same as you. What did she do? Endangered all Earth and started a half-dozen wars. Winslade came out all right, as you did, apparently. But me? I got nailed."

"Oh..." I said, catching on. She had always been one of Turov's sidekicks. But apparently, her loyalty hadn't been rewarded like that of certain others. "Well," I said, "for what it's worth, all is forgiven on my part."

Thompson looked at me. "You mean... everything between you and me? All the murders?"

That statement chilled me a little. I knew that I'd been abused in the past. Some versions of James McGill had been tortured, killed and revived again for a repeat performance. Could Thompson have participated in that particularly gruesome part of my history?

I didn't know, but I'm a man who gives out apologies and forgiveness easily. It costs my mind almost nothing to do so—as I rarely mean it when I make such declarations.

"Uh... I guess so," I said. "All of that stuff is forgiven."

She looked me up and down quietly for a second. Then she went back into action, checking my stats all over again.

"You surprise me, McGill," she said. "I couldn't have forgiven you for the same thing. For what it's worth, I'm sorry for all that's happened between us, too."

Thompson slapped me on the leg then, and she waved for me to climb off her table. "I pronounce you a good grow! Better get up there and get it over with."

"Get what over with?"

She stared at me in confusion for a moment then apparently she figured I was making some kind of joke. She slapped me on the shoulder and threw me out, shaking her head.

I stumbled out into the passages, trying to get my jacket to wrap around my chest. It wasn't easy, as I was still sticky with birthing fluids.

Gold Deck was under repair from my battle with the littermates. At least they'd removed all the gigantic bodies of the fallen.

"Centurion McGill?" a veteran with a stern demeanor called out. "Right this way, sir."

I followed the veteran, and I noted that two others fell in behind me. This wasn't good. It didn't look like an outright arrest, but it was quite possible it would turn into one.

Legion Varus had a way of eating its own when it came to difficult situations like this. People were very serious about their careers in the upper ranks. The key to rank, in many people's eyes, was never being tagged with the stink of failure. Since we lived essentially forever, a truly ambitious person could hope to rise to the very top over time.

Because of this, the brass often took a dim view of individuals who went way off-script and into the weeds. Unfortunately, that was my particular specialty.

The veterans marched me to Tribune Deech's office. Winslade was there, as was Primus Graves.

I gave them both a nod and a slight smile. As we were technically in a warzone, I didn't salute. I didn't feel like doing so, anyway.

"Centurion James McGill," Deech said slowly, coming out from behind her desk. "You're the crown jewel of this legion, if Tribune Armel is to be believed."

"Yes sir," I said, "I do think he's got a point there."

Winslade chuckled, but Deech glanced at him, and he halted immediately.

"Impudent to the last," Deech said. "Why am I not surprised?"

"Uh…" I said. "What's this all about, Tribune?"

"Graves?" Deech asked, turning to him. "Do you want to explain? He's your responsibility, after all."

"Certainly, sir. McGill, we've got to file a report on the deep-link describing our progress on this mission thus far. Your recent actions have not been successful in dislodging the gremlins from the Engine room, and therefore—"

"Ah-ha!" I said, interrupting. "I get it. Someone has to get spanked. It might as well be me, right?"

Deech glowered. "I've watched the vid files, McGill. You were sent down there twice, against my better judgment."

Here, she glared at Winslade for a moment. I guessed it had been his idea, or at least Deech was going to blame him for it.

"The resulting debacle was horrific!" Deech continued. "The gremlins sent out a delegation to entreat with Floramel. Within two short minutes, you were engaged in slaughtering them!"

"Well now—"

"Shut up!" she boomed. "I don't want to hear any excuses. Not today. Not out of any of you!"

It occurred to me, as Deech marched around the room and proceeded to blame all three of us for this gross failure, that she was one slippery customer. She was in command of the entire legion, of course. She'd placed us all in harm's way by ordering us to go down to Engineering. I'd heard more than once that she liked to set people up when she felt a mission might fall apart. That way, she could blame an underling, roast him alive and march out of it a winner.

She seemed to be doing just that now, with Winslade, Graves and I all taking the rap for her.

Of the three of us, I think Winslade was the only one taken by surprise. He'd been working hard to brown-nose this woman. He'd been smooching up pretty much nonstop since we'd left Earth. A fat lot of good that had done him. He was about to be sold down the river with the rest of us.

By the time her overly-long, irritating speech finished up, I was getting bored. I was also having second thoughts about how I was going to get out of this. The trouble was, my approach might save Winslade too. I felt I owed him nothing, but I couldn't figure a way out of helping him when I helped myself.

Ah well. Sometimes, a man's got to play the cards as they've been laid.

"...and furthermore—"

"Tribune Deech?" I interrupted. "Can I say something, sir?"

"Really?" she said, whirling around on me. "You're going to grovel? They told me you wouldn't do that. Apparently, they were wrong."

"Uh... no sir," I said. "There's no point in that. I'd rather explain my plan to move forward and win this situation."

Graves slid his right hand to touch his left wrist. His tapper blinked once, and I almost smiled. I knew right off what he'd done. He'd activated the recording option on his tapper.

More than once, Graves had recorded embarrassing conversations for use against brass later on. In this case, I couldn't be sure what he intended, but perhaps when Deech reported in to Earth he'd insert a snippet including my plan in the deep-link packet. That way, if Deech refused to utilize my plan, she'd have to explain why she'd given up instead.

"What are you talking about, Centurion?" Deech demanded, standing right in front of me.

"A solution, sir. A way out of this predicament we're in."

"You're telling me you have a way to regain control of my ship? To restore Engineering, fire-up the warp core, and continue on our way to Epsilon Leporis?"

"Just possibly so, sir—if you'd let me explain."

"You're right, McGill," Winslade said suddenly. "It's time to reveal our plans."

Both Deech and I looked at him in surprise. Was he honestly going to try to hitch a ride on my plan? Without even knowing what it was? Honestly?

"Shut up, Primus," Deech told him.

Winslade recoiled as if slapped, but he *did* shut up.

"Speak, McGill," Deech ordered me.

"Yes sir. It goes like this: the enemy—I'm talking about the gremlins now, not Winslade, or anyone else in the Legion."

Winslade made a tiny growling sound.

"Yes, yes, continue," Deech said, spinning a finger at me to indicate I should speed up.

"As far as my techs could figure out, they came on the ship that delivered the littermates. They were, in fact, the crew."

"That stands to reason," Deech said. "But it also seems irrelevant."

"No sir! The point is that the ship they came in on must still be in nearby space. Am I correct?"

Deech frowned at me. She glanced at her computer table and tapped at it.

The walls displayed the immediate situation outside our vessel. We were indeed hanging in space with another, much smaller vessel nearby.

"There it is," I said. "Now, think of it: that ship has the ability to fly in warp—otherwise, it couldn't have gotten out here. It's also pretty precise in navigation, as it had to come to this exact spot, locate our warp-path and intersect it on the fly."

"McGill," Deech began, crossing her arms and sounding bored. "Perhaps it's your lack of technical or oratory skills, but in any case I'm getting tired of this pointless speech."

"Sorry sir. I'm getting to the point. Consider this: if the enemy crew left that ship to board ours, penetrating and taking over Engineering... well then, who's minding the store back home on their ship?"

They all frowned. I think Graves got it first.

"Tribune," he said. "McGill might be onto something. The enemy ship hasn't moved since our warp-bubbles intersected. At that point, the enemy crew clearly invaded at two points, Gold Deck and Engineering."

"Hold on," I said, unable to contain myself. "You told me that the Gold Deck assault was an exercise!"

Graves looked at me then slid his eyes to Deech. She nodded to him sourly.

"It wasn't," Graves said. "They boarded and almost took Gold Deck. Your unit first distracted then defeated them."

"But what were you guys doing up there in the meantime?"

Deech shrugged, looking defensive. "We barricaded ourselves in our offices after our guards were taken out. What else could we do? We weren't in full combat gear. We had nothing but sidearms for defense."

"Right..." I said, thinking it over.

*Nostrum* had been struck at both ends at the same time. The smaller ship had almost pulled it off, too. They'd gone for the leadership and the engines, like striking the head and the belly at the same time.

"Anyway," Deech said, "let's get back to your idea. How are we going to make use of a small, alien ship? Even if it is lightly defended, we can't very well carry the entire legion to our destination."

"No," I said, "but we can make them worry. They'll have no retreat. Instead of two ships, they'll have one, and they'll only be in charge of the engines. They won't be able to navigate. I doubt they have any revival machines with them, so each death they suffer will be a permanent one."

"Hmmm," Deech said. "I like it. McGill, I don't mind telling you that your rank was in jeopardy today. Possibly, these two could have lost their positions as well. It would have been up to Hegemony."

Winslade glared at her behind her back. In my opinion, he was no longer sweet on Tribune Deech. She'd thrown him out like an old bone the moment it gave her the slightest advantage.

Turov, in comparison, had been a more benevolent mistress. She'd abused poor Winslade, sure, but she'd never strip his rank to save herself an embarrassment.

Graves, for his part, was staring directly at me.

"Tribune, I would recommend that Centurion McGill be allowed the honor of leading the boarding party."

"I second the motion," Winslade said quickly.

"I agree," Deech said in a quiet tone.

My face split into a grin.

"Hot damn!" I boomed, "and here I was, thinking Winslade was some kind of rank-climbing glory-hound who'd insist on leading all the attacks! Thank you, sirs! Thank you!"

Turning around, I marched out of the tribune's office. All of them watched me with different expressions as I left.

Winslade had his lips twisted up like a Frenchman in an outhouse.

Deech wore a questioning look, as she wasn't quite accustomed to my special brand of bullshit yet.

But Graves knew me best. There was a tiny hint of a smile on his craggy face.

## -23-

The mission turned out to be harder than it sounded, and it hadn't sounded all that easy in the first place.

"All right, let's *move!*" I boomed, waving for the veterans to marshal the troops.

"Step up, people," shouted Sargon and half a dozen other noncoms. "I want everyone right here, on the glowing ready-line."

They moved in a mass, shuffling and adjusting their gear. Unlike fighters in centuries past, legionnaires planning to fight in null-G were weighed down like pack-mules. Every soldier had to operate like a one-man spaceship, complete with survival gear and weaponry. Fortunately, we could carry huge loads without a problem.

It wasn't all love and biscuits out there, however. The trouble was that space was about the worst place a human could find himself trying to survive. Everything was trying to kill you, the radiation, the cold, the lack of air—even the enemy.

O2 hissed into my suit at a steady pace, cooling my cheek. That was a good thing, because if it ever stopped, I was screwed.

"Okay," I said loudly on tactical chat. "We've got three full units behind us, but we're the first wave and therefore, the most important."

They were listening with squinting eyes. No one was joking around, not even Carlos had the heart. Every ground-pounder hated doing trapeze acts like this outside in hard vacuum.

"What we're going to do, is pop this airlock sudden-like."

They looked at Sargon in alarm. He was standing by a big red button on the wall. All he had to do was hit the override and pull down a huge lever. Then the doors would open and suck us all out into space.

"Heavies, we'll hook you up with lines and send you as a group. But first, Adjunct Harris is going to lead the light troopers in a fast-assault dive right onto the enemy hull."

Harris looked resigned more than he looked pissed off. He'd regretted leading a light platoon many times, and today was no exception.

"Harris will find a way in," I continued, "or he'll die trying. When he does breach the enemy vessel, he'll signal us heavies and weaponeers. We'll launch then and join him, performing the final assault in a rush. Remember, we must get to their engine room or helm fast. They can't be allowed to spin their ship around and escape. Any questions?"

Several people raised their gauntlets.

"Good," I said, ignoring them all. "We're all set then. Harris? You're on!"

Startled, Harris lowered his hand. He'd had a question, just like a dozen others, but I wasn't in the mood. Wearing a sour expression, he shook his head and gave Sargon a flapping signal to get on with the show.

Sargon slapped the release, and the big lever lit up. He hauled down on it with both hands.

Flashers spun, sirens went off, but very quickly that sound died away to nothing as the doors split open to reveal a brilliant mass of diamond-like stars in a river of blackness. The air burst out of the chamber and we couldn't hear anything other than our whistling suits and the clanking of our boots.

The heavies had all locked themselves down with magnetics to resist the rush of released gas. But the light troops—they'd been given no such instructions. They rose up like a flock of birds and were sucked out into open space.

Some of them spun and thumped into the doors on the way out. I winced a little, knowing all too well what it was like to fight a battle with cracked ribs.

"You could have played that better, Harris," I complained.

"That's right, sir, if my commander had—"

I cut him off from tactical chat. There was no point in having the entire unit listen to their officers bitch at each other at the very outset of a battle.

Clanking to the edge of the sally port, I stood there peering out into the starlit scene. Damn if Harris hadn't vanished already. I could make out the ship he was heading toward, but it was pretty small and at least four kilometers away.

"Okay, when Harris sends back the go-message, we're launching next," I told Toro and her heavies.

"Why don't you send Leeson's team next?" Toro asked. "Harris might not be able to cut through on his own. Leeson has all the best techs and weaponeers—"

"Hey, hey, hey," Leeson said, stomping forward to join us on a broad tongue of metal that stuck out into the void. "We got a plan. Let's stick to that plan!"

I thought about what Toro was saying. Sure, she was trying to get out of stepping into this meat-grinder early—but she did have a point. If the problem was that Harris couldn't break in, then Leeson's people were the next logical choice.

"Toro is right," I said. "I don't want any downtime if we have to back Harris up technically. Leeson, form up on the ready-line. You'll jump the moment I give you the signal."

Leeson shot Toro a sour glance, but I pretended not to notice. Muttering, he ordered his platoon up to the line, and they stood there, looking worried. I couldn't blame them for that.

"Message coming in from Harris, sir," I heard Natasha tell me. "He sounds like he's in trouble."

"Dammit, pipe it through. I'm not getting anything."

In that moment, I realized I'd left Harris on mute. Feeling a shock of guilt, I adjusted that and heard him shout in my ear.

"By all that's holy, McGill!" he roared. "Can't you see we're under fire? We're pinned on the starboard wing of this little ship!"

Zooming in with my optics, I saw his men clinging to the sleek Blood Worlder ship. It was about the size of a lifter, but built with a narrower profile and delta-shaped wings.

"Leeson!" I boomed. "That's your signal! Go, go, *GO!*"

Startled, the auxiliary platoon jumped. At least none of them banged into anything. They leapt out into open space and used their tiny steering jets to home in on the target ship.

I grimaced as I watched sparks flying and nailing Harris' troops. They didn't stand a chance. There wasn't really anywhere to hide, and they were getting pasted on that wing.

"Toro, ready-line! We jump in ten seconds! Ten... Nine..."

I jumped on the three. I don't know why. Maybe I felt bad about letting Harris sit out there under fire without a hope.

"Scatter, scatter!" I ordered my troops as Toro's heavies began leaping behind me. "They're turning those turrets our way. Weaponeers, fly high and low out of the main column. Heavies, fly straight in. We're the targets. Sight on those turrets to see if you can get a clean shot."

Using my command rig, I was able to red-arrow targets. It was hardly necessary, as a line of orange-white sparks leapt from the enemy ship to our moving forces. They'd spotted us, and had turned their weapons our way to hose us down.

Checking casualties, I saw grim tidings. Sixteen were dead, twenty more were flashing yellow, indicating some kind of damage sustained.

Gritting my teeth, I took myself out of tactical chat and switched channels to talk on the command channel.

"Primus Graves," I said, "this is McGill reporting. We're in a bad way. There are clearly defenders, and about a quarter of my troops have been hit already."

"I can see that, McGill. Carry on. This was your idea. Failure is not an option."

"Roger that, sir. McGill out."

Switching out of every channel, I cursed for about ten solid seconds. There wasn't much else I could do. My troops were flying toward the enemy ship in what seemed like slow-motion. We weren't exactly sitting ducks, but we were slow-flying ducks that couldn't do so much as dodge or weave. Armored spacesuits aren't really built for that kind of thing.

*Splat!*

A round caught me in the right hip. It didn't penetrate my armor completely, but it did spin me around. I stabilized my flight trajectory and tried to get out of the line of fire—but it was hopeless.

More orange-white sparks leapt up to greet me, zinging by either ear. It was unnerving. Judging by the look of the incoming fire, I figured it couldn't be energy-based. It had to be something ballistic, like a turret spraying out railgun rounds.

"McGill," Graves said, "you've got to stop that incoming fire. We're sustaining pinprick hull breaches all over *Nostrum*. If it doesn't stop, I'm authorized to employ our broadsides."

Whirling around so I could look back, I saw the big transport looming behind me. The tiny strikes were indeed spraying all over the mid-section of the *Nostrum's* hull. Worse, I could see her broadsides now. They'd been uncovered and were rolling out into the open.

Sixteen wicked-looking barrels moved to track us smoothly—or rather, to track the enemy ship behind us.

What I didn't get is why the gremlins didn't just fly away. They could have—but maybe they didn't recognize the danger. Up until now, we hadn't destroyed these little buggers because we'd figured they'd damage our warp core if we did.

But at this point, the Legion Varus brass was getting anxious. They were pulling out the stops, and my unit was in the direct line of fire.

"Graves, I'm requesting back-up. Send the next unit in behind me."

"Negative, McGill. We're not going to lose another unit over this. If you can't break in, you're on your own."

Spinning back around again, I was in for a shock. I'd misgauged the distance and my speed of travel. I was right on top of the enemy ship.

Turning my big metal feet toward the hull, I fired emergency retros. That worked—but not completely. After all, my suit was no space fighter.

I landed with a grunt and a clang. Rolling, I clattered right across the skin of the ship. Inside the hull, it must have sounded like a meteor storm.

It was a close thing. Rolling and out of control, I spun off the flat top of the craft and out into open space, still falling in the direction I'd been going before I ran into the ship.

A line shot out and tagged me with magnetics. I was brought to a halt with a wrenching grunt.

The techs reeled me in and Natasha put her face into mine.

"You hit, James?" she asked.

"I'm okay. No serious damage. Get the rest of them."

She nodded and vanished.

Struggling up into a crouch, I crawled over the hull. I saw blasted turrets. None of them were still shooting at my men—at least, not on this side of the ship. On the far side, several turrets were chattering away at the men who'd missed the jump and were still tumbling out into space.

"Weaponeers!" Leeson shouted. "Crawl up over the top of the central fuselage. You're going to knock out every turret on this shit-box of a ship!"

"Belay that!" I shouted in return.

Leeson gaped at me. "Uh… what's the plan, Centurion?"

"Leeson, get your weaponeers to burn me a new hatch into this ship. You've got thirty seconds to breach her. That's it!"

I pointed over my shoulder, and Leeson followed the gesture. He saw the broadsides then. They were open and sighted on our tail feathers. If those big guns fired, they'd take out this ship, our unit—everything.

He grabbed up a wounded man's belcher, screaming orders at his confused men. There was no time to explain.

Fortunately, Legion Varus troops are used to doing crazy things under fire. We beamed the hull until it glowed, started to spark with burning metal, then slagged and yawned open.

A powerful gust of gas came blasting up into our faces. We rocked back, but our exoskeletal suits and magnetic boots held.

We kept burning, widening the hole.

The body of a gremlin, twisting and flipping as he spun, flew out of the hole like someone had shot him out of a cannon.

Leeson chuckled, but our amusement was short-lived.

"McGill, that's it. I'm out of time," Graves warned. "Deech wants this operation to come to a close. If you jump off right now, some of you might survive the blast—but I doubt it."

"Hold on, sir! Hold on!" I shouted. "We're inside the ship. Repeat, we've breached the ship."

"You're inside?"

"That's right sir. Dead gremlins everywhere."

"Get to the bridge and shut everything down. You've got four minutes. That's all."

"Easy as cake, Primus."

Even as I spoke I jumped into the breach and was swallowed up by the dark interior.

# -24-

We'd surprised the little bastards. They'd known we were out here, but they didn't seem to be masterful at unit tactics.

Quick as jumping cats, they sprang at us. Electric needles were rammed home, and ten of my heavies did a final deadly jig. A dozen more were blown up by booby-trapped hatchways and doors that seemed to be fitted with blade-like jaws.

"You've got to jump through these doors lickety-split!" Leeson said, panting and alarmed. He'd barely gotten through the last few.

"They do seem to be designed for gremlins," I agreed. "If you can't move like a gibbon, they'll shave your ass off for you."

We were walking in a crouch, another disadvantage, as we crept closer to the prow of the ship. The bridge had to be up there—it had to be. We'd chosen this path because it was the shortest, and with only a few minutes left, I didn't figure we had time to turn back and search the ship in the opposite direction.

But when we got to the very nose cone, we found nothing. There was a storage facility, a few floating gremlins that apparently hadn't been smart enough to put on a vac suit—and that was about it.

Leeson looked at me, and I looked at him.

"Ninety seconds left, Centurion."

"We're screwed."

"Oh, come on, dammit!" Leeson said. "After we came all this way? Where's that old McGill magic?"

I thought hard for a second then I looked at him. "Where are your weaponeers?"

"Outside on the hull. You can't really work a belcher in here, it's too long."

"Right... have them follow your original plan. Knock out every turret, every light—any sign of life you see on the outer hull."

"What good will that do?"

"Sixty seconds, Leeson!"

He stopped asking questions, got on his platoon channel and started shouting orders.

At the same time, I contacted Graves.

"Centurion?" Graves said, "I want to thank you and your team for giving it your all. But unfortunately, we just can't—"

"We took the ship, sir!" I shouted in triumph. "It was a close thing, but we did it!"

"Uh... but I see your men on the outer hull, firing on turrets."

"Those men are mopping up, Primus. The turrets are independently operated. We haven't killed the power yet, because we didn't want to damage critical systems. I'm hereby requesting you send the promised support. Techs first, if you don't mind."

While I made this little speech, Leeson was looking at me with big eyes. I turned away to ignore him better. He was making it hard to concentrate.

"All right, McGill," Graves said. "I'll pass on that request. Graves out."

"Centurion?" Leeson hissed at me. "Are you shitting me? We've got nothing here but a long slog! What if those techs get over here and—"

"Stop worrying so much," I told him. "A pack of techs, approved by Deech? They'll take an hour to get across to this ship. Hell, they'll have tea first."

"Yeah, maybe... but our reports... It's all there. Time-stamped and vid filed to death. We're never going to—"

Leeson was beginning to bother me.

"Are you a moonlighting hog, or are you a Varus Legionnaire, Adjunct?" I demanded.

That shut him down. Grumbling, he followed me into the depths of the ship.

Where, oh where, would a gremlin crew hide their bridge? It turned out the bridge was in the back end of the ship, right on top of Engineering. I supposed that with modern sensors, there was no real reason the bridge had to be in the forward zone of a vessel. Looking out through a window, especially in a starship, was a thing of the past.

The gremlins really didn't put up much of a fight. They squeaked and hopped around. A few more men were char-broiled in nasty traps—but we got them all in the end.

Toro said something about us being ordered to take prisoners, but I didn't like the idea. These guys were tricky. Back home, when there was a weasel or a rat in the henhouse, we never took prisoners. We eradicated the problem thoroughly.

When it was over, I slumped on the deck in my armor, tired of bending over at the waist. My back was on fire with muscular pain, and my sore muscles sang me a little song of woe as I took in breaths of stale air and relaxed.

In my limited field of vision, two faces came into view.

"Are you injured, McGill?" Graves asked.

"No sir! I'm taking a break."

He chuckled, and he looked at Deech. "He was probably sleeping like a baby."

She seemed less happy. She kicked me, and although I hardly felt it through my heavy armor, my feelings were a little bit hurt. After all, to my mind I was the hero of the hour.

"Where are my prisoners, McGill?" she demanded.

"Uh…" I pointed toward a corpse that floated past. "That one just twitched, I think."

She kicked me again, and I sat up, frowning.

"Centurion," she said severely, "exactly *how* are we to bargain with the gremlins that hold our own engineering section now?"

"Same as before, sir. With the muzzle of my morph-rifle."

"We tried that twice. It didn't work. If we go in with heavy weapons, we'll destroy the engines. How do we get home after that?"

I stretched. "Not sure, Tribune. I can't do everything around here. I don't want to be rude, but I feel I should point out that it was your idea to destroy this ship less than an hour ago. Now, at least we've got a captured vessel."

Deech heaved a sigh and stalked away, shaking her head.

Graves crouched next to me, flicking at a floating gremlin corpse. "You've sure got a way with the ladies, McGill."

"That I do, sir."

"The tribune was hoping to bargain with the gremlin invaders. She'd hoped she could use prisoners to get them to give up."

"That's an interesting plan, sir," I said, "but in my opinion, it wouldn't have worked."

"I know I'm going to regret this, but I'm going to ask anyway. Why not?"

"Because I've taken my measure of these little freaks. They don't give one rip about each other. They enjoy a good trick, and that's about it. They're tiny, twisted psychopaths."

"You could well be right," he admitted. "But now we're not much better off than when we started."

Surprised, I lifted my hands to indicate our surroundings. "What? Sir, we've got ourselves a working vessel in prime condition right here. Sure, it's on the small side, but…"

I trailed off as Graves walked away.

Natasha came to kneel next to me after the brass left.

"Are you ready for a full report?" she asked.

"Is it good news?"

"Mostly."

"Okay, give it to me."

She proceeded to rattle off facts and figures. Using our considerable damage-control facilities back on *Nostrum*, she figured in a week's time this new ship would be ready for flight—even at warp.

"How many humans could it carry?" I asked her. "That's what I really want to know."

She gave me a quizzical look, but she answered promptly enough. "Two hundred, tops. If you want food and all that—cut that number in half."

I heaved a sigh and eased myself back against the bulkhead. I'd hoped the ship would hold a full cohort, but that was out of the question. We could take a single unit, plus some auxiliaries. That's it.

Wondering if I'd wasted a lot of lives and time capturing the gremlin ship, I kicked at a floating body and smiled grimly.

*Nope*, I decided. It had all been worth it, if only because none of these vicious weasels were grinning at me now.

## -25-

Tribune Deech soon completed her inspection. She wandered around the alien ship, sneering at everything.

"Were these creatures really so dangerous?" she asked Graves.

"They took out more than their weight in humanity," he said. "I'd say they're still dangerous, as they're still holding our engine room hostage on *Nostrum*."

Deech turned her unpleasant expression my way next.

"Centurion," she said, "as I understand it, you were in charge of this operation."

"That's right, sir. But I can't take all the credit. That should kick way, way up to the top where you are!"

She twitched slightly when I said this, and I began to cement certain ideas I had about her mode of operation.

Unlike Imperator Turov, who did everything to take credit for things she never did herself, Deech played the rank game much more subtly. She delegated everything, and only took credit when the smoke cleared. If it all went well and the mission was accomplished, I had no doubt she'd be the first in line back at Central to receive her accolades as Legion Varus' commander.

But, in case it all fell apart, she was working overtime every step of the way to distance herself. The fact she *still* wasn't happy to sign her name to this mess indicated to me that she wasn't at all confident the mission would succeed in the end. On that point, we were in one hundred percent agreement.

Despite my inner thoughts, I grinned at her in triumph. I hammed it up, playing the role of the happy soldier who'd just scored a touchdown. She gave me tight-lipped smiles and tiny nods of encouragement, but that was all.

Shaking my fist overhead and whooping, I limped aboard the shuttle she'd brought over from *Nostrum* and plopped down in the VIP section up front. The pilot looked over her shoulder at me for a minute, but then she shrugged. What did she care if the brass didn't want me on their couch? It was going to be my ass if they got pissed off.

By the time Deech and Primus Graves finished their little tour and joined me on the shuttle, I was sound asleep.

Graves kicked my blood-crusted boots off the couch and sat down next to me.

"What…?" I said, startled. My hand slid away from my pistol as I recognized Graves and Deech. "Oh… it's you, sirs. What's the verdict? Is she a prize, or what?"

I made sure I injected all kinds of enthusiasm and excitement into that question. Neither one of them appeared to be as happy as I was.

"It's too damned small," Graves said.

Deech nodded grimly. "There's no way around it," she said. "This ship is no more than a lifeboat. It's not salvation."

"Salvation?" I asked. "Why hell, our problems are as good as solved!"

They both looked annoyed. Neither believed me, I could tell.

"McGill," Graves said, "the enemy holds our engine room. We've gained no valid escape route by taking their assault ship. Essentially, we're back where we started."

"Nonsense!" I boomed. "We've got them by the short ones."

"Why do you keep talking like that?" Deech demanded. "I know you're not as retarded as you pretend to be, McGill. Can't you see our situation is grim?"

"We hold all the cards, Tribune. Just let me go back into the engine room and clean them out. They've got nowhere to hide now."

She winced at the idea. "If only you'd taken prisoners. We could have talked them out of their position and arrested them."

I shook my head slowly. "I don't think so, Tribune. These tiny buggers are determined—and they don't seem to give much of a rip about each other. They might have run in fear if we'd slaughtered more of them in close proximity, but then again, maybe not."

She looked at me and sighed. "All right," she said at last. "I'll bite. What do you think would work to get them out of there and off my ship?"

"Death!" I said, grinning at her. "Mass death. For all of them."

"We tried that, McGill," Graves said. "We went in, and we were driven right back out again—those of us that survived."

"Right," I said, "but we didn't know this enemy very well yet. Now, we've got a lot of troops who've faced them. More importantly, you went in with all your troops in light gear, Primus. In my opinion, that was a mistake."

Graves gave me a blank look, but his eyes slid once toward Deech, then back again. I knew exactly what that meant. It was her idea to go in without armor. Probably, Graves had asked for heavier equipment and been denied.

Deech, for her part, looked like she smelled manure. But she wasn't shooting me down—not yet.

"You see, sirs," I continued, "I've benefited from several engagements with this enemy. I think belchers and armor are essential to defeating them. You couldn't have known that when you fought them, just as I didn't know I'd get fried on an electric needle when I first met up with these nasty little midgets."

Graves glanced toward Deech.

He wasn't playing my game. I'd wanted to keep talking to him like he'd made all the previous mistakes. But he'd brought her back into it by looking at her for a response.

"Go on, McGill," she said, rubbing her temples. "I'm listening."

"Well... that's pretty much it. We'll march in with a full unit of armored heavies, taking along techs and weaponeers to back us up. We'll clean them out even if we have to use force blades to stick every last one of them."

Deech sucked in a breath and let it out again. "Disaster," she said. "We'll perforate the hull and the core for sure. You *do* realize that a warp drive system is delicate, don't you, McGill?"

"I can only assume it is. But this time, we'll hit them from a fresh angle, with better gear. It can't miss!"

They both looked at me curiously. "What's this about a fresh angle, Centurion?"

"Oh... didn't I mention that part? I want to play the same trick I did here on this ship: I want to drill in through the hull. I've been looking at the schematics—"

"No!" Deech said. "You'll rupture the cooling jacket for sure."

"Now, hold on. I had Natasha take a look at the blueprints, and there are a few ways through the unshielded part."

She blinked at me. "Those blueprints are classified."

"Uh..."

"Never mind," she said, "let's say I give you the troops, the armor, and Primus Graves here approves the plan. Can you guarantee me we'll have our ship back and with a working engine?"

I clapped my gauntlets together so loudly they made an ear-splitting pop that caused Deech to jump in her seat.

"Hot damn!" I said. "Of course I can, sir. Are we on for Operation B?"

"B? What was Operation A?"

Tilting my head, I indicated Graves. He gave me a wry look in return.

"Oh... right," Deech said. "Primus Graves, I'm going to give you a second shot. You're in command of this attempt to regain your reputation as the best of the best. Work with McGill. Take that engine room back for me."

"That's right, sirs," I said excitedly. "Use me like a spear. I'll prong these flea-sized devils right off our ship."

Graves rubbed his right temple briefly, but he nodded. "Of course. I'll personally take operational command. McGill, you'll march into the lion's den."

"One thing," Deech said, giving me a stern look. "No explosives. No using your morph-rifles with armor-penetrating rounds for anything. Nothing can pierce those walls, McGill. The cooling jacket can't be ruptured, or we'll all die out here."

"I wouldn't dream of doing anything dangerous like that, Tribune. You have my solemn word."

We landed aboard *Nostrum* a few minutes later, and Graves hung back as Tribune Deech strode away toward Gold Deck.

"She's marching out of here damned fast," I commented. "If I didn't know better, I'd think her butt was on fire."

"McGill," Graves said, "did you really have to throw me under the bus like that?"

"Damn-straight I did. I even had to back my rig over your corpse a few extra times, to make sure. Did you notice?"

"I did, now that you mention it."

"You see, sir, I think I'm getting a handle on old Deech. She wants her wins to come clean, and her losses to come even cleaner. She'd never have approved this operation if she thought there was a snowball's chance in Hell she'd ever get the loss of *Nostrum* attached to her career."

He looked me over suspiciously. "You don't think that's a realistic possibility, do you?"

I did a shocked act, throwing back my head and putting up my hands.

"Why, no sir! *No way*. That's not even in the cards. Never was!"

He walked away shaking his head. I followed.

"How long do you need to prep for another assault?" he asked.

"Well sir... looking at the estimates, I'd say we could be ready to go in six hours."

"You've got ninety minutes. At that point, according to Blue Deck, all your troops will have been revived. Don't waste it."

"Excellent! Thank you, sir. Thank you. You won't regret this at all, that's my heartfelt promise."

"Stow it, McGill. Save it for the ladies."

He walked away, and I got down to work. I had a lot to do, and nowhere near enough time to pull it off.

## -26-

Harris glowered at the load-out. I'd just informed him each of his troops was going to have to carry a grenade.

"But Centurion," he said, "my people are trained to be light troopers. We're not demolition experts."

My hands came up, making a cautionary motion. I gave him a shushing noise as well.

All this only served to make him glower more. He smelled a big Georgia rat, and we both knew he was right.

"Look," I said. "We're not going to even mention these grenades to anyone. We're just going to carry them. Your light troops will go in first, all at once. When we get inside, I'll be right behind you with my heavies to mop up."

Harris' face was unhappy looking most of the time, but today his expression had reached a new low.

"You're asking me to suicide my platoon, aren't you, sir? That's the bottom line, isn't it?"

I heaved a sigh, looked at the ceiling for a moment then looked him in the eye.

"Yes," I told him. "The weaponeers will drill through the hull. Your lights will bounce down there, bypassing the traps in the central passages. But I'm assuming we'll hit hard resistance, and—"

"Excuse me," Harris said, "but I didn't really hear anything you said after the word 'yes'. That kind of threw me down the well."

"I understand, Adjunct," I said, "and I wouldn't be asking you for this sacrifice if I thought there was any other way."

He stared at the computer scroll we'd ironed out between us. The blueprints glowed with force-lines and planned angles of attack.

"All right," he said, "I'll do it. But I'm going to turn state's-evidence on you when this turns into the shit-show I'm expecting."

"Not good enough."

"Say what?"

"This is bound to be a mess," I said. "I want you to keep your mouth shut—by which I mean handing in a candied-up after-action report, if we retake the ship."

He stared at me with squinting eyes for a second. "All right… IF, and I mean IF, this damned ship can still fly us out of here afterward—I'm down for lying my ass off."

"Good enough."

We didn't shake on it. We didn't even smile. We just parted ways, both of us muttering about what a dick the other guy was.

But I didn't care. This whole thing was a hail-Mary op to begin with. If I didn't retake this ship, I had the feeling Deech was going to climb aboard that tiny captured vessel with a few of her biggest ass-kissers and all our whiskey. She'd let *Nostrum* blow up or turn into a museum full of legionnaires and ditch Varus entirely. No doubt when she got back to Earth, I'd be given the starring role of the village idiot in her deposition.

I'd been set up before by people who were better at it than Deech, and I had no intention of taking it quietly this time.

Seventy-eight minutes after our little talk aboard the shuttle, I found myself exiting a hatchway and clanking over the aft hull toward the engines.

Behind me, over a hundred others followed. They were pretty sullen, even for Legion Varus troops. They knew the score. They'd been taken out of the revival machines and thrown right back into the grinder.

Normally, after a hard battle, a unit was allowed twenty-four hours for R&R before they were placed back into the pit. There were only two possible reasons for such an unusually quick redeployment. One, it was a punishment by the higher-ups for failure. Two, the unit commander was crazy.

They'd all selected option number two, and I wasn't even bothering to deny it.

"All right," I said, "Adjunct Harris, distribute the special devices."

Glumly, he began pulling plasma grenades out of a huge extra pack he'd been lugging along. He handed these out, one at a time to each of his light troopers.

Sarah, a girl I'd gotten to know rather well back on Rogue World, stared at hers in dismay.

"But sir? These aren't generally supposed to be used in confined spaces. If we all—"

"That's right, troops!" Harris boomed. "We've all got an extra special present under our pillows courtesy of Centurion McGill!"

So saying, he took his own grenade, the last one, and held it high for his entire platoon to see.

"You know what Solstice troops do with these?" he asked them. "They activate them, then dive or roll under a hard target, and BOOM!"

He grinned at them, seeming to enjoy their dismay.

"Now, now," I said, waving them to silence. "I'm not asking for mass suicide—not exactly. But these little guys we're about to meet up with—well, they're tricky. I think we all know that. Some of us might find ourselves incapacitated, or otherwise in a hopeless situation. If you think you're in exactly that kind of circumstance, I want you to get some revenge out of it."

The light troopers looked sick. No one talked.

Carlos broke the spell. "These are butt-plugs, right sir? Maybe Harris' light troopers should practice with them first."

"I'm going to demonstrate on you, Ortiz!" Harris told him.

"Enough! Positions, everyone!"

We exited from the aft portal and marched over the hull of the ship. We weren't subtle. You could have heard us clanking along on magnetic boots all the way up to Gold Deck.

When we reached the stretch of hull we were supposed to drill through, I signaled Leeson. His weaponeers lit up the spot where we were going to try to break through. Carlos took that brief delay as an opportunity to talk to me.

"These sorry bastards," he said, "you're really giving it to them this time, aren't you McGill?"

"They're light troops, Carlos," I said. "You know the drill. They've got to prove themselves to rate heavy gear."

"What you mean is: they're expendable. I get that. But you might want to consider how they'll remember this betrayal in the future. They aren't total fuck-wits—at least, not all of them. They know the score."

I looked at him. "Are you volunteering to jump down that burning hole with them, Specialist Ortiz?" I asked, pointing to the molten metal in the middle of the weaponeers. "Because if you are, mark me down as impressed. That's mighty big of you."

"Noooo, no, no... *no!*"

He backed away and stopped bugging me after that. This wasn't the time to put doubts into the commander's mind, but Carlos rarely understood such moments. If a thought came into his head, he was practically forced to puke it out his mouth one second later.

"Breach!" Sargon roared.

"Widen it out!" I shouted. "Harris, drop an egg!"

He tossed a grenade into the hole, and the weaponeers cursed, ducking. After the brilliant, silent flash lit up the interior for a brief second, they went back to work, burning around the edges.

When it was big enough to let a light trooper in, Harris grabbed the one standing nearest to him and tossed her inside. Then he waved his platoon forward, wildly pin-wheeling his arms.

A dozen troops rushed down and soon a full squad. He halted the flow and crouched beside me, waiting.

We saw more blue-white flashes. Two of them.

"They're meeting heavy resistance not fifty meters from the breach," Harris said.

I checked the casualty list in my helmet. Nine names were red already.

"Crap," I said quietly. "Take your second squad down."

He stood and began to signal his squad to advance, but I shook my head and gave him a kick in the butt.

When a heavy trooper nails a light trooper with a boot that weighs a good twenty kilos, it hurts. Harris got the message. He took the lead, jumping into the white-hot, spark-spitting hole. The rest of his troops followed in a rush.

The battle was on.

## -27-

The moment Harris' group was all down, I prepared to jump after them with the heavy squads, but Leeson touched my arm.

"Suggestion, Centurion: let the light people do their jobs first."

Our eyes met in the cold glittering light of the stars. He was dead serious.

I knew what he meant. The light troopers served several critical mission roles in any legion. They were capable snipers and skirmishers in a wide open land battle, but when you were in-tight, fighting house to house or bulkhead-to-bulkhead in a boarding action like this one, well, they were best used to flush the enemy from their hiding spots. That meant they tended to die a lot, suffering the greatest casualties so that the more expensively armed heavies and specialists didn't take the initial losses.

It was the rude calculus of modern warfare. In Legion Varus, troops were almost as expendable as magazines of ammo. We essentially had an endless supply of protoplasm to convert into manpower. Hell, we could even recycle the dead and churn them out to fight again.

Weapons, armor and specialized equipment was another thing. We didn't have an easy way to manufacture more of any of that stuff.

Taking a half-step back, I waited. It was hard to do. I'd been the point man on many rough invasion missions just like the one Harris was engaged in today. Light troops always felt vulnerable and damn-near panicked when they fought in close quarters. Death was right around every corner, and if the enemy didn't get you, your own buddy with a grav-grenade might just do the trick.

Even as I had that thought, I saw three more blue-white flashes go off silently inside the ruptured hull. Moments later more names flickered from green, to yellow, to a dull red. Half the light troopers had died in the first four minutes of fighting.

"Harris?" I called. "I can see you're still alive down there. Report!"

"Centurion, sir," he said, "we could use some support! We've taken two chambers and the connecting passage, but we're bogged down now."

"Have you made it to the engines?"

"Negative, sir. We're pinned by defensive fire right where—"

"Well, get yourself unpinned. I'm sending in a squad of heavies. Toro will lead them personally. McGill out."

Looking around, I finally spotted Toro. She was looking small in the midst of her $2^{nd}$ squad. I beckoned, and she tramped forward reluctantly.

"Adjunct Toro, you're going to take point and lead your squad to support Harris."

She looked sullen. "Harris is still alive in that shit?"

To accent her comment, another blue-white flash went off.

"He's having tea in the aft maintenance shaft. You've got fifteen seconds to get your first and last man down this hole."

Toro didn't say anything else. She didn't have time. She gritted her teeth and jumped into the hole. Dutifully, her heavy troopers rushed after her, vanishing one after another like an army of tin-plated gophers.

That's what Varus troops were usually like. Surly, argumentative—but willing to die when their orders were clear.

I'd watched other legions operate differently. I supposed it was an outfit-to-outfit cultural thing. Solstice troops, for example, were like kamikazes. They prided themselves on self-sacrifice and roughing it in general. The Iron Eagles, where Deech was from, were famously professional. They were elite, and they didn't like to get dirty.

Varus people were the best and worst you could have with you. We were inventive, tenacious and resilient. It had been noted that a Varus unit was more likely to break than others, but at the same time, we were quicker to rally and return to the fight. I thought that had to do with our volatile, independent spirit.

After Toro was in the game, the fighting intensified. I could see casualties, troop concentrations and icons flaring when troops fired—but it wasn't the same thing. Getting antsy, I stepped forward and led the second heavy squadron of Toro's platoon into the breach.

They were anxious to get into the fight. I couldn't blame them. It was hard to stand around on the roof, listening to the battle without participating.

Landing with a whirr of my motor-enhanced knees, I advanced in a crouch toward Harris and Toro. Before I could get to their positions, however, Harris' name blinked red.

"Shit," I said, picking up the pace.

I called for a report, but I didn't get anything intelligible. Coming around a bend in the corridor, I saw a gruesome scene.

Harris was stretched out, face down, and dead. Half a dozen others surrounded him in a similar state, including several heavies. He had a grav-grenade in his hand, but it hadn't gone off. Could they have hit us with some kind of EMP? I wasn't sure.

Toro was still in the game, but she was clearly experiencing a counter-attack. A dozen gremlins with spear-like sticks were encircling her. She used her force-blades to slash at them defensively.

"McGill!" she called out, thrusting this way and that to force the gremlins to back off. "They've got some kind of new weapon. One touch and your armor will lock up on you."

"Set your morph-rifles to full-auto," I ordered. "Light rounds. Let's hose them down."

The heavies around me halted and adjusted their weapons.

Of all standard Earth armament, I thought morph-rifles were possibly the best. They could be used in a variety of ways, and they hit a lot harder than snap-rifles did.

We must have sent a thousand rounds downrange over the next ten seconds. Gremlins were torn apart, despite all their leaping around and dodging. There just wasn't anywhere to hide.

The last two must have realized they were as good as dead. They took the plunge, hurling themselves at Toro, who was in a defensive stance. One blade was held high, protecting her head and upper body, while the other was hanging low to cover her legs.

Rushing in from two angles, Toro thrust high and caught one—but the second midget got in low, stabbing his spear-tip into her steel-clad ankles.

She had a seizure—or at least, that's what it looked like. Moving in random jerks for a few seconds, she toppled onto the floor and died.

"Double check," I told the heavy squad as we advanced. "I want them all dead. All of them."

No gremlins hopped back up to their feet to challenge us. We brought in Leeson's specialists, and the bio people knelt beside every casualty on our side.

"It's no good," Carlos told me. "Our troops are all dead."

"Centurion…" Natasha said, moving up to my side. "I've got bad news."

"What?"

Leeson grabbed her computer from her hands and shoved it at me. That earned him a glare from Natasha, but he seemed immune to such things.

Looking it over, I began to curse.

"That's right," Leeson said, "we've punctured the cooling jacket. About seven hundred times."

"It must have been the grav-grenades," Natasha said. "That's the only thing I can think of. The density of the debris down here is perfect for shrapnel. These walls—they're kind of thin, James."

As she spoke, the chamber slowly filled with a frosty-looking gas. It was a thick, artificial fog, like something made using dry ice.

"Natasha," I said, "get every tech and light trooper alive to start patching these holes. Leeson, take the rest of Toro's heavies and sweep the deck. Hunt down the last of these gremlins—but use force-blades. Do NOT puncture the jacket and make it worse."

"I'll try," he said, and he rounded up troops to advance deeper into the ship's aft section.

"What are you going to do, McGill?" Carlos asked. "Make some gremlin stew?"

"I'm going to call Deech and ask for help."

"Ouch. When she finds out what you did to her ship, she's going to be pissed."

"Stop jawing about it! Grab some patches from Natasha and find one of these pin-prick holes. If that doesn't work, use your dick!"

Sensing I wasn't in a happy mood, Carlos scooted away.

After a moment's hesitation, I made the call to Gold Deck.

## -28-

Deech herself didn't answer. Instead, Winslade intercepted my call.

"What's your status, McGill?"

"It's all clear down here, Primus! Just a little mopping up to do. Please send in the damage control teams."

"All clear or mopping up? Which is it?"

"Does it matter? We need the crew in here right now. Send all those crewmen you've been reviving since the initial boarding. I know you've been hoarding them in the upper decks."

Winslade was quiet for a second. I thought I heard him using his tapper.

"We've been watching your vid feed when we can," he said, "but those creatures jammed most of our signals and—oh, good Lord. Are you kidding me, McGill? I'm detecting gas releases, high humidity and radiation—"

"Primus, please listen to me. If you want to see Earth again this century, you'll send me every repairman you've got. Pronto!"

Winslade made a hissing sound with his teeth. "She'll know. We'll never—"

"It doesn't matter! We're all screwed if you don't act *now*!"

I would have said more, but Winslade had closed the channel. I turned back to the aftermath. Sargon came up to me, pointing down the passage toward a closed hatch.

"Centurion? We've got most of them. But our sensors indicate there are more behind that hatchway. It's sealed and booby-trapped."

"Where does that hatch lead?"

"Aft storage and machine shop."

"Ignore it," I told him, "for now. We've got to secure the engines and the cooling system. Place four guards here and at every other exit they might be able to breach."

He trotted off, clanking and jingling in his armor. At least he wasn't giving me a lecture.

Graves led the relief team through the main hatchway. It was hanging at an odd angle, and the interior of the passage behind it had a spider web of tripwires. They took the easy way out and used grenades to clear it, but that didn't make me happy. Every blue-white flash made me wince.

"Oh," Leeson said, chuckling at me. "So *now* you're worried about explosions, huh?"

I gave him an angry stare, and he shut up. A moment later I saw him with patches, looking for leaks with an ultraviolet emitter.

"McGill!" Graves boomed as he walked in. "This is a mess!"

"Well sir," I said, forcing a cheery expression, "you've got to break some eggs to make an omelet."

A crowd of techs, mostly crewmen who'd been killed here by the gremlins in the first place, spread out and started repairing everything they could. They were soon shouting and becoming increasingly agitated as they worked.

"Throughout this battle, McGill," Graves told me, "I've been sweating in the passages outside. We couldn't track your progress due to the gremlin jamming, but we saw the flashes. You used grenades, didn't you?"

"Maybe a few… but I saw you use them too when you broke in."

He looked at me. "The cooling jacket doesn't extend this far forward. You were fighting right in the middle of the engine compartment. Right up against the core."

"Yeah... you're right."

Walking deeper into the passages with his hands on his hips, he examined the damage. Soon, he was muttering. About a minute later, he was cursing.

Finally, he turned on me. "This is catastrophic! The cooling jacket only has so much liquid in it, McGill. Are you aware of that?"

"Uh... I guess that makes sense. What are we down to?"

"Sixty percent."

"Still over half-full, huh? Not bad!"

"No. It *is* bad. This isn't a fuel tank. The core is already overheating."

"Can we, um, shut it down? Let the pile cool down for a bit?"

"No," said another voice. Natasha walked up to join us. "These drives aren't built to do that kind of thing. They're always on, always running. Part of the containment field must be kept alive and fully aligned. If it's switched off completely or knocked out of alignment, we're screwed. We'd have to rebuild it at a dockyard to get it working again."

"Um..." I said. "Could you define screwed in this context?"

"Certainly," she said crossing her arms. "It will either overload and blow up, melt down and blow up, or fuse into a solid block of molten radioactives and never work again."

"That does sound bad," I admitted.

"McGill," Graves said, rejoining the conversation. "You assured us that this wouldn't happen. You stated you could retake Engineering without disabling the ship."

"Yeah... I do recall saying something like that."

"What are we going to do if this ship is marooned halfway to Epsilon Leporis?"

"Hold a trial and perm me?"

"That's an excellent idea. I'll forward that to Deech."

Graves turned around and marched away angrily.

"I guess there's just no satisfying some people," I commented to Sargon, who'd come down the crowded passage way to talk to me.

"Sir? I don't think the gremlin jammers have been switched off yet. I've been trying to contact you."

"They probably aren't. Everyone with two thumbs left is patching holes in the cooling system."

"Well sir, we've got a pack of bio people trying to get past my men. Remember? You left us on guard."

"You mean at the aft hatch? Into the machine shop?"

"That's right."

"Let's go."

I followed him back through the ship toward the less wrecked part of the Engineering deck. There, I found a group of gawking troops in armor and a dozen bio people carrying tanks and nozzles.

"What's up, Centurion?" I asked Thompson, who I'd assumed was in command.

She turned around to stare at me.

Wincing, I showed my teeth for a second. "Sorry. I forgot they took your bars. Specialist Thompson, what can I do for you?"

"At least someone remembers I was an officer once," she said. "We've got orders from Deech, McGill. We're going in there with knock-out gas. Can your troops provide cover?"

"Uh... I don't think that's such a good idea. These little monkeys will tear you apart."

"Not if they're unconscious."

I looked at her gear and shrugged. "All right. Go for it. But they have pressure suits of their own, you know. There's no reason to think they won't be wearing their nasty little helmets."

"We've got a plan for that. The techs built it for us."

She showed me a device with a bulbous tip and a thin shaft of metal. "Just open up the hatch a few centimeters. We'll do the rest."

I nodded to Sargon's men, and I stood back a bit, watching curiously. Sargon looked at me for a moment then hastened to stand at my side—at a safe distance.

The hatch creaked open. Thompson took her lollipop thing and tossed it into the crack. Her team followed by shoving in hoses. We could hear a hissing sound as she spun the valves open on the tanks.

Once this part of the deck had been repressurized, we could see a wisp of gas coming back in through the crack.

"Did you ever…?" Sargon asked as he watched Thompson work.

"Nah," I said. "She hates me."

"That's never stopped you before. Mind you, she's kind of on the thin side."

"Hold on—whoa!" I said in alarm.

I'd caught sight of a small hand, holding Thompson's metal lollipop. It eased the object back through the crack at the bottom, and dropped it on our side again with a tiny clicking sound.

One, two… that's as many steps as I managed. I had my arms extended, my visor slammed shut—but I was too late.

The lollipop thing was a mini-grenade. It grabbed up tiny particles of broken glass, grit, even water droplets from condensation. Hurling these outward in a blue-white flash, they pierced the pressure suits of every bio on Thompson's team.

Then the gas began to flow back onto our side in earnest. How were they doing that? I didn't know, but I was certain these gremlins were the trickiest people I'd ever had the misfortune of encountering.

Thompson dropped first. I'm not sure why. Maybe it was because she was closer to the hatchway than the rest of them. Maybe the gas was lighter than air, and since she was standing instead of crouching, she got a snoot-full first.

Whatever the case, the gremlins had managed to reverse the flow of the gas and send it right back into the passage with us. One of Sargon's heavies hit the deck a moment later.

I was alarmed, thinking that somehow this stuff could penetrate armor, but then I saw he'd stupidly had his visor up.

That left me, Sargon, and two other heavies at the hatchway.

Sargon advanced, growling. He had his morph-rifle unslung and ready. I could tell he was planning to wipe the gremlins out once and for all.

Putting my hand on his rifle, I pushed it down to aim at the deck. "Thompson said she was following Deech's orders. I'm in enough trouble already."

"You want I should go in there with a butterfly net?"

"Hmm," I said, kneeling and searching Thompson's pockets. I found two more lollipop things.

Standing again, I threw open the hatch, tossed them into the midst of the scattering gremlins, and waited to the count of three.

At the last moment, I figured the gremlins might have figured out they were in trouble. They came bouncing at us in a knot. There must have been at least ten of them.

Still, I didn't let my men fire. Instead, I opened up the knock-out gas and watched it hiss, creating a cloud.

The tiny bombs went off, and the gremlins had their suits shot-through with holes. They fell a moment later into tiny heaps all over the deck.

"Nice!" Sargon said. "I would like to have killed them myself. I still could…"

"Nope," I said.

"Just one, sir? My boots are wide, and I could have an accident. Who could blame me? I hate these things."

Shaking my head, I set the local vents to exhaust. The air was quickly sucked out of the chamber. The sleeping forms quivered, choking. Before they could suffocate I closed the vents again.

"Get a bucket or something," I said. "I'm taking these up to Deech personally."

In the end, it took five buckets. The gremlins were a pretty good size.

Carrying a load of buckets with outstretched arms, I marched down the passages and right out of Engineering. I moved fast in case the little friggers sleeping in their buckets started to wake up. Before they did, I made my way to Gold Deck.

'Shocked looks' only begins to describe what I received when I brought my prizes to Deech's office. Many a noncom would have stopped me if I hadn't insisted I was following the tribune's direct orders.

Not having a free hand, I used my boot on the door. After the third kick, she opened the door irritably.

Whatever comment she'd had in mind faded away when she saw me and my buckets.

"What are you doing, Centurion?" Deech demanded.

"Specialist Thompson asked me to bring these gremlins to you personally, sir."

She looked into the nearest bucket and wrinkled her nose. "Take these nasty beasts to Blue Deck. They've set up an enclosure."

"Uh… all right. But they do know these guys are tricky, right? They're people, not animals. Smart people."

"The personnel on Blue Deck have been briefed."

Turning away, I began to march off, but Deech called me back.

"Thank you for following my orders in this instance, McGill," she said. "All your superior officers assured me you would slaughter these creatures, defying my instructions."

"I'd never do that, sir. Jealous stories about my rebellious nature have always been overblown by my detractors."

"I see…" she said. "You did get the job done again, didn't you? First, the assault on the enemy ship, then the Engine Deck, and now this… It defies logic that persons like Winslade would complain about you so much."

"Makes no sense at all."

"Very well, dismissed. I thought I saw one of your charges twitch. You'd better hurry."

Alarmed at the idea of being turned into a tree by a pack of gremlins, I rushed to Blue Deck. The bio people had me deposit them all into a holding cell for people who'd been classified as "bad grows" and thanked me.

After that, I returned to Engineering. Before I reached the blown-wide hatch, I met up with Specialist Thompson coming the other way.

"What'd you do with my specimens, McGill?" Thompson demanded. "If you jettisoned all of them, so help me—"

"Hold on," I said, "have you forgotten I outrank you now?"

She looked startled. She was rubbing her face and her neck. The knockout gas had clearly taken its toll.

"I... I'm sorry, sir. What happened to the gremlins?"

"I tried to give them to Deech, but she sent me down to Blue Deck with them."

"Oh..." Thompson said. "Thanks... How did you catch them in the end?"

I explained, and she looked sheepish. "I should have been on guard. I feel foolish."

"It's all right," I said. "If no one knows you're a fool, then you aren't one. Not really."

She seemed amused by this philosophy, but she didn't argue with it.

Deciding it was about time I checked on my unit, I moved to push past her, but she put a gentle hand on my arm.

"I've treated you unfairly," she said. "For years. I apologize, McGill, for what that's worth."

"Why, thank you, Specialist."

My eyes tracked her as she made her way down the hall. She was skinny, just as Sargon had said, but she was kind of cute anyway. Better than that, her attitude had improved drastically. It might have been the lingering effects of the gas, but she seemed nicer today than she'd ever been.

Something—call it bad genetics—made me walk a few steps after her and call out: "Hey!"

She turned, her face quizzical.

"Uh... I know we're not both officers and all, but since you were one once..."

"What are you trying to say, Centurion?" she asked quietly.

"Just that I could use a little company tonight at dinner—if you don't have other plans."

It was as weak a pick-up line as I'd ever delivered. First off, I knew better than to build an "out" into my request. That's like a car salesman telling his customer they should probably go across the street and check out those better cars on the competing lot before they put their money down. Right off, I wanted to kick myself—but the line was already out there, and Specialist Thompson was looking at me with her head cocked oddly to one side.

Slowly, not saying anything, she walked up to me and put her hands on her hips.

"Are you seriously hitting on me?" she asked. "I mean—don't you know that you and I have the worst of bad blood between us? I spent months grinding my teeth about you and your antics—"

"You're right," I said, putting up a hand in a stopping gesture. "My mistake. Don't know what came over me. Sometimes, we just can't forgive and forget."

Turning around, I walked the other way. I made a big effort not to look angry or to walk angry. Instead, I looked as disinterested and unconcerned as possible.

That worked. She came after me and touched my elbow.

"I wasn't finished," she said.

My instinct was to shake her off—but I didn't. I turned to face her.

"Look," I said, "I don't want to talk anything out. We've both died several times—maybe fifty times in my case—since those days. We're not the same people—literally. But if you can't put all that behind you, I understand."

She stared at me. "Are you honestly interested in me? That way?"

"Uh… why else would I have asked you out?"

She laughed then. "I know I'm going to regret this. I totally know it in my bones—but sure. Yes… I'll have dinner with you, Centurion."

"James."

"What?"

"Call me James."

"Oh… okay. James."

That was it. We smiled. The expression was a real one. I could tell she was still a little bemused, but I didn't care, and she seemed to have decided it was worth having a go at it.

We agreed to meet when our shifts ended, and we parted ways again. This time, when I craned my head around to look at her butt, I had to admit, it wasn't half bad. Small, sure—

everything about Specialist Thompson was small—but she was shapely enough. She was sort of the physical opposite of Kivi, for example. That didn't bother me at all. I liked variety.

Even the fact that we'd been such enemies for so many years left me curious. Maybe that was the real flaw in my mental make-up. I seemed to be attracted to women who wanted to kill me—or who'd actually done so at one time or another.

I shuddered to think what kind of a twisted, squiggly line that must look like on my psych charts.

# -29-

Back in Engineering a few minutes later, I dug into the damage reports. The clean-up efforts hadn't gone smoothly, due for the most part to the damaged cooling system. The repairs had turned into a crash effort to keep the core from melting down, and in the end, it had been a close thing.

The techs had worked hard together to come up with a solution. They'd managed to bleed off the excess heat. Floramel was credited with the initial idea, but Natasha headed up the implementation. I suspected Floramel wanted nothing to do with the mess in Engineering. She stayed in her labs instead, doling out advice. I hoped she wasn't too angry with me for killing so many of her gremlins today.

Natasha had made the hard choices in the end. She'd risked everything to save the ship.

To start off with, she'd exposed the core to space. As we were a good lightyear from any star, the exterior temperature was in the neighborhood of negative two hundred fifty degrees Celsius. That was pretty cold, almost as cold as you could get.

Exposing the core released a lot of dangerous radiation, but there wasn't much around *Nostrum* to get contaminated. After that step, they simply refilled the cooling jacket and got it all circulating again.

Sure, there were still leaks, but most were patched by now. The passages were steamy, like a sauna, as the water in the cooling jacket was pretty damned hot. Walking around Engineering was going to be difficult for quite some time.

But I didn't care about all that. Everyone who'd been muttering about court martialing or even perming me had finally fallen silent. By my standards, that made the entire mission a resounding success.

Marching back to the aft machine shop, I surveyed the damage and whistled. Floramel was there, and she looked at me oddly.

Right off, I figured she might have heard about me making a pass at Thompson. I decided to play dumb and smile a lot.

"Floramel!" I boomed, walking her way. "We did it! No, *you* did it! I left this place such a mess, I didn't think we'd ever survive."

"You can stop that, James," she said.

My heart sank. Somehow, someway, somebody had told her about Thompson. It just wasn't fair. Every woman in the Legion seemed to be in a private chat channel about my efforts to find a date. Often, before I could do so much as buy flowers, the new girl had been warned off.

None of my true worries showed on my face, of course. Instead, my mouth sagged and my eyes went big and glassy. I did my damnedest to resemble a moron.

"Uh... stop what?"

"The act. The pretense that we've beaten back a vicious assault. That we've won the day and should be in a celebratory mood."

Now, she really *was* starting to confuse me. She seemed to be talking about the battle. What did that have to do with anything?

"We did win—didn't we?"

"No, we didn't. Oh, we've slain our opponents all right—but it's Earth that was the aggressor. It's Earth that was treacherous."

She sniffled and put her hand up to her face. I couldn't believe it. Was she really so in love with these nasty little gremlins that she'd rather have seen us all permed than to see me drive them off the ship?

"Listen, Floramel, I know you liked those little guys. They sort of worshiped you. But on some level, you must know that they would have killed us all if they could have."

She shook her head and wiped her eyes. "I would have believed that if I hadn't found evidence of Earth's real plans. But they have been revealed to me—like I said, you don't have to keep pretending on my account."

"Uh…"

"In fact," she said, her mood shifting again. She became increasingly angry. "It's rude. It's border-line cruelty. These creatures came out here to defend their world. They were permed, one and all, and they didn't even manage to stop us. Don't you think a tiny modicum of respect is due, James?"

This time my dumbass look didn't have to be faked. I was totally baffled.

"Listen girl, I've got no idea what you're talking about. I really don't. If you want sympathy, you're going to have to explain what you found better than that."

"The charade continues, and I'm forced to play my part. Fine. Look there—behind those lockers. What was set up in that spot? What did the gremlins work so hard to stop from being finished and aligned?"

Curious, I walked in the indicated direction. At first, I saw nothing except a row of work benches covered in broken gear.

But then I saw what she was talking about. Two vertical poles had been placed about a meter apart.

I knew instantly what they were. I hadn't seen the like since Rogue World—but it would be hard to forget.

"This is one half of a jump-gate," I said, staring. "I can't believe it… Were they setting up to invade our ship?"

"No, of course not! Don't you see?"

She walked over, touched one of the poles, and I saw it glow in response. "These are from Rogue World. They even have our original lot numbers on them."

"You built these? Did the squids take them out here and give them to the Blood Worlders?"

She looked at me in bemusement. "Are you having me on? Seriously?"

"Um..."

"Well, let me explain things to you, Centurion. *Legion Varus* was transporting these to Epsilon Leporis. It was *we* who were planning to invade and attack *them*."

Looking back and forth between the gateway poles, and then at Floramel, I began to understand.

"We're going to invade them? I thought this was a diplomatic effort."

She laughed with quiet bitterness. She walked close and put her hand on my chest, looking up into my eyes.

I froze, both confused and surprised. She hadn't laid a hand on me since we'd left Earth.

"I'm going to suspend my disbelief," she said. "You're an officer, and you led the assault into this very chamber, but still I'm going to give you the benefit of the doubt. I'm going to trust you, James, one more time."

"Um… okay. Good. Can you tell me what the hell you think is going on? If we're not on a diplomatic mission, what are we doing out here?"

"Conquering another planet, of course. The Blood Worlders must have figured it out. They must have decided to strike first, sending an assault ship out here to intercept our approach."

"Hmm…" I said, turning over her words in my mind. "Even if this is a set of gateway poles, that's not enough to take a whole planet. We've only got a single legion. Sure, we could teleport down to their planet with suits, I guess, and set these up. But with nothing more than Legion Varus, we couldn't hope to take out an entire world."

Floramel stayed close, and her hands hadn't left my chest yet. I didn't feel any urge to push her away, so I let her explain herself at close range, so to speak.

"You're not quite getting it," she said. "I've only found two poles. Enough for one half of the gateway. The other two, I suspect, are back on Earth. Or some other planet full of troops."

My eyes narrowed. "You think we were going to invade *them* this time? Like they did when they flowed millions of troops into New York Sector some years back?"

She nodded. "Yes. What else makes sense? Why would the Blood Worlders come out here otherwise? Why would they attack our ship if this really is a diplomatic mission?"

"Hmm..." I said thinking hard. "Either they learned what we're really doing recently, or they knew it all along. Either way, Deech has been lying to us."

"That's definitely true. Do you feel bad, now?"

She looked up at me, searching my eyes. I didn't understand the question, but I knew she was very interested in the answer.

"Uh... yeah," I said, figuring that was the right response. "I sure do."

"Good," she said with relief. "There's hope for you and your bloodthirsty people yet."

Still clueless as to what I was supposed to be feeling bad about, I shaped up a concerned frown for her, and I kept my mouth shut. I just stared at the gateway poles, hoping she'd explain what she was thinking. That worked with most girls when this sort of thing happened.

"We need to talk to Deech," she said suddenly, decisively. "It's not fair what Earth's doing. It's not fair to you or your troops. You had no idea of the wrong you were about to commit."

I was pretty sure after this statement that she wanted me to feel bad about tricking the Blood Worlders.

Now, I definitely could have confessed. A better man would have done so. I could have told her I didn't give a tin credit piece what the Blood Worlders thought of me. I didn't even care if we were really going out there to conquer them.

But I knew Floramel really liked these little gremlin bastards. She was like a cat-lady, and when you're dating a cat-lady, you'd better pretend you like irritating fuzz-balls.

Right about then, it struck me that I'd just set up a date with Specialist Thompson. What crappy timing! Here I had Floramel in my arms for the first time in a month, and sure enough, it was only minutes after I'd made headway in an entirely different direction.

Sometimes, life was anything but fair.

## -30-

One thing Floramel had said did stick with me—that we needed to talk to Tribune Deech.

That was a good idea, except for one element: the part where Floramel did the talking. As usual, I decided to take the easiest course of action, and I pulled rank.

"I'll go talk to Deech," I said.

"But I'm the one who found the gateway."

"Do you think she knows that it was down here? Or do you think it was smuggled aboard by the crew?"

She made a snorting sound. She was picking up more Earther mannerisms by the day.

"Of course she knew."

"All right then," I said. "I'm an officer. She barely likes to talk to centurions, but I can probably get her attention. I'll go up there to Gold Deck, deliver my after-action report in person, and ask her about this."

Floramel looked slightly confused, but she let it pass. She wasn't as suspicious of my every intention as most girls in the legion were. For that, I was grateful.

"All right," she said, "if you think it will be better that way."

"I do. Secure Engineering and repair the drive as soon as you can. I'll go report upstairs."

I turned to go, but she pulled me back around. She searched my face, and I almost got nervous again. You never knew what a woman might detect in your face. They were like bloodhounds on a scent-trail when it came to reading expressions. I, on the other hand, barely knew what they were thinking until they started crying or something.

"James," she said. "You're not having an affair with Deech, are you?"

"Ha!" I boomed. "As-if! That old battle axe holds no appeal for me. You can take that to the bank."

"Okay," she said. "I'm sorry. It's just… I've heard things about you, and your superior officers."

"Oh…"

She had to be talking about Imperator Turov. Dammit, girls sure did like to talk.

"Don't worry," I said. "As God is my witness, I've never touched Deech, and she hasn't shown the slightest interest in me. When she thinks of me at all, she seems to want to kick me in the ass."

"Okay. Sorry."

"No problem. I'll be in touch."

Hurrying out of there, my mind was whirling all the way up to Gold Deck. Twice along the way Graves tried to contact me, but as the messages weren't marked urgent, I ignored them.

But it was when I set foot in the repaired tube leading up to Gold Deck that my tapper went red. I looked at it, figuring it was Graves again, but it wasn't. It was Winslade.

Reluctantly, I opened a channel.

"Primus?" I said, "What's up? Is this tube not working?"

Absently, I hammered on the elevator's touchscreen. It didn't do anything but blink. I wasn't making any progress up to Gold Deck at all.

"McGill? Are you finally in the mood to answer your messages?"

"I guess so. Remember, I've been in Engineering. Those gremlins set up scramblers down there."

"Really? That's the excuse you're going with?"

Getting annoyed, I hammered on the tube walls. Nothing responded.

"Are you blocking me at the tubes?"

"Ah! The light goes on at last. Before you're allowed to irritate your superiors, I want to know what this interruption is about."

He had me pissed off now. That was a bad place to be if you were a skinny weasel of a man like Winslade.

Fuming, I marched out of the tubes and headed to the stairs. As far as I knew, they still worked.

Taking six at a time, I sprang lightly up the steps. My exoskeletal suit did most of the work, if the truth were to be told.

"Well sir," I said in a voice that hid my true mood, "I'm under orders to deliver my after-action report to Tribune Deech."

"No, you're not. You're supposed to deliver it to Graves. He's your direct supervisor, and he will then submit it to me. After that, if it's deemed readable and requires no further editing, it will eventually make its way to the tribune. It's called a chain-of-command, McGill. You should look it up sometime."

"I'll do that, sir," I said, trying not to puff. I was almost there. "Now, can I please take the tube to Gold Deck?"

"No," he said. "You cannot. Did you somehow miss the import of my previous statements? Submit your report, in writing, to Graves. Winslade out."

"That prick," I said, huffing a bit.

I knew I had to hurry, as at any moment he might do a trace on me and discover I'd almost reached Gold Deck.

Straight-arming the doors at the top of the stairs, I was greeted by two guards with their weapons raised.

"Halt! Who goes—? McGill…?"

They shook their heads and lowered their weapons.

"Sorry to give you a heart attack, boys," I said. "There's something wrong with the tube."

"Winslade is what's wrong with it," one of them said. "Unless you're a Primus or a visiting hog, he's decided to keep you off Gold Deck. I'm not even sure if—"

"Tribune's orders," I said, flashing them a glimpse of my red, blinking tapper.

It was either Graves or Winslade messaging me, not Deech, but that wasn't immediately obvious, and I barely cared who it was anyway.

The noncoms waved me by, and I strode down the central passage like I owned it.

It was close in the end. I was maybe ten meters from Deech's big shiny door when Winslade's office popped open to my left.

I could tell he was ready to pitch a hissy-fit.

"McGill!"

My feet kept walking. I was maybe fifty steps from my goal.

"McGill, damn you man! I'll have you up on charges!"

Five more paces, and I turned my head. My face registered mild surprise. "Oh, there you are, Primus. Sorry to bother you, sir."

"Stop right there! Get away from the Tribune's door! I demand it!"

Twenty steps to go.

An idiot's grin now graced my face. Slowly, I let it turn into a confused dumbass frown. My pace slowed down, and I half turned toward him—but I kept walking.

He was hurrying to catch up to me. I could tell he was beyond pissed, but he was under the misconception that he'd finally got me under control. A man who knew me better, like Graves, could've straightened him out on that point.

"Sir?" I asked in a confused tone. "What's the problem?"

I was now turned around, fully facing him, but I managed two more steps backward.

"You," he said, coming close and breathing hard. "I should have you arrested. You disobeyed a direct order from a superior. Really, I don't understand—are you walking backwards?"

He'd finally noticed. There were less than six paces between me and that door, but Winslade was really on top of me now. He was in my face and then some.

One of the many keys to thwarting authority was to give the appearance of utter compliance, even while you kept doing your own thing. Usually, this meant your progress was slowed, but never quite completely halted.

According to this principle, I took another backward step toward Deech's door.

"Oh, no you don't," Winslade said. "I'm Deech's liaison. Her chief of staff. No one goes through that door without going through protocol first."

"Primus, sir, I assure you I have absolutely no intention of going around you to meet the Tribune."

One more step. I wasn't even sure how close I was now, because I didn't dare turn my head to look.

"Hold it right there," Winslade said.

He made a move on me then. It surprised me, as he should have known better. He reached out one of those long-fingered, frog-like hands and grabbed hold of my wrist.

Now, you have to understand I'm a big man. I'm a good two heads taller than Winslade and more than double his weight. What's more, I was still wearing battle armor as I'd been fighting for my life only a few hours earlier.

My face darkened, and he saw the threat there.

To my surprise, he didn't snatch his hand back in fear. He hung on.

"That's right," he said in a hissing tone. "You go ahead and strike me. I've had enough of your insolence."

Behind him, I could see the guards I'd slid past earlier were advancing. Their hands were on their pistols. They began to trot when they caught sight of the situation, jingling as they came.

It was now or never—and I don't like giving up on a thing once I've set my foot on a path.

My fist flew. It was wrapped in steel, and Winslade never had a chance. There was no time to dodge, or block—not that blocking with one of those skinny arms would have done anything other than break yet another set of bones.

My whistling gauntlet flew right toward his wincing, lip-curled face and kept on going.

The truth was, I hadn't been aiming at Winslade at all. I'd been letting fly at an equipment locker that was behind him.

*Wham!* A crashing sound of metal-on-metal filled the passageway. If you've ever slammed a fist or a foot into a thin metal locker, you know they sound like a kettledrum when you nail one.

"What's going on out here?" Deech demanded behind me.

She'd finally come out of her office to investigate the near-riot in the passageway. That was what I'd been counting on.

"McGill? Winslade? What are you two doing? Having a childish fight?"

"Tribune," Winslade began, "this man is a menace. He simply won't obey orders. He won't observe the most basic protocol—"

"Shut up," she said in a deceptively mild tone.

To his credit, he closed his mouth with an audible snap, and his voice shut off like magic. It was enough to make me wish I'd be a tribune someday, just so I could shut him down like that.

Deech stalked forward, eyeing me like I was the turd in her punchbowl.

"What have you got to say for yourself, Centurion?"

"I've found something, sir," I said. "In Engineering."

"You found *what*?"

"Something that's not supposed to be there."

She glared at me for a moment, then her eyes widened in alarm. I gave her a slight nod.

By then, the MPs had arrived.

"We're sorry sir," the veteran said. "McGill said he had orders to meet you. We didn't—"

"And so he did," Deech said smoothly, never taking her eyes off mine. "Go back to your duties—all of you."

This last she directed at Winslade, who was sputtering. For once, it was his mouth that hung in dumbfounded amazement.

I gave him a little wave as I followed Deech into her office.

## -31-

Deech circled her desk like a shark. I stared at the wall behind her like it was interesting.

"Drusus warned me about you," she said. "Armel did too—he all but bribed me to have you permed."

"Permission to speak, sir?"

"By all means! You've worked so hard to barge in here, it's almost flattering."

"Armel hates me, sir. And I hate him. You can, and should, disregard anything he says about me."

"What about Drusus? Should I value his opinions?"

I hesitated for a second, but I couldn't bring myself to make up any tales about Drusus. She probably wouldn't believe them anyway.

"No sir. He's a good man. His words should be heeded."

She nodded. "That proves the point. He said you're honest—when it matters."

As she hadn't asked any questions, I didn't say anything. She did one more trip around her desk before facing me.

"So, I take it you found something unexpected in Engineering. For your sake and mine, I pray you didn't damage it."

"Gateway posts. One set. They're secure, and they're undamaged."

"Good. We were worried the enemy would use them to transport troops aboard *Nostrum* and take the ship. It seems obvious now, in retrospect, that this had to be their plan all along. Naturally, I need to swear you to secrecy regarding—"

I cleared my throat loudly.

"—would you like to say something, Centurion?"

"Yes sir. You see, my mama didn't raise no fool."

"Is that right?"

"Yes Tribune, it is. The gateway posts were brought out from Earth by *us*. What makes sense is that the matching pair of posts is back on Earth—not on Blood World."

She canted her hip and rested her butt against her desk. Her arms crossed under her breasts, and her eyes narrowed to slits.

"What are you saying, McGill?"

"That I understand the plan. That I know Earth doesn't mean to do any diplomacy out there at Blood World—we mean to invade."

Her butt came up off that desk like she'd been stung. She stepped up to me and put a wagging finger in my face. I hated that, but I didn't let on.

"Listen to me, Centurion. You're speculating. You can't know any of this. What if we were just hoping to set up a commercial connection with the Blood Worlders?"

I glanced down at her for the first time. "It doesn't matter what *I* think, Tribune. Someone has tipped them off. That's why they attacked our ship. They did a pretty good job of it, too, bumping us out of warp and all."

She began to pace again. I watched her this time, and I found my mind wandering.

"Is that all you wanted to report? That you found these items, and you're concerned about them? Was that really worth barging up here and ruffling poor Winslade?"

"That's most of it, sir," I admitted. "But I also wanted to know what you knew about this. I thank you for being so forthcoming."

Coming close and peering again, she seemed to be trying to figure me out. If she had any idea how many women had given me that same expression... well, she'd be alarmed, that was for sure.

"Keep silent about this. Pretend you didn't see it, or that you forgot. Do you understand?"

"Forgot what, sir?" I asked, letting my face go slack and my eyes wide.

"That's excellent..."

"Tribune? What about the enemy?"

"The Blood Worlders? We'll make friends, or we won't."

"No, I wasn't talking about them. We've got someone else out there, maybe even here, aboard ship. Before we left, I heard Claver was coming along."

She stopped pacing, and her lips squirmed for a moment.

"I don't know how you could have heard such a rumor."

"Well," I said, shrugging, "when you're on a ship for months, secrets are hard to keep. Can you tell me why a person of such low reputation might be traveling with us?"

"He's an agent. Nothing more. Someone had to make initial contact with the Blood Worlders."

"Ah..." I said, catching on at last. "Right... Claver was the one who helped them invade Earth in the first place. He's got the connections, but I'd say he's not the most reliable go-between."

"We know that," Deech snapped. "But we had no choice. The prize is too great. Think of it—billions of trained and equipped loyal troops. Remember that we're facing a new war soon."

"Right. We promised the Mogwa we'd fight a border war for them."

I recalled the meeting well. Grand Admiral Sateekas, commander of Battle Fleet 921 had cut a deal with Earth. We promised to build up and fight for the Empire—but as far as I knew, who the enemy was had yet to be revealed.

"Is Claver here?" I asked. "On Gold Deck?"

Deech didn't answer, but she didn't have to. Her eyes wouldn't meet mine.

Claver was a merchant and six different kinds of traitor. But he knew all about gateways and the people of Blood World.

"Is that the real reason Winslade is keeping people away from this deck?" I asked.

She made an irritable gesture with her hands. I took this as a dismissal and retreated toward the door.

"McGill," she said from behind me as I put my hand to the touchpad. "Keep quiet about all this—but keep me informed if you learn more. Privately."

"Uh…" I said, knowing how this was going to look to people like Winslade. "Okay, sir."

"Don't worry about Graves or Winslade. I'll inform them of this new arrangement. Dismissed."

Exiting the office, I hardly felt like I'd won any battles. Hell, Carlos was probably making up sex-stories about me and Deech already.

Winslade gave me some growling threats as I passed him, but his tapper beeped in the middle of his tirade.

"Better take that," I advised.

He glanced down, saw it was from Deech, and his eyes widened.

"No…" he said. "Don't tell…"

I gave him a tiny grin. There was no point in fighting it. The rumors were going to fly anyway. The way I figured it, a man might as well get some mileage out of that kind of thing while he could.

Defeated, Winslade shook his head and slunk back into his office.

The noncoms at the tubes looked me up and down as I approached, but as they had no orders about me, they let me pass with nothing more than suspicious looks.

An hour later, I finished washing off my battle armor and the skin underneath. Twenty minutes after that, I reached Specialist Thompson's door.

She stepped out into the passages and eyed me shyly.

It was kind of weird, taking this woman on a date. She'd been among the very first to try to get me permed. Hell, she'd almost managed it.

The fact that I'd reversed things on her back then and managed to get the upper hand had never sat well with her.

She'd died as a result of our disagreement, and she'd put me on trial for murder.

Of course, it's hard to convict a man for murdering you when you were standing right there, especially when the evidence showed you'd been trying to kill him first with a needle full of toxins.

Despite all of that baggage, we had a pretty good time. We ate some dinner, drank some booze, and checked out Green Deck.

Most Legion transports had a Green Deck. By day, it served as an exercise yard. By night, it turned into a public park. It could grow trees, had a realistically simulated sky and even a stream with a small lake in the middle.

Long term flights being what they were, humans needed a little R&R now and then. Couples found spots here and there to have a private moment under the artificial, high-resolution stars.

We didn't end up doing anything out there, though. We went back to her quarters instead, which were relatively private since she had only one roommate with opposite duty-shifts.

Apparently, she didn't like public displays of affection, but once we hit her bunk—well, let's just say that I was taken by surprise.

## -32-

My love-life had always been turbulent. I could recall a day when I'd been good at sneaking kisses at the water fountain in elementary school. Sometimes, I'd gotten myself chased around by irate girls, or even hauled into the office of one weary-faced principal or another.

While the techs repaired our engines, I became concerned that Floramel, Natasha, or someone else was going to figure out I'd been quietly seeing Specialist Thompson. Luckily, she wasn't bragging about our relationship. Maybe she felt a little ashamed, as she'd no doubt complained about me for years to whoever would listen.

I caught a break when the engines flared back into life, however. On that very day, they shipped Natasha back to Earth.

Now, I don't want to give the impression I didn't care for her, or that she'd done anything wrong. Hell, she was probably going to turn out to be the luckiest member of Legion Varus when the dust settled on this mission.

The thing was: Natasha loved new tech. Consequently, she'd spent a lot of time poking around on the gremlin ship. She'd learned how to operate it, and when the time came for *Nostrum* to move on, Deech didn't want to just leave the ship behind.

"This is a valuable find," she told me and Natasha. "I know Specialist Elkin is one of your primary assets, McGill, but no one is more qualified—"

"You can have her," I said, breaking into Deech's delicate talk.

"Really? No arguments?"

"I'm a team player, Tribune," I lied. "Through and through. You're right, the gremlin ship needs to get back to Earth in one piece more than I need an able tech. Recognizing that, I'm not going to be pigheaded and argue about this transfer."

"Thank you, James—uh, Centurion," Natasha said.

She was the third party on the call, and I knew without asking she was desperate to fly her prize back home to Earth.

So, it was settled. Natasha took off, greatly reducing the odds my visits to Thompson's bunk would be discovered. Not just that, Earth really *did* need to see this new kind of starship and dissect it for intel. It was a win-win all the way around.

Once the gremlin ship took off and vanished among the stars, heading home, *Nostrum* did the same, heading in the opposite direction.

The rest of the flight out to Blood World went pretty smoothly. My weird fling kept going with Specialist Thompson, and the ship zoomed through the lightyears without a hitch.

Unlike me, the brass was feeling nervous. I could tell that much. They weren't sure what the Blood Worlders were thinking. Everyone realized that we might arrive and get blown out of the sky as we approached, by whatever served them for a fleet.

Once Epsilon Leporis hove into view, and we came out of warp, I noticed we were pretty far from the big orange star. Not just a few million kilometers, either. We were more like a hundred times that—more than a day's flight from the target planet.

Right off, I contacted Kivi. Of the three tech girls I knew, she was the biggest gossip, and the least likely to follow pesky rules.

"Kivi?" I asked.

"Why are you calling me *now*?" she asked. "Is that bio already tired of you? Or is it the other way around?"

There you go. That was pure Kivi. Somehow, she knew about me and Thompson, even though we rarely appeared in public together. But that's why I'd contacted her in the first place.

"I know you're on the feed from Gold Deck," I told her. "Hook me up."

She hesitated. "Why should I?"

"Come on, Kivi. I want to see what's what. These Blood Worlders—we're not sure if they're in a good mood today or not."

"No one is sure of that. Did you see how far out we were when we exited warp?"

"Of course I did. Hook me up, girl, dammit."

She finally did so with a dramatic sigh.

A thready vid-stream came to my tapper. It had to go through several proxies, scramblers and illicit tunnels to get to me, so the quality wasn't perfect.

"Hot damn…" I said, studying the vid. "They don't seem to have much of a fleet. At least, we can't see it."

"That's right. Just a few small ships, like that assault ship they sent out to greet us."

"Maybe that's why they're worried about us…" I said thoughtfully. "Maybe they're scared of *Nostrum*. After all, we've got a full bank of sixteen broadsides. That's a whole lot of fusion shells we can land on them if we wanted to."

"Why should we? We aren't here to conquer them."

Kivi's words made me squint. I almost asked her if she was *sure* about that, but I held off. After all, she didn't know about the gateway posts I'd found, and I'd sworn myself to secrecy on the topic.

Still, she had me thinking. Why *were* we out here, exactly? The brass back home had talked about some kind of diplomatic mission, as if Legion Varus was an outfit full of tea-drinking ambassadors. Sure, we could use their troops, but how did sending Legion Varus to the scene further that aim?

The cover story just didn't wash with me. At the very least it was incomplete. Varus had always been good at just one thing: killing stuff.

"Thanks for the vid, Kivi," I told her. "McGill out."

My tapper went berserk about ten minutes later. I was worried someone had traced down the piggyback signal Kivi had shared with me—but it wasn't that.

Officer-chat had lit up, and I tuned in.

"To all my sub-commanders," Tribune Deech began, "Legion Varus has been asked to present itself in full parade-dress. We will honor this request, unexpected as it is. Accordingly, every unit is to move to the top of their respective modules and—"

I didn't even hear the rest. I was already running back to my module. On my unit's channel, I was shouting for my adjuncts and noncoms to cinch-up every boot and wipe every nose. We had a bit of showmanship to perform.

Usually, the entire legion didn't display itself for foreigners. We generally only did it to show off in front of crowds on Earth, or when we were replacing another legion at a given post. Clearly, this arrival was going to break that tradition.

"Harris, get out the banners and make sure the troops haven't forgotten how to stand in a line. Toro, gather every soldier into the module and slam the door. Leeson, get them kitted up and formal. We're on display in ten!"

I'd given each of my three adjuncts jobs that best fit their personalities. Harris had long been our most senior noncom, so it had been his honor to bear the unit colors. I could count on him to get that kind of gear into the right hands and make sure it was displayed right.

Toro was a busy-body. She knew where every wandering soldier could be found and how to catch them. Leeson was a stickler for clean kits and matching socks. I knew the troops would look good if I put him on the task.

By the time I got to the module, the place was a hive of activity. We had ninety percent of our troops in the cube, and they were pulling on boots and slapping down visors like there was no tomorrow. Noncoms and officers stalked among them, pointing out flaws and kicking asses.

With three minutes to go, we raced up to the top of the module and lined up on the roof. Already, the feed from Gold Deck was flickering on the ceiling—but no one had taken the spotlight yet.

Leeson, my senior adjunct, joined me in front of the unit.

"I don't like this," he said quietly. "First, these Blood World freaks attack us on the way out here. Now, they want us to give them a little parade. You think maybe they want to nail us while we're all lined up like ducks, McGill?"

"Could be," I muttered.

Harris stepped up to stand on my other side. "Is Leeson panicking yet?"

"A little," I admitted.

"What a sorry excuse," he chuckled. "Tell him I found a spare set of balls in the flag box he can sew on, but he has to give them back after the parade."

I glanced at him, and Harris grinned at me. I wanted to grin back, but I couldn't undermine Leeson that way. Sure, he was a worrier—but he had a point.

"Harris, sound the horns. Have them fall in."

Harris did as I ordered, and over the next thirty seconds a rabble of some hundred and twenty legionnaires turned into a crisp square of soldiers.

It was just in time, too, as the big screen overhead went live. Tribune Deech stared down at us like the face of the Almighty, who she thought of as a competitor.

"Legion Varus—is this all of them? Where's the eleventh?"

She was talking about the eleventh cohort, which was an auxiliary cavalry group. At one time, Winslade had commanded such a group on Machine World. They'd taken away the cohort, but they'd left him a primus.

The eleventh began to flood out onto the parade grounds only seconds after Deech complained. Their big metal dragons clanked and buzzed as they walked. As I'd once led men in dragons, I felt for their commander. It simply took more time to suit up and move around a ship in vehicles like that than it did to put on armor and hold a flag.

Deech herself was quite a sight. She looked better than she had when I'd first met her, as she'd died a few times and her hawkish broken nose had been fixed during a revive. She looked to be about thirty-five, but the Lord only knew what her actual age was.

All that said, it was alarming to have anyone's face looming on top of you. Deech's mug was at least a hundred meters wide and almost twice that in height. It looked like my troopers could have crawled into one of her dark nostrils, even though that was an illusion, of course.

"All right," she said after staring at us for a time. "They're ready. Connect the feed to the locals."

*The locals.* So, that's what we were calling the bloodthirsty, genetically altered population of Blood World? My, how times had changed since they'd invaded our green Earth several years ago.

Another face loomed beside the first.

My breath caught in my lungs. The second face was nothing like what I'd been expecting.

I'd met Blood Worlders before, you have to understand. The first time, they'd invaded Dust World while Legion Varus was busy trying to eradicate the local inhabitants. At that time, they'd served the Cephalopods. Some years later, they'd invaded Earth.

Now, at this third meeting, I was in for a surprise. The face that looked at me wasn't a twisted giant, a leering gremlin, or a disgusting slaver—it was almost a normal, human face.

But it wasn't quite the same as ours. The features were more beautiful and shapely. The neck was longer, too.

She was a tech-smith. A human bred for brains and scientific know-how.

The most alarming thing was her resemblance to Floramel. The two could have been sisters.

## -33-

"She looks like your girlfriend, McGill," Carlos said. "Or should I say, your ex-girlfriend—ow!"

Sargon had slammed his fist into Carlos from behind. As he was the nearest noncom, it was his job to keep the mouthy troops quiet. Carlos was wearing our lightest armor, little more than a ballistic vest, and it was easy to deliver hurt right through that with a metal gauntlet.

I didn't even look at Carlos, much less answer him. I was fixated on the face that peered down at all of us. She *did* look like Floramel, but with darker, sleeker hair and eyes that were so blue they were almost clear.

"Earthers," her sweet voice said. "I am Gytha. You're welcome here. If you don't discomfort us, we will tolerate you."

It wasn't the warmest welcome I'd ever heard, but at least I knew she meant it. Her kind didn't know much about lies and deceit. An Earther could smile and laugh while they knifed you in the back—but one of these tech-smiths would probably look troubled.

Chiding myself not to read too much into her pleasant and familiar appearance, I tried to keep my perspective. I knew I shouldn't let my past associations with her kind color my judgment. It could be these nerds were an entirely different breed than Floramel's folks. After all, we'd traveled hundreds of lightyears to find them.

Deech reappeared then. A split-screen formed and the effect was even more alarming than before. The women were side by side, and both of them were too big to take in all at once. It was like sitting in the front row seat of a movie house with binoculars, or being under the close scrutiny of two curious goddesses.

"Thank you, Gytha," Deech said. "I trust you find our soldiers impressive?"

"She's fishing for compliments?" Carlos asked aloud, "that's pathetic."

"Shut up, Ortiz," Harris said.

In Deech's defense, we *did* look good. Each cohort was broken into ten units of a hundred troops, led by a centurion. Every unit had a flag, just as the Romans had so many centuries before us. The flags were red with gold print that identified our units.

The banners were just for show, of course. These days we didn't need flags to know who to follow on the battlefield. We had tappers, internal displays inside our helmets and many other high-tech gizmos to do that job. We only broke out the old gear on special occasions like today—but it did look impressive.

Gytha studied the ranks of troops.

"On the first metric, you fail," she said.

Deech's face fell. It was instant and undeniable. Knowing how most people worked, I knew at that moment that these two were never going to be friends. Deech wasn't a woman who would easily forget a slight, real or imagined.

"And what might that metric be?" Deech asked stiffly.

"Bitch-fight!" Carlos said, laughing.

I fully expected Sargon or Harris to belt him one, but a glance in their direction told me they thought it was pretty funny, too. It was going to be up to me to straighten the boys out.

"A little respect would be nice to see, Adjunct."

That was all I said. Harris rounded on Carlos, his face suddenly wrathful. Maybe he was extra pissed because Carlos had managed to engage him and embarrass him. Whatever the case, a stream of low-volume threats ensued, and Carlos looked subdued.

"The first metric is one of numbers," Gytha explained. "Let me demonstrate the inadequacy."

Her face vanished, and in its place a mass of glinting dots appeared. Haze drifted over them, an orangey-brown haze. It took me a second to realize what I was looking at, and it wasn't until someone else said it that I knew the truth.

"Littermates," Leeson said, sucking in a breath. "A hundred thousand of them—maybe a million. See each one of those glinting squares? That's nine of them—or maybe more."

He was right. So tiny that we couldn't make out any individuals, they sprawled over a vast area. The camera's viewpoint must have been that of a satellite or a drone, because it moved rapidly. An endless river of metal-encased troops stood at attention on what appeared to be a rust-colored desert.

"What a shithole of a planet," Harris said under his breath.

I had to agree.

"You see?" Gytha asked, her voice transmitted over the high winds that blew over her vast army. "We have a thousand times your number."

"But," Deech said between clenched teeth, "we're on a transport. Did you honestly expect us to bring a million troops with us?"

"Not directly," Gytha responded.

That perked up my ears. Did she know about the gateway posts? Was that a snide, or accidental, reference to them?

"You're correct, however," Gytha continued. "In that numbers are not a fair test. That's why I'm allowing this meeting to proceed."

"This chick seems to have forgotten that we kicked her troops' collective butts just a few years back," Leeson remarked to me.

"I'll make sure to bring that up to her," I told him.

"The second metric is therefore called into focus," Gytha said. "We will greet you in the pit when you arrive."

The image flickered and went black.

"Of all the..." Deech said. Her tremendously magnified mouth was squeezed pin-prick small and tight. "Legion, dismissed!"

The screen died entirely. Horns blew, and we were sent back down into our modules.

"What in the blue blazes was that about, McGill?" Leeson asked me.

I glanced at him, somewhat startled that he thought I knew the answer to his question.

"Uh... I'd say those two women aren't going to get along."

Leeson laughed. "I know that. But what's this about a pit? Are they talking about some kind of knife-fight like we did to get into this craptastic adventure in the first place?"

Not wanting to lie, I nodded my head. "Stands to reason. Why else would they have selected us in the manner they did?"

"Shit..." he whistled. "I'd hoped it wouldn't end like this."

Clapping my gauntlet on his armored shoulder, I walked past him. "It's not over yet, Adjunct."

"Where are you off to—if you don't mind my asking, Centurion?"

I glanced at him. "I'm going to ask the one person who might enlighten me about Blood Worlders."

Leeson looked around then came up to me. "You talking about Deech? Is it like they say, McGill?"

"What's that?"

"Are you, uh, involved with her, too?"

I frowned. One slip-up with Imperator Galina Turov had stained me forever. Every joker thought I was chasing top-brass tail on a daily basis.

"Not at all, Adjunct. I'll tell you about it when I get back."

Leaving a curious pack of soldiers behind, I quickly found my way down to the labs.

Floramel was there, studying a component she'd taken from the gremlin ship.

"Floramel?" I asked. "Did you watch the assembly?"

"No," she said.

"Why not?"

"Because I knew what I'd see. And I know, James, why you're here."

"Uh... okay, I'll bite. Why?"

She turned around slowly, but she still didn't lift her eyes to meet mine. "You want my permission to see another woman."

That line stunned me. First off, I was already seeing another woman as Floramel had sworn me off a good two months back. Second, I'd never asked for such permission in my long and storied life.

"Hmm," I said, not sure how to proceed.

"You don't have to be shy," she said. "I give you your freedom."

"That's... that's very kind of you."

"Gytha is a lovely girl, younger than I, more clear of heart, mind and eye. She—"

"Whoa, whoa, whoa!" I said. "What's this about Gytha?"

She looked up and met my gaze for the first time. "Didn't you see her? Didn't you find her lovely?"

"Uh..." the truth was, I had done so. But I wasn't thinking about bedding the woman. It seemed to me unlikely that we'd ever actually meet in person.

What I was thinking about was my fling with Thompson. Floramel didn't seem to have any concept of how these relationship things worked. You couldn't leave a man like me high and dry for months and expect him to stick around. Hell, we'd only spent a few nice nights together.

But I decided to drop all this drama and get back to the real reason I'd come down to see her.

"Floramel," I said, "that Gytha girl looks a lot like you."

"For good reason. She's my sister."

My face must have looked slack with amazement, because Floramel shook her head.

"Not in a literal sense, not exactly. She's related to me. All of the tech-smiths who served the Cephalopods are related. After all, we come from a very small genetic pool."

"Oh, okay," I said. "I get it now. That was what I wanted to confirm. She's a Rogue Worlder—or an offshoot of the same stock."

"A rude way to put it. We're not cattle, James."

"I know, I know. Sorry. But I also want to know if you knew these people would be out here before we arrived."

"We couldn't *know*. We could only hypothesize. We've been out of contact with this colony for a long time. But the likelihood was there."

I moved close to her, frowning at the tools in her hand. She was tinkering with some gizmo that looked like the guts of a microwave oven.

"Are there more colonies full of warped humans like Blood World, Floramel?" I asked her. I was in deadly earnest.

"I don't think so. Rogue World is gone. There are a handful of us at Central on Earth. Here, on Blood World—that's probably the greatest number of my kind that remains among the living."

"And what about the pits she spoke of? What should we expect there?"

"Death. Yours, or your opponents. Nothing else will free anyone from those places."

"That's encouraging," I said, and I thanked her again.

Walking out into the passages again, I thought about Floramel, Gytha and Specialist Thompson.

Didn't good things always come in threes?

## -34-

In the middle of the night, ship's time, we slid into a wary orbit over Blood World. As we approached we watched the gremlin ships, but none of them charged at us. No missiles came zooming up from the planet, either.

Primus Graves came knocking at my door first thing in the morning. It was a good thing I was used to getting up early now. I wasn't embarrassed when I flung the door wide.

We observed Blood World via my desktop, which was really a computer. It had been connected up to a live feed from Gold Deck.

"It's all quiet down there," I said.

"It won't stay that way for long," Graves said. "Not once you and your crew start to mix it up with those giants."

The vid stream showed what they called *the pit*—a cratered region of Blood World that was particularly hot and nasty-looking.

"Is that in the middle of one of their cities?" I asked.

"Yes—well, the ruins of a city. The craters take up about eighty percent of the inhabited area. From our orbital recon, the buildings surrounding the crater appear to be deserted and somewhat radioactive."

"Sounds inviting."

He twiddled the touchscreen and zoomed in closer. We peered at the landscape.

"They don't have any trees?" I asked. "Just those big, mushroom-looking growths?"

"Looks like they'll throw some shade."

"Yeah, but so does a rock."

Graves looked up at me sharply. "Are you whining about this assignment *now*, McGill? You knew what all of this training was coming down to, didn't you? If you didn't want to do this, you shouldn't have worked so hard to win those contests back at Central. You should have let Armel take the prize."

I nodded, knowing he was right. It was a curse I had. I enjoyed winning, and I frequently burned tomorrow to pay for a good time today.

"McGill," Graves said, looking me in the eye. "I'm meeting with you today because we're starting the first contest. They'll grow in intensity with each round, but you're going to have to choose your representative for the first heat—right now."

"My representative?" I asked.

"Right. The first contest will involve only two fighters. One from our side, and one from a challenging group. That's all we've been told."

"Just one man?"

"That's what I said. I'm leaving the choice up to you. Send whoever you want."

My face contorted. The situation wasn't what I'd expected.

*One man.* I was going to have to decide who it would be. Graves could have made that call, but he'd passed the buck. That was a curse and a blessing at the same time.

I thought about my options. I could send Harris, or Sargon. There were a few others who were of equal skill.

We knew nothing about the layout down there, except that it was hot and deadly. That was about all the intel we had thus far.

"I'll go," I said.

Graves nodded. "I figured as much."

"So why didn't you just 'volunteer' me?"

"You know the answer to that. A man's commitment to battle is always stronger if he's made the choice to participate."

I nodded. "You want to know why I chose myself?"

Graves shrugged. "You're pretty good on your feet. But that's not all of it. You want to scout the land for the next round. Who could do that better than the centurion who's going to command the next mission?"

"Exactly. You know me better than I thought. It's disturbing."

Graves rumbled, his form of laughter. He reached out a gauntlet and gripped my arm for a second. "You'll do just fine down there. You might even win."

"Thanks for the confidence, sir. When do I ship out?"

"Immediately. Come this way."

It was a set-up. It had been from the start, I began to realize, from the minute Graves had knocked on my door. As we walked down to the shuttles, everyone seemed unsurprised. They handed me gear and briefed me like airline people punching tickets.

"Centurion, set your air conditioner to high and keep it going," a bio told me. At least it wasn't Thompson who'd been given the task of seeing me out the door. "It's hot down there, and very dry. You'll dehydrate in ten minutes if you're exposed."

"Got it."

I passed the cursory fitness test and was placed on a shuttle. I had a morph-rifle, heavy armor, a single grav-plasma grenade and basic survival gear. That was the arrangement, apparently. We were to present them with a single man in standard infantry gear.

The shuttle dropped like a bomb. We split their clouds and plunged toward the cratered surface at an alarming pace. I guessed our brass wanted us to make our arrival look as intimidating as possible.

Fortunately, I'd never suffered from vertigo, a fear of heights, or much else in that department. My pilot didn't seem to have much in the way of nerves, either.

When we pulled up from our screaming dive, the whole ship rattled and stuttered to a violent stop. The skids thumped down, and the pilot looked at me.

"That's it, McGill," she said, staring at me through a shaded visor. "End of the line."

"Wish me luck," I said.

"Luck."

She smiled briefly. I couldn't see anything except her mouth. It was a nice-looking mouth.

"Say… are you the one who will fly me back up to *Nostrum*—I mean, if I live through this?"

"That's right. I'm staying right here. A front-row seat."

"If I put on a stellar performance," I said, "how about you and I have a drink afterwards?"

She snorted, and she shook her head. "You just won my boyfriend a bet—sorry."

"No problem. A man has to try."

She watched me unbuckle and double-check my gear. Just before I hit the airlock, she called after me.

"Hey, McGill?"

"Yeah?"

"Good luck. I mean it for reals this time. You've got huge balls to go out there on a new planet and go up against an unknown opponent. I appreciate that."

"Still no drink though?"

She laughed. "Can't."

"All right. You wait right here. I'll bring you back something on a stick—maybe a bug's head or whatever…"

Climbing out of the airlock, I heard a blast of friendly air go by. That air had first been canned all the way back home. It made me feel nostalgic, as I knew I was leaving the last vestiges of Earth and humanity behind.

## -35-

My boots crunched down on Blood World soil, and I looked around, checking my tapper for readings.

The atmosphere was quite breathable. That wasn't really a surprise as this planet was inhabited by genetically altered humans. The air was mostly nitrogen, with oxygen second and argon in third place. The other stuff like carbon dioxide was too high, but not toxic.

Essentially, this part of Blood World was a desert, kind of like the Sahara back home. The temperature was hovering at around forty-five degrees Celsius. That wasn't good. At that heat level, I would dry out fast, especially since the humidity was only four percent.

But enough of such minor worries, I told myself. This contest was to be an open-air, open-ended struggle. Once I left the immediate vicinity of the shuttle, anything could happen.

I surveyed the landscape. There were low hills around me in every direction. I was walking in the depths of a crater roughly two kilometers in diameter. There was strange vegetation, mostly shed-sized leathery growths with sloping tops. They looked like lumpy mushrooms, but they weren't as wide and flat as mushrooms usually were back home. They were more conical in shape.

Besides that, the region was littered with boulders, spiny shrubs and cracks that ran every which-way. The cracks attracted my eye first, and I headed for the largest of them. If I could find one as big as a ditch, I'd have cover.

A hundred steps. That's all I was allowed to take before things kicked into gear.

Way overhead, I saw drones. Those were the cameras, the vid-streaming system for all of Blood World to watch this contest. They weren't supposed to drop down below the edge of the crater, which was at least a hundred meters above my head.

I figured the Blood Worlders were probably watching closely, and I knew Legion Varus was recording every second of this via high-atmosphere optics. It was a little intimidating to know I was performing in front of a live audience of possibly billions.

Something buzzed overhead. Glancing up, I saw the camera-drones were still hanging high overhead. It didn't look like any of them had moved.

Insects then? If that had been a bug, they sure had big ones out here!

After six or seven more steps, one of them went into a whining dive. Instinctively, I stepped out of the way, and an explosion splintered the ground where I'd stood. Shrapnel rang off my armor, denting it all around my shins and legs.

"A frigging suicide-drone?" I asked nobody.

Swinging my morph-rifle high, I looked for targets. I spotted two of them that were way under the limit.

Shrugging, I figured they were fair game. I thumbed my rifle's muzzle aperture to its widest setting and began lazing the sky overhead.

Two more drones fell like stones, but they didn't explode. I'd wrecked them.

The last one I didn't see at first, but I could hear it making a buzzing approach. It was coming from the opposite direction.

I spun around and spotted it. The tiny disk had dived low, zooming along at about ten centimeters off the deck. The little bastard was going to take my leg off at the knee, I could tell.

Even when dialed to the widest setting, the cone of fire on my morph-rifle wasn't going to do it this time. The drone was in too close already, moving too fast.

Reversing the rifle, I took a big chance. I swatted at it, like a batter trying to nail a low-ball coming in over the plate.

It worked, sort of. The drone splattered on the stock of my rifle. But that wasn't entirely good news, as the explosive charge it was carrying detonated, blowing the butt of the gun clean off.

My head was ringing inside my helmet. I did a systems check and a health check. All good. My armor integrity was over ninety percent still, and although my heart and breathing were at elevated rates, that was only to be expected. If that drone had gotten through to me, I'd have lost a limb at least.

The bad news came when I inspected my rifle. Unlike in older, traditional weapons, the stock on a morph-rifle wasn't just a block of wood or polymer. It held a sophisticated high-energy battery. With that gone, the rest of it was a fancy walking stick.

Tossing the weapon aside, I began to run. My armor was still powered and the exoskeletal systems picked up my legs and propelled me at an alarming rate.

I don't mind telling you, I was kind of freaked out. I'd expected to face a heavy trooper, maybe, or a tracker. But this—could it be a gremlin out there, throwing his toys at me from a good hiding spot? I had no idea, as I'd yet to lay eyes on my opponent.

Fortunately, I reached the wide crack in the ground I'd been advancing toward before anything else deadly was tossed my way. Diving in, I made myself right at home, letting dirt sift over my metal boots and trickle down on my helmet.

My eyes scanned the environment, especially the sky, but I didn't see any more drones. Maybe my opponent had a limited number of such sophisticated weapons available. That would be fair, at least.

Scooting along in the trench, I found it kept getting wider and easier to navigate. The bottom was filled with sand and gravel.

My legs kept churning. My plan was to put some distance between me and the initial contact point. If you can't locate your enemy, get the hell out and come back under your own terms later. That was my motto.

Ten minutes passed, and I found another crack, breaking off from the first. A fork in the road. One way led toward the crater walls, and the other back toward the center.

The safe play might have been to keep moving away from the initial contact-point. I still didn't know who I was fighting or where he was—although the enemy was clearly in possession of advanced technology.

I took the twist that went back the way I'd come. Maybe running off wasn't going to help at all, as the sun was already dipping low. It would be dark soon, as Blood World's rotational period was only about thirteen hours long, and who knew? Maybe this guy was nocturnal.

I had my secondary weapon, a pistol, out and ready to go. Now and then, I checked my single issued grenade and knife as well. Both were still with me and fully serviceable.

But in order to apply any weapon, I needed to locate my opponent. The fact he'd thus far eluded me kept me grinding my teeth as I doubled-back toward the shuttle.

That's when I realized something. The shuttle I was approaching—it wasn't mine. It was an Imperial shuttle, that was clear, but it wasn't the same one I'd come flying down aboard.

Frowning, I decided to take a chance. I climbed up out of my trench and after looking around furtively for about thirty seconds, I trotted toward the small ship.

It sat there, as if waiting for me.

"McGill!" a voice crackled in my headset. It was Winslade. "You're in violation of some rule or other. The Blood Worlders are warning us that unless you desist, you'll be disqualified, so whatever you're doing, knock it the hell off!"

"Roger that, Primus," I said, and I stopped charging at the shuttle.

But there it was, not ten meters away.

I *had* to have a look. I'd come so far, risked so much—I had to know.

Rushing up to the front windshields, I saw they were open. The blast shields had been peeled down to afford a good view of the action.

There in the pilot seat sat a creature I could easily identify. It looked startled and quivered slightly at my brief inspection.

The weird-looking thing wasn't very big, maybe a meter long from stem-to-stern. A hard glossy shell covered its central thorax. Several thin limbs sprouted from under this shell at various angles. The wrinkled-up face in the middle of the whole thing was vaguely humanoid, and it wore a scared expression.

It was a Skrull.

Generally speaking, the Skrull were a peaceful species. They were highly technological, and usually served on ships that they rented out to the inhabitants of Frontier 921. They possessed, in fact, the Imperial patent on FTL travel in this region.

As I high-tailed it out of the area, complying as fast as I could with the rules I'd flagrantly violated, my mind was left whirling.

Could the Skrull be butt-hurt about Earth's recent advances? We'd gone from a single, low-tech planet to being the supposed masters of three hundred planets in a very short time. Worse from their point of view, we'd been given the okay from the Core Worlds to violate their patent and start building our own starships. Maybe that was why they were out here fighting against me.

It was a working theory, at least, but I was certain I didn't yet understand the full picture.

My helmet buzzed again, and Winslade spoke into my ear. The contempt in his voice was palpable.

"That was so close, McGill. You're such a fool sometimes. We had to insist you were confused, and beg for a pass on that last stunt of yours. If you pull anything else, other than defeating—"

"It's a Skrull," I said, getting bored with his little tirade.

"What?"

"My opponent, the guy in the second shuttle—they're Skrull."

"Are you mad? That's utterly impossible. The Skrull aren't a violent species. Did it ever occur to you that the Skrull pilot you saw might just be a chauffeur?"

"Yeah, it did, but I rejected that idea. This enemy, whoever he is, is acting the way I'd expect a Skrull to act."

"And how, in your wild imagination, would an impossibility like a killer-Skrull behave?"

"He'd be a chicken-shit," I said with certainty. "Just like this guy is. He's trying to kill me at range while hiding. I still haven't laid eyes on the little bastard."

"That doesn't prove anything, McGill, but I must get off the channel before we're accused of cheating again. Winslade out."

Completely certain of my discovery, I paused at the next spot where I'd found cover. Slinking under the umbrella coverage of a giant mushroom, I crouched low and waited.

Sure enough, a few minutes later I saw a Skrull crawl into view. I'd predicted the exact location where he'd emerge. He slipped up out of a narrow crack in the ground nearby.

To be sure, he didn't exactly stand tall and beat his chest. No, not this weasel. He crept out into the open just far enough to scan the horizon. Every few seconds, he dodged down into that crack again.

It was no wonder I hadn't found him earlier. He was so much smaller than I was, probably no more than thirty kilos soaking wet, he'd been able to hide in the countless bolt-holes on the crater floor.

Hmm… How to get him? It was going to be like hunting up a gopher on my grandparents farm back in the day.

Coming up with a plan, I set up my grav-grenade. They had timers and other optional fuse settings. After adjusting the grenade's tiny brain with my tapper, I stood up and walked out into the open.

I didn't walk toward the hiding Skrull. Instead, I walked away at an angle, never looking his way.

As I passed another skinny trench, I set the grenade for a proximity-kill and tossed it in. Then I moved away and crouched about fifty meters off with my back firmly directed toward my trap.

It was a big risk. Doubtlessly, the Skrull had other types of weaponry besides his cache of drones. If I kept my back to him, he might just sneak up and off me.

But Skrull were cowards through and through. I knew he'd see that trench I'd passed by, and he'd feel an urge to squat in it. That crack in the ground represented all kinds of cover, from which he could screw up his courage to move on me.

Even as I pondered my plans and began to worry that it was taking too long, that it wasn't working—I heard a singing sound and saw a blue-white flash behind me.

Smiling, I stood up from the worthless pile of sticks I'd been pretending to be interested in. I walked back to the spot and picked up the mangled corpse.

Less than an hour later, I arrived back at my shuttle, where I tossed the body into the pilot's lap.

She shrieked and pushed it off, cursing.

"Told ya," I said pridefully.

She gave a sigh and squared her shoulders. "Disgusting."

After that, she wouldn't talk to me the whole way back up to *Nostrum*.

I laughed, because it was funny—and because I was still alive.

## -36-

"A *Skrull?*" Deech demanded, poking at the corpse on her desk. Her lips were curled back so far I could see her gums. "Is this some kind of a joke?"

"The joke was on me," I said. "I was freaked out down there at first. Imagine, landing on an unknown world, all the while expecting some dumb giants to come at me. Then, I get blitzed by drones and—"

"Yes, yes, McGill," Winslade said. "We witnessed most of this. Possibly, we should dismiss the centurion now, hmm? Would this be a good time, Tribune?"

He looked at Deech expectantly, but she was still puzzling over the dead Skrull.

I didn't argue with Winslade, as I would just as soon go wash up and grab some chow. Strategy sessions bored me unless I was about to go into battle—often, they bored me even then.

"No…" Deech said. "This is very strange… I'm hoping for new insights from our reigning champion. We will continue discussing the matter."

Winslade made a rude sound with his lips. "I'm sorry Tribune, but I must say I've had much more experience with this particular man than—"

"Get out," Deech told him in a deceptively mild tone.

Winslade's mouth cinched up tight. He nodded, shot me a venomous glance, and turned toward the exit. I gave him a little smile in return. I couldn't help myself, even though I knew that slight would cost me later.

After Winslade had made his prissy exit, Deech glanced up from the small corpse on her desk to face me.

"What possessed you, Centurion, to risk this entire venture for the sake of curiosity?"

"You mean when I looked into the windshield of that shuttle?" I asked, shrugging. "I wanted intel. It's much easier to beat an enemy you know."

Deech nodded thoughtfully. She stopped prodding the Skrull and walked out from behind her desk.

That was when I noticed her outfit. Her uniform was *tight*. Normally, Deech didn't go around in boots and cinched up clothes the way some ladies did. This was unusual, and smart-clothes being what they were, it couldn't be an accident. She had to have a plan in mind—but what could it be?

I kind of hoped she hadn't altered her appearance for my sake. She wasn't my type.

Deech crossed her arms, propped her butt up against her desk, and eyed me like I was some kind of bug.

"You judged a peek into the enemy lander was worth the risk?" she asked. "Throwing it all down on a single cast of the dice?"

"Uh... maybe I'm missing something here. Aren't we just going through these contests to impress the Blood Worlders?"

"Yes, of course. But it's more than that. Now that we've reached our destination, I suppose we can discuss the matter more frankly."

"Sounds good to me," I said.

Deech looked at me seriously. "We're trying to become their new masters, McGill. Earth needs troops. Tough troops that can survive in our transports. These people are human-related at least, which means that our standard life support systems will sustain them. The short version is that we want them on our team. A war is coming, you know."

"Yeah..." I said, thinking about the agreement we'd made with Grand Admiral Sateekas a year or two back.

Earth had opted to build up our military and eventually go to war with an unnamed power. In return, we were allowed to keep control of all the Cephalopod worlds.

The only trouble was our relative lack of numbers. Earth was just one small planet. To govern hundreds of worlds, you needed a lot more than a few elite legions and a thrown-together fleet.

Her words made me think. She was right: the Blood Worlders were human, more or less. If they could be convinced to serve us instead of someone else we'd have a ready-made army to wield.

"I pretty much get all that, Tribune," I said. "But what I don't understand is the idea that I was risking something big. What would have happened if I'd lost this battle to the Skrull?"

She sighed. "We haven't discussed that previously because we didn't want to overwhelm you—but these contests are single-elimination. If we lose one, we're out of the running."

"Out of the running for what? What exactly is the prize? They aren't going to declare themselves to be our slaves, are they?"

"It's better than that. Slaves sometimes rebel. They will ally with us—following our orders."

They tell me I'm not the quickest man in the Legion, and they're more right than they know, but it sounded kind of like slavery to me.

"I see…" I said. "What about those gateway posts I found in the hold? What's their purpose, if not to invade this Blood World?"

Deech looked at me like I was six kinds of a moron. She lifted her butt off her desk—and wow, I got way more than I'd bargained for in a single glance. Her pants were so tight I could see her religion.

Fortunately, she was too distracted to notice where my eyes had wandered.

"Think about it, McGill," she said. "What if we succeed on this mission? What if we actually do gain a billion soldiers to fatten our ranks? Would Central want to send a fleet of transports all the way out here to pick them up?"

"Ah… I get it. The gateway isn't going to be set up to bring our troops here—it will send *their* troops back to Earth. So we can load them up in transports whenever we need them."

"Finally," she said, shaking her head, "you grasp the situation. Now, let's discuss tomorrow's contest. You've beaten a single Skrull—not exactly an astounding feat. Tomorrow, we must send a full unit to face another challenger."

"Uh… are we talking about fighting a hundred Skrull or something?"

"I'm not sure what we'll meet on the field of honor, but the one thing they *won't* be is Skrull. The Skrull have lost. They've been eliminated."

"Oh yeah. Right. Okay then, I'd like to go spit-polish my unit, if you don't mind."

Deech looked me up and down. "Why would you assume *your* unit has been chosen to represent Earth?"

"Um… am I wrong?"

She squirmed a little and shook her head. "No, you're not. No other group would make sense now. But McGill, don't get cocky—or rather, don't get any worse about it."

"I swear I won't, Tribune."

"Good. Now, get out of here before I come to my senses and send someone else."

I walked out of her office, giving her one more back-glance on the way out. Yes sir, there was no getting around it: she was doing her best to attract a mate today. Nowhere in her mannerisms had I detected any hint she was interested in me, however.

Curious, I decided to play out a hunch. As I passed by Winslade's desk, I crashed my fist down on his desk.

He had his boots propped up there, but his feet swept themselves down to the floor right-quick. Alarmed and annoyed, he planted them on the deck and stood up.

"What's the meaning of this, McGill? Can't you respect a superior for one second?"

"I'm angry for your sake, Winslade."

Confused, his rat-slit eyes narrowed even farther than normal. "What are you talking about?"

"Haven't you heard? The rumor mill says Deech is dating a primus. That's just dirty. Graves shouldn't be pulling this kind of thing. He's got to be a century older than she is, for one thing."

Winslade's face underwent a series of contortions. At last, he settled into a snooty expression. "That's ludicrous."

"Yeah? How do you know? Do you see how she dressed herself today? Her uniform is so tight her—"

"Yes, yes, I know. I shouldn't say anything, but for your information, I've been taking the Tribune to dinner lately."

I feigned shock, and let my expression quickly morph into a leer.

"Congratulations, Primus!" I said loudly. "Imagine that, bagging the CO! I stand impressed!"

Winslade began hissing at me. "Shut up about it. That's not public knowledge, understand?"

"Oh... yeah. Right. Sorry about that. Best of luck to you, you sly dog!"

With that, I left him. He looked kind of ruffled, but he looked happy, too. I didn't begrudge him his moment of pride. Even a ferret like Winslade deserved to catch a fish now and then.

## -37-

That night I made a mistake. I let Specialist Thompson into my room.

We'd been sneaking around for nearly a month, but that had gotten old, and after my safe and triumphant return from the pit, she'd wanted to celebrate.

We opened the first bottle, and by the time we'd finished it, we were already making love. That's when my tapper started buzzing.

Glancing at it, I saw no red. That meant whoever was calling wasn't my superior, and therefore they could wait. Probably, it was one of my troops fussing about our plans for the morning.

I'd tried to impress upon them that we couldn't do much other than carry our basic gear down to Blood World and figure out what to do when we got there. That was upsetting to the likes of Leeson and Toro in particular, but that was just too damned bad. This time, they weren't going to get to line up all their ducks in a row. The Blood Worlders didn't play it that way.

Forgetting about the buzz, I put both hands back on the bio, and I let her have her way with me. For a skinny girl, she sure had a lot of energy once she got going.

"Specialist," I said, "this is an unexpected treat."

"Don't you think it's time you started calling me Evelyn?"

"Oh... sure, Evelyn. Sorry."

She didn't seem upset, and things continued to grow more heated. My bunk was making a squeaking sound, but I decided to ignore it.

The door chimed not ten seconds after I'd had that thought, and Evelyn froze. "It might be important," Evelyn said. "Maybe you should answer it."

I let out a growl of frustration.

"It's just some nervous Nellie freaking out about tomorrow," I told her. "Just ignore it."

We tried to keep going. Really, we did. But this visitor didn't seem to be capable of catching a hint. Whoever it was, they chimed and knocked about every thirty seconds for the next two minutes.

Finally, I got up with a roar. I pulled my clothes on and threw open the door.

It was Floramel. She had the gall to display a surprised expression.

"I was beginning to think my tracer was wrong," she said. "Were you asleep?"

"Uh..." I said stupidly.

Behind me, Specialist Thompson didn't run away. Far from it. She stretched luxuriously on my bunk and looked at Floramel with a slight smile.

I knew what that meant. Most women were either embarrassed in this situation, or pissed off. The fact that Thompson was happy—maybe even amused—meant she wanted to show me off—like a cat with a mouse in her mouth teasing her neighbors.

Floramel finally noticed her and stood dumbfounded.

"You... you have a visitor."

"Um... yeah. What's up, Floramel?"

A series of thoughts ran through her face. Now, you have to understand that Floramel is a genius. She was born and bred for intellectual pursuits. But somehow, for all of that, she was a relatively innocent when it came to matters of the heart.

Because of this, when her face crumbled, my heart fell with hers.

She was crushed.

Maybe I'd known she was going to react this way. Maybe that's why I hadn't made it crystal clear to her that we were no longer a thing. After all, she'd pretty much dumped me. After that plus a few months without so much as a dinner-date, you'd think any woman would know it was over—but Floramel hadn't been brought up on Earth.

"I'm sorry," she said. "I'm interrupting. I'm sorry."

"Hold on, Floramel. Let me explain."

Floramel was turning away slowly, stunned. She walked out into the passageway and stood there for a moment. I moved to follow.

"Let her go, James," Evelyn said behind me.

That was a different tone. She didn't say it sweetly—not at all. I could hardly blame her, but in that instant, her voice brought back unpleasant memories. She'd once been an officer trying to get me permed, and I could hear a commanding, mean note come out of her.

"I'll be right back," I said over my shoulder, and I followed Floramel.

We stood out there in the passage. She turned away from me—her face was blank and lost. I talked to her back, and I didn't try to touch her.

"Look," I said, "you had to know we were drifting apart. You had to know a man like me can't be shunned for months and—"

"I was a fool," she said. "I always play the fool among neuro-typicals. We're just too different."

"Oh, come on..."

"I came to talk about Gytha. I'm sure you're not interested, but I needed to explain something to you."

"Okay, okay, tell me. I'm not sure I'll ever meet her, but I—"

"You will," she said. "If you keep winning, she'll want to meet you personally. She's cold, James. Not like me. She's much more dedicated."

That was an alarming statement as I considered Floramel to be one of the most dedicated people I'd ever met.

Floramel turned around, and I could tell by her expression she was serious.

"You have to be careful around her. She's not what she seems."

"Uh… okay. Is that it?"

"Yes, I'll be going now. I'm sorry to have caused you an inconvenience."

"It's not like that. I'm the one who should have talked to you. I just kept thinking you'd figure it out. Any Earth girl would have."

"Again, our cultural differences sabotage us. I should stick to my own kind—too bad they're so dull."

She walked away then, and I stared after her. *Damn*, she was a lovely woman. Evelyn couldn't hold a candle to her in the looks department. On the flipside, my little bio-specialist was as hot as a firecracker. It was all a matter of preference, I supposed.

Heading back into my room, I found my firecracker's fuse had gone out.

"Out of my way," she said, pushing past me.

"Hey! Wait a second," I called after her. "I came back to *you*!"

"Not good enough, James."

That was it. Both women had left in a huff.

Just wandering around bumping my nose into relationships wasn't cutting it these days. I had to work on my relationship skills.

## -38-

The reddish, Mars-like disc of Blood World filled my horizon a few hours later. This time, I wasn't a lone man riding down on a shuttle. Instead, my entire unit was strapped into the lifter with me, and we rocketed downward together.

As Leeson was my senior adjunct, I'd tasked him with doing the mission rehash and the pep talk.

"Here's the deal," Leeson said loudly. "We're going to face an unknown group of enemy soldiers. There should be an equal number of them as there are of us. Remember, the last contest featured a single Skrull, so I wouldn't freak out about the unknown part."

A wave of muted laughter swept the group.

"All we have to do is defeat them and we're in the clear. Any questions?"

Carlos shot his hand up. I felt the same pang Graves must have had when he saw me open my mouth.

"What is it, Ortiz?" Leeson asked with a weary sigh.

"Do we get to use a revival machine?"

"That's negatory. We'll get off the lifter with what we can carry—that's it."

Harris raised his hand next.

"Adjunct?" Leeson asked, calling on him.

"How are the Blood Worlders defining 'defeat' in this case?"

Leeson's face faltered, and I knew why. We'd talked about this quietly before we'd boarded the lifter. The answer was upsetting, so we'd decided to sidestep it.

"Um…" he said. "There's a big crater down there. If either side runs outside of it, they're out."

Carlos jumped in, smelling dirt. "Out of the fight? As in, free to sip a beer and watch braver souls mix it up in the arena?"

"Uh… no. McGill?" Leeson turned to me, his face uncertain.

Being the centurion meant the buck stopped on my plate—along with the toughest questions.

"Here's the real deal," I told them, having decided there was no point in sugar-coating the facts now. They were suspicious, and any more dodging would only lower morale as they began to speculate. "We can't get out of the crater until the enemy force is a hundred percent dead."

They looked at me, and I looked back at them flatly. This stare-down continued for about two seconds.

"Thank you, sir," Adjunct Toro said. "You've confirmed my darkest suspicions. No one is going to call this off early. No one is going to get to run off into the desert and sip a beer."

"Nope," I said firmly. "The Blood Worlders aren't big on retreating, not unless a high-end commander orders it. They'd rather die. Anyone exiting the crater will be slaughtered by the locals like the disgusting dog they are."

You could have heard a pin drop. The difficult part for them to swallow, I knew, was the thought that *we* might be the ones on the losing side of this contest. What if *we* were the ones running like hens and being cut down to the very last man?

"This isn't my best pep-speech," I admitted. "But facts are facts. When reality is grim, and it can't be candied-up, I think the truth is called for. So, there it is. Go ahead and have a good cry if you want to."

No one made a sound. Not even Carlos, who looked like someone had stepped on his dick.

Their grim but accepting attitude made me proud. Varus troops were a lot of things, good and bad, but we weren't wimps. We could suck up punishment and keep marching.

About five minutes later, the lifter's skids hit the ground. Harris and his light platoon were the first to deploy, with orders to fan out and scout the perimeter.

"Go! Go! GO!" he roared, chasing his lights out onto the dusty plain.

They scampered like rabbits, and he trotted after them. As an officer, he'd been given a breastplate and a heavier kit, but he still carried a snap-rifle like the rest of them.

Toro's group stood and formed up next, jogging down the ramp in two columns. Heavy soldiers in full armor, their boots made the deck plates ring. They were all regulars and veterans, with a couple of specialists thrown in. They formed the solid core of our force.

I followed Toro while Leeson marshaled his auxiliary platoon behind me. His was a mix of troops with lots of techs and bio people. They also had more than their share of weaponeers and two light artillery teams.

Outside, the sun was going down. That caught my attention right off. The swollen orange fireball known at Epsilon Leporis was six times as big as Old Sol was back home. But the combination of the dirty atmosphere and the local sun's weaker output made the day less dazzling than it might have been. Reddish stars were red because they were cooler, after all.

The minute we were all on the ground, the ramp rolled up. The lifter took off and left us behind in a swirl of grit. There wasn't so much as a "good luck" call from the pilot.

"We're pulling back toward the crater wall," Leeson said. "Please cover us, sir."

"Right," I responded on tactical chat. "Harris, are your rabbits posted?"

"There's not enough cover out here... but we're placed as best we can be."

"Leeson," I said, "have your techs unload buzzers. Locate the enemy fast. No holding back."

"On it."

We talked and moved professionally. So far, we hadn't made any kind of contact with the enemy. That was good.

Our planning had been thin prior to deployment. It really hurt to have no idea what you were going to be facing. The basic thinking of my adjuncts was that we had good firepower at range, and the enemy might not. Accordingly, we would try to put as much land between us and them as possible at the start. With luck, we could shoot them down as they came in.

We'd had our lifter set down in the most open, sand-box region in the crater. Digging in close to the crater walls, we hoped to set up at vantage points that commanded all approaches from across the pit. With any luck, the enemy would be simple tactically and charge into our guns.

Leeson's artillery teams hustled toward an outcropping of leaning stones. Harris' people were mostly on their bellies, sighting on everything that moved. Toro's heavies had spread out, but they were marching behind Leeson's auxiliaries. In case the enemy jumped us, they were supposed to defend the softer troops.

Some of the brass, Winslade in particular, had suggested we cheat by placing a full unit of heavies into the fight. Why have lights and bio-people in a vicious pit fight?

The logic had held water for many, but Graves and I had prevailed upon Deech in the end. We'd been worried that changing out our standard equipment would be noticed, as the enemy had recently engaged with our units and knew what they typically looked like. Also, it was never a good idea to go into combat with a hodge-podge of troops that didn't know how to work together effectively.

In the end, Deech had overruled Winslade. She might be wearing skin-tight clothes for him, but she wasn't interested in giving up command.

Winslade had twisted up his lips, but he'd said nothing.

"McGill!" Harris roared in my ears.

"Talk to me!"

"We've got contact, sir—half a kilometer behind us."

"Pass me the feed."

I reviewed the vid stream. It was from a buzzer, I could tell by the sickening motion. The insectile drone flew over a large formation of troops.

The enemy had no landing vehicle. Instead they were sprouting out of pods that fell from the sky and sank into the ground.

"We should have rushed them," Harris said regretfully.

"Yeah…" I agreed. "But we didn't know. Now we do."

"Saurians… Steel World's finest, no doubt. It's been a long while since we tangled with dino troops."

I watched the vid intently. A hundred theropods climbed out of the cocoons they'd ridden down from orbit. They had armored bodies, long tails, and soap-bubble shielding.

"Shields," Harris said in disappointment. "They'll be hard for a snap-rifle to penetrate."

"At least I don't see any juggers!" I responded in the cheeriest voice I could muster. "These are just dinky blue-bellied lizards."

Harris snorted.

We both knew the truth. Even the smaller raptor-types were bigger than a man.

"Orders, Centurion?" Leeson called out.

"Stick to the plan. Set up your artillery and—"

That's when the first wobbling shell arced up and down again, falling between Toro's retreating heavies and Harris' skirmish line. A black acidic mist rolled out of the shell when it cracked on the hard ground.

The battle was on.

## -39-

"Leeson!" I shouted over command chat. The general tactical channel had become too crowded with troops calling out for medics.

"I'm still here, McGill."

"What's your status? Are those 88s set up yet?"

"No way. Give me ten minutes."

"You've got five, after that I'll kill you myself."

"Roger that."

Waving to Toro and her men, I trotted quickly back toward Leeson's position. More smoking bombs were falling among my men. They seemed to be targeting Toro's heavies, probably because they were the most visible targets at the moment. Leeson's people and Harris' rabbits had some cover by now—but not Toro's solid core of troops.

Sure enough, when the next warhead splattered down, it fell where Toro and I had been standing. Harris' people weren't even touched.

"Keep low, Harris. Dig in a little, if you can. They might rush us."

"And what the hell are we supposed to do with snap-rifles against shielded heavy infantry?"

"It's just like you taught me, Adjunct. You'll dance like monkeys and distract them until we're set up. Skirmish, man! Skirmish!"

Harris muttered some choice words about my questionable heritage then ordered his troops to engage the enemy.

Snap-rifles could operate in auto, semi-auto or sniper modes. None of these settings could knock out a tank, but they had solid range and were hard to ignore. Each round hit harder and faster than any gunpowder driven bullet—but that wasn't the best feature of the weapon.

What really made them stand out was the number of rounds a man could carry. Snap-rifles used magnetic accelerators to fire, rather than gunpowder. That made each round very small, not much bigger than a BB, and our troops could easily fire a thousand shots without running out of ammo.

Tapping into our buzzer feed again, I saw white sparks showering off the leading saurian troops. The air was filled with the unmistakable snap and whine of accelerated metal slivers being sent down-range at fantastic speeds.

Doggedly, the saurians marched forward. Their armor wasn't powered, so they walked slowly. What their kit lacked in speed, however, it more than made up for in survivability.

The saurian troops soon spotted some of their tormentors and began nailing them. Smoking limbs—that was all that remained after one of them lobbed a shot on top of a light trooper.

In the meantime, the bigger shells kept falling. They took out a heavy now and then, as they'd walked the artillery up to catch Toro's hindmost troops.

"Ready!" Leeson announced suddenly in my headset.

I'd never heard a more welcome announcement. Before I could even give him the order to fire, he took the initiative and twin beams sizzled over our heads. Somehow, he'd managed to get some elevation and set up his 88s with a good command of the field.

Toro's heavies threw themselves facedown into the dirt, and we all strained to look at the enemy.

The front rank of the saurian infantry melted. They were scattered, and they were shielded, but it didn't matter. The 88s swept their beams over them, like twin lawnmowers cutting two careful lines. A dozen enemy troops went down, and the rest scrambled for cover.

A cheer went up. My troops had needed a victory, and they'd finally gotten their first one.

"Leeson," Harris said, "I take back all the shit I was muttering about you."

Leeson laughed. "We've got plenty more where that came from! Cycle down, recharge, sweep back—"

That was as far as he got. Six black spheres were sailing overhead. They plunged down, seemingly at random, popping all over the rocks where Leeson had set up his ambush.

"Leeson?" I called out. "Leeson!"

"He's gone, sir!" Sargon said. "We lost one of our gunners, too."

"Take command, Sargon. Man those 88s and sweep them again. Toro! Get your heavies up off their asses! Advance and support Harris. We have to break the enemy line!"

All around me, the heavy troopers climbed to their feet and moved with purpose. There was no cover to be had on the high rocks. Leeson's platoon was in a pall of acidic smoke to prove it. The time was ripe for a charge.

As Toro's platoon began rushing past me, I joined them. I was wearing a heavy kit, the same as the rest of these boys. One more morph-rifle might turn the tide in a tight battle.

The heavies seemed to appreciate my participation. Too many officers liked to sit in bunkers in these situations, powdering their swollen posteriors while grunts risked it all.

"Harris," I said, "take what's left of your people and pull out. Flank south, get around behind their main force and see if you can take out whoever is throwing these acid-balls at us."

"I've only got—"

"I don't care if it's you and a one-legged possum! Take out those enemy gunners!"

"Roger that," he said resignedly, and his signal cut out.

He was probably cursing me with the mic muted, but I didn't care.

As Toro's troops rushed forward in a ragged line, the saurians spammed us with flashing explosives. They were firing mini-missiles, nasty little weapons the size of sparrows. They homed in on our armored butts.

"Buzzers! I need buzzers and jammers!"

We all switched on our jammers, and most of the mini-missiles exploded in confusion or just plain missed. Three, however, found targets. Men were turned into tumbling piles of junk, blood and smoke.

Slowing down to a crouched advance, we peppered the saurians with fire. Toro and I lit up red arrows on key targets. Concentrating fire without being told, our combined rifles tore several more saurians apart.

Then we met their line, and the battle got personal. Human troops let their rifles dangle and extended force-blades from their armored forearms. The enemy troops were shielded, however, and they fought with blades of their own and superior strength.

Certain relationships soon became apparent. The saurians were larger and stronger than any human, and they had shielding. Our force-blades, however, had greater reach and our powered suits made up for our lack of muscle.

Overall, the human troops were more offensive, while the saurian troops were better defended. One on one, it could go either way.

Fortunately, we outnumbered them at this point. Having endured several deep cuts from our 88s, the saurians didn't have enough bodies to stop our advance. We pressed them back, oftentimes with two humans taking down a single dino.

We were beginning to cheer, to sing, to roar with the knowledge we were winning—but then the battle shifted again.

The sky darkened. My faceplate went black, and indicators began blinking red inside my helmet.

"Acid-shells!" I shouted. "Break off!"

The enemy had clearly decided we'd beaten their main force. In response, they'd decided to melt all of us, human and lizard alike, down to bubbling puddles of flesh in the sand.

We scattered, some men coughing blood when the acid ate through the polymer fittings in their armor. When we were clear, I did a quick count.

Toro was gone. Veteran Johnson was gone. I had less than a dozen heavies with me, and some of them were shedding their smoking armor or limping.

Looking back, the only good news was that none of the saurians seemed to be walking out of that black roiling cloud. Not one.

"Harris!" I called out on command chat. "What's your position? Report!"

"McGill, we're sneaking around to their south flank. We don't have a good firing position yet."

"Can you see the gunner crews? Who's nailing us with these gas shells?"

"They're dug in, sir. I can see the sources, but I'm not in a position to snipe at them."

"Can you assault their position?"

There was no response for several seconds. "Harris?!"

"Maybe, sir," he admitted at last. "I'm still counting heads. They've got about as many heavy troops in their camp as I have lights. I'm assuming their artillery teams are weaker—but as I said, I haven't seen them yet."

I felt sweat run down into my eyes, making them sting. The remaining heavy troops under my command had all found a rock to hide behind. They were exhausted, pouring what precious water they had into their faces and gasping for breath. We weren't ready to press another attack and support Harris if I ordered him in now.

"All right," I said at last. "Hold your position. Look for opportunities. Those mortars, or whatever they are, have to be taken out. They're killing us."

"Agreed… Centurion? There is one combatant out here that I'm not able to figure out."

"What are you talking about?"

"A man, sir. A single man. He looks human enough, anyway."

"There's an actual *human* with the enemy troops?"

"Yes. In fact, he looks like he's giving orders."

That perked me up. "That sounds like cheating to me. Take snaps of the guy with your tapper. Send me your best."

The images came in soon thereafter, and my jaw sagged inside my helmet.

Almost at the same time, as if he knew I was on to him, a familiar voice buzzed in my helmet.

"This is the commander of the Saurian forces," the voice said with a mild Texan accent. "With whom do I have the pleasure of speaking?"

It was Claver. He was the most infamous trader—and turncoat—Earth had ever given birth to. He was also the slipperiest man alive in the galaxy today.

## -40-

The orange sun beat down on my helmet. I let the air conditioner cycle down, then I opened my visor and felt a wave of hot steam escape my suit. An equal amount of oven-hot dry air rushed in to replace it.

Overall, the drying effect was a net positive in my view. I slammed my visor back down soon after, worried about another acid-bomb, and I felt the cooling effects of my hissing air conditioners as they kicked back on again.

"Claver?" I asked, responding to him at last. "Who let you out of your cage?"

He gave me an evil chuckle. "James McGill…" he said. "I never thought we'd cross paths again, but I shouldn't be surprised after that cluster Deech orchestrated back on Rogue World. You're living proof that Deech is as shit-off stupid as Drusus."

"We haven't got much time to talk, Claver," I said. "This is about over."

"What? Are your men all dead already? That's disappointing—almost embarrassing."

"You called me. What do you want?"

"Peace!" he said loudly. "Tranquility too—and I've got good prices for both."

I shook my head. "Sounds like bullshit meant to distract. I'm afraid I'm through here. See you in Hell, Old Silver."

He'd never liked it when I mentioned his old nickname. He'd been proud of it for years, as he hadn't died for a long time. I'd fixed that situation, and his silver hair had been turned back to its natural black again with my help.

But today, he didn't growl at me for mentioning it. He seemed relaxed, easy-going.

"Hold on boy," he said. "Don't be so hasty. I've got a proposition for you."

I was silent for a second. I knew I shouldn't listen any further. I should shut him down, block his channel, and ignore him until he was as dead as a cockroach under my heel.

The trouble was I couldn't be sure I was winning this fight. By my estimates, both sides had lost about half their strength. We were now taking a break, hugging rocks and licking wounds—but the conflict was bound to start up again. After all, the only escape from this pit was death for one side or the other.

"Talk fast," I said at last.

"Over this unsecured line? Do you have any idea who's probably listening in right now?"

"Uh,... everyone in the star system?"

"Bingo! And here I thought you were living proof that a man can live without a brain. I stand corrected."

His insults ran off me like piss off a duck's back. Later on, if he kept talking, I knew I'd lose it and throttle him or something—but not now. I was thinking too hard about how I might gain an advantage by talking to him.

I weighed the pros and cons of parleying with Claver. I could let the battle continue until it reached its final conclusion. Win or lose, what would be would be.

But if I talked to him, I might learn more about the bigger picture. About why we were struggling on this rock with aliens we'd once called friends. About why, in God's name, Claver was out here commanding saurian troops.

"Okay," I said at last. "Meet me in the middle with a white flag. No weapons. No backstabbing."

He snorted. "A good, old-fashioned parley, huh? All right, I'll bite. I'm a sucker for the classics."

And so it was arranged. Harris and pretty much everyone else in the unit thought I was completely insane, but I didn't care. I was in command, and I wanted whatever information I could glean.

Harris had an entirely different take on the idea.

"All right, sir!" he said. "I'll set myself up for a clean shot. I'll take it myself. You don't even have to say hello, just stand clear and let me take him out."

"That's not how I want to play it, Harris."

"What? Are you shitting me? You're really planning to get up on him, nice and personal, and do it yourself? Have you still got your daddy's knife hidden up your ass?"

"Nope, I'm not doing it like that, either. I want information, and I plan to get what I can with no tricks."

"Information? What the hell for? I'll give you some information: It's them or us, McGill! This is all about murder, the dirtier the better. Don't be giving him an easy kill on us."

Harris was excited, but I didn't feel I could let his disrespect pass.

"Adjunct," I said, "are you saying you're going to disobey my orders?"

"What...? No sir! No... I'm just saying this is a foolish move, and I object strenuously."

"Objection noted. If Claver kills me somehow, you have my permission to fill him with nails. McGill out."

My tapper and the inside of my helmet continued to buzz and flash, but I ignored every caller. I got up and trudged out to the designated meeting spot.

Once out there, it was deceptively quiet. But I knew Claver had to have his lizard troops watching, the same as I did.

Claver stood with a bored stance. His helmet was off, and he was squinting in the blazing sun.

"Nice day," he commented. "Don't you agree?"

"It's so dry I suspect the trees would be bribing the dogs—if they had trees or dogs on this rock, that is."

He snorted at my joke and eyed me seriously. "You'll have to take off that helmet if you want me to talk."

"Why?"

"Because I don't want any recorded audio, dummy. What's inside your head, anyway? I know they can't stack shit that high."

For a second, my hand twitched toward my pistol, but it wasn't there. As part of our deal, I'd left my weapons behind.

Claver noticed my movement and laughed. "You know what your problem is, McGill? You're too easy to manipulate. Too emotional. It's like talking to an old woman with an itch."

Having had enough, I turned around and started walking away.

"What the hell?" he called after me. "Don't you even want to know what I'm doing out here? No curiosity at all?"

I stopped. He had me. He knew it too, and that's why he was heaping on the insults. That was his way of enjoying himself. If he had a man on the string, he pulled and yanked and flicked at that string, loving every minute of the other guy's helpless dance.

Taking my helmet off, I tucked it under my arm and waved for him to talk.

"That's more like it," he said. "I've got jammers going, but you could still record me. Now, I'm feeling better."

"Then talk already, dammit!"

"Okay, okay. You met Gytha yet?"

I blinked and nodded slowly.

The left side of Claver's mouth twisted up into a smile. "I bet you like her, don't you? Well, you should be careful. She's not like her sweeter sisters back on Rogue World. She's a cast-iron bitch, and that's no lie."

"Is that all you've got?"

"No, no, not by a long shot. We've got some dealing to do, you and I."

"Dealing? I don't think so. What's there to deal about?"

"This planet. The next war on the Frontier—oh yeah, I know all about that. Earth's on her own now. You *do* realize the Empire handed you a pack of rebellious worlds and took off, right?"

Unable to deny it, I nodded. "That's a fair assessment. What can you do about it?"

"I can give you three billion troops. It used to be nine billion—but, you know, there were casualties recently. This planet wasn't always covered in fallout."

Despite myself, I felt stunned. I looked around at the dusty air.

*Six billion lost?* That was grim. The Blood Worlders had paid harshly for their loyalty to the squids.

"How can you get them to join us?" I asked him. "What influence can an old peddler like you possibly wield out here on the fringe?"

The best way to get Claver talking had always been to sting his pride. He was pretty big on himself, and if you could get him into a defensive mood, he might brag about all sorts of things.

Frowning, Claver shook his head. "Rude. Just plain rude. Your momma failed in her first duty, turning out a young man who respects his elders."

Turning my head to the north, I studied a pile of boulders, as if I was seeing something interesting. Then I turned back to Claver.

His suspicious eyes followed my glance then went back to my face.

"Is that where Harris went with his snipers?" he asked. "Did you think I didn't notice when he disappeared from the battlefield?"

I shrugged and checked my tapper in boredom. "We're going to have to wrap this up. It's going to be dark soon."

"Here's the essence of my offer: I can throw this fight. These dumb lizards are trained to follow me. I'll order them to march right into your 88s until there's nothing left but a few tails sticking out of an ash-heap."

"We can beat them without your help."

"Maybe. Maybe not. The stakes are high, McGill, and Earth needs this army."

"I might be interested," I said. "If you'd answer a few more questions first."

"Don't you even want to know what I want for this service?"

"That was my first question."

He laughed again. "Okay. Fair enough. You might be thinking that I want the galactic key again—but that's old hat. Sure, it's nice, but the Empire is a toothless old man with a chill. The frontier—this is where things are happening now. Right here."

"So? What do you want?"

"I want legitimacy. A planet of my own. Somewhere full of docile workers would be nice. I've got three worlds scoped out for the job."

I blinked in confusion. "What makes you think I can deliver anything remotely like that?"

"Not you, moron. Deech can do it, with her deep-link reporting back to Earth. I'm offering a valuable planet. I'm only asking to trade you for a less valuable planet. Your role in this deal is to play the go-between."

I craned my neck, looking at the sky. "You know they're watching this, don't you? Don't you think the Blood Worlders are going to be suspicious about us talking here so long?"

"Fortunately, most of the Blood Worlders are fools—not that Gytha though. You're right to think we have to watch out for her. But don't worry, I've got an excuse for this parley. That's all part of the plan."

"Let's pretend I'm interested. What's the next step in this show? Even if you let me beat your lizards, that won't be the end of it."

"No," he admitted. "It's a down payment. You'll have to revive me on your ship—I have to die at the end of this round, of course, in order for you to be declared the winner. Once I'm aboard your ship, I'll talk to Deech and give her more intel. Enough to help your side win the final round."

"What will we be facing next?"

He looked cagey all of a sudden. "You've got all you're going to get from me for now. Is it a yes, or a no?"

I thought it over for a second, then I nodded.

He began to smile, until he saw me extend a force-blade from my right arm.

We weren't that far apart. Maybe he'd forgotten that my armor always had a weapon built into it.

Thrusting my blade deep into his chest, I gave it a twist and let it sizzle in there.

Shaking, knees buckling, he collapsed in a heap. I stood over him. His mouth was open, with drool and blood making a dark stain on the sand.

"I accept your terms, Claver," I told him. "It's a deal."

He died quickly, and I walked away from the mess.

"McGill!" Harris shouted in my ears as soon as I was far enough away from Claver for his blocker to be ineffective. "You old sly-boots! That was wild!"

"Centurion," Sargon shouted before I could answer, "you've got incoming! Watch your six!"

"Sargon," I said, "get those 88s sighted on me."

"Already done, sir. But that's extreme range for these babies."

"I know. Harris, when the acid-shells start to fly, spot the enemy. You've got to go in and pop them if you can't snipe them."

"Roger that," he said in a deflated tone.

In the meantime, I began to run. Not flat-out, mind you, but moving at a good clip back toward our lines.

The remainder of the saurian heavies pursued me, but they weren't fast on their feet. Mini-missiles were my big concern. They snapped and whined nearby, blasting up chunks of sand and rock. I ran into what little cover I could find, putting some of those mushroom-cap things between my back and the enemy lizards—but that didn't help much. Their missiles chewed the mushrooms down fast.

My helmet was on by this time, and it was a good thing I'd thought of it. Black roiling clouds burst nearby, causing me to carom off at an angle whenever one came down.

"We've spotted them, sir!" Harris shouted. "They're dug in all right. My snipers are engaging now, and I'm sending another team down to close-assault their nests."

I could see shiny flashes bouncing off Toro's surviving troops. They wanted to come out and meet me, but I ordered them to stay low. They were one of the final cards I could play in this struggle.

Enraged after witnessing what looked like treachery on my part, the saurian troops seemed hell-bent on my personal destruction. They doggedly followed me, taking sweeps from the 88s when they crossed the open land where Claver and I had met. They pressed on despite their losses.

In the end, I almost made it to our lines—but not quite. I caught one of those missiles in the spine.

Knocked off my feet and spun around, I found myself making a strange, continuous wheezing sound. Air was escaping me, but I wasn't really breathing. It was more like a long, low howl of pain and shock.

Forcing my eyes to focus, I saw three lizards catch up.

I'd died like this once before, long ago. My first death had come under the claws and teeth of raptors like this, in fact. It was the death that played most often in my nightmares to this very day.

But before they could tear my steaming guts from my body and run around with bloody trophies in their wet muzzles, I saw the 88s sweep over all of us.

The world went white, and we were all turned to ash together.

## -41-

Voices slowly impinged on my universe.

"What's his score?" a female voice asked.

"A ten... See that? A frigging *ten*!"

"That's what I call a good grow."

I didn't open my eyes right off, as I knew they were bleary and sore. The dimmest light was always blinding right after a revive.

"James?" the feminine voice called softly. I felt her breath puff over my ear.

I knew that voice. I knew she was someone who could be evil or sweet. Part angel and part devil, Specialist Evelyn Thompson was the kind of woman who often attracted me. I'd long accounted this as one of my many flaws.

"Evelyn?" I croaked, using her first name, as she'd done for me.

She almost giggled. That wasn't a normal sound for her, either.

"You're okay," she said. "You died hard in the crater. I watched it—but you're doing great now. Your revival scores are topping the charts."

"Do you... do you forgive me? For Floramel?"

"Yes," she said, running her fingers through my wet, sticky hair. "I forgive you. After all, you won the battle. But let me warn you: not everyone aboard this ship is so happy with—"

I heard the revival chamber's hatch snick open and shut again.

"Ah..." Winslade said. "Our sleeping beauty awakens again, hmm? Well Specialist, hurry up and give him a goodbye kiss. He's got some explaining to do."

Surprising everyone, Evelyn *did* kiss my cheek.

My eyes fluttered open. I snorted and released a laugh. My nose ran, but I ignored it.

Coughing up stuff I'd rather not name, I sat up and fumbled my numb arms into fresh sleeves.

Winslade watched impatiently. "I swear, McGill, you'll be late to your own perming in the end."

"As long as I get to watch yours first, sir," I managed to rumble out.

Winslade huffed out the door, and I staggered in his wake.

When we reached Gold Deck, I figured I was going to have to talk the brass into reviving Claver and talking turkey with him—but I'd figured wrong.

Claver was already there in Deech's office. Winslade waved me inside with a smirk and closed the door, staying on the far side of it.

Turning around, I was shocked to see Deech and Claver talking in calm tones.

"Was everyone in on this from the start?" I demanded.

"Everyone but you, apparently," Claver remarked.

Deech sighed. "The situation is... complicated, McGill. Not every lower echelon officer is informed when—"

"When traitors are stalking the halls?" I finished for her.

She frowned. "That's a very rude tone. I'm going to excuse it, but only because you just handed Earth another victory. Don't get too cocky, however. No one is irreplaceable."

Grumbling to myself, I found a chair and stretched out in it. While I listened, Claver and Deech wrangled about various details of the bargain.

Claver wanted his own personal planet-sized playground, but Deech wanted to buy him off cheap. She offered him a shipment of goods and a transport to carry them in. They just weren't seeing eye-to-eye.

"Tribune," Claver said, "you're being miserly. Worse, you're doing it at the wrong time. The stakes are much too high in this case to quibble about a few billion credits one way or the other."

"I disagree," Deech said. "It's your cooperation that's barely required. Legion Varus may well win this contest outright, in which case everything Earth paid will have been wasted."

Claver sucked in a breath and let it out in a long sigh. "Winslade was right about you," he said.

Deech looked annoyed and adjusted her clothing. "What exactly does that mean?"

Claver looked at me suddenly. They'd both been ignoring me for the last ten minutes, and I was ready to fall asleep.

"McGill!" Claver shouted.

"Huh?"

"Would you pay me a planet to seal this deal?"

Deech shot daggers at me with her eyes.

"Uh…" I said. "It's not really my place to say."

"I know that. Just give us your honest opinion."

"Well…" I said thoughtfully. "It does seem to me that when something is so close to a done deal, it's worth a little extra to make sure the outcome goes your way. I mean—given that the stakes are so high."

Claver turned back to Deech, crossed his arms, and grinned. "You hear that? He's as dumb as a hog's fart, but even McGill knows when to squeeze and when to give generously."

"McGill," Deech said in a dangerous tone. "Get out. I'm not sure what you're doing here, anyway."

"Yes sir," I said, getting to my feet.

Turning, I walked to the door and reached for it, but I heard an odd sound behind me. Was that the distinctive tone of a needler singing its deadly song?

Turning back around, I saw a sight I wasn't expecting. Deech was slumped dead on the floor with a perfectly round needle-hole in the back of her neck. Claver stood over her, his hands on his hips, clucking his tongue.

My hand reached for my sidearm—but I realized it wasn't there. I had no weapons on me. Winslade had marched me up here fresh from a revive. There was nothing but a wad of spacer-blues in my clenched fist.

Claver looked at me speculatively. "You know, I was going to send you down in the next contest. Really, I was. But after that display of untrustworthy behavior the last time we met, I changed my mind."

"You don't belong on this ship, Claver," I said. "Much less in command of anything. I'd kill you where you stand if I was armed."

"Maybe—but you're *not* armed!" Claver said, tsking and tapping his temple with his needler. "Keep your fingers away from your tapper, McGill."

I froze. I'd been reaching for my left forearm with my right hand, but Claver was too cagey to let me call security.

"You see?" Claver said in a conversational tone, "this is all part of the problem. Your mind is flexible, and you do possess a certain degree of horse-sense... but really McGill, it's just not good enough."

Confused by his talk, I was looking around the room for something to kill him with. Weapons came in a wide variety of forms. I'd found you could use almost anything to hurt a man if your heart was really in it.

The door behind me opened then. Winslade popped in. He gave a little gasp when he saw Deech on the floor.

"Contact security, Primus!" I shouted.

"Instantly!" Winslade said, and he brought up his tapper.

Instead of contacting anyone, he took a snap of me and of Deech lying on the floor.

Claver released a nasty chuckle. "There's a man capable of planning ahead," he said. "I think in the end, you were right about this all along, Winslade. We can't trust McGill. He's just too much of a beast."

"Every man has his advantages and his limitations," Winslade replied in the tone of a man quoting a proverb.

That was it for me. I understood that Winslade was in on this conspiracy, and I didn't like it. Claver's insults had been rankling me all along, and I didn't think Deech deserved this kind of treachery in any case. Say what you will about the woman, she normally played things straight.

Winslade had gone and taken advantage of her, seducing her, playing the suck-up like only a master could. She'd bought into it so far she'd even tried to dress sexy for him. Turning on her now? That was just plain wrong.

Two of my stiff fingers jabbed Winslade in the throat. He staggered back, gagging. I launched a hammer-blow with my left, which just caught his temple as he fell away from me.

Claver laughed. He was close behind me.

I whirled, but he had his needler in my face.

"Perfectly played, boy! You're like a puppet without strings. You got me back on the planet, I'll admit that. A shameful moment. But now, you've finished this little Greek tragedy I've set up in the tribune's office."

My fists flew again—but after all, I'm just muscle, sinew and bone.

The needler sang, and I had a new dime-sized hole in my right cheekbone. Burning, losing control of my body, I slumped down on the deck.

"You're going to stay asleep for a while now, McGill," Claver said with amusement. "You're going to make an excellent alibi. Sweet dreams, dummy."

As I lost consciousness and died, my final thought concerned this particular grow of James McGill. He'd been a fine specimen. I couldn't recall ever having achieved a revival score of ten. Not in any of my uncounted past lives.

It was a damned shame.

## -42-

As was often the case, I awoke with the same lingering thoughts I'd died with.

"I was a *ten*," I muttered.

"What's that? Did he talk?"

"I didn't hear anything."

Two voices were speaking in hushed tones. They were both women, and they seemed familiar, but my brain wasn't quite able to identify them yet.

I was coming back to life. My eyes fluttered, but they didn't want to open all the way.

"Hack the console again," the first one said.

I recognized her now. That was Specialist Thompson—Evelyn.

"It's done. Be quick, every time we get into the data core it leaves a trace."

*Floramel.* The second voice had to be hers. But how could these two girls be working on my revival together? The last I'd heard, they hated one another.

"McGill?" Evelyn hissed in my ear. "Are you ready to move yet? We've got to get out of here."

Summoning what little strength my fresh body had, I sucked in air, coughed it back out, then forced myself into a hunched sitting position.

"What's the rush?" I managed to slur.

"Listen to me, James," Floramel said.

I could smell her natural, hot-sweet scent. She never wore perfumes, but she never seemed to stink, either. Not even to my new nostrils, which had never sniffed anything before.

"What?" I managed.

"This is an illegal grow. We got your data, we charged the machine with stale materials out of the tanks, and we revived you. But we've got to get out of here. The revival machine will log this usage."

"Help me up," I said, without demanding any further explanations.

The two women did as I asked, and I staggered off the gurney. They staggered with me, almost buckling under my thick arms. Neither one of them was a weight-lifter.

With each step and each breath, I became more human. Stronger, more alert—and I found I was slowly growing pissed, too.

Standing on my own at last, I nearly tore my jacket apart as I pulled it on over my slimy limbs. Why was it that liquids made you slip on the floor, but they made clothing stick to you like glue?

"I'm going to kill Claver," I said with certainty. "Maybe Winslade, too."

The two women exchanged worried glances.

"It isn't time for killing," Floramel told me. "Not now."

"What's our situation, ladies?" I asked.

"You're on the run," Evelyn said. "If we're caught in your company, we'll be arrested and put up on charges."

"Do you have a plan?"

"We do. Follow me."

Thompson led, I followed, and Floramel brought up the rear of our group.

We were still aboard *Nostrum*, I could tell that much at least. Checking my tapper, I caught up on more vital information. It was the middle of the night, ship's time. I'd been dead for perhaps a dozen hours.

"I take it I'm not supposed to be revived," I said.

"Hush," Evelyn said gently. "We'll tell you more soon. Just keep moving."

I glanced at Floramel. She looked troubled, but that could have meant anything. After all, I could only assume I was an accused killer in her eyes.

We made our way aft, to Engineering. Floramel worked her magic on the hatchways. They were secure—but she was a tech.

We passed several bored crewmen, but they did nothing more than give us a curious glance. My stern eyes and the centurion's red crest on my shoulder kept their gaze from lingering.

Whatever slander Winslade had put out about me, it seemed like it hadn't included an all-points bulletin. After all, why warn people about a dangerous madman *after* he was conveniently dead? It could only cause uncomfortable questions to be asked.

When we reached the machine shop, I frowned.

"What's back here, besides the gateway posts?"

They looked at me. The light went on in my fridge.

"You want me to go somewhere? To get out of your hair?"

"You have to go back to Earth, James," Evelyn said. "You have to warn them. Deech is dead. We think Winslade did it, but—"

"It wasn't him. It was Claver. They're working together."

Specialist Thompson's eyes widened. "He's back? He's aboard this ship?"

"Yes. Winslade and Claver cut some kind of deal concerning Earth's ownership of Blood World. This contest to show mastery—it's a sham."

"Not entirely," Evelyn told me. "The Blood Worlder's really do respect this process. Ever since the Cephalopods were taken down by us, they've been lost. Three billion warrior slaves in search of new masters."

I frowned. "Uh… how do you know all that?"

She shrugged and looked down. "Well… as you must know, I've had dealings with Imperator Turov for years."

Slowly, ever so slowly, I began to figure a few things out.

"You're still working for her, aren't you?" I demanded.

Evelyn wouldn't meet my eyes. "Yes," she said.

"So… this whole romance-thing we've been having? That was all a setup? A way to keep tabs on old McGill?"

Specialist Thompson shrugged. Her face had reddened a little.

"I don't know," she said. "I hated you before, remember? But you did charm me, over time."

"Oh, that's nice! Shit…"

Floramel watched the two of us having this conversation, but she wasn't saying anything. That told me a lot.

"You're in on this too, aren't you?" I asked her. "Are you working for Turov too?"

"No," she said, "but Specialist Thompson told me about it. She needed my help to get your data copied out of the core. I didn't want to do it—until she explained the true nature of her relationship with you."

My mouth hung open. It was a thing that just happened to me in moments like this.

Sure, I'd been surprised when Claver and Winslade had gone off the rails and pinned Deech's murder on me. But this was personal.

"You're telling me your feelings for me are real, not manufactured like miss prissy-pants over here?"

"James…" Evelyn said. "We're wasting time. For what it's worth—I don't hate you anymore."

"That's great," I said. "That's really cool."

Floramel had set up the gateway posts. They'd never been powered-up before to my knowledge. I was surprised they weren't under guard—but I guess the techs figured they were safe enough down here.

"We'll have to tap the main engines to get enough power," Floramel said. "The jump to Earth is a long one."

"Why don't you gate home, Evelyn?" I asked with a hint of bitterness.

"I have other missions to perform. You don't."

"That's cold," I said. "Ice cold—but all right. I'll go back home. I'm not sure why I would bother coming back, but—"

"You probably won't have to," Specialist Thompson said. "Just get Turov on the deep-link. She can talk to Winslade and the crew. If Winslade understands that his secret dealings are public knowledge back home, he won't be able to complete his plans."

"I don't entirely get it," I said. "What's so incredibly valuable about Blood World anyway? I know they've got troops, but—"

"Think, James," Thompson told me. She touched my cheek with the back of her hand, but I pulled away. "How many credits would it take to train and equip three billion ground troops?"

I stared at her for a long moment. "A whole lot," I admitted.

"Exactly. Floramel? Are we ready?"

Floramel watched the two of us. I felt a pang. I'd ditched her, and it now seemed I'd made the wrong choice.

On impulse, I leaned forward and gave her a chaste kiss. She looked startled, but she didn't dodge.

The gateway posts began to thrum. They were active.

"Where do I come out?" I asked, looking at the glowing poles dubiously.

"Central, probably," Thompson said.

"Probably..." I echoed.

Setting my beret at an appropriate angle, I stepped forward—and vanished.

## -43-

    I've taken many teleportation trips before. Usually, I'd done it with the aid of a protective suit. Long jumps tended to burn the traveler with radiation and friction created by various manipulated fields.
    But the gateway posts worked differently. Unlike teleportation suits, they didn't cast a man adrift in the cosmos like a one-man starship. Instead, they connect two points in space together, linking them via some trick of entanglement.
    The result was that my trip from Epsilon Leporis to Earth took mere seconds to complete. I saw no stars, and I experienced no sensations on this long journey. Over three hundred lightyears were crossed in the time it took to breathe a few puffs of air.
    Only, I couldn't breathe. I couldn't move at all. I felt as if I'd been stuck in stasis. That had been my lot in the past, watching the world move with great rapidity while I was stuck crawling through time at a very different pace.
    To me, it seemed like my mind wasn't in synch with my body. My body was frozen, but my mind was racing. It was quite disturbing. It was like being paralyzed but aware.
    Then, not a moment too soon, it ended. My sharp walking pace had turned into a stumble, and I put my hands on my knees while the world swam around me. I gasped like a fish on

land. Psychologically, I felt like I'd been suffocated—even though it was all an illusion.

"Who the fuck are you?" demanded a voice.

Looking up and regaining control of my breathing, I realized I was inside some kind of glass box. The glass looked thick and tough. It was probably ballistic glass, bullet proof.

Beyond the glass, I saw a group of hogs. They were noncoms, mostly, with a centurion in charge. All of them were armed, and they held their rifles at their shoulders.

"I'm Centurion James McGill," I said, slapping my legion patch. "Legion Varus."

They relaxed a little. "What are you doing here, McGill?" the officer asked. "No one is due to come out of there for days."

"Something's gone wrong," I said. "The mission is in trouble. I'm supposed to report to Imperator Turov."

The hog immediately began working his tapper.

"Who are you contacting?" I asked.

"The Equestrian's office," he said. "If anything happens down here, I'm—"

"Hold on, Centurion," I said. "When I said something's gone wrong, I'm talking about treachery."

He stopped tapping at his arm and looked at me. "Are you saying that Drusus has gone bad? Didn't he run your legion originally?"

"Are you contacting Equestrian Drusus directly?" I asked him. "Because if you are, I'm all for it."

He snorted. "Are you kidding? He's serious brass. I'm calling his staff."

"That's when it becomes a problem."

His expression shifted to a frown again. "His staff? His staff is compromised?"

I didn't say anything. I just stared at him flatly.

Normally, this kind of tactic might not have worked. But there had been many bouts of strange shenanigans in Central in previous years. No hog officer could be unaware of that fact.

One thing about hogs that made them easier to manipulate than a star-faring legionnaire was their natural tendency to play it safe. After all, if they'd been born with real balls, they wouldn't have signed with the biggest, most boring service of them all.

The hog opened his mouth to say more, but he never got the chance. I lifted my tapper. My fingers had been working just as quickly as theirs had.

Imperator Turov's sly face looked out of the tiny screen.

"Gentlemen," she said. "Please let Centurion McGill out of the protective enclosure. I would appreciate it if you'd escort him directly to my office."

None of them were about to disobey a direct order from someone of Turov's rank. Drusus was one notch higher—but he wasn't watching right now.

Grumbling a bit, they let me out of the glass cage. Half of them rode up several hundred floors with me.

They didn't look at me much, and they said even less. I could tell they wanted to unload me and the stink of misconduct I represented ASAP.

On Earth, it was a fine sunny morning. My tapper updated and said it was 10:20 am. Right away, I began feeling cheery. I'd missed Earth. Blood World sucked in comparison.

Turov didn't let me into her office right away. She summoned her own squadron of hogs to surround me first.

Without so much as a statement of intent, a hog noncom began searching me. I spread my hands and legs—but suddenly, he was on his back on the deck. I'd swept his feet from under him when he was off-balance.

"Oh hey," I said, with simulated concern. "Let me help you up, big guy."

Growling, he grabbed my hand and squeezed. He did have an iron grip. I was almost impressed. A twist of the wrist, however, allowed me to gain control of his hand with one of mine. Humans have several weak points in their skeletal structure, and having been a veteran myself for some years in one of the meanest legions in Earth history, I knew them all.

Hissing in pain and doing a little spin, the hog found himself face down on the deck again.

"Damn, boy!" I shouted in his ear. "Have you got a case of vertigo, or something?"

Another trooper put a rifle up against my spine about then. I had a plan all ready for him—but there was an interruption.

"Don't shoot him," Turov said, standing in her open doorway. "I know you really, *really* want to—but don't."

The gun barrel in my back retreated. I straightened up and smiled at the man at my feet.

"No hard feelings, hog," I said.

He got to his feet, glaring and showing me a lot of teeth. I smiled back, knowing I'd made another friend.

"Get in here, McGill," Turov ordered.

"Imperator," said the man who'd been enjoying the floor so much. "You can't trust that man. You shouldn't be alone with him."

"I know that," she said resignedly.

She closed the door in his face.

Turning around with her hands on her shapely hips, she gave me an acid stare of rebuke.

In return, I ogled her. *Damn*, I'd forgotten how good a superior officer could look after hanging around Tribune Deech for months. Now, don't get me wrong, Deech was fine and decent woman. But Turov? She was like a doll possessed by an evil spirit.

"Still looking good, Galina," I said.

The Imperator and I had shared many inappropriate moments in the past. Because of that, I'd always felt a certain familiarity with her when we were alone. Sometimes, that went fine with her—but this clearly wasn't one of those times.

"Don't call me that," she snapped. Her eyes were full of suspicion. "Dare I ask the most basic of questions?"

"Fire away, sir."

"What the hell are you doing on Earth?"

"Well now, that's a funny thing. I found these goal posts in the basement aboard *Nostrum*, and—"

"Cut the shit, McGill. Who sent you?"

"Your sneaky honeypot agent did."

She cocked her head to one side. "Specialist Thompson?"

At those words, I felt a twinge. Her instant recognition confirmed my worst fears. Thompson *had* played me like a fiddle.

If there was one thing Galina Turov wasn't, it was dumb. She caught the shift in my expression. Her voice lowered.

"Is she still alive, James?"

"Yeah, sure... Last I checked."

"You didn't perm her or anything, did you?"

"Why would I want to do that?"

We eyed one another. After studying my face, she relaxed a little.

"All right," she said. "Thompson wouldn't have sent you unless the situation was critical. Brief me."

I did so, with only a very few key reservations. I even threw in a few details from my sexual escapades with Thompson for good measure. Turov rolled her pretty eyes when I did that.

Naturally, I left out anything that reflected badly on me, such as when I'd murdered Claver out of turn. I also failed to mention much about Floramel's involvement in the rampant scheming. I figured I'd already broken that girl's heart, so why make it worse by putting her on Turov's radar?

Galina began to pace when I'd finished, so I helped myself to her liquor cabinet. It was a testament to how hard she was thinking that she didn't admonish me for taking liberties.

"Hmm..." she said. "This is complicated, and it feels incomplete. I can only surmise you're holding back critical information for your own purposes."

People often divined all sorts of deep thoughts, sinister plans and semi-amazing powers due to simple gaps in my knowledge. I'd found over the years it was best to let them do so.

"That's not just a lie, sir," I said. "It's a *damned* lie!"

I'd spoken with such false vehemence, she appeared to be convinced.

"Of course it is..." she said thoughtfully, not believing me for a second. "I can't tell you how upset your information has made me, McGill. None of this was supposed to happen—not like this."

"Uh... how was it all supposed to go down?"

"Isn't it obvious? Armel was supposed to win at the end. When your legions fight in the final contest, Earth can't lose.

Either one legion will win, or the other will. In my estimation, it should be a simple matter for Germanica to defeat Varus. That's why Varus was chosen to face them in the first place."

I blinked. I tried to stop that reaction, but I didn't manage to do it in time.

Fortunately, Galina was strutting around and fuming so much that she didn't notice my shocked response.

*Armel*? The tribune of Legion Germanica? As far as I knew, he wasn't even out there at Blood World. I was confused, but I kept pretending I knew what was going on. Turov was letting gems of wisdom fall on the floor at random.

To cover my mood, I drank a shot of her scotch, made a face, and then poured another. When she walked by, I absently pressed the tiny glass into her hand.

She paused, looking at it in confusion for a second, then threw it down her throat and handed the glass back. I went back to pouring.

"The plan was foolproof," she said. "We sent out a legion to impress the Blood Worlders. They need new masters, and we require countless slaves willing to die."

"A match made in Heaven," I said, toasting the air.

"Exactly. To make certain we won, we sent *two* legions. One was representing Earth directly, and the other was supposedly hired on by a third party. In the end, of course, that would turn out to be Earth as well, or someone under our control."

I was beginning at long last to grasp the nature of her scheme. It sounded evil, underhanded, and thus highly likely to succeed. By having two players in the contest, the odds we'd win were much improved.

"So then," I said thoughtfully, "why is Thompson so convinced things are going wrong?"

"That should be obvious. Claver wasn't supposed to be leading saurian troops in any battles. Winslade wasn't supposed to be shooting Deech, either."

"Okay, but—"

"Winslade is a puppet," she continued, "so it all comes down to Claver... I don't know what he has in mind, but I don't trust him at all. That's why Thompson sent you to inform me of the situation. She's there to keep an eye on the operation."

Her words troubled me. They shouldn't have, but they did. I'd kind of liked Evelyn, and it hurt a little to know her passions for me had been bought and paid for.

I poured another shot, slipped it into Galina's hand, and she downed it absently.

"I was a fool to let Claver get involved at all!" she said, waving her hands around angrily.

"Uh-huh," I said, sipping more scotch.

We were drinking the good stuff, and it went down smoothly. However, as I was fresh from the revival chamber with an empty stomach, I soon felt a rumble deep inside. I fished some stale chips out of her cabinets and munched on them.

"Really?" she said, letting her eyes focus on me at last. "You're eating now?"

"I'm hungry."

"You're always hungry."

I shrugged, conceding the point.

"Here's what you're going to do," she said, outlining a new plan. "You're going back out there—to Blood World."

I released an unhappy grunt.

She ignored that and began to tick off a list of instructions on her fingers. I watched her fingers, drank, and slowly began to frown.

"Galina," I interrupted at last, "I'm not on your payroll any longer. I work for Drusus. Why shouldn't I ride the elevator up a few floors and ask for his opinion on this whole mess?"

Her teeth clenched.

"So… here we are at last. The shake-down. I've been expecting it. What is it you want, McGill? What will bend you to my will?"

Looking at her thoughtfully, a smile crept over my face.

She caught on immediately, and she took a step toward me. She shook her head and tsked.

"Really? *That* is what you want? Haven't you learned anything from your experience with Specialist—?"

That was as far as she got, because I grabbed her and kissed her.

She melted quickly. Maybe it was the booze, or maybe it was her commitment to gaining my support. Whatever the cause, she made love like she meant it.

It was perfectly possible she was enjoying herself, of course. That's what it *seemed* like to me at the time, but I wasn't sure I could tell the difference anymore.

My faith in women like her had been shaken for good.

## -44-

My return to *Nostrum* almost went unnoticed.

I'd taken care to walk through Engineering like I owned the place, and as far as that went, I figured I'd succeed.

Sure, various crewmen looked at me funny now and then as I passed them by. But I figured they weren't suspicious, they were just wondering why an officer from the legion they were transporting was wandering around in the guts of the ship.

Before I got to the big hatchway, which had been repaired and now looked kind of shiny, a tech caught up with me.

She tapped her finger on my back. I almost kept walking, but I knew that if she'd been ordered to keep an eye out, she would report me. The fact she felt safe enough to walk up and touch me indicated she wasn't thinking I was some kind of threat.

Therefore, I spun around, manufactured a smile, and asked her a question.

"What is it, Specialist?"

She looked me up and down once. Her expression was one of slight confusion.

"Aren't you supposed to be on one of the lifters, sir?" she asked.

My eyes widened slightly, but I managed not to look too alarmed. "I'm on my way right now," I said. "Thank you for your concern."

Exiting with broad strides, I let my long legs carry me at a pace that was beyond what a normal person would call walking. When no one was looking, I checked my tapper.

Messages were flooding in. Timers, warnings—the cohort had been ordered to drop. I was late for deployment on Blood World.

I shifted into a trot which transformed into a dead run. I reached the lifter bays just in time.

Graves was there, like a hostess offering people a seat. He saw me coming, smiled faintly and shook his head.

"Where have you been, McGill?" he asked. "I had to order your unit aboard myself."

"Sorry sir," I said, "I was unavoidably detained."

"Right…" he said with a rumbling laugh. "What was her name?"

"Uh… something Russian-sounding, I believe."

He puffed out his lips. "You've got to stop employing blockers when you go off-grid with a girl. I covered for you this time, but this has got to stop."

"I'd dearly appreciate this chance to redeem myself, Primus," I said. "I promise nothing like this will ever happen again."

Shaking his head, he went up the chute to ride with the pilots. I sat down in the midst of my unit. They all looked at me with a wide variety of expressions. Some—the women mostly—appeared to be disgusted.

Only Carlos looked amused.

"Another hard night with the ladies, huh, McGill?"

Normally, Sargon or Harris would have belted him one for smart-mouthing the CO—but they didn't seem interested in defending my honor this time around. Apparently, everyone thought I'd abandoned my post and wandered off to chase some tail.

I wanted to tell them the truth, but I couldn't. It was frustrating.

"There are things at work here," I said, "things I can't discuss."

"Really? Are we talking about parasols and butt-plugs?"

That was enough for Harris. He backhanded Carlos, causing a trickle of blood to run from the corner of his mouth. After that he finally shut up.

Deciding it was time to take back my command, I opened a channel and spoke loudly into every ear in the unit.

"We're about to deploy on Blood World again," I said. "You've all been there. You all know the score. Last time around, we won the contest. This time, we're going to win again."

They shuffled and studied their boots. A few raised their eyes to meet mine briefly.

"Fortunately," I said, "we're not going down alone this time. We've got the entire cohort with us. Nearly twelve hundred troops. I've talked to Graves, and we're not going to be put on point this time."

That was a lie, told because I needed to bring them a win. I'd only checked out the roster moments earlier and noticed we were set to deploy on the southern flank. Probably, Graves hadn't been sure I'd show up, and a unit without a centurion wasn't anything a primus would send in first. Leeson could have been placed in charge, as he was the senior adjunct, but Graves didn't have the utmost confidence in him.

A ragged cheer went up from my unit. I'd delivered good news, and I'd made it sound like I'd negotiated on their behalf. They were perking up now, looking interested. They all felt they deserved a reward after having suffered the day before.

"Whatever we face down there, be it man or alien, we're going to win! Know that in your hearts, and it will come true!"

I ended there, and a few shouts of "Varus!" rang out. They weren't all that enthusiastic, however. I'd made sure to end with talk of an unknown enemy.

It seemed to work. People began speculating among themselves about what we would have to deal with down there instead of giving me sullen glances. They weren't thinking of me being AWOL any longer. They were worrying about what they might soon discover crawling and humping over the hot sands of Blood World. That was just where I wanted their minds to be: in the game.

The lifter came down with a plunging finish. I was proud to see not a single member of my unit flipped up his visor to puke. If that wasn't proof we were professionals, I don't know what would be.

The big ramp went down, cracking to let in a blazing orange line first, then yawning wide. Like a dragon's mouth, the lifter released a vast rush of troops.

Two full units of light troops led the charge. They scattered fast, setting up wide lines to cover the rest of us. My unit came out sixth, well to the rear. It was a pleasure not to be expecting death from the first minute.

Slamming gauntlets like drumbeats, Sargon and the other vets shouted until they were hoarse. They all but chased our unit toward the south. When we got to our deployment rally point, we realized our asses were pressed up against the back wall of the crater.

"That's both good and bad," Leeson said, walking up to me. "We can't get hit in the tailpipe—but we can't retreat, either."

"Right," I said, studying the cliffs.

In my mind and the minds of the others, we were thinking of our last struggle in this crater. The lizards had started throwing shots at us right away. There hadn't been much breathing room. We naturally assumed today might be fought in a similar fashion.

But it didn't play out that way.

"What in the nine hells of Rigel is that?" Leeson called out, pointing into the sky to the west.

We all looked, and we watched a hulking ship lift off. It was a weird one. Visible flames shot out of undercarriage. The engines, whatever else they were, couldn't be called "clean" by any stretch of the imagination.

A massive blast of black smoke roiled across the crater.

"Kivi?" I called out. "Analysis: is that vapor toxic?"

"Just a second..."

She got out her computer and her optical scope and connected the two. The scope swiveled around like a goose's head on the end of a long neck and studied the cloud.

"It's toxic, but not deadly. Not enough acid to eat through anything… It's basically particulate exhaust. Some radiation, but not too much."

"Looks like something that would come off a tire fire," I said. "All right, everyone should keep their helmets sealed just in case."

We began to dig in then. We had two pigs with us—big drones with stumpy legs and loud engines. They buzzed and thumped the sand. Shovels descended, and they edged forward, plowing up trench lines in seconds.

The second the trenches were dug, my troops jumped in. They widened the trenches, throwing all the dirt up in the direction of that strange enemy ship to form a berm to shoot over.

In the meantime, I walked over to Harris. He was one of the most senior troops in the cohort, and he'd seen three times as many planets as I had.

"Harris, what did you make of that ship?"

"Pretty strange."

"No recognition? Nothing tugging at your memory?"

"Nothing," he said, shaking his head. "Kind of strange…"

"What do you mean?"

"Well, I've seen all sorts of Imperial transports, and I'd bet my last credit that contraption wasn't built by anyone from Frontier 921. I doubt it was from the Core Systems, either."

Squinting at him, I made a decision. It was time to contact Graves.

The primus was online, of course. I had the text stream option going on command chat for the whole cohort. His lines were the most common, if not the longest running.

"McGill?" he answered privately. "What is it?"

"Any ID on that ship yet?"

"Negative. No tech in the cohort has a listing for that configuration in their knowledge base. They're puzzling it out, but the pervading theory is that since the Skrull lost their exclusive license to build ships, some other race might have developed their own lifters."

"Hmm," I said, "Harris thinks it isn't from this province. He's convinced it isn't Imperial, or even knock-off Imperial."

Graves hesitated. "He might be right. Keep your eyes peeled. As everyone knows from the briefing you missed this morning, the plan is to kick-off on the defensive. We have no idea what we're facing, so we'll let them throw the first punch."

I didn't like the plan, but I could hardly complain now. I was stuck with it.

Graves signed off, and we went back to digging and setting up defenses. Kivi and the techs deployed a string of defensive drones and auto-turrets in front of our position. Leeson's 88s were set up in makeshift puff-crete bunkers, and troops were laying their rifles over humps of dirt all along the line.

It was Della, in the end, who sounded the alarm.

She was a Dust Worlder, and that meant she was the final word in paranoia. While the rest of us were looking forward to where the enemy ship had taken off a half hour ago, she was looking everywhere else.

"McGill!" she called into my helmet. "They're behind us!"

I spun around, staring at the tall cliff-like walls of the crater. The walls were a hundred meters high, made of reddish clay and crumbling stone. I didn't see a thing.

"Della?" I called back. "State your position! Mark the enemy if you have a bead on them!"

Nothing. Not a word came back.

My eyes flicked down to Della's name, which was lit up inside my helmet to indicate she was the one in contact with me.

Her name was as red as fresh blood. Della had been killed.

## -45-

Della meant a lot me as she was the mother of my only child Etta.

Sure, we didn't always get along. The first time we'd met, she'd killed me—the second time too, as I recalled.

But all that aside, it was a personal affront to me that someone—or something—had managed to sneak around behind us and nail one of my best scouts without even showing their nose.

"SNIPER!" I shouted on tactical chat. That reached pretty far, at least to the units setting up camp ahead of us and to our right.

Naturally, I had no idea if it had been a sniper or not. But if you want to get a couple of hundred heads turning in an alert fashion right now, there's no better announcement you can make.

While my unit ducked and looked around every whichway, guns at the ready, I contacted Graves.

"Contact sir!" I said. "One troop down. She said they were behind us. That's all I know so far."

"McGill? Switch to audio on command chat."

He disconnected, and I did as he'd ordered. Immediately, a flood of reports began coming in.

The information was confusing. The enemy was reported to be on the walls of the crater itself, or maybe buried in the dirt at our feet. Whatever the case, a dozen soldiers had already been taken out with no confirmed sightings on our side.

"All right Centurions, listen up," Graves said. "We're facing a sneaky enemy. Locate your dead, mark the spots for everyone, and we'll see if we have a pattern."

We did so quickly. There was an option to select any red name and highlight it. Everyone in my unit or the rest of the cohort could see where Della had died. She had indeed been on the crater wall.

"Harris!" I shouted. "Take a squad of lights and patrol that wall. Watch your six, these guys are sneaky!"

"Yes sir! Thank you for this golden opportunity, sir!"

I ignored his veiled complaints. Harris never liked to do his job. You'd have thought he was born behind a desk.

"More like a golden shower," Carlos said, laughing at my side.

"Specialist? What are you doing away from your post?"

"I've been ordered to inspect the casualty, sir."

I glanced Toro's way. She was hunkered down in the trenches with the top of her helmet barely visible. It was just like her to send a lone bio out to take a sample. Then again, maybe Carlos had been pissing her off all day.

"Carry on," I told him, and he ran off toward the crater wall.

Before he even got there, snap-rifle fire erupted. Harris and his troops had fanned out and were walking along the bare slopes of the crater. They were shooting at something up-close, but I was damned if I could make out what it was.

"Harris! Report!" I shouted.

But he went down before he could come back with a word. I squinted, not sure what I'd seen. His light troops were backing up, wildly spraying the sand all around them. It was as if they were shooting at the air.

In rapid succession, more light troops were cut down. I stared. Blood was everywhere. They'd been sliced in half, most of them. Cut from chin to crotch. Blood sprayed, turning black when it welded with the hot sands.

"...stealth..." that single word had rasped its way out of Harris' throat. "Invisible... mothers..."

"Leeson!" I roared. "Sweep that crater wall with the 88s! Slag all that sand to glass, *now*!"

Startled, Leeson began shouting orders. He spun his twin light artillery pieces around and released uneven gouts of energy.

Our retinas burned with the dazzling light. As big and hot as Epsilon Leporis was in the sky above, the big guns were brighter.

Harris' squad was all down by the time the beams rolled over them, and if they weren't already dead, it was probably a painless blessing to finish them off.

What was interesting, however, was the series of white explosions that rippled as our 88s burned the open sand. At first, I thought maybe we'd found some buried mines and set them off—but then the white puffs of vapor dissipated, and I realized they'd been steam.

"Keep going!" I ordered. "Burn them off."

In the end, we melted down twenty-two bodies on that crater wall. I was gratified to note that a solid third of them weren't human.

"Toro! Get your heavies out of that hole and advance!"

With some reluctance, she got her platoon moving. They poked around in the ashes and crunched on the slag, but I could tell they were nervous. When a pocket of steam whiffed up from one body, a heavy skittered back like he'd wet his armor.

"Report!"

Carlos was the one that called back in. He had balls when it counted. Kneeling over one of the burnt bodies of the enemy, he gave me what he could, including a vid feed from his body cam.

"They're melted down instead of turned to ash completely," he said. "I'd guess these creatures have a higher water-content than humans. I'd say they weigh more too—a couple hundred kilos."

"What kind of weapons do you see?"

"Um... swords? That's what I'm seeing. Metal blades at least a meter long. The way the human remains look, I'd say the edges are molecularly aligned to be super-sharp."

"Why the hell would an enemy with a sophisticated stealth suit carry a sword?"

Kivi jumped in then, she'd been listening in as were many in my unit.

"I'd have to guess that other types of weapons would give them away. Maybe if they fired a gun while stealthed our sensors could pinpoint them."

Her theory did explain how they'd managed to stalk us without being noticed for so long.

After reporting all this to Graves, he relayed some details to the rest of the cohort, then he came back online with me.

"You turned the 88s on them?" he asked. "That was a good response. Those wide beams are inescapable. Have your techs set up every form of sensor you've got? Something has to work."

I relayed that order, but I didn't have much hope. We'd already deployed motion sensors, optical beams and even sonics. The enemy had slipped through it all.

Worse, they'd managed to take down an average of twenty troops in each of our units along the back of the crater. We'd lost nearly a hundred men, and we'd only killed a handful of them. In some cases, the stealthers had escaped without a single loss.

My eyes turned toward the west. Out there, that's where they were now, plotting their next move. Clearly, this first attack had been a test. They hadn't committed their full forces. Estimates were that as few as fifty had done all this damage.

We were in a war of attrition, and so far, they were slightly ahead.

## -46-

A transmission came into my helmet about fifteen minutes after I'd talked to Graves about the stealthers. Since the emblem showed the caller was a primus, I assumed that Graves was calling me again.

But it wasn't Graves.

"McGill?" Winslade's voice said in my ear. "Is this *really* Centurion James McGill?"

"Uh... yes sir. What can I do for you, Primus?"

"You can stay dead, that's what. I don't understand how you managed to catch a revive at all, much less how you got down to Blood World again."

"It's good to hear your voice as well, sir."

"McGill..." he said, "I saw your name on the rosters just moments ago, and at first I flew into a rage. Now that I've recovered, I'm calling to make you an offer."

"Glad you're feeling better, sir. What kind of a trade are we talking about?"

"Your existence will be permitted to continue for a small amount of effort. I know cooperation doesn't come naturally to you, but perhaps your self-preservation instincts will overcome your natural proclivities."

"I don't know, sir..." I said thoughtfully. "My instincts are notoriously bad."

"Indeed. Let me spell it out for you: if you want to get out of the revival queue in good time on your next go-around, you'll lose this contest. Let the Vulbites win."

"The Vulbites? What the hell are Vulbites?"

"Seriously? You people *still* haven't managed to identify your opponents? I'm disappointed in Graves."

"Well sir, I don't know beans about Vulbites, but I have no intention of losing this fight. You do realize that every living Earther on this planet has to die to make that happen, right?"

"Of course I do. But death is merely an inconvenience for Varus legionnaires. I'm shocked you would whine about it. What's important now is making sure Varus does *not* proceed to the final round."

"Ah…" I said, starting to catch on at last. "You're trying to fix the game, aren't you? Let's pretend I'm interested. How am I supposed to throw this battle? I'm only in command of one unit out of ten, you know."

"Expand your mind," he said. "Imagine—just for a moment—that you're not the only officer upon who's neck I have a functioning lever."

I frowned. I didn't like the sound of this at all. If Winslade was going up against Turov, well, anything could happen.

"You're talking treason, sir," I said. "You're aware of that, aren't you? What you're suggesting is the worst kind of treachery against your own species!"

He sucked in a breath and let it out in an exasperated sigh.

"No it isn't, you imbecile. I want Earth to win this game in the end—probably more than you do. The trouble is that I don't trust the script as it is written. These Blood Worlders are gullible, but there's a limit. How can they watch two human legions struggling in the final heat and not realize the game was rigged from the start? Our opponents are sure to protest."

"Oh that," I said. "You mean Germanica is winning their fights too? I'm surprised. I haven't seen them fight a single battle in this pit, and none of our observing techs have seen it, either."

"That's because more than one arena exists. There's a similar crater on the far side of the planet—but wait a moment… How did you know Germanica was involved?"

"Well, it stands to reason. Armel's army of wimps did take second place back at Central."

"Yes... but I smell a rat, here. A two-meter tall rat with an inflated sense of self-worth."

"You'd best catch him fast. Rats will tear up an attic—even the wires in your tram, sometimes."

"Enough with your embarrassing sense of humor. Will you obey me or not?"

"Tribune Deech is supposed to be running this legion. Why don't you revive her and have her talk to me?"

"Again you express your loyalty to false gods. At least you're consistent, McGill. Deech will stay dead until this entire affair is at an end. You'd best remember that before you consider crossing me."

"Hmm..." I said. After a moment's thought, I did what came most naturally to me: I lied. "I'm going to go with you on this one, Winslade. Sure, I owe you a trip through the revival machine—but I'll play your game anyway. What do you want me to do, shoot Graves behind the ear?"

"No, no! Nothing so crude and direct, please. Just improvise as you go and stop killing Vulbites effectively. They'll go on to the final and face Armel. At that point, their fates will be sealed. Agreed?"

"Uh-huh. Have a nice day, sir."

I moved to disconnect, but the call had already ended. Winslade was like that. Sometimes it seemed like he was in a race to end a call first.

Frowning, I stared at the battlefield. We still hadn't seen the enemy we were up against. They were like ghosts out there on the cracked sands.

Kivi sauntered up to me and looked me up and down.

"Who was that?" she asked, pointing at my arm.

"What? You saw me look at my tapper? Can't a man play a bit of porn to relax?"

She put her hands on her ample hips.

"That call wasn't from Graves. It was from the ship. Who was it?"

That was the trouble with techs, especially the extra-nosy ones like Kivi.

"Wrong number," I said, turning away. I surveyed the battlefield while she wandered off, frowning.

Her radar was up, and that meant other people were watching me, too. How did Primus Winslade expect me to get everybody killed if they were suspecting me already?

Graves began talking over command chat then, and this time he was talking to all his officers.

"Commanders, we've got to get into this game. I don't see any point to sitting here on the defensive any longer. That didn't work the first time, and every minute we wait gives the enemy more time to plan out the perfect stealth assault."

I felt my heart sink. I figured I knew where he was going with this idea.

"We're going to mount an offensive," he continued. "Assemble a full platoon from every unit. Advance, seek and destroy. Stay close, but don't hump each other. This enemy must be flushed out into the open. You've got five minutes until go-time. Set your tappers and don't disappoint. Graves out."

A general assault? To me, it seemed like a worst-case move. Like something a World War I general would have come up with and transmitted down to the men in the trenches.

On the bright side, maybe we'd lose because of it. Then I could pretend I'd gone along with the plan to make Winslade happy later.

## -47-

My first instinct was to send out the light troopers to run like rabbits. The trouble with that was Harris was stone dead, and so were most of his troops.

"I want to make a mixed squad up front," I announced. "Leeson, you're in command. Keep those 88s alive and ready to sweep out any surprise attackers we run into. Toro, you're coming with me. We'll take all the remaining lights and one squad of your heavies—oh, and give me Sargon too, Leeson."

"Sargon? He's my best man on the artillery!"

"Stop complaining," Toro retorted angrily. "You've been sipping tea in a trench."

"Unprofessional, people," I told them.

They did shut up, but I knew it was only temporary. I'm not sure if it was my leadership style, or the fact that Varus had always attracted complainers, but it did seem like my supporting officers were never fully satisfied.

A few minutes later a tone rang out of our tappers, and we charged onto the open field. Advancing into the blowing dust—there was a wind up now—I felt edgy. These stealthers could be anywhere.

We marched a full kilometer before anything happened. That's when the unit on our flank ran into trouble.

"Contact!" a cry came over tactical chat.

My helmet said the call had been relayed from another platoon about two hundred meters north. We had no visual on them, as there was an intervening outcropping of boulders.

"Let's take the high ground," I said, jogging toward the boulders. "Lights, sweep the perimeter of these rocks. Kivi, set up some buzzers."

"They're not detecting anything."

"Well, mark the dead from 4th Unit then. That should clue us in to where the action is."

She trotted ahead of me with the lights, and I moved with Toro's heavies in the wake of the faster troops. Toro came to my side.

"This is crazy," she said. "What the hell are we doing splitting our force and coming at a stealthed enemy piecemeal? It's like Graves *wants* to lose this battle."

My step faltered. I looked at her then I spun around, facing back toward our lines, toward Graves in his central spot behind 5th Unit.

"You've got a point there..." I said. "Everybody, hug these rocks!"

We swarmed the wide hump-shaped boulders and crouched on them. From one point of view, we were sitting ducks up there. But if the enemy wasn't using ranged weapons, they'd have to come uphill to get to us.

The scene on the open ground ahead was a mess. Two platoons were out there, fighting ghosts. Sometimes they got someone, and a wet spot burst into view. But just as often, a trooper was cut down by an invisible meat cleaver.

"Light troops, sniper-mode!" I ordered. "Get to the top of these rocks and pick a man. If he seems engaged, fire at the ground right in front of him."

They scrambled up and began taking potshots.

"Heavies," I said, "sling rifles, extend force-blades. Poke at every shadow, leaf or—"

A scream rang out. It was Kivi. She was down at the bottom rung of our rock pile, setting up sensors. She'd been hit, and her arm was off at the shoulder.

But she was a Varus girl, through and through. Shock might come in time, but for right now, she was pissed off. She had out a knife and advanced, slashing ahead of herself wildly, blindly.

Without being told, several of my troops fired bursts around her. A Vulbite popped like a water balloon, and I rushed to the spot.

Carlos was at my side, working on Kivi.

"She's lost a lot of blood," Carlos said, "but with a good spray-down, she might be able to function."

"Don't worry," I told him. "I'm not offing anyone. We've got no revival machines in this crater. We're going to die hard, every last one of us."

While Kivi panted and groaned, Carlos sprayed nu-skin like there was no tomorrow. A coating of fresh pink cells grew over her stump, adhering to her suit, her hair—everything. Now was not the time for finesse.

In the meantime, I squatted over the Vulbite. It was my first good look at the enemy as we'd crisped most of the others to ash.

Slicing open his silver, rumpled suit, I saw a mess inside. It was... bug-like.

"I hate bugs," Kivi said. "Especially big bugs."

"Looks like a centipede," Carlos said. "But with a wet carapace. Man-sized, wet skin... I'd say this is some kind of aquatic or semi-aquatic creature."

"Like a frog?" I asked.

"Sort of. It probably lives in a swamp, anyway."

The thing had curved mandibles. They looked like fangs with fingers at the end. Bulbous black eyes glistened above that horror-show mouth.

"Damn," I said, "I thought I knew ugly until I saw this thing."

A few more attacked our line, but with heavies wielding force-blades and lights backing them up at range, the enemy didn't fare too well. Vulbite's often got in close and nailed a trooper, but the swords didn't always pierce the heavy armor. If that initial surprise attack didn't kill the trooper outright, they were doomed as force-blades slashed laterally where they had to be standing. Cut down in the middle of their segmented bodies, the Vulbites didn't live more than a few seconds after that.

In case Graves was interested, I relayed my vids including effective tactics to HQ. It didn't take long after that for him to contact me directly.

"That's good work, McGill. Your platoon is doing better than most."

"Maybe that's because you marched us into a slaughter on purpose."

Graves didn't answer immediately, but at last he sighed.

"Winslade talked to you too, huh?"

"That's right, Primus. I'm surprised you listened to that weasel."

"McGill, not everyone thinks like you do—not even in Legion Varus, the most independent-minded outfit in Earth history."

"Sir, Winslade killed Deech. Are you aware of that fact?"

"Is this rumor or what?"

"I was there, sir. I was in her office. Claver was there too."

"Claver? Are you serious?"

"Yes sir. As God is my witness, this is a plot of some kind."

Graves sighed again. "Let's say I decide to believe you, Centurion. Even if you did just wander in late from a tawdry night in Engineering."

I released a puff of air. "Sir, I *died* yesterday aboard ship. You caught me returning fresh after an unsanctioned revive, not a night of glory."

"And how did you get out of that queue at the revival machine if Deech didn't? Never mind—don't answer that. I don't want to know. Since we're laying our cards on the table, I'll give you a piece of information from Floramel: she says these stealth suits aren't something to be expected from Vulbites. They don't have much in the way of advanced tech."

"Huh..." I said thoughtfully. "That kind of makes sense. Their drop-ship looked kind of low-rent now that you mention it."

"Exactly. Let's talk about our current situation. Winslade was legally declared Deech's exec. We're honor-bound to follow his orders."

"That's why she's staying dead."

"Regardless, he's legally in charge of this legion. Even if we wanted to arrest him, he's up on *Nostrum*, and we're stuck here in a blood-soaked crater."

"Yeah…" I admitted. "We have to solve that problem first. Here's my idea…"

I began to outline my strategy, and Graves listened. By the end, he was chuckling.

It did me a world of good to hear his spirits had been uplifted.

## -48-

After ordering us to pull back from our first disastrous offensive, Graves reorganized our units. Some platoons were down to ten or less men, and they were folded into other groups to get them up to full strength. By the end of this effort, we had seven units that could fight with near one hundred percent effectiveness.

It was kind of an unusual situation for a Varus force to have to deal with. Generally, after we took heavy casualties, we'd sit back and take a break until our troops trickled back in from the revival machines—but we didn't have any of those to rely on this time.

Using weaponeers on the front line of our force, Graves ordered them to crank open the apertures on their belchers to maximum dispersal. Set up that way, they were about as effective as flame-throwers. They couldn't punch through armor, but they could still burn wide swaths of territory.

At the side of each weaponeer on the front line, we had regular troops with guns at the ready. If the belchers lit up a target, everyone had been ordered to blow it down.

The system worked like a charm at first. We advanced slowly, our front line being about three hundred infantry strong. Behind that, we brought everyone. There was no point leaving people behind in holes. Non-combatants dragged 88s in the center of the mob. Our rear guard was made up of a few more weaponeers and heavies with force-blades extended.

"Contact!" boomed a deep voice up ahead. It was one of our weaponeers, a man named Eric Roth.

Ahead of him, the target was obvious. Even when you're invisible, getting hit by a heavy beam that's burning at around five hundred degrees centigrade hurts. The enemy transformed into steaming explosions. Alerted, our troops hosed them down with small-arms fire.

We must have killed a hundred Vulbites that way without a loss on our side. They came at us, to be sure, from the front and flanks, even at the rear of our line. But as soon as they were within about a hundred meter range, they were spotted and gunned down.

"That's the trouble with these sneaky guys," Roth said with joy in his heart. "They have to get in real close to do any damage. This is working great!"

I should have told Eric not to jinx it. Not to brag so hard that the lords of fate decided they'd had enough—but I wasn't sure if he'd have listened to such defeatist prattle out of me anyway.

Things changed about when we'd made it halfway across the field. I was impressed to think the enemy had had time to consider our tactic and respond to it so quickly.

All of a sudden, the ground at our feet exploded. Vulbites sprang up out of the ground, hissing and slashing with their overly-long swords.

One did so within a meter of me. It was a shock. One second, there'd been a lot of laughing, happy troops around—feeling an early certainty of victory. The next, a dark patch of sand had exploded, and a blade was flashing.

The sword nearly got me. An overhanded chop came down, shaving off an epaulet of my armor. If I'd been a light trooper or a tech—well, it would have been all over. The monster would have lopped off a quarter of my body—from collarbone to pelvis on the left side.

But as it was, I caught nothing more than a close shave. The blade took off my shoulder armor on the left side, exposing skin and flesh to the searing dry heat of the atmosphere pouring into my suit.

The skin of my shoulder and about a quarter inch of muscle had been shaved away as well, leaving a patch a good ten by ten centimeters across that was exposed and bloody.

My left arm didn't work right after that, neither the flesh part nor the exoskeletal power-assist.

Deciding now wasn't the time to worry about flesh-wounds, I drilled the Vulbite with my morph-rifle at point-blank range. I pretty much put the muzzle against his midsection and let her rip. The Vulbite was shredded and fell, squirming.

Doing a quick rotation, I took stock of the situation. All around me were struggling forms. By lying in wait underground, they'd managed to get into our midst where their swords weren't such a disadvantage.

Hustling, I joined a hundred other survivors to help people put down their attackers. The work was messy. We lost a hundred, and they'd lost the same by my estimation.

Kivi was one of the unlucky ones. She'd survived the initial surprise swing, but her Vulbite had wrapped itself around her body and squeezed, biting through her thin armor. Nearby troops shot them both, and the Vulbite died with fangs sunk into her neck.

"Dammit," I complained. "Graves!"

"What is it, McGill?"

"Should we pull back? Regroup?"

"Are you kidding? We're winning by two to one at least. We're already on an even footing with these Vulbites. If we press the advantage, we'll break them soon."

I looked at the centipede-thing wrapped around Kivi.

"I don't know, sir," I said. "These things are bugs. They don't seem to get scared and run off. At least, I've never seen it happen yet."

"Get your head in the game, McGill. Regroup, improvise and press ahead. We're winning this right now."

Reluctantly, I called my shrunken unit back together, and we marched onward.

We were on their turf now, past the half-way point in the middle of the crater.

We continued advancing until I spotted something ahead, something that gave me a good reason to pause.

"Unit halt!" I shouted.

Graves didn't take long to notice my section of the formation was falling behind the rest. "McGill? What are you doing out there?"

"I'm forwarding you the vid feed from my optics, sir," I said, and did so.

An officer had a different kit than the standard issue for a grunt. My gear had longer range vision and more options than a helmet worn by the average man on the line. That was because people with too many gizmos tended to play with them instead of focusing on completing their mission.

"Well..." Graves said, "I'll be damned. Is that a human out there? A human woman?"

"Yes sir. And I'd say she's like Floramel—a genetically bred science type."

"Of course..." Graves said. "That's why this bug culture that can barely build a drop-ship has incredible stealth technology. Someone gave it to them."

"This contest does seem to be full of cheaters, sir."

"Take her out."

"Excuse me, Primus?"

"You've got light troopers left. You've got line of sight. Kill her."

"Um..."

"Are you feeling bad again, McGill? She's not supposed to be in this pit. She's cheating, you said it yourself."

"So I did," I agreed with a sigh.

I reached out and snagged the snap-rifle from a dead recruit's body nearby. Forcing my bad arm to operate, I lifted the butt to my shoulder, sighted—then stopped before I pulled the trigger.

The woman out there was easily visible through the scope on the sniper rifle.

But there was more. At her feet, I saw the unmistakable shapes of a dozen or so smaller creatures.

Tiny limbs, leering eyes—they were gremlins.

*Pop! Pop! Pop!*

I fired my snap-rifle. Three gremlins did backflips and scrabbled in the dust, dying.

The woman got up from her knees, alarmed. I stood up and approached, changing my helmet's external speakers to maximum volume. That was pretty loud, as an officer's kit was meant to be heard a couple hundred meters away.

My helmet buzzed.

"McGill?" Graves said in my ear. "I'm watching you. I sense you're going AWOL again. Is that right?"

"Sir," I told him, "please have a little faith. Give me a few minutes. I'm going to try some diplomacy."

"Diplomacy? Are you out of your mind?"

"Maybe sir. Maybe. Just give me a few minutes, and all our troubles might be over."

I closed the connection before he could answer. Sometimes that worked—at least for a few minutes.

"Gytha!" I shouted, because I'd recognized the woman in the midst of those gremlin bastards. "Gytha, surrender now, or I'll put you down!"

Startled, my own men stood and followed me. Most of them hadn't spotted the cheaters yet. They weren't kitted for long-range vision, and after all the surprise attacks their attention had been focused on repelling the next wave of Vulbites that might be sneaking close even now.

At last, Gytha spotted me.

She was no soldier. I could tell that right off. A trained fighter's instinct would have been to hit the dirt—but instead, she'd stood tall and looked for who was calling her name.

"Stand down!" I shouted at her. "Surrender!"

"How?" she asked.

"Put your hands up! Put them on your head and lace your fingers together."

She did so, moving slowly. She looked bewildered and angry.

As I approached, I did my best to keep her in my sights. I saw her face, her eyes. She was just as pretty as Floramel, but with darker features. I hoped I wouldn't have to kill her. If I fired, she'd probably be permed.

Her eyes flicked down to her sides. I saw her give a tiny nod.

The gremlins saw her nod, and they moved to obey her.

## -49-

Halting and sliding the scope from side to side, I saw them now. A dozen or more. They had devices in their hands, and they were manipulating them.

"Unit halt!" I shouted. "Unit withdraw slowly!"

But it was too late. The gremlins, seeing that we were pulling back, activated their devices.

All around me, a dozen nozzles sprang up. They began pumping out gas. A moment later, there was a spark.

My troops were in full retreat. I fired sporadically at the gremlins and Gytha—even though I couldn't see her any longer.

The gas ignited. It was some kind of aerogel, an airborne explosive.

A terrific ripping sound tore through the air, reverberating off the distant crater walls. Small avalanches were triggered, and a massive cloud of dust swirled into the sky.

My unit was hit hard. We'd been killing Vulbites right and left, but now, with this underhanded maneuver, our fortunes had been reversed.

"Dammit!" I shouted, letting my helmet carry my voice to whoever would listen. "Gytha, you're nothing but a red-handed cheater!"

Quiet prevailed for a short time. But at last, over the groaning of the wounded, the crackling of fires that were still burning here and there, I heard a faint cry come back.

"You cheated first!"

Hmm... That was a shocker.

She was right, of course. Sort of.

"Truce!" I called out. "Let's talk for a minute!"

Another brief period of quiet ensued. But at last, I got my reply.

"I saw how your truce went with the saurians!"

*Damn*! She had me again.

Sighing, I felt there was nothing for it. I had to take a chance.

Stripping off my helmet and dropping my gun, I ripped loose a shred of my shirt through the damage in my armor, under my wrecked epaulet. It wasn't all white, there was drying bloodstains on it. But I figured it would do.

Walking forward into the desolation of dead and dying, I marched toward her, toward the spot where I'd last seen her.

When I topped a rise, I found about two dozen gremlins crouching and peering up at me. They snarled and showed their teeth. Their eyes were slitted like angry cats.

In their midst was Gytha. She, like Floramel, seemed to be treated like a goddess by the gremlins. They shifted uncomfortably around her, as if she was sacred and I was some kind of offensive being from the abyss.

Vulbites were there too, watching. They were further off, shifting in and out of their cloaked state. The bag-like stealth garments they wore could apparently be turned on or off at will.

"Gytha?" I asked, and she came forward warily.

"What do you want, human? What evil trick is this?"

"No trick this time. When I killed Claver before, we had agreed that he should die. He's alive now, revived on our ship."

She cocked her head and walked around in the low part of her shallow refuge.

"You didn't shoot me. You shot the homunculi around me—but not me. Why?"

I didn't answer instantly, because I had to think about it. I had been shooting for her, in reality. Firing blindly as I pulled back. If a round had struck her—well, we wouldn't be having this conversation.

But that reality wouldn't buy me any favors, I was pretty sure of that much.

"It's not right for one leader to shoot another by surprise," I lied. "How can there be any discussion if one or the other is dead?"

Gytha nodded slowly, seeming to accept this particular line of bullshit.

It was about then that I realized she was very suspicious—but in the wrong way. She expected me to make a physical move on her. To try to slay her whenever I was able to do so.

That was a very reasonable fear, but she didn't seem to equally appreciate the threat of guile. Sometimes, words are better than bullets when they're applied by a talented man.

"So," she said at last, "what is it that you'd like to talk about, leader of Earth?"

That made me pause again, but only for a moment. I decided it was time to let all pretenses fall to the wayside. I wasn't going to give her any more breaks.

"You figured it out then? That I'm in charge of Earth—of all humanity?"

"Of course, and I'm glad you're not bothering to deny it. We're not fools here on Blood World."

"Clearly, I underestimated you folks."

"Something you do at your peril!"

About then Graves began bombing my tapper. He was doubtlessly wondering what the hell I was doing out here. Armor suits had extensions that docked with a man's organic tapper, giving a similar interface on the inside of the left forearm.

It kept blinking, but I turned my left arm away from Gytha so she wouldn't notice.

Gytha walked around, fuming. "You treat us like children," she complained. "That's been the most galling thing about you basics. But to answer your question, your real rank was obvious after I carefully considered the evidence. As you must realize, we've received vid reports from our initial attacks on your ship."

"Naturally we knew about that," I said, lying harder every second.

"Your subterfuge was poorly done. Every time we struggled with your people, McGill was there. When our force took Gold Deck—you freed it. When the final assault came against Engineering—you were there again."

"Uh-huh," I said. "I guess I got cocky."

"You took it to the point of insult when the charade continued here on our homeworld. McGill? Alone in the first contest? Leading the second? Then claiming after all of that to be a subordinate in the third? I don't think so!"

"My apologies. The essence of warfare is to keep the other guy guessing."

"Excuses for dishonor are in and of themselves dishonorable."

I thought about apologizing, but I was betting she wouldn't think much of that, either. Hers was a warrior culture, after all. She looked like Floramel, but she was an entirely different stripe of nerd.

"The gall of it!" she went on. "You called a long list of fools your master! Winslade, Deech, Graves—one absurdity after another! Leaders *lead*, they don't sit back and talk! It's insulting that you believed we could be so easily fooled."

All I did was nod. Smart people really liked to be right about everything. I found the easiest way to trick them was by admitting their deepest suspicions had been correct all along.

"Okay then," I said when she'd wound down some, "where does that leave us right now? We've killed a lot of people in this crater today. Was it all a waste?"

"Not at all. We're learning about you basics, and you're learning about us. You hold life in small regard because you can recreate it. We hold life with even less regard because we're true warriors."

"Yeah..." I said, not totally following her logic. "Let's talk about your cheating in this contest—"

"NO!" she shouted suddenly, taking a few threatening steps toward me.

Behind her, like dogs who'd been waiting for this signal, every Vulbite and gremlin surged with her. I realized if she even ran toward me, they'd all join in. It was like dealing with a wolf pack where she was the alpha.

Fortunately, she turned away and began stalking around her shelter in a circle, looking pissed.

"Um... what did I say—" I began.

"*You* are the cheaters! You basics are the *worst*! The Cephalopods were chivalrous in comparison! We always knew where we stood with them. They were masters, we were slaves. Clarity was always maintained."

"I get it," I said, becoming annoyed. "It's okay for you to cheat—but not us. That's what you're saying, isn't it?"

Gytha narrowed her eyes at me. "I don't like you. I don't understand how Floramel could let herself serve a basic at all."

It was my turn to be suspicious. "That's it then, isn't it? You're looking for a master—but you don't really want it to be us. Earth men aren't good enough to serve?"

"No," she said. "We've seen your kind many times before. We were once—according to legend—like you. But no longer. You're weak. You're a race of natural slaves. You aren't our brothers. We'd prefer to serve another."

"I see..." I said, thinking about it.

The Cephalopod Kingdom had created this place about a century ago—maybe longer. They'd brought humans from Dust World as breeding stock. They probably abducted humans before that to kick off the colony.

From Gytha's point of view, these captured humans that were brought here from time to time must have seemed weak. They were, after all, the ones the squids had been able to catch. They hadn't been genetically altered and trained to serve as dogs of war.

The squids had kept bringing them in to supply fresh genes which were needed to stabilize the herd. But Gytha and the others had never seen Earth's best.

"Ah..." I said as if I'd come to a great conclusion—which I sort of had. "I get it now! You're talking about Dust Worlders!"

Gytha's eyes were slits again. "What are you saying?"

I laughed. "Don't you see? Those people were captured slaves. Cast-offs. Losers who couldn't fight properly to defend themselves. We counted ourselves lucky every time those big ships came down and carted some of them away. They weren't even worth feeding, if the truth were to be told."

Della would have pulled a knife on me if she could have heard what I was saying about her people, but fortunately, she'd died hours ago.

Gytha stared into the distance. "That's very interesting..." she said. "I can almost believe it... The circumstances fit... The weak are captured, the strong remain. You've shown you can fight. You've shown you're strong..."

I didn't say a damned word. When your opponent is making your argument for you, that's always the best policy.

She looked at me suddenly, with a different light in her eyes.

"Perhaps we've made a serious error," she said.

"How so?"

"We've rigged the game. Earth can't win."

"Hmm..." I said. "Then you're right. We've got a big problem."

"We didn't think we wanted to serve you," Gytha told me. "You have to understand that."

"Oh, I get that part all right. You screwed up."

She glared at me.

My wrist was flashing again, so I answered this time. I figured that if I didn't, Graves might well launch an attack.

"McGill here!" I said in a cheery tone.

"McGill!? Why aren't you answering your tapper, dammit?"

Gytha shook her head and paced. "You can tell him to stop pretending you're his slave. It's an insult."

"Graves," I said sternly, "I'm in the middle of an important negotiation. If you want to win this contest—I'm talking all the way to the end of it—you'll stop interrupting and give me more time."

He was silent for a few angry seconds. "Fine. But if she ends up pregnant, McGill, the legion isn't paying the bill. You hear me?"

"McGill out," I said, shutting down the connection.

"What was that?" Gytha asked. "What did he say to you?"

"Something disrespectful. I shall punish him severely when I return."

Gytha nodded, seeming to accept this.

"I can end this contest," she said. "You have the upper hand. The audience is watching, but discussion isn't entirely unknown to us. They're bored by it, but they'll accept it."

"Uh…" I said, "okay, that sounds pretty good. Varus will go on to the final match-up, right? And there we'll face another legion of Earth—we know about that, by the way."

She flapped her hand unconcernedly. "Of course you do. Earth set it up."

"Er… right. Anyway, Earth will fight Earth, and no matter who wins Blood World will serve us. How can there be a problem?"

Gytha laughed at me. I hadn't heard her laugh before. It was kind of a sexy laugh.

"Please don't play the fool any longer," she said. "I don't know why you bother. Does it bring you some kind of pleasure?"

"Just explain the problem, as you see it."

She shrugged and paced. "You. You are the problem."

Now, I can attest that any number of women had told me that. It was practically a mantra for a girlfriend of mine around about the fifth week of dating. But in this case, I was baffled by Gytha's meaning.

Accordingly, I sat quietly until she explained it to me.

She heaved a sigh. "You can't lose the battle," she said. "Maybe you honestly don't realize that. You *must* win—Varus must win. But at the same time, Germanica must win. It's an impossible situation."

"Uh…" I said. "Because I'm Earth's leader?"

"Exactly. You really don't understand? Are Earthers so very different? My people won't follow a loser. They all know who you are—they're not fooled. So, if Germanica wins, that means you must personally die in this arena along with all of Varus. The Blood World populace will have just witnessed

Earth's warlord perishing. They'll never follow Earth after that."

"Ah…" I said, beginning to catch on. She meant I really *was* the problem—or rather, the Blood Worlder perception of me was at the core of it.

I had to admit, I'd been pretty heroic over the last couple of days. If they were keen on me, watching me lose might be hard to take.

"Well then, Germanica can't be allowed to win."

"Precisely. Damned if you win and damned if you don't. What I don't understand is why you're not fighting in Legion Germanica. Why is that?"

"Uh… history. Tradition," I said.

She shook her head. "That's a pathetic reason to lose a planet."

There was clearly something about this situation I wasn't getting. Wracking my brain, I tried to figure out how to get her to reveal it to me without revealing anything in return.

Gytha looked me over thoughtfully. "I can see this took you by surprise. I can only surmise that you planned to throw the last fight as Varus, and you didn't understand how that would impact our viewers."

"Right…"

"It's all coming clear to me now," she said. "You thought you could fool us. You thought you could hide your true identity until the very end. The Warlord of Humanity participating and losing—because you thought we were stupid. That we wouldn't recognize you for what you so obviously are."

"Um… thanks for the compliments."

"None are necessary. But now at least, I think you understand our difficulties. Germanica fights for Earth. Varus fights for Rigel. Such a strange twist of fate…"

Gytha was wistful, almost dreamy. She looked quite enticing in the dying light of the sun. We'd talked so long the big orange fireball that lit this planet by day had sunk over crater's rim.

But I wasn't in a dreamy mood. Not at all. Something she'd said… *Varus fought for Rigel?*

"Rigel…" I said. "Do you know why they wouldn't come here and fight for themselves? On the field of honor?"

She looked at me sharply. "Of course they wouldn't. That's not their way. They're the opposite of Earth men. Earth hires out her best to war for others. Rigel is fantastically rich, and they believe in hiring others to fight for them."

All of a sudden, I felt a little sick. My gut was falling away from me.

I knew my legion. I knew Earth. I knew all my masters, and how they thought.

They loved money. Big money. And when a diplomat of Earth saw money, they would do almost anything to get it instead of a war.

So that was it. Varus had sold out, not Germanica. I'd had the wrong idea all along.

And that was why Gytha had said Earth could not win this contest, that no path led from here to Blood World joining us.

If Legion Varus lost this battle I was in the midst of right now, it would mean that Legion Varus had been eliminated. As I was Varus' hero—and supposedly the champion of all Earth—that wouldn't sit well with Blood Worlders. They wouldn't go along with it.

On the other hand, if Varus won this round and lost the next, then the same problem would apply. They'd have to watch me lose.

Finally, if Varus won every round to the top, it would still be a disaster, because Varus had sold out to the Rigellians—whoever the hell they were.

We'd reached an impasse. I couldn't think of a way for Earth to win this struggle, even though it seemed that Gytha was rooting for us now.

"How about this," I said. "Let's end the current struggle, play it out, and we'll see if I can figure a way out of our PR problems in the final round."

Gytha frowned at me, not quite getting it.

"So… you want to continue fighting? It seems kind of pointless."

"Well, you guys made up the rules. To the death, and all that."

"Yes..." she said, looking dejected.

"Uh... you don't have revival machines on this planet, do you?"

"No," she said, not meeting my eye. "But you have the upper hand now. The Vulbites can't face you without stealth—it will be no contest."

Advancing into the pit, I took slow, careful steps. The gremlins didn't like it. They circled around like small, bristling dogs. I didn't care, as they had no charged needles to stick me with. They appeared to be here just to help fit the Vulbites with stealth gear.

"Gytha," I said, "I like you, and I don't want to see you get permed."

She eyed me, looking up at last.

"What can be done?"

Reaching out both hands, I grasped her shoulders firmly. She looked a little shocked.

"Listen," I said. "I know you don't like to cheat. You have your honor to think about—but you should run out of this crater. Just do it wearing a stealth suit. The Blood Worlders will never know."

"Are you going to harm me?" she asked, looking at my hands. "In the middle of a truce? What despicable beings you—"

"No, no," I said. "I'm just demonstrating that I like you."

This technique had worked before on Floramel when I'd first met her. Their kind only touched when they were considering mating or violence. I was hoping it would fluster her and get her to think outside the box.

"You assail my person, and yet council that I flee? Ah! I understand! You want sex."

"Um..."

"I've been approached like this upon occasion, but never by a basic. You behave more like one of our slavers."

I dropped my hands back to my sides. "I want you to survive the day."

"I understand, but it can't be. I won't dishonor myself by slinking from the field of battle."

I laughed, earning myself a quick frown.

"You've been cheating all along!" I jeered at her. "You aren't supposed to be down here in this pit, distributing tech to these centipedes. What difference will it make if you sneak out? Even if you'd won, there wouldn't have been any honor in it."

She looked at the sands. It was getting dark now, and the sky had turned purple.

"Your words hurt me more than you can know. I will go—ashamed."

"Aw now," I said, worried I'd overdone it. I'd only wanted her to save herself. "I'm sorry if you feel shame. Humans—basics I mean—we can be callous."

Gytha gave me a dark look. "Then know that we, too, can be heartless."

I believed her.

"Here's what I'm going to do," I told her. "I'm going to walk out of here. In ten minutes, we're clearing out the rest of the Vulbites. If you're still standing here, well, I guess you've made your choice."

After this pronouncement, I walked out of her camp. A few gremlins skittered along behind me for a time, but they soon vanished into the night.

After a long walk back to our lines, I sought out Graves. He came up to me with his arms crossed and his face flattened into a grimace.

"There you are. Did you have a nice date, McGill?"

"I've had better," I said. "She's giving up, by the way."

After I explained the situation, Graves ordered the legion to advance. I tried to slow him down, but it had been about ten minutes by then anyway. I wondered what Gytha had decided to do.

Hours of methodical fighting ensued—if you could call it fighting. It was more of an organized slaughter. We marched, burned Vulbites, and kept advancing. After a while, they didn't even have stealth suits anymore. Maybe they'd run out.

It took until dawn bled into the skies overhead. Weary, I checked the dead.

There were no humans among them, unless you counted a handful of gremlins. Apparently, self-preservation had won out in the end.

Gytha had fled.

## -50-

Dead tired, we returned to the lifter and rode up toward *Nostrum* in orbit. The strange planet we knew as Blood World was stretched out below us.

I tuned my tapper into the ship's external cameras. Looking down at the planet, I figured nothing in my experience had come closer to Hell than this place.

The lifter slid around the planet, rising up and slipping back into darkness. The edge of dawn fell far away and behind our relatively small ship.

After staring down for a time at their dull city lights, strewn in patches over the globe, I realized something: most of their cities had one or more jagged holes in the middle of them.

The crater we'd been doing battle within was just one such example. We hadn't been fighting in the wilderness—it'd been smack-dab in the middle of one of their torn-up population centers.

"Fusion bombs," I said, looking at the evidence and yawning. "Too small for anti-matter. Must be fusion."

"What are you talking about, McGill?" Carlos asked me.

I turned to him, mildly surprised to see him alive. Most of my unit had died down there this time around.

After explaining what I was looking at, I shared the feed. Carlos whistled.

"You're right. So many blasted cities... No wonder the radiation levels were high—it must have happened years ago, but still..."

"What I don't get is how living plants can grow down there in those hotspots. Wouldn't they die?"

We were baffled by these questions until we got back to *Nostrum*. Once there, I looked up Kivi. She'd been revived and was back to work in the labs.

"It's been years since those bombs were dropped on their cities," she told me. "I'd say the hotspots have had time to cool. Hiroshima was only radioactive for a few weeks, remember."

"Years, huh? I guess it wasn't us who blew them up, then. Who did it?"

"We don't know. This is the frontier—it's pretty rough out here among these stars, past the fringe of the Empire. The Cephalopods have been in plenty of wars before they faced us."

That reminded me of something Graves had told me long ago, so I headed to his office but found it empty. I made myself at home, and when he arrived, I looked at him through half-closed eyes.

"McGill?" he asked. "What are you doing here? You should be on your bunk. We've got another battle to fight tomorrow—one last round and this will all be over."

Before explaining to him that we were in a bad way as far as winning the contest went, I asked him about the Blood Worlder cities.

"We're not sure who did it," he said. "The Blood Worlders aren't talking—I don't think they trust us. They're isolated and paranoid."

"With good reason."

"Huh... I guess so."

"This is what you meant, sir, isn't it? When you told me how I shouldn't wish for the Empire to end too soon?"

He looked at me seriously. "You remember that, do you? Your own shoe size is probably a mystery, but not that comment I made years ago?"

"The fringe of the fringe," I said, using his desk to look at the stars and the reddish-brown planet below us. "That's what Earth is. This place—this is past the fringe. We're into the frontier. Where one species can war with another without any fear of repercussions."

"That's right. A galaxy where anything goes. Do you like it?"

I shook my head slowly. "I can't say that I do, sir."

"Now you know why I've fought for the Empire for nearly a century. I don't like the Galactics. I don't even like the hogs who run Earth—but this is the alternative."

Startled, I glanced over at him at the mention of fighting for a century. Could it be? Varus had been founded in 2076... Had Graves really signed up with this legion back then? That was almost ninety long years ago. No wonder he shrugged off each revive like a bad night's sleep.

"The good news just keeps coming, sir," I said, then I launched into my explanation of our predicament.

At first he stared, and then he frowned. By the time I was done, he was glowering in a sour rage.

"We've been duped. I can't believe it—no, that's not true. I *do* believe it. We've got to talk to Winslade."

"Uh... he might not be too keen on meeting up with me again."

"I'm sure he won't be. But this is big."

Walking across Gold Deck to Winslade's office, which had formerly been Deech's office, we touched the door—but it didn't open. We rapped politely after that—still nothing.

MPs came trotting up behind us about twenty seconds later. We slowly dropped our sidearms and raised our hands.

The moment we'd been disarmed, the door popped open. Winslade came out like a skunk out of a hole.

"Well, well, well," he said, "to what do I owe this dishonor?"

"We won your battle for you, Winslade," Graves said. "You owe us a moment to talk."

"Really? Do I? I was thinking more along the lines of a stint in the stockade, or possibly a quick execution until your fates might be decided later on Earth."

"You don't want to do that," Graves told him.

"You're wrong. I *very much* want to do that."

"We can't win tomorrow," I said. "I talked to Gytha personally."

"I saw that via the drone cameras. I shuddered when you grabbed that poor girl. Really, you should be prosecuted for taking such liberties."

"But you couldn't hear what I was saying," I pointed out. "Aren't you a little curious? Aren't you wondering why we came here together and gave ourselves up so easily?"

The left corner of Winslade's mouth twitched. I'd introduced doubt into his mind, and I could tell he didn't appreciate it.

"Tell me your latest lie, McGill," he said in a weary tone. "I can see that it's burning to get out of your mouth."

"Not out here," I said, nodding toward the unsmiling MPs. "Let's go inside where we can talk plainly."

Sighing, he stepped aside. A pistol was in his hand, and he waved it at us. We moved into the office and the door snicked shut.

"Don't try anything," he said, pointing toward his desk.

Something sleek and black squatted there. Surprised, I saw an automated turret on a tripod had been set up and activated.

"That's a safety violation," Graves complained.

Winslade found this amusing. "Is it really? I'll be sure to file a report at Central when we reach home. In the meantime, I'd recommend that neither of you make any sudden movements."

We shuffled, moving almost in slow motion as we found seats. I leaned back in my chair, and the turret twitched each time I rocked back and forth in it.

"Now, make it quick," Winslade said. "I'm preparing to meet Armel on the field of honor."

"We know all about that—we know that Varus is supposed to lose."

He looked at each of us in turn. His eyes slid rapidly back and forth, until he was satisfied.

"I see," he said. "This is disgusting. This legion has no security at all. Nothing is sacred. Who ratted out the plan?"

As he said this, he put his pistol down and sat behind the desk. I frowned, as I wasn't quite understanding what was going on.

"Um…" I said, "So you're not part of some kind of coup?"

"Not, not really. It was all a show."

"Where's Deech then?" Graves demanded.

He shrugged. "She's alive and well on Armel's ship."

My mouth sagged low.

"What?" I demanded. "That's impossible! I—"

"You know nothing," he said. "Before we left Earth, Central hatched a plot to win this struggle for Blood World's support. Two legions would enter the contest, and no matter which one won the fight, we'd be awarded the prize."

"Yeah, yeah," I said. "We know about that. Why did you and Claver kill Deech?"

"That was a hasty alteration of the original plan. Once both legions began to win their battles, we realized we'd made a mistake. We couldn't allow both to reach the final contest. By killing Deech, it was surmised Varus would lose—but we didn't."

"That's right," I said. "We won against all of y'all!"

I slapped my hand on his desk, and the turret stuttered, lighting up.

"Oh…" I said, sitting back slowly. "I forgot."

"No, no! By all means, make more aggressive displays, McGill."

I sat still, and the turret went back to slowly rotating and scanning the room.

"Varus was calculated to be the less effective legion," Winslade said. "It was decided that Germanica should win in the end. Varus was only a failsafe from the beginning. So, Deech was killed and revived aboard Armel's ship with legion Germanica."

"You killed me, too."

He shrugged. "You got in the way. In any case, we couldn't just transfer her over there via a shuttle. The Blood Worlders are watching closely. Death and revival was an expedient to move Deech. By now, she's been briefed and is doubtlessly giving them any information she can to defeat us in the final battle."

"Such a carefully laid plan," Graves said wistfully. "Too complex, too twisted—it was bound to go wrong in the end."

Winslade frowned at him. "What do you mean? It's time you two began talking. What are you doing here, bothering me? I've got a battle to lose in the morning, if you don't mind."

I spilled my guts then. I told him all about Gytha, the way the Blood Worlders were seeing this fight, and all the rest of it.

By the end, his mouth was hanging open slightly. It did me a world of good to see that.

"You've got to be kidding!" he exclaimed, beginning to pace around the room.

He made agitated gestures, so much so that his turret began tracing his movements instead of ours.

"I can't believe this!" he said at last, spinning around to face me.

I sat in my chair, deadly still.

"I'm going to have to leave you out of the fight tomorrow, McGill," he said. "You can see that, can't you? If you're not there, the Blood Worlders won't be rooting for you."

"I don't know if that will work," I told him honestly. "They see me as their future ruler. The one they're willing to lay down their lives to follow into battle. If I don't show up—I don't know."

"You *can't* show up, because you *can't* win—but you can't be seen to lose, either! Damn! Why do you always make such a mess of things?"

"I don't rightly know, sir. My momma always said my teachers asked her that exact question on every back-to-school night. Every single one."

"I'm out of options," he said, fuming. "I'm going to have to kill you, and televise your corpse. We'll make up some reason as to why you've been deposed. Something disgraceful will do nicely—"

As he spoke, he went over to his desk, snatched up his pistol and aimed it at me. He stepped around the desk again to get a point-blank shot.

One thing I've been gifted with, being a well-grown man of two meters in height, is an amazing length of bone. My feet, for example, always surprised people. When they sat in a booth at a restaurant, it was almost certain they'd kick me, or I'd kick them—I was just too damned lanky to fit into places made for normal folks.

So it came almost naturally to me to relax my long legs and shove a size fourteen boot into Winslade's path. He was walking and talking so fast, he never saw it. I guess he was too focused on burning a hole into my skull with his laser pistol.

Going down in a heap, he scrambled to get up—but that's when things went totally wrong for him.

His turret, which had been following him around the room with heightened interest, had finally decided it had had enough.

Making a rattling sound, it pumped a good fifty rounds into him. He spun around, flopped onto his back and gargled.

Graves and I got up out of our chairs carefully. We stooped over the steaming corpse.

"He doesn't smell too good," I commented.

Graves released a rumbling laugh. "That was the funniest damned thing I've ever seen, McGill. Did you really plan that?"

I shrugged. "Improvised, more like."

"What are we going to do now?"

Frowning, I shook my head. "I'm not sure, Primus. I think I should hit the hay and sleep on it."

Graves touched the top of the turret gently, turning it off.

"You do that," he told me, rumbling with laughter again.

## -51-

After a good night's sleep I found myself refreshed in the morning. I'd taken a trip to Blue Deck late last night to get my shoulder fixed, but other than a patch of itchy nu-skin, I was right as rain.

At breakfast, I left my unit and sat among the officers. That was unusual for me. I generally stayed with my men on the morning before a battle.

"McGill?" Winslade asked in a tone that indicated disbelief on his part. "What gall you have... Do you know I just got revived an hour ago?"

"There's more than one way to get a good night's sleep, Primus," I said in a cheery tone. "Sorry about yesterday, sir. My feet just get in the way sometimes. It's an awful habit of mine, sprawling like that."

He stared at me like he was a cat eyeing a flea. Getting up from his top table, where he'd been sitting with a load of other primus-level brass—all ten of them—he came over to my table.

Unconcerned, I shoveled food into my face. That was one good reason to eat in the snooty officers' mess. The food tasted better. They got omelets made to order, and fresh fruit in three different varieties every morning.

"You know, I've got half a mind to have you arrested," Winslade said. "I can do that, you know. Deech is serving with Armel, leaving me officially in charge of Varus."

"She's over there ratting us out, I'm sure of that," I agreed. "Sit down, take a load off."

If he'd meant to intimidate me, he'd failed. We both knew it.

Maybe it was the fact he couldn't really afford to arrest me or shoot me on the spot. We were dropping back to the pit in around an hour, and I had fans down on Blood World. They wanted to see me. Apparently, I had an avid following.

"McGill," Winslade said, "don't speak of that humiliation with the turret, and I won't launch any reprisals against you. Deal?"

"Uh…" I looked up in surprise. I hadn't thought of him wanting to keep it a secret, even though in retrospect, it was obvious he'd want to do so.

The trouble was, I'd already shown the vid around. I'd been running my body-cams, and a few of them had caught all the action. Kivi had already cooked up a repeating loop of Winslade's riddled corpse doing what looked like an infinite series of summersaults. My unit had laughed until tears ran.

Winslade's face began to narrow at my hesitation, so I spoke up quickly.

"Got it, sir. I guess I'd already forgotten about it. Hell, why would I want to admit to endangering the life of a superior officer? That's no way for a man to get ahead in rank."

That was the sort of thing Winslade would have thought to say, so it convinced him.

He nodded and relaxed, sitting back and poking at his omelet with a fork. It was one of those fancy jobs full of spinach and sprouts and the like. No wonder he was so skinny.

"Good to hear," Winslade said. "I've got a plan for today's activities. Do you want to hear it?"

"Hmm…" I wasn't really interested, but I'm always willing to make conversation.

"First off, you won't be dropping with us. You'll be dropping with Germanica."

I blinked in confusion. "What, sir?"

"That's right. You're marching with them today. These Blood World yokels won't know the difference. As long as they see you on the winning side, they'll be pleased enough."

My eyes narrowed at him, and I shook my head. "But sir? How can I drop from their ship? It's orbiting on the far side of the planet."

"Oh damn!" Winslade said, slapping a hand to his forehead dramatically. "How could I have forgotten?"

He made such a face of confusion and anguish that I was sucked in for a moment—but only for a moment.

Some people say I'm slow on the uptake. Not in a physical reflex sort of way, but in a complex concept sort of way. But in this case, I was able to do the math fast and my hands leapt across the table for his skinny neck.

They made it there, too. I grabbed him, and I throttled him— but the beamer he had in his other hand—the one under the table—was already squeezing the trigger.

A hissing, burning sound ripped the air and my guts blew out. They went all over the mess hall. Men jumped to their feet cursing and dancing out of the way.

Squeezing still, I tried to finish old Winslade before I died—but I failed. I'll forever feel the disappointment.

My head slumped down, and I made gargling sounds. My fingers began to go limp, and Winslade pried them loose one by one. He gasped and choked.

That was the last thing I remembered hearing aboard *Nostrum* that fine morning.

\* \* \*

I returned to life aboard *Actium*, Germanica's transport. This happened right away, but to me it seemed to be an eternity later. Time is funny when you're dead.

"Off the table McGill—no violence, please."

The Germanica bio-people watched me warily. They stepped back—well back—when I got up into a sitting position.

"That was dirty pool," I said, releasing a low laugh that sent me into a coughing fit.

One of the women handed me a squirt bottle of water and danced back. I sprayed myself off and leered at them. One was thin, and the other was kind of chunky.

To me, that seemed odd. People rarely gained weight in Legion Varus. To do so was to invite a recycle from your CO.

"What's got you two so nervous?" I asked.

"Let's just say you have a certain reputation," the chunky one said.

"All good I hope?"

The thin one blew a puff of air through her lips, relaxing. "You don't look like you're going to murder anyone. You're a good grow. Get yourself cleaned up and report to Deech."

"Where is she?"

"Gold Deck, of course."

Shrugging, I climbed off the gurney and moved toward the uniform locker.

"What are you doing, Centurion?"

"Uh… getting dressed?"

"The shower is right there. Don't get slime into one of our uniforms—it's disgusting."

Surprised, I turned in the direction she was pointing. They did indeed have a shower installed just a few steps away. I climbed in, blasted off the sticky goo and felt a lot better when I pulled on a uniform a few minutes later. These Germanica pukes had a good idea there. It seemed so… civilized. I wondered if I could talk the Varus bios into adding a shower stall on *Nostrum*.

"Thanks for the revive, ladies. If either of you are looking for a date later tonight, let me know."

They looked startled and tittered a little. Apparently, they hadn't heard everything about me.

Thinking about that on my way up to Gold Deck, I smiled. The day might not be a total loss after all.

Internally, I was pretty steamed of course. Winslade had shanked me pure and simple. It was downright embarrassing for a man such as myself. I should have seen it coming.

His idea had seemed like a good one, too. I'd come up with zip after my full night's sleep. I'd been kind of hoping something would jump out at me this morning.

And it had—just not in quite the way I'd figured.

## -52-

Gold Deck on *Actium* was just like Gold Deck on *Nostrum*. If anything, the officers up here were even stuffier.

"James McGill…" Armel said as I walked in unannounced on a strategy session. "How good of you to crash our party."

"McGill," Deech said, jerking a thumb back toward the door. "Out. We're planning our attack."

"No, no!" Armel exclaimed. "Don't send our hero packing! Come back. Witness the seeds of destruction. Legion Varus is doomed, and it's only fitting you should know the nature of her overdue demise."

I wavered for a second, but then Deech nodded. I walked up to the table they all huddled and stared at a holographic map.

As usual, Germanica had the best. They always had the good stuff, the most expensive gear the Galactics allowed humanity to purchase.

The holotable, accordingly, was spotless and vibrant. It had all kinds of automated icons and scripts you could activate.

And the graphics? I thought I was looking at the real thing.

"Looky there!" I said, pointing. "Those Varus lifters are *perfect*. Right down to the wolf's head emblem on the side."

Deech set her mouth into a grim line and gave me the death-stare. Any girlfriend I'd ever dated could have told her I was immune to that.

"Can you make the troops get out and deploy?" I asked.

My questions seemed to make Armel happy even as they upset Deech. He grinned and twiddled fingers near the Varus side of the table.

"Certainly," he said, and sure enough, troops poured out of the lifters.

"Hot damn," I said. "How come we don't have tech like this on *Nostrum*?"

"It's a waste of funds," Deech said with a sniff.

"Look close, McGill," Armel said. "Maybe you can see yourself if we zoom in a little more…"

Hunching over, I stuck my face into the map, drinking it in. This was better than the best gaming rigs.

A few of the Germanica brass snickered—but I didn't care.

"Armel, please," Deech said. "Let's stop fooling around and finalize the plan. We've got less than an hour before the lifters drop."

"Oh, but my captive lady, we've already done so."

At the mention of her being a captive, Deech frowned at him and crossed her arms. I could tell she wasn't enjoying her stay aboard *Actium* as much as I was.

"Look here," Armel continued. He made a flourish over the map, and it accelerated in time.

Both sides exited the lifters in good order. Varus was committed to the field faster, it looked like. I thought that part of the simulation was accurate. We knew how to hustle.

But when both groups formed up into lines, the Varus units looked more ragged. They advanced sooner, before all their heavy equipment was even out on the LZ.

"An early assault?" Deech asked. "You think Winslade will try that?"

"It fits Varus behavioral profiles. Light troops probe almost immediately. They hope to find the enemy off-balance. They search for early intel in order to take advantage of any weakness—it's a very aggressive strategy."

"A damned good one, too," I tossed in, but they both ignored me.

"Now watch," Armel said. "We've anticipated them. We catch the scouts with a surge of heavies—they're meeting now."

The timescale was greatly increased. Each second was a minute of time on the simulated battlefield.

The Varus lights met the Germanica heavies and were repelled with catastrophic losses.

I watched transfixed as the Varus troops fell back to their lines, beaten. I had to admit, we did tend to get a bloody nose early-on.

"The enemy has been admonished, but not yet beaten," Armel said. "With deliberate stratagems, we move in for the main struggle."

While the Varus troops circled the wagons and dug in, Germanica advanced slowly. Their light troops crept up on the walls of the crater to find good sniping positions. Their main body of heavies and artillery advanced in the center.

About two minutes—two simulated hours into the struggle, the battle was joined for real. A preponderance of gear and planning allowed Germanica to wear down the Varus troops.

It was bloody on both sides, but Varus was outgunned and outmaneuvered. Germanica was shown mopping up the broken Varus troops a simulated hour later.

"What do you think?" Armel asked us with his eyes alight. "Was it not glorious? I've watched it countless times—even before we set sail for this godforsaken rock."

"It could work out that way," Deech said. "It fits the profiles. Your plan is a good one."

"No it's not," I said loudly. "It sucks."

Armel spun around on one heel. He clasped his hands in front of himself and eyed me with displeasure.

"Ah, the master speaks—no-no!" this last he said to Deech, who'd clearly been about to yell at me. "Don't reprimand this wizard. This prophet. This man of visions. Tell us, Nostradamus, where have we gone wrong? I must hear your concerns."

I waved a big hand across the field, making the landscape shiver as it passed through it.

"Just about everything. You clearly programmed the simulator to examine typical Varus behavior and extrapolate—but that's a flawed premise."

They looked at me curiously.

"Please, do go on," Armel said.

"I will, because Germanica needs to win today. Winslade isn't Deech, or Drusus. He's much more cautious. He wouldn't throw out an early attack with half his light troopers. Not against Germanica."

For the first time, Armel looked uncertain. "You don't think he'll follow the same playbook?"

"No," I said, "I don't."

"But it doesn't matter!" Deech said at last. "It doesn't make any difference, not really. This isn't a real contest, it's a setup. Winslade knows he's supposed to lose. He'll do that, if only to enrich himself."

"Ah!" I said, imitating Armel in my mannerism. "At last, you've set your finger upon the real problem: Winslade isn't on our side. He has no intention of letting Germanica win this contract."

They all had their mouths open now. Squinty eyes, slack jaws... I'd seen these expressions often when I really got on a roll.

"All right, McGill," Armel said, making a pffing sound at me. "I'll give you your pleasure. Why would Winslade attempt to win? Has he been bought off? Is he so angry with your regular abuses that he desires revenge in a blinded fury?"

"Nope. The trouble is... he's not Winslade."

That dumbfounded them.

"He's Claver," I said. "I realized it once I grabbed him—when I saw his expression in the mess hall. It wasn't the sort of rat-look Winslade would give me. It was Claver's face, being masked by one of his projection boxes."

"You are mad," Armel said quietly.

"I wish I was. That would make today an easier day—but I'm not. You see, I've grabbed Winslade by the throat, and Claver too. They aren't the same. Winslade, he's a skinny fellow. All strings and bone. My fingers and thumb can almost touch when I throttle him, when I squeeze hard enough."

330

They were staring now with a mix of amazement and worry. No one said a word. Not even the staffers laughed.

"This man—he was *big* in the throat. He didn't look that way due to the projection box, but he was disguised—I'm sure of it. As I died today, I had a few seconds to think: who might be wearing a projection box, have cause to pretend he was Winslade, and who possessed a fat neck?"

"Claver..." Deech said, her eyes unfocused and searching nothing.

"Bingo!"

"This is absurd," Armel said, giving himself a shake. "Such fantasies! No wonder you Varus types get wiped every other mission."

"No," Deech said, "it's true. At least, the part about illusion boxes is. When I took over Varus, I was briefed in detail. I'll show you the vids."

I stepped away from the table while she paired her tapper with it and began playing classified vids. Some of them I'd taken. Some had been made as far back as Tech World, where the Tau wore faces and clothing that were as ethereal as the simulator on the table.

## -53-

When Armel was convinced he could be in trouble, he came to me again. I was led to his private office.

"Here," he said, pouring us each a drink.

"Should we be drinking before battle, sir?"

"Of course. This is gin. Do you know what the British used to call this particular spirit, centuries ago?"

"Uh… no sir."

"Dutchman's courage. The Dutch invented gin, you see, and they dosed their men liberally before marching them into the cannons."

I sipped my drink while he gulped his. I considered telling him that a small pistol was sometimes referred to as a "Frenchman's pecker" in my part of the woods—but I figured that wouldn't make him happy.

"You have to talk to me seriously now, McGill," he said.

"Um… what else do you need to know, sir?" I asked. "All you have to do is assume you're fighting against Claver—Old Silver—and plan accordingly. That should about do it."

"Old Silver…" he said in a dazed tone.

"Yeah. Isn't that what you used to call Claver when he was in your legion?"

"Yes, of course…" he said, looking haunted. "Did you know that Old Silver was always in trouble—even long before you met him? Even before I came to command Germanica?"

"No… but it stands to reason. A man like him can't hide among normal people for long."

"Indeed not. He's one of the first legionnaires, you know. A very old soul, as they say. There have been whispers…"

He had me curious now, so I leaned forward and peered at him.

"Whispers about what, Tribune?"

Armel took another gulp from his glass then set it down with a knocking sound on his desk. The desktop glowed around it, a shimmering blue, waiting for instructions.

"There have always been whispers about the long-term effects of countless revivals. How they might warp a man's mind with successive small errors introduced over time. It has been hypothesized that, given enough recycles over a century or more, the personality of the individual involved might become permanently altered."

"Makes sense, I guess—but not in Claver's case. Wasn't he called Old Silver precisely because he didn't die much?"

Armel leaned forward. His voice lowered, as if he was imparting a dark secret. "That's right—but that's because when you met him he wasn't *allowed* to die often. In the early days, his role was the opposite. He was killed many, many times."

"Why?"

He shifted uncomfortably in his chair. "In the old days, when we first began to take contracts and venture out into space—things were different. Our histories from those times… well, they're darker than you know."

All of this was interesting, but it seemed unimportant to me right now.

"Okay," I said. "I get it. I know that Earth's legions were, at times, even deployed to eradicate rebels on Earth herself."

"Exactly! When Hegemony was established as our worldwide government, not everyone wanted to embrace the Galactics. Not everyone wanted to be part of the Empire."

"Okay… so you're saying Claver comes from that time?"

"He does. As do a few others—your man Graves, for instance. He comes to mind. Did you never wonder why it took him nearly a century to rise to the rank of Primus? Well… not everyone in Central trusts him still. Not even to this very day."

"I see… but what's all this got to do with Claver's behavior now?"

"They held back his rank for many, many decades. Just as they did with Graves. The revivals—they twisted him. Claver's dangerous now. He's mean-spirited and ruthless."

I laughed and gulped my drink. "Tell me something I don't know."

Armel looked at me seriously.

"All right, I will tell you something new: If Claver is commanding Varus today, as you claim… we're in trouble. We might not be able to defeat him."

That comment floored me. If there was one thing in the cosmos that didn't fit Armel's personality, it was humility. He thought he was better than everyone. For him to admit he was in trouble—the situation had to be serious.

"How do we beat him then?" I asked. "Will he send his lights out in an early, unsupported attack?"

Armel waved my words away as if they offended his ears.

"No, no. Of course not. He's no fool. I'd rather fight a dozen Winslades. Pardon me, but you must go. I have to think."

So saying, he got up and went to his liquor cabinet. Apparently, that's where he did a lot of his "thinking" these days.

It was my cue to exit, so I took it. I walked out and headed down to the lifters.

Before I got there, a person I hadn't seen in a long time caught up to me and matched my stride as best she could.

"Centurion Leeza?" I asked her. "Wow… it's been since Tech World, hasn't it?"

"Indeed it has, McGill," she said with one of those foreign accents that sounded faintly British.

Leeza was a tall one with narrow hips and suspicious eyes. Today, the object of her suspicion was clearly me.

"Uh…" I said. "I haven't raided the officer's liquor cabinet yet. I swear."

Her face flickered with a smile at our shared memory. "I know. You just got here. When I heard you were revived on

*Actium*, I traced you to Gold Deck. I waited outside until Armel finished your briefing."

"Oh..." I said, already entertaining ideas of a date. Somehow, getting to know a Germanica girl sounded interesting. I'd never managed it before.

The trouble was that even if this battle went well, one or the other of us would probably be dead. Then we'd be revived on different ships.

Shrugging, I decided to make the best of it.

"So, why'd you look me up?"

"You've got to drop with someone's unit. You're to be embedded with me."

"Sounds good. Let's review the troops."

Centurion Leeza reintroduced me to her legionnaires, calling me a "battlefield asset" and an "advisor" to be taken seriously. She made it pretty clear I was a visitor, with no official command capacity.

For my own part, I smiled and nodded to all of her adjuncts and noncoms. In return, they eyed me like I was a road-kill soufflé.

Packing with Leeza's unit into a lifter, I was geared up in heavy armor and given a belcher to lug around. That was a nice surprise. I'd been a weaponeer back in the day, and I'd always kind of missed the role.

*Actium* was equipped with ten lifters, just like *Nostrum*. When the time came to start the battle, both of the larger vessels spilled out their assault ships in a swarm. Riding down with the rest of Leeza's unit, I experienced a nearly nostalgic emotion as the lifter screamed down to a harsh landing on Blood World.

The landscape was familiar—but not identical. The crater we'd landed in this time was different. I could see that right off. It was much larger, for one thing. It was a good ten kilometers across with an oval rather than a circular shape. Apparently, two bombs had made divots in the landscape here, one overlaying the other.

The city surrounding the mega-crater was bigger than the other I'd visited, too. More importantly, it was still inhabited. It gleamed with lights and people. I could see them gathering around the edge of the crater as our jets wound down to a rumble.

The battle started on the night side of the planet this time. We landed and jogged out onto the rough surface. We could see a ragged line of figures circling the crater on all sides.

"Are those civvies?" I asked Centurion Leeza.

"I sure hope so," she replied.

It was a fair sentiment, so I let it ride. We trotted a long distance away from the lifters before they roared up into the sky again, leaving us on the dirt.

I flipped up my visor for a sniff—it wasn't good.

"Smells like a city dump," I commented.

"That's the living city around us. Not all of them are still inhabited after the planet was bombed—but this one is. They smell better when they're vacant."

"Um… okay. About that, do you know who bombed them, Centurion?"

She looked at me seriously. "No. No one seems to. Either the squids forgot to tell them, or they forgot themselves."

I nodded, but I doubted *everyone* had forgotten the truth. Someone knew the whole story. Whatever it entailed, the people of this harsh planet clearly had a right to be paranoid.

## -54-

We were deployed by cohorts onto the field of honor. We didn't line up like Napoleonic Era fools, however. We took cover, fanned out, and advanced into the brush.

There was more organic material here than there had been in the last pit I'd fought in. Big mushrooms still dominated, but spiny plants with crooked branches like fingers were everywhere in between.

As Leeza's group was a light unit, I was stuck with a pack of snap-rifle toting troops. Playing the part of a weaponeer, a heavy belcher thumped on my shoulder. I'd been issued a breastplate and a heavier protective suit than the regulars—but it wasn't a powered exoskeletal rig.

"Getting tired, Varus?" Leeza's top noncom called out to me.

A few of his buddies in light kits grinned.

"Nope," I lied. "I've been looking forward to the workout. It's been hours since I fought those Vulbites."

They looked a little disappointed, and I made an effort to make my long strides seem smooth and untroubled. For laughs, I began to outpace them.

Now, there's something deep in the human psyche that just hates the hell out of being beaten in a race. Just watch people in a shopping line or a slow-down point on a highway if you want proof.

The veteran raced after me to catch up. I could hear him puffing, and all his assigned squaddies were in his wake.

There was no way I could keep up my pace for long, of course. I'd sprinted ahead, and my legs were about a mile long, but I knew they'd give out pretty soon as I had about fifty more kilos of gear than my pursuers did.

Accordingly, I twisted and dove into a ditch, sliding into a position to sight along my belcher's optics.

Alarmed, the lights all hopped after me and threw themselves onto their bellies.

"Did you see something?" the veteran puffed. "Are we under fire?"

"Nah," I said, "I just thought this was a good spot to fire from. See the terrain ahead? I've got a little elevation, but not enough to be exposed on all sides."

Frowning, the veteran looked over the quiet landscape.

"Why don't you take your bunny-rabbits forward a ways? I like to have a screen for my belcher."

He looked at me, spat deliberately, and then moved away in a crouch. His troops followed, fanning out.

As it turned out, I almost felt bad for these Germanica pukes. After all, I'd arguably been to blame for their bad luck.

Snap-rifle fire erupted. They were single-shots released at long range. Two of the light troopers pitched onto their faces—their chests were blasted open.

"Sniper!" I shouted. It was a bit late, but better late than never, I always say.

The lights were crawling like snakes in every direction. The veteran made it back to my hole and slithered in beside me.

Face full of dirt and hate, he snarled at me.

"You *knew* they were there!" he accused me. "They're your troops!"

"Nah," I said, sighting along my belcher.

At long range, a belcher was still an effective weapon. Even a kilometer away, it could knock out a soldier, small gun emplacement, or even a vehicle without a trace to give away your position.

Some said the belcher was antiquated. That a shoulder-launched smart missile was a better weapon. Under certain circumstances, I had to agree. But it was the sheer versatility that made the belcher a good weapon. You didn't have to carry extra ammo for it, just recharge it now and then. It might overheat if you held the trigger down too long, but so did a lot of weapons.

What I liked most about it was the fact I could tighten down the beam to a narrow stream of energy no bigger than a man's skull or crank it wide to take out a dozen unarmored targets at once.

Now was the time to tighten it down. Spotting a Varus sniper, I placed the reticle on her chest and fired.

No recoil. No drop-off due to range. Nothing complicated like that. The beam simply connected two soldiers for a split-second—then one of them was dead.

My unannounced shot startled the Germanica veteran a bit. He began sweeping the field with his scope.

"Two o'clock," he said.

"Take the shot, I'm after another sniper."

"Check it, McGill," he said. "It's a nest of them. They're setting up an 88."

That got my attention. "Damn," I said. "So far forward? Advancing so fast with artillery? That's aggressive play."

The veteran said nothing.

I sighted and fired, letting the beam go for nearly a full second. I played it over the nest, destroying the weapon, the gunner, and one of the team who'd been dragging it.

We had to duck after that as a storm of counter-fire came back our way, pinning us.

"That was a mean shot," the veteran said. "Sorry about suggesting you were on the other side. Clearly, you're not."

"Apology accepted, Vet. But now I think we should exit this position and seek new cover. They've got us flagged. Lord only knows what's coming next."

The battlefield had been steadily heating up during this early encounter. Both sides had moved forward, gaining ground rapidly. We'd met, and now sporadic exchanges were transforming into an all-out firefight.

Crawling deeper into Germanica territory, I saw lots of stuff fly overhead. Mushrooms jumped and caught fire. Spiny bushes were lashed as if hit by a sudden windstorm, crumbling apart to show the white wood within the black bark.

Along the way, the vet caught one. I felt kind of bad about that—but I kept crawling.

When I reached Leeza's trench line, I crawled inside and lay on my back.

"Are you hit?" she demanded, crawling right over my body and checking every inch of my armor.

"I caught a couple of rounds in the back of my breastplate—but it held."

She released a gust of air, sighing in relief. "What's wrong with you?" she demanded. "I've been calling for five full minutes."

"Yeah... I was kind of busy."

"What possessed you to race right up into contact with the enemy?"

I hesitated. I sensed that telling her about foot-racing her vet wasn't going to impress.

"Uh... I guess I wanted to convince your people I wasn't a Varus spy."

She shook her head. "Such foolishness. You're an officer, and you're critical to this mission. Where's the squad that was with you?"

"The rabbits? Um... I don't think they made it."

Leeza spoke through clenched teeth after that. Knowing women pretty well, I felt sure this was a bad sign. All hopes of a date with her after this vaporized.

"Armel has ordered me to help you withdraw to the rear lines," she said.

I looked at her questioningly. "Help me withdraw? Is that anything like placing me under arrest?"

"If it needs to be that way, then yes," she said flatly.

Shrugging, I got up to follow her.

Leeza moved furtively. "This way. Don't stand up straight and make a target out of yourself, please."

Moving in a fast crouch, I followed her through the winding trench lines. The firefight was still hot, but the sounds of it soon faded behind us.

At last we reached a set of four pigs—big drones that could move a lot of weight. The pigs were digging a hole—a deep hole.

"What's that? Four meters straight down?"

Armel came swaggering up to me. "*Precisely* four meters," he said. "And I'll make it your tomb if you don't stop taking chances."

"A bunker?" I demanded. "That's what you're doing, digging an officer's latrine in the middle of a death-fight? This might be over, Armel, before you finish this hole."

Armel's eyes were red and his voice was slightly uneven. I could tell he was mildly drunk. I felt like asking him if he was as full of courage today as an old-time Dutchman.

"Yes, it's a bunker. But it's not for me, fool. It's for *you*. I should have placed you under arrest immediately, it would have helped everyone."

"No offense," I told him, "but I've been under arrest before. Many times, in fact. Not once did I find it helpful."

Armel chuckled. "Then you shouldn't have run off like a madman to the slaughter. You shall stay in this bunker and let my sweet Germanica do her job."

The bunker was done in a few minutes. After the puff-crete dried, we retired within.

"You've even got a desk down here," I marveled, running my hands over it.

"The better to coordinate my counterattack."

I shook my head. "There's not going to be one."

Armel narrowed his eyes at me. "What do you know about it?"

"Claver has decided to push hard. He'll probably keep going. Let's take a look at the front."

Warily, Armel activated the desk and brought its graphics to life. He depicted the known positions of friendly and enemy units all over the battlefield. Already, Armel's forces had been pushed back, and they owned only a third of the limited territory.

"Looks like an all-or-nothing play to me."

"Such madness!" Armel exclaimed. "Why would he do such a thing? Take such early risks?"

After thinking for a moment, I nodded to myself.

"He doesn't know we know he's Claver. He must have figured we'd expect timid action—something Winslade would do."

"Ah... Therefore, he moved boldly right from the start. You might be right. The essence of strategy is deception."

"What are you going to do in return, sir?" I asked him.

He shrugged. "I'm going to fight it out. Let Varus come. We're digging in every minute. If they persist in an all-out attack, I will suffer their abuse while delivering my own. In time, the enemy will run out of steam, as you like to say in your part of the world."

Tapping at his graphics and figures, I kept frowning. Varus was losing troops, but they were gaining ground. The crater wasn't really big enough for twenty thousand troops to fight in the first place.

"It's getting crowded," I said. "Don't you think we should make a stand where we are? Your units are still falling back on both flanks."

Armel eyed the scene. "It is our way to defend by giving ground. Varus is paying for each step with blood."

"Maybe," I said, "but what if he pushes some of your troops right off the field?"

"My troops aren't an undisciplined mob, McGill. They know what will happen to them if they try to exit this crater."

I fell silent for a time, watching the battle unfold. Varus was very aggressive—unusually so. After a time, I found an option that allowed me to place cohort and unit IDs on both sides. Scanning Varus, I quickly found the 3$^{rd}$ Unit of the 3$^{rd}$ Cohort—my unit.

"They're on the front lines... the southern flank."

"What's that? Did I hear you say you wanted another drink, McGill?"

"Uh... might as well, Tribune."

He chuckled and whirled around with a sloshing tumbler of liquid in each hand. He had ice tinkling in there. How had he managed to bring ice down from *Actium*?

Taking a glass, I toasted him.

"To victory!" he shouted, tossing back the entire glass in a gulp.

It was my chance, so I took it.

I wasn't sure this was the right thing to do—but I was certain Armel's plan had a fifty-fifty shot of winning at best.

I thought I could do better.

Before the tribune could lower his beverage, I swept his legs out from under him. He slammed his skull onto the puff-crete floor of the bunker.

Checking his carotid with two fingers, I was pleased to feel a thready pulse. At least I hadn't killed him.

Refilling my glass and pasting a goofy smile on my face, I walked calmly up the crude puff-crete steps and out into the night air again.

Centurion Leeza was still up there, unfortunately. She frowned at me immediately.

"What are you doing out here?"

"Just catching a little night air."

She caught my bicep and tugged, seeking to pull me down the stairs again. "You're supposed to stay put in this bunker."

I ignored her tugs and lifted my drink to my lips. "It smells a bit off down there," I said. "The tribune—he might have had too much."

Leeza looked me in the eye.

Fortunately, my eyes can lie almost as well as my mouth can.

She made a wild sound of frustration. "Again? *Now?*" she demanded.

Letting go of me, she trotted down the steps into the dim interior of the bunker.

Walking away, I turned off my tapper and sipped my beverage. The troops gave me odd stares, but no one tried to stop me. Centurion Leeza seemed to be too busy trying to awaken Armel to sound the alarm.

Taking a few extra turns in the dark trenches, I was soon lost from view.

## -55-

Making my way to the front lines wasn't all that easy. I had to crawl on my belly sometimes, and at others I had to run from gunfire.

But I made it.

Lying low, I ripped off my Germanica jacket and the patches on my armor. My gear had friend-or-foe id systems, so I had to shed my belcher, too.

For a full ten minutes I was in the middle of the battlefield, lying face down like a corpse.

The Varus troops soon crept near. That's when I dared to speak to the nearest of them.

"Hey!" I said in a harsh whisper.

A light-trooper whirled around and threw herself on her face. She let loose a full-auto burst in my direction. Fortunately, I was in a depression of ground under a torn-up spine-bush. The bush shivered, but no accelerated slivers of metal found me.

"What the heck…! I'm Varus, girl! Check your HUD!"

"There's no contact. Nothing. You're not—"

"My tapper must be damaged," I said. "I'm Centurion McGill, 3rd Unit, 3rd Cohort, under Graves."

She paused. "McGill? I heard you weren't going on this drop. You were arrested."

I laughed. "Does it look like I'm back on *Nostrum* to you, girl?"

She was just a recruit, and she wasn't sure. She called for back-up—which was what I'd hoped she would do.

Sargon showed up with a platoon of heavies. I couldn't have been happier if I'd seen my own dead-and-gone grandma.

"Sargon! Tell her who I am, man!"

"McGill? Is that really you?"

"It damn well better be, or I'm out a bundle on size fourteen boots."

Sargon laughed and came forward, grabbing my wrist. He heaved me to my feet and clapped me on the shoulder.

"How do you pull stuff like this, sir?" he asked. "I don't think I could get away with it for one second."

"You couldn't," I agreed. "Take my advice and never try."

We walked back toward the Varus lines. We were challenged several times, but each time Sargon vouched for me, and they let me pass with suspicious stares.

"What shit did Winslade spread about me this time?" I asked Sargon.

"Some crap about you being dead and having gone over to the other side to help them beat us. Called you a traitor and all."

"Figures," I said. "You want to know the real truth—?"

I broke off, because someone had shoved a carbine barrel into the crack between my helmet and my breastplate.

"Why don't you tell me about it instead, McGill?" Graves asked.

"Uh... hello sir. Good to see you on the field of battle again. I thought old Claver would have left you for dead in the revival queue."

"Claver? What are you talking about?"

I told him the whole story then—or most of it. I left out what I'd done to Armel. Graves was squeamish when it came to mutinous behavior, even if it had been done for a good cause to a rival legion.

"So..." he said. "You're claiming Winslade isn't Winslade? He's Claver in disguise, trying to win this battle when he shouldn't?"

"That's about the size of it, sir."

"Why's he doing this?"

"You believe me, sir?" I asked, startled. "Just like that?"

"Yes. I know Winslade. He's not behaving the way I'd expect. His moves are strategically sound and bold."

"You're right, that's not Winslade at all. As to why he's doing it—he wants the Rigellians to win the contract. He must have made some kind of deal with them to give them Blood World. When I fought my unit against an equal number of saurians, he told me he'd help me win. Why would he do that? Why did he want Varus to win so badly, right from the start?"

"Because he's betting on Varus," Graves said thoughtfully. "Now, he's playing Winslade's part because he didn't trust him to win on his own."

"I could hardly fault him there."

"Me either," Graves sighed, "but I still don't see what we can do about it."

"What? Really? I thought that was plain as day, sir."

He looked at me, narrowing his eyes. "You aren't suggesting...?"

"I sure am. Put him down like the dog he is. Frag his ass like yesterday's creamed beef, sir!"

Graves had his stubby carbine up again. He pushed it into my face.

"I don't like when you talk like that, McGill."

"I know, Primus. It's distasteful and rude. I must apologize sincerely. But you see... the thing is... he's not our legit commander. He's an imposter."

"I'll take it to the rest of the staff. I'll file a formal charge."

Snorting, I fought back a laugh. When Graves was in this kind of a mood, you didn't want to laugh in his face.

"We're on the battlefield, sir. Fighting hard. No one is going to listen to that. By the time they even acknowledge your complaint, this will all be over."

"Sirs?" Sargon said. "If I might offer something?"

"Why not, Veteran?" Graves said.

"The Varus officers will never listen, even if they think you're right. They hate Winslade. Right now, they're kicking ass, and they like it. They won't want to give Claver up—not until this shit-storm is over."

"Hmm..." Graves said.

He pulled the muzzle of his gun out of my face. It was an absent-minded gesture. I could tell he was thinking hard.

"Old Silver..." I said to him. "He goes way back, doesn't he?"

Graves looked at me suddenly. In the dark, his eyes reflected the starlight.

"What do you know about that?"

"Armel told me things. Freaky things about errors in duplication."

"Forget whatever he told you. That's all unproven allegations from the past."

"Forget what, sir?"

Graves nodded. "That's better. All right. I'll go kill Old Silver. The rest of you try to slow down the advance—at least for now."

Graves walked away into the darkness.

"What a cold fish," Sargon said. "Even for Graves, that was some cold shit."

"He's not like us, that's for sure."

Sargon craned his head around to look at me. "What was all that about errors in duplication?"

"Funny, I don't remember."

Sargon stared at me for a second then he shook his head. "That's right. I don't remember either."

About an hour later, our tappers lit up with an announcement.

"Primus Winslade," Graves voice said, "the acting Tribune of Legion Varus, has unfortunately fallen in battle. As our most senior remaining Primus, I'm taking over command."

Seniority was more flexible in our legions than it had been in the past. Due to multi-year deployments on distant worlds, and the very long careers of some officers, it wasn't a simple matter of deciding who had first been promoted to the rank of primus and selecting that officer.

Other factors applied, such as the original commissioning date of the officer in question. Years in service at the rank of centurion, for example, weighed in an officer's seniority when he moved up.

To the surprise of many of the other primus-ranked officers in Varus, Graves was the most senior officer. The acting officer could bypass that system by announcing a second in command of the appropriate rank—but Winslade had neglected to do so.

"That sly dog," Sargon laughed. "I didn't think Graves had it in him."

I shook my head. "I doubt there was anything sly about it. He probably walked into the command post, shot him, then turned off the disguise box when the staffers freaked out."

"And you think they just went along with it?"

Shrugging, I threw my hands in the air. "What other choice did they have?"

"Yeah…" Sargon said. "He probably didn't even change his expression when he did it. That does sound like Graves' style."

Privately, I disagreed with Sargon.

Graves didn't like a lot of people, but Old Silver was pretty high on his private shit-list.

I therefore suspected Graves had grinned—just a little—as he gunned him down by surprise.

## -56-

Graves ordered the front lines to stop attacking and fall back. Legion Varus lost the initiative.

Tired, injured and limping, our legion pulled back to our side of the line where they'd dug trench-works. Except for the extensive command bunker Claver had put down, we had little in the way of a defensive line.

Seizing the opportunity, Germanica surged after us. They didn't let us rest. They pushed and pushed.

Somewhere along the half-way point, in the middle of the huge crater, Graves ordered Varus troops to stop retreating and make a stand. The trouble was our trench-works had been dug farther back. Graves had ordered them to fight over open ground.

It was a mistake, of course. It was meant to be a mistake. I wondered if it hurt him to give that order.

I took a moment in the confusion to walk to the crater's edge, and I surrendered to a patrol of Germanica light troopers.

It was a close shave, I don't mind telling you. They almost gunned me down on sight, even though I'd removed all my legion patches.

After identifying myself and asking for Centurion Leeza, I was arrested and hustled to the rear lines again.

Centurion Leeza was pissed—but Armel was furious.

"You had the temerity to strike your superior?!" he asked in a tone that bordered on disbelief. "In Germanica, such an act is punishable by immediate execution. Afterward, we hold a trial to decide if the miscreant will be revived or left dead forever."

"Permed for a punch?" I asked. "That seems kind of prissy to me."

He blinked in response to my words, and Centurion Leeza squinched her eyes closed as if she was experiencing a private pain.

"*Prissy?*" Armel demanded. "I know in my heart I should not ask this, but I feel compelled to do so anyway. Calling the punishment extreme, yes, I could understand that. But this word you use is wrong. In what manner can a harsh penalty seem *prissy?*"

"Well," I said, "it must be a difference in legion culture. You see, in Legion Varus, we don't take injuries—or even death—all that seriously. It happens all the time. So, if one man hits another they might get fined or thrown into the stockade for a night. But nobody whines about it. In fact, it's kind of embarrassing to make a big deal out of it. We find it... unmanly."

He scowled at me, but he removed his hand from his forehead. There, I saw I'd split open the skin both above and below his right eye. They'd sprayed it with a flesh-printer, but you could still tell.

"Unmanly..." he echoed. "Such a culture you must have. Undisciplined. Barbaric. It would be best if your legion was disbanded. I've said as much for years."

"May I point out that I've pretty much handed a victory to Germanica? That's why I did it. You'll win this pit-fight now. Graves is doing his best to throw in the towel without seeming to."

"We've lost thousands of troops," Leeza said. "It hardly feels like he's giving up."

I threw my hands high and laughed at them.

"There you go again! More sour grapes. Varus had Germanica on the ropes, but they pulled back, letting you grab the initiative. You now outnumber them and you're pushing them off the field. What more do you people want?"

"A good perming would be nice," Armel said, eyeing me with distaste.

I got the feeling that he wasn't used to injuries, much less death.

"To a Varus man," I told him, "there's something faintly disgusting about a soldier who's touchy about a little bump on the head."

"Get out!" Armel shouted, thrusting his finger toward the bunker exit. "Leeza, stay with him. He must survive until this is over. After that…"

He made a throat-cutting gesture.

I was led out into the open air, where I breathed easier. "Damn," I said, "I could smell his breath all the way across the room."

"That was the mess on the floor. You smashed a bottle of fine gin when you tripped him."

"Are you sure?" I asked. "I think it came out of his gut."

Centurion Leeza wasn't sweet on me anymore. I could just tell. She led me to a trench, sat me down in it and posted half a dozen guards around me.

"Don't let him leave," she said. "If he needs to take a piss, he can do it in the trench." Then she stalked away.

One of the noncoms stared at me. He was a black guy who chain-smoked stims when the officers weren't looking. I watched his latest stim glow red in the middle of his face.

He offered me one, but I refused. In the distance, the battle still raged on. It seemed farther away every minute. They were still driving Varus back.

"Did you really knock Armel flat?" the smoking veteran asked me at last.

"Sure did."

"After he invited you into his HQ? After he gave you a drink, and shared all his intel? That's some rude behavior, McGill."

"I needed to run some errands. Armel didn't see things my way."

"So you cold-cocked him?"

I shrugged. "He got in the way."

The veteran's eyes narrowed. He flashed into anger.

"Don't you try any of that shit with me, McGill. I'll put you face down in this trench and piss on your back!"

"Sheesh," I said, looking around at the group. "Did you guys get your feelings hurt? What a bunch of babies! You Germanica friggers whine more about minor injuries than hogs do."

These statements didn't seem to please anyone, but at least they stopped complaining all the time. They gave me the stink-eye instead.

Overhead, the camera drones were thick. I wondered what the home audience was thinking.

About twenty minutes later, I got my answer to that question.

"McGill?" whispered a female voice.

I looked around in confusion. The Germania gang guarding me had stepped away and stood in a lazy circle. I sat in the trench bored and ready to go back to my ship.

"Who's that?" I asked in a harsh whisper.

"Gytha."

I looked around slowly, and I thought I could tell where the voice was coming from. She was next to me in the trench. I could feel her body heat in the cool night air.

"You stealthing again? What's up?"

"Shhh," she hissed in my ear, closer than ever.

I felt two small hands on my shoulders. I wanted to hunch up, but I tried not to move.

"Listen," she said, "I came to tell you this isn't working. The news streams—it's not convincing."

"What's not convincing?" I asked.

"Hey," the veteran with the stims said, turning his head to frown down at me. "Shut up down there. You can say your prayers later—for all the good it will do."

The other Germanica troops laughed and shifted comfortably. Things must have looked pretty good to them. The battle was clearly going their way. At the far end of the crater, I could still hear steady gunfire, but it wasn't the raging storm of a half-hour ago.

"You can't end it like this," Gytha said. "All of Blood World is watching you right now."

My eyes drifted up to check on the camera drones. It did seem like there were more of them up there than I'd seen previously.

"They're all wondering why you're on your knees in this pit. It looks like you've surrendered. The populace is confused—they will riot in the streets soon."

"They really don't like confusion then, huh?" I whispered.

"No. They like a hero. They've chosen you. They don't understand why you're being humiliated while your army marches to victory."

"I get it…"

A boot struck the back of my head. Knocked forward, I grunted.

"No one said you could talk, Varus!" the veteran told me.

Then he made a mistake. He spit on me.

Now, a man like me can take a lot of abuse. I've been tortured, murdered, beaten and strangled plenty of times. Throw in a few poisonings and even having my guts eaten out of my belly while I watched—I'd seen it all.

But spitting on a man? That's just an insult without a cause.

"Throw that stealth suit over me," I told Gytha. "Over both of us."

"No."

"Why not, girl?" I whispered. "It's roomy enough, those Vulbites were big."

She was silent for a second. "It's too intimate. Such close contact—it isn't done."

*Wham!* A fist slammed into my ear. My helmet was off, and it hurt pretty good.

"I said: Shut! Up!" the veteran roared.

A scattered round of laughter went up from the group.

Becoming almost as annoyed with Gytha as I was with the Germanica troops, I reached for her in the dark. She was invisible, but in order to talk to me she was very close.

A quick up-down motion was all it took. I grabbed that bag-like stealth-suit she had over her head and pulled it over myself as well. She made a small gasping sound.

Seen from the inside, the stealth-suit wasn't completely transparent, but it wasn't opaque, either. It was kind of like being inside a loose weave garment that reminded me of a gunny sack.

"What the fuck?" a voice said a few seconds later.

"Where'd he go?"

Lights played around us on the dirt, but I sat still. It was weird to see the light shine right through our bodies and strike the ground underneath us. It was as if we were transparent, but I knew the suit was bending and refracting light around us.

My hand reached up and clamped itself on Gytha's mouth. I sensed she might be thinking about screaming.

"He must have slipped away!" said one of the Germanic guards.

"Shit-shit-shit!" the veteran hissed out between clenched teeth. "Find him, or it's your ass!"

Footsteps crashed around in the dark. They were looking all over—but they weren't searching the trench. Why should they? They'd all shined lights into that particular spot and seen it was empty.

"VARUS!" a man shouted, but I didn't even move.

Inside the stealth suit, I could see Gytha's shadowy face clearly enough. Her eyes were wide with shock.

I eased my hand away from her mouth.

"You have dishonored me," she whispered. "I should kill you."

"Uh... can you do that later, maybe?" I asked. "I'm in a bit of a hurry."

"Let go of me. You're violating my person."

"I'm up against you because we're both inside a one-meter bag!"

"No wonder these men hate you so much."

Sighing, I considered knocking her out and leaving her in the trench. The trouble was, these Germanica friggers weren't totally dumb. They'd find her, and they'd know she had something to do with my escape.

If they didn't recognize her, they might even kill her. Life was cheap to a legionnaire, but Gytha had never been scanned for revival as far as I knew. She didn't even have a tapper to record her mental engrams. She might be permed.

Not sure what else to do, I stood up, lifting her with me. I carried her like a kid.

I was lucky she wasn't carrying any weapons. The look on her face told me I'd have been dead otherwise.

Heading toward the crater wall, I ran with her in my arms. She squirmed, but she didn't try to gouge out my eyes or anything. For that, I was grateful.

Once we were out of the Germanica camp, I crouched down and waited.

"You want me to release you here?" I asked. "I can let you run up and out of the crater, but I need your stealth suit to fix things."

She stared at me with an odd expression on her face.

"You are very forceful. I thought you would demand intimacy."

"Uh…" I said, thinking that over for a second. Finally, I got it. "Oh, no, no, no. I wasn't going to do that."

"You behave like a littermate put out to stud," she said. "I'm no brood-mother."

"Right… of course not."

There was a lull in the conversation while I reviewed my tapper. My inbox was full of nasty messages. Among them were automated battle-updates from Legion Varus. They were down to ten percent effectives.

"Do you find me unattractive?" Gytha asked.

She was sitting next to me, and we were hip-to-hip under that stealth-suit. It was kind of like being wrapped up inside a blanket together.

The truth was, she was a lovely girl, but my mind was on other things.

"Listen," I said, "I'll take you on a date sometime if this all works out. But right now I've got to leave you here."

I ditched her then, lifting the stealth suit off her and standing in it. She stood uncertainly.

There were snipers everywhere, and I was sure most of them were looking the other way—toward the front lines—but you never knew.

I grabbed her shoulders, turned her around so she aimed uphill, and gave her a slap on the butt to get her moving. It was what my dad might have done to a horse that didn't know which end was up.

Gytha looked alarmed, but my prompting worked. She began trotting up the hill.

Moving down into the camp again, I took one glance back.

I thought I could see her at the top of the crater. She was part of the crowd now. I hoped she wouldn't catch a stray round. I'd heard a number of Blood Worlders watching the battle from the lip of the crater had died that way.

Then I forgot about Gytha and moved through the Germanica trenches. They were almost all empty, except for their dead. The fighting was all on the other side of the crater.

There wasn't much time left, so I got a move on.

## -57-

By the time I managed to sneak my way back to Armel's bunker, they were in victory celebration mode.

The camera drones were buzzing overhead, too. There had to be thirty of them up there, humming away and streaming the scene from every angle.

"Germanica has won!" Armel shouted, throwing his hands high.

I could tell he was very aware of the cameras, and he was hamming it up for them. Centurion Leeza and a crowd of other officers had gathered around.

Most of them looked weary. Many were wounded. At least Varus had given them hell.

A booming crack of gunfire rang out in the distance at that moment, making everyone look up to the edge of the crater.

Up there, two squads of littermates stood in perfect order. Two squads of nine, walking three by three, began marching down the wall of the crater.

"Ah," Armel said, "they come to honor me at last."

We all watched the procession, transfixed. But for me it wasn't the towering giants in their armor that attracted my eye. It was the smaller figure between them. If I wasn't mistaken, Gytha walked in the center. She was alone and clearly in charge.

Inside my stealth suit I frowned. I sure hoped she wasn't harboring any ill-feelings.

The heavy troopers stood nearly three meters tall. Even at that height, they weren't lanky or thin of build in any way. They were hulking brutes wearing polished heavy armor that reflected our lights with dazzling beams.

Each of the giant figures carried a massive high-tech rifle that fired a large, accelerated round. I knew from experience those guns could put down a legionnaire or stop an air car with a single shot.

In addition to their rifles, they carried thick blades. These were slightly curved and had a bright leading edge. Wielded with the unnatural power of the heavy trooper, they could chop off limbs. They weren't utilized with any kind of finesse, but rather treated like meat-cleavers in close combat.

The procession approached us, and Armel ordered his troops to stand back.

"Make way! Make way!" he shouted—his delight was obvious on his face.

The Germanica pukes backed up, scowling. There was no love lost between basic humans and Blood Worlders. We'd been mortal enemies up until now.

Armel, however, was beaming.

"This is a fine day! Look! The sun rises in the east!"

It was true. The skies were turning orange as the fierce star we called Epsilon Leporis spun slowly into view, coming over the edge of the crater like the eye of an elder god.

The night was over, and short though it may have been in hours, it had been long and hard-fought for the thousands who'd died in this bloody pit. All told, I estimated that less than two cohorts worth of Germanica's troops had lived to see the dawn—and Varus had been wiped out.

The survivors gathered to watch the ceremony. They came up out of their trenches, smeared in filth. They lined the hills and even the crater walls themselves.

At the top of the crater's rim, a great throng grew. Thousands stood silently, watching us.

Armel loved it all. He walked in a tight circle, unable to contain his glee. His heels kicked up with every step, such was his level of excitement.

Standing off to one side, I had to crush myself against the outside walls of his bunker in order to avoid being bumped into. The stealth suit still hid me from view, but it wouldn't stop anyone from noticing they were touching a ghost.

"This is a fantastic moment for Legion Germanica!" Armel announced. "We've won an entire *planet* for Mother Earth! Let it be known for all time that we have gifted this prize to humanity, that we have reunited our species, brother and sister. All those who were once pitted against one another in war are now allies!"

It was a pretty speech, I had to give him that. It even sounded like he meant it.

Glancing up, I saw the camera drones shift a little. They were focused on Gytha now. She walked forward in a ceremonial fashion. She was wearing a white garment. It looked kind of like a white sheet clasped at the shoulder by a golden sunburst.

Stopping to stand in front of Armel, she stared around at them all, regal in her manner.

*Damn* was she a fine-looking woman. She had an exotic look to her, an ethereal beauty that usually only existed in holo-vids and re-touched ads back home.

"Blood has been owed," she said in a loud, clear voice. "Blood has been paid. This contest is over."

Then, she did something none of us had been expecting. She reached up with her fine-boned fingers and touched the emblem at her shoulder.

Her garment dropped away, and she stood there as nude as the day she'd been born.

A murmur went up from the audience. We were no strangers to nudity—even if Gytha was an especially nice-looking specimen. But this whole thing... it seemed like some kind of ancient rite. A pagan festival from our distant past.

Just how different were the Blood Worlders from normal folks back home? If some of them decided to settle on Earth in the future, I wondered if they would bring such archaic practices to our world. I shuddered to think how they might fit in.

"Who shall claim this prize?" Gytha asked, looking at Armel.

We all froze for a second. I think there were about a thousand brains ticking like clocks, processing this new input. Was Gytha the prize—or part of it?

I guess it made sense in a way. She'd been the ruler of this world, so it was only fitting that she'd give herself to whoever the new master was going to be.

That kind of thinking had to be the squid influence. It seemed clear to me. Cephalopods only understood two possible social roles in their society: you were either a master or a slave—or possibly both relative to others higher or lower than you on the food chain. Still, I couldn't imagine what a squid would want with a human woman, pretty or not.

I could hear audible gasps from the Germanica troops when Gytha made her offer—especially from the women. There were a lot of scowls, too. I'm sure they were as shocked as I was.

But not Armel. He was grinning like it was his wedding night.

He bowed deeply, and with a sweep of his hand, he caught Gytha's fingers in his, bringing his lips to brush against her knuckles.

That's when I made my move. I pushed forward, knocking people out of my way.

It's easy and kind of fun to bull your way through a crowd when you're invisible. Everyone should try it some time.

People growled when I jostled them aside. They turned angrily—but then a look of shock came over them when they realized there was no one there to yell at.

They staggered away as I advanced. I felt like a shark fin cutting through the waves.

"Stop!" I boomed.

Armel's mouth had just opened after his lingering finger-kiss. Frowning, he straightened with Gytha's bare hand still in his gauntlet.

Everyone turned to look in my direction.

Whipping off the stealth suit, I tossed it down and stood tall.

"No!" I said. "I claim the prize!"

"McGill?" Armel growled.

His face registered disbelief, but it quickly down-shifted into rage.

A dozen officers surged forward, seizing me from every direction, but Armel waved them back. Reluctantly, they released me and stepped away.

Gytha made no move to cover her nude body in any way. She seemed completely at ease standing buck-naked on the worldwide vid network.

"A challenge has been issued," she said calmly. She looked at Armel. "How do you respond?"

Armel's face had been squirming like a toad on a spike this whole time. His cheeks had turned an awful shade of purple.

He stared at me. His right eye twitched where I'd sent it smashing onto the floor earlier. I got the impression the nu-skin he'd sprayed on it was itching him something fierce.

"I will face the challenge!" he roared.

## -58-

The situation had not gone the way I'd expected. In truth, I was kind of pissed off.

Armel knew the score. Earth needed to impress these people. We were just playing a game for them, putting on a show.

Wasn't that how you impressed any culture when you met up with its members for the first time? We were supposed to politely participate in whatever tea ceremonies, feasts, feats of strength or intellectual contests they thought were important. We weren't supposed to take this kind of pageantry personally.

But *noooo*…! Not old Armel. In my humble opinion, he was guilty of the worst sin of all: pride.

"You're blowing it," I said to him quietly.

His eyes flashed at me angrily. "I will *not* yield in front of billions. You have sown the seeds, McGill. Now, it is time for the harvest!"

I had no idea what he was going on about, and I didn't much care. I looked at Gytha hopefully.

But Gytha, for her part, appeared to be more curious than alarmed by this turn of events. She watched the two of us with interest.

Was that a gleam in her eye? Did she *like* the idea of two men fighting over her? I got the impression that she did.

*Dammit.*

Seeing there wasn't going to be any help coming from her to talk Armel out of this, I sighed.

"All right," I said. "What do we do now?"

"You fight, of course," Gytha said. "To the death. On this planet, only blood can settle a disagreement."

The camera drones overhead looked thicker than ever. There must have been thirty of them buzzing around up there by now, maybe more.

They'd been racing in from all directions, flying to us from every corner of the crater. Apparently, no one wanted to count the dead or recap the action anymore—they wanted to see this new wrinkle we'd added to the show.

Armel was calm again. I watched as he puffed himself up. His nose lifted up into the air with growing confidence.

"As the challenged," he said, "I will choose the manner in which honor is satisfied. A duel, McGill. You will meet me with crossed swords. No armor, no other weapons. Right here, right now."

"A duel?" I asked, narrowing my eyes.

"Yes. Do you yield in fear?" Armel asked.

"Hell no!"

"All right then. Centurion Leeza!"

With two rapid claps of his hands, he summoned Leeza. She walked up to us, eyeing Gytha's naked body indignantly.

"Tribune?" she asked.

"Your unit failed me today," Armel said to Leeza without even looking at her. "Now, you will help witness this event. Honor will be served."

"Great," she said.

"Get the wooden case. You'll find it behind my desk."

Leeza stalked away in annoyance. While she rummaged in his bunker, Armel kept trying to stare me down. I returned his stare with my best slack-faced, dumb-assed expression. Sometimes, that threw people off.

He stripped off his armor, so I stripped off mine to match.

When Leeza returned with an old fashioned hardwood box, I broke the deadlock with Armel and checked it out.

"Is that real cherry wood?" I asked him.

"It's rosewood, imbecile."

He opened the case with a dramatic flourish. Sure enough, there were two long, skinny swords in there. They looked like a pair of meter-long toothpicks to me. The metal was dark, rather than bright, and I got the feeling the swords were really old.

Grabbing one, I flexed it in half, and it snapped back.

"Pretty good steel," I commented.

"They're family heirlooms. Relics of a better day. Two hundred years ago—"

Slashing experimentally, I clipped the top of his head, making him duck.

A few hairs floated down.

"You done yapping yet?" I asked.

Snarling, he grabbed a sword and strode a few paces off. Then, he turned to face me.

"Salute, you baboon," he said snapping to attention and bringing the sword up vertically to his face.

I did the same, and he slashed it down in an arc. It made an impressive sound as it cut through the air.

I wasn't really a swordsman—sure, I'd been taught the basics, but Armel had clearly studied fencing seriously.

Way back when I'd signed up with Varus I'd been tested in a fight with a robot using a blade like this one, and there had been refreshers since then. The legion thought it taught balance and discipline for a soldier to be familiar with all sorts of weapons.

But real pro fencing is another thing entirely. I had to resort to what I knew, which was knife-fighting, and my force-blade training.

Unfortunately, a rapier is a weapon that requires a different approach to succeed.

Armel came at me with his body turned sideways and his weapon arm extended. His other hand cocked behind him for balance. I did what most people did when someone lunged at them, I gave ground.

Our weapons touched, sparked, and he slid his blade over mine. He almost nailed me in the heart right off. I don't mind saying that it spooked me.

I managed to beat his blade away as I was stronger and had more reach.

He came at me again, and I was running out of room to retreat. There were open trenches behind me, but I couldn't spare a glance to look for them.

Rather than fall into one and be skewered like a dog, I decided to launch a clumsy counterattack of my own. My only real move was to slap at his blade and thrust. He fell back smoothly, caught my blade with his, and it slipped past him.

I tried again and again, making rapid thrusts, staying on the attack. He shuffled back, parrying with ease.

Then he began to smile.

"I am your master, McGill," he said.

To prove it, he riposted and nailed me in the shoulder.

Geez, that hurt! It felt like he'd chipped the bone. Blood ran down my bicep and although I was able to ignore the pain, I knew my arm would soon weaken.

We separated, sides heaving. He came at me again, and I countered. Neither one of us was moving too seriously. He was still grinning, and I was beginning to dislike that grin.

"Children should never be allowed to play with a man's weapon," Armel announced, and his blade dipped to thrust low.

I skipped back, but I was too slow. He nailed me in the foot. I countered with a vicious slash—you weren't supposed to slash with these things, but I didn't care.

Crippled up pretty bad, I was limping and painting the stones with blood.

Armel sniffed, stepped back, and made a flippant gesture with his fingers. "Switch," he said.

"What?"

"Your right side is finished. Try your left. I will stand until you're ready."

Thinking about it, I decided to trust him. Why would he jump me now? He could have nailed me in the gut that last go-round by my estimation.

Taking the sword in my left, I felt only slightly less skilled. A Varus man soon learns to be as close to ambidextrous as possible. It just came with the job as we got wounded often.

Then, that sick bastard jammed his sword right through my left knee.

He left me hissing with that one, giving me a clucking sound as he walked around in a circle, raising his hands high.

Germanica troops whooped and hollered. They loved it.

Hurting badly and slow on my injured legs, I took a shot when his back was turned, but I'll be damned if he didn't whip his blade around, slapping mine so hard I almost dropped it. A red line was drawn across my wrist as well.

Armel turned to survey the damage with the air of an instructor who's failed to teach a bumpkin. He put his hands on his hips, made little sucking sounds with his mouth, and shook his head.

"So pathetic," he said. "A dismal performance, even for a man of low skill such as you. All four limbs, useless."

Rage was coursing through me now. I don't know where it comes from, but I've got a bad temper in me at times like this.

I wanted to hurt Armel. I wanted to hurt him bad. My mind raced, trying to come up with a way—then, I had it.

My face split into a grin of my own. I took his sword and broke it over my good knee. I dropped the two pieces on the rocky ground, where they clanged and clattered.

"Oh, damn!" I called out, shaking my head. "I'm *sooo* sorry! I bet those swords were important to you, too? Huh?"

After staring at me with insane eyes for a moment, Armel lost it.

I've seen that happen before—hell, I've done it myself—but this particular meltdown caught me by surprise. After everything I'd done, all the bad blood between us, what had really set him off was breaking a sword? Go figure.

He came at me, and there was no room for doing much. I managed to shift a little, so the deadly tip didn't go right into my chest. Instead, it thrust through my guts.

He pushed it deep, all the way to the hilt—that was his only mistake.

A real kill was a cold-blooded thing. You were supposed to thrust deeply, piercing the organs, then step back out of the way. Let shock do the work, or blood-loss.

But he wanted to hurt me just as badly as I'd wanted to hurt him. He drove that sword through my belly until most of it came out the other side.

That's when I grabbed him. He was in close, and I wasn't about to let him go.

I'm a big man, by anyone's accounting. My hands were each twice the size of his, and I stood a head taller. When fencing or shooting, that didn't matter much—but in a clinch, everything changed.

Maybe I should have strangled him. That would have been the more usual approach. But I was pissed off by this time. Pain, embarrassment and just plain being tired of his shit worked on my mind creating an awful concoction.

So, I grabbed him, bent his sword arm over my knee, and broke it.

He gave a cry of rage and pain. He released the sword, which was still stuck through my guts. He tried to retreat, but I had a good hold on him.

I only had one working arm, but I still found it easy to throw him on his back. Standing over him, I looked down, panting.

"Do you yield?" I asked.

His eyes blazed. "Never!"

Nodding, I pulled his own sword out of my guts and thrust it through his heart. It wasn't a fine thing—it was simple butchery.

Armel died snarling, on his back, with his whole legion watching.

I hoped it would give them all nightmares.

# -59-

After the duel was over, I was in a pretty bad way.

"Anyone got a flesh-printer handy?" I asked, but they all sneered.

Only Centurion Leeza relented. She took a can of nu-skin spray off her belt and tossed it to me. It fell to the ground, rolling away.

I went after it slowly, painfully, but a long graceful arm picked it up for me. I straightened up, and I met Gytha's eye.

She was radiant. She looked enamored, and she was still naked.

Taking my right arm in her hand, she began to spray a thick foaming coat of fresh cells. They adhered to wounds all over me, stinging and tickling. She sprayed until the bottle was empty then tossed it aside.

"You have won," she said. "As I knew you would."

Forcing a smile, I nodded. My eyes drifted up to the drones that hovered around us still.

"You hear that, Blood World? I command this legion, and my troops won the day. Serve me, and we'll fight together!"

There was no cheering. The Germanica shitheads were sullen, but they didn't try anything.

"It's done," Gytha said, taking my arm.

My blood stained her hands.

"What next?" I said. "I don't want to pass out in front of everyone."

"No, no! That won't do. Come with me, we must remove you from view."

I began limping toward Armel's bunker, but she squeezed my arm, halting me.

"Don't walk that way. You must appear strong."

Gritting my teeth, I sucked in a breath and walked as normally as I was able. It's funny how adrenalin pumping through a man during a fight can keep the pain at bay, but the second your brain knows it's over, you feel it all.

Each step was agony. Each movement sent fire through my wounded belly in particular.

Gytha had stopped the bleeding, but I was pretty cut up inside. My guts had fresh holes I'd never been born with. I could feel one chamber spilling into another, swelling my internals.

Somehow, I made it to the bunker and slammed the door shut. Sprawling in Armel's chair, I sighed and leaned back until it creaked in protest.

"Ahhh…" I said, "that's better. Can you get me a drink?"

"Alcohol? But you have an injury in your digestive tract."

"You don't say?" I chuckled, but I stopped immediately because it hurt. "I hope your people loved the show."

"They did. Reports are coming in—they're accepting the victory. The final struggle seemed to convince them Earth basics aren't weak."

"Fair enough."

She poured me a glass of straight gin. It tasted pretty bad, but I didn't care to explain mixed drinks to her.

My mouth was soon numb, and the rest of me slowly followed.

Gytha, in the meantime, was pulling off my clothes. For some reason, I thought she was planning on nursing me back to health—but I'd thought wrong.

She climbed on me and mounted up, right there on Armel's chair.

I almost pushed her off, as jostling me around right now was going to hurt my gut pretty bad. But after looking her over, and seeing the earnest look in her eyes, I decided to give in.

Gytha had her way with me then. I was pretty sure it was a first for Armel's field office.

Unfortunately, before either of us had finished—I died.

* * *

When I came back to life, I found myself in familiar territory.

"What's his Apgar?"

"A low eight—I guess it will do."

They helped me off the table. I felt sore this time—but not in the guts. It was more of an all-over ache.

"Did you guys used expired plasma?" I asked.

"We never do that, McGill," the bio said.

Frowning, I realized I recognized the voice. It was Specialist Thompson.

"Hey, Evelyn!"

"Don't call me that."

One look at her eyes, which were downcast and all business, and I knew it was over.

"Did you ever really care?" I asked her.

She paused with her poking and prodding. "Did you?"

"Hell yeah!" I said with enthusiasm.

"I don't believe you."

"Oh, come on. I didn't take money to seduce you."

That line earned me a slap. I let her get away with it, but when she pulled back to take a second shot, I caught her wrist.

"You're hurting me, Centurion."

As this conversation developed, the orderlies in the room fell quiet. They had big eyes and exchanged surprised glances.

I let her go and got off the gurney. Pulling on a uniform, I regretted that there was no shower to step into.

"You know," I said to Evelyn, "you guys really should put a shower in here. If I could wash this goop off, I'd feel a lot better about going back to the front."

She sniffed at the idea. "I'll make sure to mention that to my CO," she said in a sarcastic tone.

"Germanica does it."

"Why don't you sign up with them, then? Or better yet, desert and go down to your girlfriend on Blood World."

Turning around, I put my hands on my hips. "Are you serious? Is that what your problem is?"

Something in my tone sent the orderlies skittering out of the chamber. In the old days, when I'd been a noncom, they might have tried to kick me out—but now that I was an officer, they bailed out and left Evelyn to face me alone.

Trying to calm down, I remembered who I was and turned away. I headed for the door. When my hand was on it, I heard Evelyn sigh behind me.

"I'm sorry."

She'd said it fast and quiet—but I figured she probably meant it.

"Me too," I rumbled, then I left.

In a bad mood, I headed for my module and my long-empty bunk, but my tapper began buzzing. Someone had put a change-alert on my revival status. The damned computers always tattled on a man these days.

It was Tribune Deech, so I didn't have much choice. I answered it.

"McGill?" Deech asked. "Is your head on straight?"

"I'm good-to-go, sir."

"Excellent. Clean up, and present yourself on Gold Deck in your dress-blues."

That was a surprising request. I kind of liked the implications.

"Will do, sir."

A few minutes later, I was whistling in the shower. Ten minutes after that, I arrived on Gold Deck. Hell, even the tubes were working again.

"Centurion?" Winslade asked as I approached. "What are you doing here?"

I stopped and appraised him.

"What are you doing?" he asked again. "That's a demented look on your face—even for you."

"I'm considering throttling you, sir. It's the only way I can be sure you're not Claver."

Winslade made a pffing sound. "Of course I'm Winslade. Claver was arrested and executed half-way through that nonsense in the pit."

"Yeah? Who did the good deed?"

"Graves. He did it down there in the pit... It's disturbing, actually. What if he'd guessed wrong?"

I'd known all about this, naturally, as I was the one who'd put Graves up to it. Still, it was fun to make Winslade sweat a little.

Winslade's account did give me one piece of vital information: apparently, Graves hadn't told him I was the one who'd spotted Claver. That was just as well, I figured.

Nodding, I stepped past him—but he snapped out a thin-boned hand to block me.

"You still haven't told me—"

"Deech summoned me. Dress-blues, she said. See this? I'm wearing my Dawn Star."

The Dawn Star was a silver four-pointed medal—a high honor. I'd received the award after helping to send the Mogwa battle fleet back to the Core Systems a few years back.

Oddly enough, Winslade didn't seem impressed. He looked me up and down, then let me pass in disgust.

That was a good thing, because my mood had been shifting into a dark zone. If he'd riled me up any further, I might have punched him and spent the night in the brig.

Deech let me in the moment I reached her door. Graves was waiting inside as well.

They stood up and congratulated me. That was damned unusual, but I took it in stride.

"McGill," Graves told me. "I thought you were dead as a mackerel after Armel ran you through. That you managed to beat him after that—well, mark me impressed."

"Nah," I said, "never count out a Georgia boy. There's always a little more juice left in a man like me."

"Indeed..." Deech said.

I thought it was a strange thing to say, but I didn't complain. After all, I was the hero of the hour, and it seemed like people were acknowledging that fact for once.

"Is that why you summoned me, sirs? For a hearty congratz?"

"Not just that," Deech said. "You have a few more duties to perform. You must be present in the morning for the review of the Blood World army."

"Uh... down there? On the planet?"

"That's right," Graves answered. "You'll review the troops while they parade around in their full kits."

"But that's not all," Deech said. "Ah... Graves, could you excuse us?"

His eyes slid from me to Deech, then back again.

"Are you sure about that, Tribune?"

"Quite sure," she said sternly.

Shrugging, Graves walked out.

My eyes followed him. Graves was acting like I was going to face something unpleasant. Perhaps he knew what this was all about. I certainly didn't.

"Tribune?" I asked when we were left alone.

"Centurion..." she began. "Are you a loyal soldier? A man who would give his life for Earth and Empire?"

"Um..." I said, already not liking where this was going. "I think I've proven that by giving my life a hundred times or more, sir."

"Yes, of course. You're a decorated hero. Perhaps that was the wrong way to ask..."

"Tribune? Could you just get to the point and tell me whatever it is you're holding back?"

"All right. McGill, we've won Blood World—no, that isn't quite right—*you* have won Blood World."

"That doesn't sound like a reason to be so down in the dumps to me, sir."

"No, you wouldn't think so. But here it is: the Blood Worlders aren't satisfied with the generalized concept of James McGill as their hero. In order to march into our gateway by the millions—they want you to be there. To command them personally."

Deech met my eye then, and what she was saying began to sink in.

"Are you serious? They want me to preside over this dirt-hole planet like a king, or something?"

"Or something. In particular, you'll function as Gytha's consort. That shouldn't be too painful for you, hmm?"

"Uh…" I said, my mind whirling.

I liked Gytha in the most basic way a man could like any beautiful woman, but to abandon Earth? My family?

"You're asking too much, Tribune," I said.

"There will be perks. You'll be made a primus. Perhaps, in time, we can arrange for your family to be transported out here to join you. All you have to do is get these people to march a few million troops between our gateway posts whenever they're needed. It should be a very cush post."

My mind was racing. I felt like I was being permed. No more Earth? No more Georgia? No more Legion Varus?

"How long, sir?" I asked. "What kind of a term are we talking about?"

Deech gave a tiny shrug. "Years, I should think. No more than a decade, surely."

I felt sick. I'd walked in here on the top of the world, but Deech had managed to bring me down hard inside of five short minutes.

"Well?" she asked. "Will you do it?"

"Do I have any choice, sir?"

"None whatsoever."

"All right then. Put me down as a volunteer."

"Excellent. Your cooperation was assumed, naturally. You'll be departing for the planet shortly. You can ride in my lifter, inside the command module. You'd like that, wouldn't you?"

"Uh… sure thing, Tribune."

Stunned, I was dismissed. I marched back out of her office and headed for the tubes.

Outside the big viewing ports, I could see Blood World in all her stained, dirty, rust-orange, ugly-assed glory.

Was this really to be my home? For a decade or more?

I couldn't fully grasp the concept.

## -60-

I could almost hear the trumpets blare—but they didn't have any trumpets on Blood World.

Thousands—no, *millions* of troops stood in a vast array before me. They didn't form a parade, not exactly. They marched up in a single, threatening mass and stood at attention before Gytha and me.

We stood up on a pedestal together, side by side. The pedestal was big—more of a stage, really—built with stone chunks and smoothed over by puff-crete.

It wasn't lovely. It wasn't even decorated, but in typical Blood Worlder fashion it was very functional.

From that shared perch, we were a good ten meters above the massive host of troops. They stood before us in the roaring desert heat, their ranks stretching out for as far as my eyes could see.

"You guys really go in for the ceremonies," I told Gytha.

She glanced at me curiously. "Isn't that the norm for Earth? Our oldest vid documents show standing armies like this."

"In the old days, maybe. I guess you guys must have some historical footage to go by. Did you bring it here from Dust World?"

"We must have. The Cephalopods didn't let us keep much from our heritage, but what we do have is full of marching armies. Pride, Service and Sacrifice."

She listed these three words as if they were some kind of a slogan. I had the feeling they were—for her.

The squids were bastards any day of the week, but I felt they'd outdone themselves with my kin here on Blood World. They'd manipulated their bodies and their minds, seeking to form an army that was unstoppable.

To compound the sin, we Earthers had come along to take advantage of these people. They were eager and felt lost without their old masters, and I'd helped to provide them with new ones.

The army saluted then, all at once. I never saw or heard a signal that kicked off the salute, but I did hear the deafening unified shout that roared out of a million mouths at once. Wincing, I fought the urge to put my hands over my ears. I didn't think that would look hero-like.

"McGill?" a voice spoke into my headset. It was Graves, and he sounded business-like as usual. "We're ready at our end."

Looking over my shoulder, I saw the massive arch behind us come to life. It lit up with coruscating colors, mostly a pinkish-white with big moving patches of silver that drifted like clouds.

The arch was a huge gateway. It was a military-issue portal, built by our tech-smiths back on Earth for this precise purpose.

It was, of course, much bigger and more elaborate than the single-file gateway posts we'd brought with us from Earth. To get that kind of tech out here, with huge generators and heavy metal coils and all, the legion had used the small gateway posts we'd brought with us.

The idea was ingenious to me. We'd brought out a small unit, set it up, then walked through that to haul out this much bigger contraption. A small army of techs had built it piece-by-piece in the open desert.

The stage I stood on, stone though it was, had a massive fusion generator buried inside. I could feel the thrum of it, coming up into my boots. The truth was it set my teeth a little on edge.

"Looks good down here, Primus," I told Graves. I had to speak loudly to be heard over the din the troops were making.

I turned back to the army to see what the fuss was about.

A brigade of giants had just arrived. These weren't the small kind, like the littermates. They were much taller and thicker. Each one was a true monster, six meters in height or more. They carried massive energy projectors. Glittering shields of force wrapped around their bodies in a glassy nimbus.

To greet their big brothers, the littermates wailed and caterwauled like demons. I expected these monsters to press ahead, marching through the spherical portal we'd made for them—but they didn't. Not yet.

Gytha gave my hand a squeeze.

"The brood-mothers are coming!" she said excitedly.

This grabbed my attention. I'd never seen the females that had supposedly birthed all these monstrosities. Not knowing what to expect, I craned my neck and leaned this way and that.

"Where are they?" I asked finally. "All I see are some flower-girls walking under those giants."

Gytha frowned. "Those are the brood-mothers."

My mouth gaped. "How could those tiny women give birth to something six meters tall?"

"They don't gestate the giants in their bodies," Gytha said in a tone that indicated I was of substandard intellect. "Their eggs are harvested, and the offspring are grown in breeding facilities."

"Huh... sounds kind of dull."

She let go of my hand, and I got the idea I'd insulted her somehow—but I didn't care. I wasn't too keen on my new role as troop-reviewer anyway.

"Is this about over?" I asked her. "When they start marching through, we should take a break."

Gytha gawked at me. Her face told me I'd said something shocking, but for the life of me I didn't know what it was.

"This is the Marching of the Host," she said in a formal tone. "These brave soldiers are willing to die for you. The least you can do is stand and watch them!"

"Uh... sure."

After a few thousand brood-mothers did a little bit of fancy-footwork, they stepped aside at last. The giants then began marching up the steps to the stage, two abreast.

Gytha and I stood off to one side, letting them pass us.

They were impressive—but they also stank. Each one cast us in a deep shade briefly, and I could feel a gust of their body-warmth puff into my face as they marched by.

Trying not to look disgusted, I took to holding my breath briefly as each puff came, and then sucking in some fresher air as the next pair approached. It left me feeling light-headed.

"Is something wrong?" Gytha asked.

She'd been watching me. That was a bad thing. Ever since I'd been a kid in church and school, after a while, some lady had started watching me. They'd always frowned. Eventually, I knew that frown was going to turn into an outright scowl.

"I'm fine," I lied.

Gytha turned back to the passing giants. Her face soon brightened. She didn't seem to notice the puffs of stink, or to think these huge freaks were disturbingly close. It was all normal to her.

After a full frigging *hour* long parade, the last giant stepped through and vanished.

The littermates started howling again, and I took a deep, deep breath.

"We've got to take a break," I told Gytha.

"It's not done."

"What if I have to piss?" I asked. "You don't want me to pee my pants in front of the army, do you?"

She gave me a cold look. "Then go behind the stage. Hurry up, before the main army begins the march. There are ten times as many troops in the next March, so empty yourself well."

Shaking my head, I stepped away toward the back of the stage. I really did have to pee—that part had been no lie.

What happened next was an accident. I will swear to that for all eternity—up, down, and sideways, even in the bright light of God's grace.

I walked into the portal and vanished.

## -61-

Stepping out into the blissfully cool, fresh, open air of Earth, I felt like I'd found Heaven.

Unfortunately it was only New Jersey Sector, but I'd gladly take it in a pinch.

The giants were there, setting up camp. They'd come through with survival packs and weapons, but Earth had provided them with a camp here just north of what the locals called Wharton Forest. It was farm country, open land that hadn't been eaten up yet by the mega-cities along the coast.

No one was looking, so I hopped down from the creaking steel ramp and found a dark place to take a much needed leak.

"Aren't you Centurion McGill?" a voice asked behind me.

"Uh… hello?" I said, turning and zipping up. "What can I do for you, Adjunct?"

The woman was a Hegemony tech, and she wore that same frown I'd seen on Gytha not moments earlier.

"Sir…? Aren't you supposed to be on the other side of this portal?"

"I am, and I'm going back in a second."

Right about then, I heard the thrumming of the fusion generator die. It had been under the ramp, just like the one buried under the stage back on Blood World.

With the sound of receding power, I saw the portal flicker then go out like a light.

"Hmm..." I said. "Did you techs turn that off?"

"Of course, sir. The giants are all through. This camp can't hold a million troops. They're placing the heavy troopers up in Nova Scotia. There's another rig up there—but sir, you must know all this. They must have briefed you."

My mind fell back to that briefing. I'd been kind of tired after my latest revive and disaffected by the prospects of being deserted on Blood World to play mascot. I recalled having taken a well-deserved nap.

"Hmm..." I said. "I might have missed that part. So, they're parking the army in more than one spot?"

"Yes, our new gateway tech is much improved. Those tech-smith people, the ones who came from Rogue World, they've moved us decades forward in transportation technology."

"You don't say..."

I was looking at the dead portal, and it occurred to me that I might be in some trouble. On the far side, three hundred odd lightyears away, Gytha was probably beginning to wonder where I'd gone.

"Sir?" the tech asked me. "Aren't you supposed to review the troops? All of them, I mean? It's going to take at least another twenty hours for the entire force to march through into Nova Scotia."

"Twenty hours? Really?"

She shrugged. "They're supposed to jog, and they'll go through nine at a time—but still, a million troops takes a long time to march by."

I read her nametag then. Samantha Sladen. It seemed like a nice name.

"What's it like?" she asked, taking a step closer. "Being out there on Blood World, I mean?"

"Well Adjunct, I'm feeling kind of hungry. Maybe I could tell you the story while we get a bite to eat."

Startled, she looked me over. For just a second, I could tell she was considering the offer, but she shook her head at last.

"No, I can't. I've got a crew to run. Maybe later."

I nodded, smiling, but I didn't think there would be a later. I had to get the hell out of here—and fast.

A few hours after I'd returned to Earth, I was walking backwards down the turnpike. My thumb was stuck up and out. Several trams whizzed by, but no one even looked at me twice.

I was headed south. I'm not sure why, as Central was up north. Maybe I was homesick.

Whatever my reasoning, my mind was happier than it'd been in months. I don't like to talk a planet down, especially when I'd just served there—but honestly, Blood World sucked hard. By comparison, most of the places I'd seen in my long life qualified as genuine slices of paradise.

After another hour of walking, I heard a different sound. It wasn't the clattering whir of a tram. It was more of a whooshing sound, the sound made by fans and repellers angled to push away the gravitational forces of the Earth.

An air car landed behind me, and a figure climbed out.

I knew her. Despite my predicament, I grinned and waved.

"Hello, Imperator!"

It was Galina Turov. She must have traced me using my tapper.

She was pissed, and I could read that mood in every hip-swinging stride she took in my direction.

"James McGill…" she said. "Why have you gone AWOL? This time, I mean?"

"Uh… it was the funniest thing, sir. You're not going to believe it."

"No, I'm not—but try me anyway. I'm curious."

I told her about the endless parade of troops, and how long it took. She looked as unsympathetic as the last few ladies I'd told about that.

"Then," I said, "I stepped away to take a leak. Gytha told me to go to the back of the platform—I swear she did! Just ask her."

Galina crossed her arms, plumping up her breasts, and I tried not to stare. Sometimes she did stuff like that just to throw a man off.

"Go on," she prompted.

"Well… I stepped through the portal by sheer accident. I mean, it was right there. Did you know that the globe-like field they generate can reach out and pick up a man who gets a little too close? It's like a jet engine on a carrier."

"I hadn't heard that, no."

"Well, it can happen. Anyways, I ended up here at the wrong end of the portal. I tried to go back—really I did. But there was this cute little adjunct named Sladen, and she—"

"You're kidding me, right?" she interrupted. "This all ends with you being distracted by some woman you just met?"

"No, no, not at all! She just told me I couldn't go back through. That's what I meant to say."

"Why not?"

"Well… they'd, uh, shut it off already. By the time I tried to step through."

Turov nodded thoughtfully. "So, no one ordered you to come back to Earth?"

"Like who?"

"No one in particular."

"Um… nope."

Galina chewed on that for a few seconds.

"You know what?" she asked at last. "As strange as this may seem, I do believe you, to a point. It's just the sort of lame-assed thing you might do."

Surprised and delighted, I immediately walked over to her air car and climbed into the passenger seat.

Galina came to the window and looked inside at me. "What do you think you're doing?"

"Um…"

"Do you realize you're a deserter? That I should, for the good of Earth, perm you right now in the street?"

"But I thought I was a hero," I pointed out.

"That is unfortunately correct. It's the only thing holding me back from executing my duty."

"Well then… can I hitch a ride?"

"No way. Get out. You can walk to Central—and by the way, it's in the opposite direction."

She kicked me out of her car, climbed in and flew away.

I was left on the puff-crete strip, baffled and annoyed. Why'd she gone to all the trouble of coming down here? Just to make me squirm?

No... She'd wanted to know if I was pulling something more significant than avoiding Blood World. She'd wanted to know if I was working for someone—like Drusus, maybe.

## -62-

It took me a full day of walking, but I made it to Central around midnight. I crashed at a friend's house then made my way to the big building the next morning at the crack of dawn.

The guards eyed me curiously. "Aren't you supposed to be deployed, Varus?" the senior hog asked.

"That's right, but they've got these new gateways set up. I've been called back early."

He frowned. "That might be why I'm not seeing your name on these rosters. Well, your tapper checks out, and I've gotten an approval to send you upstairs. Follow the arrows, please."

With a nod and a smile, I did as he told me. I took an express elevator to the four hundred seventh floor, stepping out when the blinking arrows on the carpet told me to.

One thing that was always disconcerting about the legions was being ordered around by automated systems. No one called you half the time. They just sent a drone, or triggered a computer script to light up arrows on the floor. This was one of those times.

What was disturbing about it was how impersonal it was, and the fact that the system rarely told you what your final destination was.

I hadn't been dealt with like this for at least a year, except when making drops on planets. They usually reserved this level of impersonal treatment for clueless recruits. Maybe somebody was trying to make a point.

The office I ended up at contained a person familiar to me.

It was Claver.

He sat behind a desk with his feet up on it. He looked at me when I walked inside, and he sneered.

"You're as slow as a dancing bear on those two feet, McGill."

"Why didn't you fly out to pick me up if you wanted to talk so bad?"

He snorted. "I can't leave. I caught a revive downstairs—don't ask how, I'm not going to tell you. But even though I'm breathing again, I can't just walk outside. The guards check everyone going in or out—just not those of us wandering around inside."

There was a pistol on the desk. Claver had it sitting there right out in the open, but his hand wasn't near it. From this distance, it looked like one of those alien-made jobs from Tau Ceti.

I was disarmed at the moment. They'd asked to check my weapon at the lobby, and I hadn't put up a fuss. I hadn't expected to need it.

Without being asked, I slid into a seat across from him. I was closer to the pistol that way—but not quite within snatching range.

"So," I said, "you've been waiting here for me? I'm flattered."

"Don't be. I'm here to deliver a message."

"What's that?"

He leaned forward, his face screwing up into an expression of rage.

"You are a card-carrying moron! You blew it back there on Blood World! Millions of lives—maybe billions—will be lost now."

"Uh…" I said, unsure where this attack had come from. "Most people think I'm a hero."

He laughed bitterly. "I'm sure they do. But that's only because they're as dumb as you are."

"Look, Claver," I said, getting tired of his act. "Is that really why you came here today? To yell at me?"

"Partly, yes. But I must explain the rest in order for your lowbrow intellect to comprehend the true situation. You see, I had a deal cut back there on Blood World."

"Right. To sell out Earth. To give the Blood World troops to another planet."

"Not another planet, another *empire*."

"Wonderful. That makes your treason all the greater."

"Dummy…" he said, shaking his head. "I cut a deal with the Rigellians. They promised not to invade Earth's domain if they were allowed to win and keep Blood World. I arranged the contract hiring out Varus to do it—but you guys stopped me."

"Rigellians? You mean those things they call Vulbites?"

He made a flapping gesture with his hand. "They use Vulbites sometimes. They use lots of different kinds of troops. Most of the groups in the contest were sponsored by them."

"So they were cheating too?" I asked. "Just as much as Earth?"

"More so. Did you really think the Skrull were interested in running Blood World?" he chuckled and shook his head. "Dipshit… Anyways, the point is they were willing to take Blood World and call off the coming frontier border-war."

Frowning, I thought back to my conversation with Sateekas on this topic, more than a year ago. "Grand Admiral Sateekas said we'd have to fight a growing power in a neighboring province. Rigel is out past the edge of the Empire entirely."

Claver leaned forward. "I can't believe you were paying attention! Just goes to show you even the lamest student in school can still earn a gold star for the day sometimes. Let me explain: the Empire's borders used to go out past our province. A century or so back, Rigel was in another province, number 929."

"Why didn't he say that?"

Claver shrugged. "Sateekas is old. To a Mogwa, a century isn't all that much time."

"You mean he forgot?"

"Hell no. They never forget a loss. That's why they want Earth to reconquer 929 for them. To the Mogwa, it's just one more rebellious region, waiting to be subjugated again."

I found all this to be alarming. It sounded to me like the Empire really was in decline, losing provinces along its ancient borders.

"If this was so damned important," I complained, "why didn't you say something about it when we met in the crater?"

"Would you have believed me?" he demanded. "Would you have let me win on behalf of the Rigellians?"

"Maybe..."

"How about 'never in a million years' instead?"

"You might be right," I admitted. No one trusted Claver.

"Well then," he continued, "we've now come to the other reason I'm here."

So saying, he snatched the pistol off the desktop. I reached for it too, but he surprised me. Like a swamp gator, he was pretty fast when he wanted to be.

"I came to tell you about your immediate future," he told me. "Think of me as your modern-day prophet on the mount."

"Let's hear it," I said, waving my fingers at him like I was bored—which I was.

"You're in some pretty deep shit, cowboy," he said, leaning forward and lowering his voice. "I want you to thoroughly enjoy the new frontier war you just kicked off with the Rigellians. Every life that's lost in the days that follow this one can be traced directly back to your red hands—and it's going to be rough, punk."

Claver lifted his gun then, and I flinched. I was expecting to take another unplanned trip through the revival machine.

But instead, he put the gun to his own temple and calmly blew his brains out.

Afterward, I slowly puzzled it out. Claver had somehow snuck a revive at Central, but he'd only used that life to berate me, then check himself out again.

His corpse was still wet and sticky behind the ears. He'd been fresh from Blue Deck.

I couldn't imagine enduring a birth and death just to yell at somebody. It had to be the single oddest use of a lifetime I'd ever seen.

It was almost spooky…

* * *

When Drusus discovered I was on Earth again, he called me immediately.

He was kind of pissed. I expected him to send me right back out to Blood World using the portals—but he didn't.

He said it was because they didn't want me back.

"Gytha really said that?" I asked him via my tapper.

"Apparently, you made quite an impression. Gytha felt stood-up. She had to cover for you, making up excuses for literally hours as her troops marched by into that portal by the thousands. At last, when it was all over, she was so angry she contacted Tribune Deech and stated that you were banned from her planet."

"But… she's still honoring our deal, right?"

"Yes, for now. Earth is no longer on the best diplomatic footing, but in retrospect, I don't think Gytha was going to tolerate you for long, anyway."

"Hmm… that happens with me and women sometimes. They tend to blow hot then cold soon after. It's a sheer mystery."

"Right, McGill. Here's the deal: I'm demobilizing you. You'll retain your rank of centurion, because you did well all things considered, but you'll get no active duty pay as of the end of this call."

"Got it, sir."

He disconnected and I whooped. I was going home! I'd be short a few paychecks, sure, but such was the price of freedom.

Down in Georgia Sector, my family was overjoyed to welcome me back. I didn't tell them anything about Gytha, or how I'd almost been marooned on her strange planet. There was no point in freaking them out now that I was safe and sound.

The only sad thing was I'd missed most of the summer. Etta was going back to middle school soon, and she didn't like that idea at all. I strongly suspected her teachers felt the same way.

"Dad?" she asked me on my first night home.

"What's up, Pumpkin?"

"Do you have to call me that?"

"It makes me happy."

She sighed. "All right. You know what would make *me* happy?"

"What?" I asked, with just a hint of wariness in my voice. I tried to stop doubt from creeping in, but with this girl, there was no telling where a request might go.

"Nothing weird," she said, catching my tone immediately. "I just want to see where you went this summer."

I blinked at her. The whole Blood World project had been classified. Even the location and existence of that planet was a secret—not that I figured anyone cared much now that the mission was over.

"Sure," I said, shrugging.

Stepping up to her star-scope, I tapped in the official name of the star, Epsilon Leporis, and it began whirring and zooming. A few moments later, we had a clean view of the star. Another thirty seconds passed, and we got a shot of the planet itself.

"That took a long time," she said, eyeing her instrument.

Suddenly, she looked up at me in surprise. "Three hundred lightyears? You went outside the boundaries of the Empire? Past the frontier? Is that even a former Cephalopod planet? Did you even know where you were, Dad? Half-way to Rigel?"

"Uh..." I said, suddenly understanding why things were classified.

Etta looked at me with big eyes. "That's why the others aren't back yet, isn't it? It's too far out. How did you manage it...? No ship could get there so fast and—"

My big hand moved of its own accord, and placed itself over her mouth—gently.

She didn't bite me. She just stared with those big, shocked eyes. The best part was that she *did* shut the hell up.

"Now listen, Pumpkin," I said in a calm, measured voice. "Didn't we have a little talk about not upsetting this machine, here? Just in case it's listening?"

Her eyes swept back to her star-scope. They were so big around I thought they might pop out of her head.

"To answer your question, honey: of course not!" I told her. "*Nobody* goes halfway to Rigel! *Nobody*. The entire idea is silly."

Calmly, I took my hand away from her face and reached out to touch the star-scope. I activated its local auto-search feature, which was programmed to find something interesting in the area. Dutifully, it panned up and to the south, spotting a summertime meteor swarm.

"There! Doesn't that look nice?" I asked Etta, giving her a pat on the head.

She hated that, and usually when I did it she informed me that she was no dog. But I knew it would give her the correct message: *stop talking*.

She took in a deep breath, looked into the scope, and began cooing about the meteors. Damn, she was good at bullshit. It must be in the genes. If I hadn't known better, I might have believed she cared right now about a few burning dirt clods hitting our atmosphere.

When we'd finished with star-gazing for the night, I headed back to my shack to sleep—but I didn't make it.

The light was on inside, and I hadn't left it that way.

My shack is about as basic as you can get. It has electricity, and sometimes the heating and cooling works. But I'd installed a few gizmos such as automatic lights. You could turn them off, but I usually didn't.

They were on motion-sensors, and unless that frigging tomcat from the Bentley farm down the road had managed to break-and-enter, someone was inside my place right now.

I didn't go to the front door. I crept around to the back window instead. It was blacked out, of course, so I could sleep-in when I felt like it.

But there was a crack in the casement, down low. I put my eye there and looked inside.

A figure sat on the couch. The shape was female, slight-build, fidgety fingers…

All of a sudden, I knew who it was. Yanking an axe out of the stump out behind my place, I stalked around to the one and only entrance.

The door crashed open under my foot. I stood in the entrance, axe in hand, filling the doorframe.

"What are you doing here, Thompson?"

Specialist Evelyn Thompson jumped half out of her skin. She dropped the magazine about floaters she'd been paging through. She had a terrified look to her, and I didn't see a weapon.

Thinking that I might have made a mistake, I forced a smile and set the axe aside.

She watched it with fascination.

"Chopping wood?" she asked.

"Sure," I lied. "We've only got a few months to go before winter sets in."

"I'm really sorry. I knew you lived back here, and I saw you with your daughter—I didn't want to intrude."

"So… you came back here and broke in?"

She shook her head. She still seemed to be a little freaked out. "No, the door wasn't locked."

"Oh… right. You want a beer?"

Evelyn watched me move to my fridge and rummage inside.

She began to get brave again, so she stood up and put her small fists on her hips.

"How'd you even know I was in here?"

I shrugged. "Sometimes people come here to mess with me. I have ways of detecting that. Did Turov send you?"

She got up and walked toward the door.

"Hey," I said, "was that the wrong question?"

"Yes, of course it was. I'm not on anyone's payroll tonight."

"All right. I'll take your word for it. Sit back down and have a beer."

"No," she said. "I shouldn't have come. I was just feeling a little guilty after all that's happened—but it can't work between us. You're too crazy, too paranoid, too hurt."

"Hurt?" I snorted. "By what?"

"By what I did. You know."

"You mean where you slept with me for money?"

Glaring, she pushed past me and ran out into the yard. She kept going despite a few shouts I sent after her. Finally, I was alone in the dark.

Shrugging, I turned to go back inside, but I saw another, smaller figure moving in the trees.

"Etta! Now, don't you go and kill her! She was just a visitor!"

Etta came out of the shadows reluctantly. She looked angry and downcast.

That was a bad look on my girl's face. When she did something bad, she felt bad—and feeling bad pissed her off. It didn't make any sense, really, but that's how it went with her.

"What'd you do, girl?" I asked, stepping down off the porch to where she stood in my tiny yard.

"Nothing…" she said, but I wasn't convinced.

"Come on," I said. "I've looked less guilty with blood on my hands."

"All right… I found her tram. That's all. She can fix it tomorrow."

"Aw, dammit girl."

Sighing, I walked toward the lane. There, in light of the Moon, sat an unfamiliar vehicle. All four treads had been disabled.

I looked around, but I didn't see Evelyn anywhere.

Going back to the family garage, I got out the tram and began rolling out into the street to look for her.

A few hundred meters away, I flicked on my brights.

There she was, walking toward town with her shoulders hunched and angry. Sometimes, it seemed like every woman I knew was angry about something.

I rolled up beside her, but she kept walking. She didn't even look at me.

"Come on, Evelyn," I said, "let me at least give you a ride to town."

"You're dangerous," she said.

"Yeah, that I am. Come on, get in."

She glanced over at me. "You've got your axe in the tram, don't you? Is this supposed to be some kind of ritualistic killing this time? Something you've been planning for years?"

"Uh…" I said.

Turning her words over inside my skull twice, I figured I might just know what she was talking about.

"Are you still mad because I killed you that one time? That must have been twenty years ago."

"No, I'm not mad about that. I'm mad because you destroyed my tram. How'd you even get out there so fast? No, wait! I have it!"

She stopped walking, put her fists on her hips again, and glared at me. "You did it *before* you came busting into the room, didn't you? That's why you had the axe!"

"Sheesh," I said. "I'll tell you what really happened, even though it's embarrassing."

Evelyn paused, squinting at me. "Well?"

"Get in. I'll drive you back to town."

"I'll hitch a ride."

"Look," I said in a reasonable tone, "if I'd wanted to kill you, girl, you'd already be dead."

She thought that over, saw the logic of it, and finally climbed in. She crossed her arms and legs tightly and sat up against the passenger door.

I told her about Etta then, my wild-animal daughter.

For some reason, this made her curious. She stopped pouting and asked a few questions. I realized after a time that she was intrigued by the thought of a Dust Worlder-Earther hybrid.

"We're not two different species," I told her. "You've met Della. That's Etta's mother. She's human enough."

"Oh…" Evelyn said in disappointment. "I was visualizing offspring between you and one of those things the squids bred on Blood World."

"Lord no!" I said, laughing. "She's no genetic freak, half-littermate or something."

We fell silent for a time, but then she broke this new ice as we got close to town.

"I'm sorry," she said. "I should never have come down here. I tried to call you when *Nostrum* got back from Blood World, but your tapper just bounced everything I sent at it."

I shrugged. I had it set for priority-only calls. If the brass wanted me, they could get a message through—or someone on my friends list. But Evelyn wasn't either of those.

As we got closer to town, she suddenly got agitated.

"Let me out," she said.

I looked at her. I'd begun to entertain certain ideas. Perhaps the night was recoverable. Maybe if I took her to the Gator Farm, a local bar and grill that stayed open late, I could change the mood.

"James," she said. "Just stop the tram here and let me out. Please?"

I looked at her. She had true pain in her face.

What was all this about?

Looking around, I was suddenly on the alert.

We were on the outskirts of Waycross. Most of the town was shut down, with nothing in sight but streetlights and late traffic gliding this way and that.

"All right," I said, stopping the tram.

She got out, and she started to run away, but then she came back. She leaned into the driver's side window and kissed me.

"I'm sorry," she whispered. "For everything."

Then she was gone again, her shoes slapping on the pavement. Surprised, I didn't even get in a word.

Then I saw it.

An air car was parked across the street. It was a familiar shape: long, sleek, and darkly painted.

It was Turov's air car. I couldn't make out the driver. It could have been Winslade, Claver, or even Turov herself—it didn't matter.

Evelyn climbed into the air car, and the vehicle shot into the sky. Locals craned their necks out of their crappy trams to watch.

I didn't bother. I did a U-turn, and I headed back home.

Walking back to my shack, I felt low. The whole thing had been another trick. Evelyn was still working for Turov, and I'd been her mission for the night.

She'd failed—but I wasn't sure if that was a good thing or not. I was pretty sure I'd have enjoyed my night more if she'd managed to fool me again.

The stars shined on my back. After I'd spent so much time in the dark, they seemed bright to me.

When I was back home and digging out a beer, a shape came to my door and tapped. It was Etta.

"She's gone, isn't she?" she asked. "I blew it for you, didn't I? I'm sorry."

I gave her a sad smile and a hug.

"Nope," I said. "Your instincts were right this time. That one—we can't trust her. Never again."

Confused, but happy about the praise, Etta headed off to bed.

I sat out on my porch in a rocking chair, wondering what Evelyn had been after. She hadn't wanted to kill me, that was for sure. She must have wanted information, or just to worm her way back into my life to keep an eye on me.

I'd been paid to spy before—but I'd never had anyone spying on *me*. It was a different feeling, and I found that I didn't much care for the sensation.

Star-gazing without the help of Etta's scope, I tried to count all the places in the sky I'd visited. It was strange to think that those cold, gleaming lights up there had been shining for countless years before I existed, and that they'd continue to shine countless years after I was permed someday.

Getting a little drunk, I noticed the bugs were nipping at me, but I didn't worry about it. I fell asleep on my porch sometime after midnight, and I dreamed of people and planets I'd forgotten about long ago.

Books by B. V. Larson:

## UNDYING MERCENARIES

*Steel World*
*Dust World*
*Tech World*
*Machine World*
*Death World*
*Home World*
*Rogue World*
*Blood World*

## STAR FORCE SERIES

*Swarm*
*Extinction*
*Rebellion*
*Conquest*
*Battle Station*
*Empire*
*Annihilation*
*Storm Assault*
*The Dead Sun*
*Outcast*
*Exile*
*Gauntlet*

Visit BVLarson.com for more information.

Printed in Great Britain
by Amazon